VOLUME TWO OF THE

YALE EDITION OF THE

UNPUBLISHED WRITINGS

OF GERTRUDE STEIN

under the general editorship

of Carl Van Vechten

with an advisory committee

of Donald C. Gallup, Donald

Sutherland, and Thornton Wilder

MRS. REYNOLDS

and Five Earlier Novelettes

BY GERTRUDE STEIN

with a foreword by Lloyd Frankenberg

NEW HAVEN : YALE UNIVERSITY PRESS

London · Geoffrey Cumberlege · Oxford University Press

1952

ON FIRST MEETING MRS. REYNOLDS

by Lloyd Frankenberg

A preface is to point the way. This will be to ask directions.

On first meeting Mrs. Reynolds, what are your impressions? Is this a novel about your impressions on meeting Mrs. Reynolds? I think it is, as well as a novel about Mrs. Reynolds, about war and peace, about anxiety and tranquillity, boredom and delight, fear and courage, middle class virtues, saints, miracles and predictions, and the shadow cast by Angel Harper. And it is the celebration of Angel Harper's death.

If this is a novel in which the reader is one of the characters, it will be a different novel for each reader. For some it will be another bundle of repetitions, like the much laughed at, very widely quoted, and usually misquoted, "Rose is a rose is a rose is a rose."

No wonder Gertrude Stein had this phrase made into a seal and, for the cover design of *The Autobiography of Alice B. Toklas*, into a circular design: It is her style in embryo; at once vague and precise. The precision is in the way it follows the vague way our minds mull over things. This is not written speech, nor is it spoken speech. It is a transcription of the motion of thought. If we let it, it can release a flood of associations. I

v

think of a flower, a color, a girl's name, a Shakespearean quotation, an Elizabethan connotation, a feminine colloquialism, the verb to rise: rows and rows of them find their way to me like arrows.

This is both delightful and maddening. It is not the way I am used to having my thoughts thought for me by other writers: think *this;* feel *that;* believe *me.* Rather it says: think what you will, feel if you must, believe or not. I find it exhausting, this being thrown on my own resources. And whatever I do think, feel, believe, there is the suspicion that Gertrude Stein intended more.

Anything new is irritating. And her style is new. No other writer has anything quite like it, this identical pun, so different from Joyce's multilingual play on words. This is metaphor that exposes unlikeness. A rose may be a rose, but no two are alike. Her repetitions imply disconnection; the roses follow each other, but without sequence. It is a bringing together and a separating in the same breath.

So in these novels one day is very much like any other and very different. So too with months, winters, years, stars, names, and people. Everything contains its opposite. When we think of anything we sense its absence as vividly as we realize its presence.

Perhaps Gertrude Stein's work as a whole might be called a study in attention, including inattention. Does it all stem from her early experiments under William James and Hugo Münsterberg with "Fluctuations of the Attention," "The Saturation of Colors," and "The Place of Repetition in Memory"? In his illuminating book, *Gertrude Stein: A Biography of Her Work,** Donald Sutherland suggests that it does; that here may be found the principle underlying all her future work, "the idea that present thinking is the final reality."

How different this is from Joyce, with whom her style, because it too is "different," has often been confused. The Jesuit-trained Joyce, conceiving of the present as a palimpsest of all the past, packed more and more of that past into his words so that, at the end, they achieve a maximum saturation, an ultimate density of interrelated associations. The philosophically and

* (New Haven, Yale University Press, 1951), pp. 7, 40–41.

medically trained Gertrude Stein, in her pursuit of "the immediate moment" (or the "prolonged" or "continuous present" as she came to call it) often seems to be chasing all historical meaning clean out of hers.

What she chooses to attend to and to ignore at different times determines her different styles. In her early writings, such as *Three Lives,* she concentrated on exploring "interior reality." Here the problem was to exclude everything that did not contribute to her conception of consciousness. To quote Sutherland: "First the word had to have not its romantic or literary meaning but the immediate meaning it had to the contemporary using it . . . The second necessity was to destroy 19th century syntax and word order, which could not follow the movement of a consciousness moving naturally." If this was an extension of the "realism" of Flaubert and of Henry James' preoccupation with states of consciousness, her reading of the Elizabethans, too, gave her "a precedent and model for an extremely loose syntax which could follow the immediate interest and impulse of the consciousness, whether lively and extravagant or simply ruminant."

From the subtly realized, individual speech-rhythms of these stories, Gertrude Stein went in an almost opposite direction in *The Making of Americans.* This is still interior reality, but of types rather than of individuals; of "everyone who ever was or is or will be living." "Everyone always is repeating the whole of them," she says, and bears it out with frequent re-beginnings, protracted repetitions, and a shifting sequence of time and events.

Still later, in such books as *Tender Buttons,* she turned to "exterior reality"; to a writing as self-contained as furniture, fruit, or a landscape.

It is not my purpose, even if I could, to enumerate or account for her many changes of style and intention, but to suggest some of the paradoxes and apparent contradictions in her life and art. One of the first of her generation to settle in Paris, in 1903, she became one of the most patriotic of the expatriates, writing indefatigably on American themes. Coming from a comfortable background (although her own income was modest), she wrote most tellingly in *Three Lives* about the servant class and about

Negroes. A personified Mecca for most of the avant-garde writers and painters of her time, she displayed in *The Making of Americans* a warmth of affection for the American middle class that was almost totally unreciprocated. From being one of the least read of important American writers, she became, with her autobiographies, one of the most popular. In these, where she intended to record events and personalities in the "biographical" sense, she wrote a simple, lucid, and lively prose. Yet the paradoxes continue. This intensely subjective, or "interior," writer, when she came to write her autobiographies, put them into the mouths first of her friend Alice B. Toklas and then of "everybody," so as to present Gertrude Stein objectively while maintaining a subjective point of view.

Mrs. Reynolds is the last long novel Gertrude Stein wrote before her death in Neuilly, France, in 1946. In the light of hindsight the earlier, shorter novels, "Marguerite" (1932), "Bartholemew Arnold" (1932), "Hotel François Ier" (1931), "Brim Beauvais" (1931), and "What Does She See When She Shuts Her Eyes" (1936), all seem preparations for *Mrs. Reynolds*.

On first meeting, Mrs. Reynolds is already Mrs. Reynolds. Later on she is not yet Mrs. Reynolds although she is called Mrs. Reynolds and it is predicted that she will become Mrs. Reynolds.

She likes predictions and generally manages to live up to them. She becomes Mrs. Reynolds. Is that her fate, to become what she is?

It is also predicted that when she grows up she will have more than a mile of strawberries, and a garden choked with box hedges. She is very happy about these predictions, at least the one about the strawberries. We are told that it will come true, but I don't remember its being mentioned again. Is this omission as significant as the repetitions? Does it mean they were there, the delight and the ordered tranquillity, but they were overshadowed?

If this novel is more than repetitions, the repetitions will mean something different to every reader, the novel will be rather a different novel, the characters will have different features and live in different places. We are not told what country this is. It

viii

might be the United States. It might be England. It might be France. Is it all three?

What of Mrs. Reynolds? Is she a nice, pretty, healthy, and well-born woman who is also quite empty-headed?

"It takes courage to be courageous said Mrs. Reynolds." Also she likes roses to be roses, and she does not think that stars are worlds. They are what you see in the sky, stars. She has no imagination? Yet "She thought she would prophesy for every day in every month not for herself but for everybody else. She knew she could if she would."

On the first page we are told:

> Mrs. Reynolds never sighed, she sometimes cried but she never sighed.
> All the world knows how to cry but not all the world knows how to sigh.
> Sighing is extra.

Throughout the book, and more and more, Mrs. Reynolds does sigh. She has good reason to. What is this apparent contradiction? Did Gertrude Stein forget what she had started out with? Is she being deliberately inconsistent? She sometimes, it seems to me, is; it is part of her "inner realism."

What is "extra" about sighing? Nervously, it is a sign and release of hypertension. Emotionally, it is a recognition of the inevitability of repeated experience; a symbol for growing older. To cry is to respond to something new or at least unexpected. Is Mrs. Reynolds a baby? She is baby, child, and grown-up. She carries her past and her future about with her: memories and predictions. In the mind these coexist; they are on the same plane.

In *Mrs. Reynolds* this plane is not the continuous present. It is written in the past tense. Yet it gives me the sensation of being an immediate past, of being a present moment continuously becoming the past. Even the future, when it is thought of, has already gone by.

This effect is heightened by the predictions. What is to come, having been foretold, has taken place, as in the 7th century prophecies of Saint Odile, the patron saint of Alsace: "Saint Odile had said, listen to me my brother, I have seen the terror in forests and mountains where the Germans shall be called the most war-like people of the earth."

The future is all contained within the time-span of the novel, 1889 to 1945, and especially and increasingly 1939 to 1945. No prediction goes beyond it, except the following. In 1853 Saint Godfrey prophesying the second World War, concludes:

> In 1948 there will be an appearance of revolution.

> In 1980 an era of Anti-Christ will exist for sixty years.

> Mrs. Reynolds read it all and showed it to every one and it was all true and she knew it was all true and it all would come to pass.

> I do not said Mrs. Reynolds care about what happens in 1980, why would I, said Mrs. Reynolds.

> When she dreamed again she dreamed of meat.

If the future, in this novel, does not extend beyond V-E Day, the past too, except for the prophecies, is all but obliterated. Beyond the mention of a nurse and some cousins of her grandfather, we are told nothing of Mrs. Reynolds' origins nor of those of anyone else in the book. Has the historical past been wiped out by the eternal past of these years? We are not told where she was born nor the year of her birth. Only the day of the week is given: it was a Tuesday.

She attaches great importance to Tuesday. Is this the pride we take in anything that distinguishes us? "Sometimes people wanted to give her a Thursday but she never took it, never noticed they wanted to give it to her." Is this the fulfilment of another prophecy: "Tuesday's child is full of grace?" Does it refer to the gods of war: Zeus' Day, or Tiu's Day? "That was the day they made peace from war and that was the day they made war from peace. And it was a Tuesday." To which war, to which peace, does this allude? Armistice Day, 1918, for instance, was a Monday. These questions are directed to that reader who is the opposite of the reader who regards the repetitions as just repetitions. They are addressed to the scholar who will one day try to pin them all down.

Mrs. Reynolds is never called by her first name. (Could it be Grace? she is sister-in-law to Hope, no blood relative, and Hope has entertained Angel Harper.) Nor is Mr. Reynolds. We never see Mr. Reynolds, although we sometimes hear him, agreeing a little too quickly as with an adversary. Yet they go to bed very early, we are told, sleep very happily and soundly, and are childless.

All this makes for an unwritten novel; a novel we try to supply as we read. The usual events of ordinary living, the going out and the coming in, the talking to people, the feeling well or ill, sad or happy, are wrenched loose of the contexts in which we customarily think of them, in which we live them, and made extraordinary. They prepare us for the miracles that rather casually occur: "Clothilde, Raymonde and Adele gave birth to Joseph." Why not? If a miracle is a miracle, why should it not be preposterous? The unusual is like everything else.

"His best friend," it is said of one of the friends of one of the minor characters, "was the widow of a tea-king, and she liked to wander in the rain in wooden shoes and carry an umbrella.

"She felt she was a Chinese heroine."

And what of Angel Harper? Angel Harper is unusual. He is announced by clouds. He begins by being a neighbor, although nobody really knows him until he goes away and later becomes a dictator. Then his name is on everybody's lips, in everybody's dreams. He is in his own dreams: "Gloomy is when Angel Harper dreamed."

Joseph Lane is another and more remote dictator. He begins by being not quite a neighbor. Nobody knows his age. At one point he is thirty, but not in relation to anybody else. Consequently he is unpredictable. Like Harper he is associated with forebodings, but of what? Does Lane lead to the future?

Everybody knows the age of Angel Harper. It is harped on. (Is he a relic of the past? Does his name imply haranguing?) More and more, everyone fears that Angel Harper will live to be a year older. Until finally, mercifully, "Angel Harper was not fifty-five alive." The past is ended. The novel is over.

Why doesn't Gertrude Stein say right out that Angel Harper is Adolf Hitler, and Joseph Lane Stalin? Is it because they are not? Because they are everybody's fears and thoughts and dreams about them? Are their names euphemisms for death? for birth? the fear of living? of reaching the menopause? of giving birth? of growing old? Are they all of these, and more: an equation of the extraordinary anxieties of our time with the ordinary anxieties of all time?

Through it all, interwoven with the dramatically minimized pity and terror, runs an underthread of serene confidence. The mile of strawberries is there, each plant carefully wrapped in straw from the rain.

In many ways *Mrs. Reynolds* is the culmination of Gertrude Stein's narrative style. This might be called a style by repetition, transposition, and accretion; to which must be added omission. Rather than developing by means of a beginning, a middle, and an end, its effect is one of endlessness.

It is a question how much each reader can tolerate of this endlessness. Gertrude Stein makes openly the kind of repetition that goes on inside our heads. It is this ease with what makes us uneasy that makes us resentful. She can be boring to the point of fascination, and fascinating to the point of boredom.

When one reads judiciously, the boredom tends to disappear, like the taste of resin in Greek wine. What is judicious? This will depend on each reader's octaves of attention. Often she exceeds my own span and I have to stop. But after the resentment whatever I may have been reading of her returns. When I read it again, I find that my own mind has grown more limber. For this I should be, and am, grateful, and expect to be more.

Meet Mrs. Reynolds.

CONTENTS

MRS. REYNOLDS

A NOVEL [1940–1942]

PART I

Chapter 1   It takes courage to be courageous
said Mrs. Reynolds.

She said it used to be Sunday and now it was Tuesday.

If it were Sunday and Tuesday, well it would be a day too much.

Mrs. Reynolds never sighed, she sometimes cried but she never sighed.

All the world knows how to cry but not all the world knows how to sigh.

Sighing is extra.

Mrs. Reynolds was a pretty woman and she had never been unwell.

Her husband was a nice man he looked nice and he was nice.

He was not well and strong but he could get along very well.

They were a good-looking couple and they had begun life and were going along. They had gone along.

They had a sister-in-law named Hope who was the wife of Mr. Reynolds' younger brother.

Mrs. Reynolds liked roses to be roses. That is the way she felt about roses. She felt that way about all roses.

I

She had a nephew, he was quiet and worked from morning until evening, he liked to do it. He had always known another boy who also was quiet not quite so quiet but quiet and who did not work quite so well from morning until evening but well enough. They had always known each other, they went to school together, they were both twenty-five years old and then they went to be soldiers and they were both killed by a bomb on the same day.

Mrs. Reynolds was very sorry about that, her eyes were filled with tears and she said he was dead, she knew he was dead because they had been told he was dead. They were both dead.

Mrs. Reynolds and her husband did not mind wind and rain, they did not mind heat, they did not like snow very much, it made Mr. Reynolds stay in the house and it kept Mrs. Reynolds from going very far, they often talked about dates in cakes and they often talked about bread in soup, they also often talked about eggs and butter but most often of all they talked about guinea hens and geese. They liked that the best of any subject of conversation. Of course they listened to the news, they had well not exactly an adopted son but one who could never become one and his name was Roger.

They often lost a dog, that is he did not live and they considered this very bad luck.

Mrs. Reynolds never complained but she told about it.

Mrs. Reynolds was quiet and easy, when she said, well, she meant well. She did.

Mrs. Reynolds is not all about roses, it is more about Tuesdays than about roses. Mrs. Reynolds had many kinds of Tuesdays. There were the Tuesdays that came after Mondays, there were the Tuesdays that came before Wednesdays, there were the Tuesdays that came after the first Sundays there were a great variety of Tuesdays and it all began with the Tuesday when Mrs. Reynolds was born. That was a Tuesday.

That was the day they made peace from war and that was the day they made war from peace. And it was a Tuesday.

On Tuesday getting better makes it worse and on Tuesday getting worse makes it better.

2

Mrs. Reynolds was very well born. She was born on Tuesday. Tuesday.

And then the next day was Wednesday and she was a day old on Wednesday.

Mrs. Reynolds accepted that.

When she had accepted that everything else followed, commenced convinced and followed. Thursday followed Wednesday and Tuesday followed Monday and there was Sunday and there was Saturday and there was Friday.

A little while after Mrs. Reynolds was born she knew the days of the week just like that.

She was born on Tuesday and there was no confusion. She knew it could be worse and she knew it was better.

And she never did care about Thursday. Thursday was never a day that came and went. To let it alone meant just nothing.

Mrs. Reynolds was never careless nor too careful, she seemed not to let everything alone but really she was careful of it, not too careful but quite careful.

Thursdays were different she was never careful of Thursdays.

Sometimes people wanted to give her a Thursday but she never took it, never noticed they wanted to give it to her. Paid no attention to it, never asked any one to take it away, simply did not notice a Thursday.

Mrs. Reynolds was careful to do so.

Her brother-in-law first met his wife Hope on a Wednesday. Her cousin Mr. Vine first met Mrs. Rose on a Saturday.

This had nothing to do with Mrs. Reynolds having been born on Tuesday, she knew that there was nothing to do, the stars had arranged it that she was to be born on a Tuesday. Nothing could stop it and she was born on a Tuesday.

She was sure that the stars had so arranged it and that there was nothing possible but that, she believed it and so do I.

Mrs. Rose was fond of flowers and fruits, she liked trees and plants.

She always said she would like to have fruit-trees growing on the sunny side of a wall. Mr. Vine always said he would put a goat on the wall to live there and nibble the fruit-trees.

3

Mrs. Reynolds having been born on a Tuesday, went on to be a little girl baby.

She had a very nice baby-carriage and she easily commenced to talk and walk.

Very very much later Mrs. Reynolds' husband had an adopted son called Roger. He was very thin, Mrs. Reynolds tried to fatten him, she did succeed in getting him into the habit of eating a very great deal but he always remained just as thin. Mrs. Reynolds said it was because he had eaten too much soup when he was young. Too much soup has a tendency to keep one thin.

They did not know what day Roger had been born and so Mrs. Reynolds decided that he should always have his birthday not on a Tuesday but always on a Friday. Which became a habit with him, Roger always had his birthday once a year on a Friday, he could choose whichever Friday pleased him but he could only have one.

After a while Roger went away and nobody ever knew what became of him.

So after Mrs. Reynolds had commenced talking and walking she went out with her nurse every day and she always had something to say, she said, well are they coming. She always said that. Of course they very often did come.

She had said after they did come, Will they come quickly will they.

And then she said, are they coming and then she said Are they coming quickly.

She was about six years old before she stopped asking that.

She began to say let us play that they are not coming, let us play that they are not coming quickly.

She was almost seven before she stopped saying that.

She continued to be a little girl. She had a cousin who was older, and who had a mother. She did not look like her mother. Their mouths were not shaped alike.

They both liked to work hard that is to say the mother did and the daughter did too. If the mother worked hard she was not tired, if the daughter did, well she was not tired either. Much as they had to do they always did it. Any day.

4

Mrs. Reynolds never said how do you do to her cousin, not for any reason, but there was no reason to say how do you do to her cousin or to her cousin's mother. The mother naturally enough was a widow. The daughter never married that is she had not married when Mrs. Reynolds was Mrs. Reynolds, but to wait did not bother her and later on waiting was like being there. And he came, not to stay and not to go away, but she had seen him. Mrs. Reynolds knew it she did not know him but she knew it.

Mrs. Reynolds then after she had been born on Tuesday went on being a little girl until she went to school. That was not the same thing. She learned to read out loud. That changed everything.

She quite liked studying. She did not like music or geography. She found music lugubrious, all music, and she found geography uninteresting.

Much later her husband's brother who married a girl named Hope was professor of historical geography. He could tell all about roads and plains and hills and their connection with history. He did not often but once in a while he did explain something. Mrs. Reynolds said yes I see, they were coming but they did not come. Yes yes said her brother-in-law pleasantly.

Mrs. Reynolds' husband had a distant cousin, who was a captain in the army and his specialty was geography. He was married and had five children, and his wife's mother had been put away because she was crazy, a great many in her family were, but she herself was very sensible and a good manager and all her children except the third one were very happy. He the captain never at any time said anything about geography. To be sure they never saw him very often, but they did quite often at one time see his wife and the five children. None of the children nor the wife ever said anything about geography.

So Mrs. Reynolds who was still a little girl went on studying and explaining quite enough.

She did not even care to hear people whistle, she had a brother who was always whistling. She did not really mind but she thought it was lugubrious.

Arithmetic went very well and spelling. A tune did run through

5

her head sometimes, not a tune exactly but a thing, it said, they look like men, they look like men, they look like men of war, it came into her head, she was around thirteen then, it came into her head between sleeping and waking. She did not think the tune lugubrious but she knew that they would not come.

Then she was a little older she was sixteen.

Fortunately sixteen was not any older.

At that time she knew some one who kept cows, and these people always were losing a little calf who would well not run away but get away. Mrs. Reynolds when she was sixteen liked to hear it getting away and then seeing it brought back again. It gave her a happy feeling. She said it is coming, and when it came she said it is going, and whichever she said last she liked to say and she said the last last.

When she was sixteen eighteen was so far away it was not interesting but she never lost her interest in Tuesday. She never longed for Tuesday but there it was.

Sixteen was not more necessary than fifteen but fifteen was a has been.

Mrs. Reynolds felt like that. She did when she was sixteen.

When she was sixteen she had a distant cousin who had a brother who had a son and that son liked his hat to match his socks and his hair. Most people like to match their eyes but he did not he liked to match his hair. Not that his hair was red or anything like that. It was just rather a pale color.

He was not very active but he liked to stand. If he stood he was quite comfortable and he told her that she was to be Mrs. Reynolds. That was his prediction to her, he predicted that she would be Mrs. Reynolds.

Later when she was seventeen she said it was predicted that she would be Mrs. Reynolds.

When she was seventeen she was often enough ready to see anybody who came even when they did not come. They sometimes passed along. It was a nice way to come and they often came that way. Mrs. Reynolds she was only seventeen then and not Mrs. Reynolds had her seventeenth birthday on a Tuesday.

On Saturday and Wednesday, she had a brother who knew some one who was a doctor and whose wife liked gardening, she the wife always said that something was going to happen on Saturday or Wednesday. Mrs. Reynolds when she was seventeen said she would wait for Saturday and Wednesday but she herself had always been born on Tuesday.

Then Mrs. Reynolds was eighteen but she was not yet Mrs. Reynolds. She had a friend who had a wife and three daughters, there might have been four daughters but as one of them had died there were only three. They all three looked as if they were very pretty girls but the oldest one who was a very pretty girl never gave it away, she talked about it but she never gave it away, she said she never did because she was born on a Friday.

The second one who was really very pretty was very busy passing examinations that is to say getting ready to pass examinations, she wanted Mrs. Reynolds who was not Mrs. Reynolds yet to come with her and pass examinations but Mrs. Reynolds did not care to get ready, if she was not already ready for anything and she mostly was ready for anything she was to do, she did not care to get ready and she certainly did not care to get ready to pass any examination. Then there was the youngest daughter, well she really was not a pretty girl but she might have been, but unfortunately her features did not make her pretty. She was quite comfortable as she was and that was all of that.

Mrs. Reynolds was now nineteen. She was coming nearer to being Mrs. Reynolds, she was not really Mrs. Reynolds until she was twenty-three.

She stayed with a friend who had a whole mile of strawberries, they were all in one row, nice bushy plants that just followed close on one another, the whole mile and under every bit of the mile they had put straw and so even when it rained the strawberries were good, they were a very large variety almost like a small tomato and they were called country strawberries. Mrs. Reynolds she was nineteen then and not yet Mrs. Reynolds liked this mile of strawberries very much. A friend of these friends who was staying with them predicted that some day when Mrs.

Reynolds would be Mrs. Reynolds she would have an even longer line of these strawberries than were here and this prediction was highly pleasing.

She who made the prediction was a funny woman, she liked candy made of honey, she liked to keep money, that is to say if there was a certain sum to pay she liked to make believe that she had paid it all when she had not when she had kept back the last bit, she also liked to tell about what happened to her and well nobody knew but she did like to tell what had happened to her. A prince had wanted to marry her but she refused him and married a baker. A friend of the prince had wanted to give her a wedding present of a house and a car and she had accepted it and then he had gone away. She had liked having a dog and when it was killed she cried for three days, and candy made of honey was no consolation. She always accepted a gift even when it was a dog which snapped and was disagreeable, she kept him, and once in a while she made a prediction, and she predicted that when Mrs. Reynolds was Mrs. Reynolds she would have more than a mile of strawberry plants and when Mrs. Reynolds was Mrs. Reynolds she did have more than a mile of strawberry plants and that pleased her and also because it had been predicted to her.

She was nineteen then and then she was twenty. She was not yet twenty-one.

When she was twenty she had a friend and this friend had a garden and in this garden there were box hedges, the garden was all made into circles and squares of box hedges and they were lovely and smelled of box when they were clipped and they were clipped every two months. Mrs. Reynolds, she was not Mrs. Reynolds then she was only twenty and she was not Mrs. Reynolds until she was twenty-three. She stayed in the country in the house that had the garden filled with box hedges and she liked these hedges. There there was a woman she was staying there too and she was not a strange woman but she did say strange things. She said one day that she considered that servants were nothing but utensils, in fact said she that is the way I feel about them, well yes utensils. Everybody thought her saying this was very shocking.

Then she said and box hedges, box hedges are not like servants

8

they are not utensils, everybody thought that her saying this was very shocking and she went on, and you she said looking at Mrs. Reynolds who was not Mrs. Reynolds yet, you will some day when you are Mrs. Reynolds you will have a lovely garden and it will be full so full that there will be no room for anything else it will be full of box hedges. Mrs. Reynolds, she was not Mrs. Reynolds yet she was only twenty always liked predictions but she could not quite settle in her mind whether this was a prediction, she could not quite settle it in her mind, yes or no.

The woman who made the prediction was not a strange woman, not at all. She had three daughters, one of them was a nun, one of them was a trained nurse and the other one was a bridge teacher. She herself had a brother who was very distinguished, and whenever he had a little stain of any kind on his hand he always sucked it off but he was he really was very distinguished. He once lost his memory but that was only for a very short while, after that, he became a mayor and was very distinguished very distinguished indeed, and they never wanted any one else, they only wanted him.

And so Mrs. Reynolds was then twenty-one.

She went pale at twenty-one just a little pale, she had been quite rosy until then and later on she was pleasantly rosy again but at twenty-one she was quite a little pale.

When she was pale she was twenty-one.

Just then her cousin had a lover, he was young, had very large eyes and he was tall and he had a brother whose name was George. He and his brother were really devoted to one another although they had nothing in common, George liked drinking liquor his brother did not, George wanted to marry, his brother did not, George was heavyset and his brother was thin and being thin and having large eyes he was a lover and George was not. Well anyway he the lover did notice that Mrs. Reynolds was twenty-one and that she was quite pale then. He said to her is it because it is Tuesday. No said Mrs. Reynolds, she was not Mrs. Reynolds then, no because today is not Tuesday, it is Monday, tomorrow is Tuesday.

It really did make a difference, it is hard to believe that there

9

is such a difference between Monday and Tuesday but there is. Anybody who has ever been through anything knows that.

And so the cousin's lover said how satisfactory it will be when there is Monday. Yes they all said. Yes he said it will be satisfactory, so very satisfactory. But and his eyes his large eyes were sad, yes but it will never happen, it will always be Monday after Sunday and before Tuesday, always.

And that is true enough and that is what they all said.

Gradually she was not any longer twenty-one and so gradually she was not pale any more, and pretty soon she was twenty-two and even quite as pretty as she ever had been as well as being twenty-two.

Then clouds began to come that is she began to see the clouds there were in the sky, rosy clouds and dark clouds and white clouds and silver clouds. Whichever clouds there were, she noticed them and she looked at them.

There was a daughter of a friend of her mother who always listened while she talked about the clouds she saw.

This daughter of the friend of her mother's was the oldest of four girls. She used to cut their hair, and she made them look quite fashionable and then she more or less cut her own hair, she was the only one of the four of them who could cut hair like that. And then they all put their hair up in hair curlers, they liked it better than a permanent, and besides their mother did not like them to go to a hair-dresser's, and then they would fluff out their hair and they all looked very well, none of them really pretty, but they all four of them looked very well, they had a brother but he only sat and read. So she the oldest of them was always listening when Mrs. Reynolds, she was not quite yet Mrs. Reynolds talked about clouds.

She said about clouds, look at that cloud, every time I look at that cloud I know there is to be going on being clouds and I am sure they are black clouds and not white clouds. And if there are white clouds well after all black clouds can be rosy clouds as well as white clouds and black clouds can be silver clouds as well as well as white clouds. Now look at that cloud she said to the daughter of her mother's friend, now look at that cloud, there are lots of clouds but look at that cloud now what does it look like. Well, said the daughter of her mother's friend, yes and if that cloud is followed by other clouds what does it look like, if you can tell me what it looks like I can tell you what it looks like said Mrs. Reynolds, she was not Mrs. Reynolds yet.

They both sighed. I know what it looks like, said Mrs. Reynolds, it looks like that cloud and that cloud well I hate to say it out loud, but it looks like a cloud, well I don't know quite what to say about that cloud, and she sighed. The other sighed too.

The cloud disappeared but it was true there were clouds.

So one day they were looking at clouds and there were some white clouds but they were far away and there were some rosy clouds but they turned to grey, now said Mrs. Reynolds, she was not Mrs. Reynolds yet, now said she to the oldest daughter of her mother's friend now you just tell me what that cloud looks like not the rosy cloud not the white cloud but the grey cloud, now you just tell me. Well said the other, yes well said Mrs. Reynolds yes now I think I just think that that grey cloud well no it is the white that does look like a white dog, do you see it looks just like a white dog, the grey cloud well it looks like well I just do not want to say what it looks like, do you see what it looks like she said, and the other said yes, well it does said Mrs. Reynolds.

And then one day they were looking at clouds, and everything was just filled with clouds lots and lots and lots of clouds and as they were looking at the clouds Mrs. Reynolds said, now what do you think of that cloud now that is what I call a silver cloud, it is not a white cloud and it will not be a white cloud because a silver cloud never is a white cloud. No said the oldest daughter of her mother's friend, no, No said Mrs. Reynolds, she was not Mrs. Reynolds yet, no silver cloud well silver clouds have to change and if they change what will they change to, there is no way to know what they will change to, and she sighed and the other sighed too.

And they looked at the silver clouds and they did change, they changed to other clouds.

And that day, Mrs. Reynolds she was not yet but very nearly Mrs. Reynolds, that day she happened to see three very very large dark red slugs climbing a tree, they moved very slowly very very slowly but they did move. They moved very slowly and not always up but they did move and she did not wait to see she had other things to do but she did know that they were going up the tree which they did do.

And so she said, she would not look at clouds any more, she just would look at the sky and see if it was going to rain and just leave it like that, and she said to the eldest daughter of her mother's friend, The trouble with clouds is that they can always be clouds. And the other said yes, oh yes.

And now Mrs. Reynolds was twenty-three and this year she was to be Mrs. Reynolds.

She was now twenty-three and it was through Epie and her brother that she was to meet Mr. Reynolds.

One night it was nearly morning and she dreamed that there were five artichokes blooming in the garden. A little later she met Epie and her brother Leonardo. Leonardo was a musician who neither played nor sang nor composed. But he did know every prediction and he knew it had been predicted that she would when she was twenty-three become Mrs. Reynolds. He introduced her to Mr. Reynolds and before she was twenty-four she was Mrs. Reynolds, as had been foretold.

Mrs. Reynolds and Mr. Reynolds were quiet and busy. Before he met her he had been in a war and so he had to be careful as to what he ate but she knew, she had not been in a war but she knew. He had lost two brothers in the war and then he had a younger brother and the younger brother died, so Mr. Reynolds was the last of four brothers and he was married to Mrs. Reynolds. Very much later and in another war he lost his only nephew, and Mrs. Reynolds had nephews and they the Reynolds never had any children but they did not sigh, it was easy to be peaceful morning and evening.

So it had been predicted that she would be Mrs. Reynolds before she was twenty-four and she was.

Mrs. Reynolds' grandfather's cousin was a lawyer, he was a

12

lawyer but he knew a lot about eating and cooking and he wrote a book about it, and he had a daughter-in-law and a grandson and the grandson married a widow with five children. The grandson never had a child of his own.

They all including the stepchildren were present at the marriage of Mr. and Mrs. Reynolds.

There was also a cousin whose mother was very charitable and her daughter always said so and the son-in-law always said so and they had three children, none of them married happily. They were all present at the marriage of Mr. and Mrs. Reynolds.

There was one more cousin whose mother was alive and whose father was dead and who had a brother. The brother was a doctor and married an Egyptian and he had three children two of them twins and the children came home but he never did. His sister was also a doctor, she did not marry until she was older and then she was almost immediately enceinte, and looked very thin and pale and stammered a little. Her husband was an engineer and had disappeared but not for always.

Anyway she was present at the marriage of Mr. and Mrs. Reynolds.

They settled down to a pleasant life quiet, and active, and they had neighbors.

On one side was a family there had been a very old father and he was dead and there was a fairly old mother and she was active, there was a very gentle very blue-eyed son and he had married a rather gaunt wife and they had a child and it might have been a boy but it was a girl and its name was Jenny, it was as gaunt as its mother and as blue-eyed and gently smiling as the father and it had a god-father who was Colonel Isaac Courageous, and they did not see him often but once in a while, he was small and blue-eyed and very careful and not particularly pleasant and he had a wife and a daughter and the daughter sang and predicted, she could predict diseases and she could predict property and she could predict ages, and she was tall and rather stout although both her mother and her father were very small.

On the other side of the Reynolds lived Mr. Reynolds' younger brother and his wife Hope.

13

The parents of the wife sometimes came and stayed with them but mostly they had other kind of people with them.

The ones they knew best were two men.

The one was Angel Harper. He became very well known but they did not know him any more then.

The other was older he was Joseph Lane. He had bushy eyebrows and was older than any of them and it did not make any difference to him how young he was or how old he was.

Mr. Reynolds' younger brother always stayed in bed when anything happened, nothing much does happen but when it did happen and it happened the great part of any winter, he stayed in bed, his wife Hope did not stay with him, she went out, and he did not like to stay alone but he did, he stayed in bed.

The wife of the younger brother of Mr. Reynolds adored the cracked voices of little dogs. Her name was Hope and she never had a little dog nor did she want to have one.

Her name was Hope and she was interested in mushrooms. She particularly liked wild ones. She sometimes had a pleasant voice but very often she was teaching. She could prepare boys and girls for college and she did not like walking. They did not have very much money in fact very often they did not have any but she did not mind being poor. She was often very quiet, she was always quite polite and she always inquired for the other members of the family when she met any one. She was very often used to be asked with her husband and as very often he could not come she was very often used to not going.

She and her sister-in-law were neighbors but it would not be very likely that they would be either going out or coming in at the same time.

Anyway neither the brothers nor the sisters-in-law met, they really never met.

Mrs. Reynolds was quite fond of her husband's god-daughter a girl of twelve, and sometimes had her to stay with her. She looked like Mrs. Reynolds you never can tell these things but they do happen.

To be sure Mrs. Reynolds had small features and dark blue eyes and mediumly brown hair while the little girl had sandy hair and light blue eyes and might come to have rather rugged features.

Mrs. Reynolds once said, she was speaking of unpleasant people, they will not handle them as easily as they did us. Here they drank champagne there they will be filled up with water.

That is what she meant when she said it.

She probably thought they would be drowned.

If some even a good many are drowned it probably would be easier. Very well then.

The god-daughter of Mr. Reynolds said to Mrs. Reynolds, the birds are flying high in the sky today, sometimes they fly high and sometimes they fly low.

And then she went on eagerly, it is true and they tell me so the birds fly high when the air is light but not simply in delight, they fly high because the air is light and all the insects are carried high by the light and the birds fly high to eat the insects that are up so high in the sky and when the air is heavy the birds fly low because just below there are the insects and they eat them up so, the birds look as if they were there just to have a happy time and just to tell anybody who knows whether there is going to be rain or not like the barometer does but not at all that is not the reason why they fly high and low, I know it said Mr. Reynolds' god-daughter to Mrs. Reynolds, I know it is so because my god-father told me so.

Ah yes said Mrs. Reynolds yes it is true but it is not that that makes anybody be sad.

Mrs. Reynolds was very content any day, any day was quite a pleasant day, quite, not altogether, but quite, a little more than quite, any day was a pleasant day.

Take today.

When Mrs. Reynolds slept and any one awakened her she would turn her head and still asleep would say do not take the water away water should always be kept for flowers.

So any day was a pleasant enough day.

Fish were sympathetic to Mrs. Reynolds but not bees.

And after that each one in his or her own way was troubled.

On these days Mrs. Reynolds would say, The sun moves so fast that it is impossible to keep one's feet in the sun.

Mr. Reynolds had a cousin who was a judge.

Judges should not mix much with people.

There was one judge who had a sister and one friend, that friend talked all the time and the judge said from time to time yes Oliver yes Oliver.

There was another judge who wrote poetry when he did not judge and he had a wife and a little boy and the wife died and the little boy lived with her father and her mother so that judge had no one. There was another judge and his wife liked hunting and fishing and she hunted and she fished all the time and when it was a closed season for hunting and fishing she was busy preparing for the open season that was to come, she liked to train dogs to hunt truffles too and so the judge had no one.

The cousin of Mr. Reynolds was never married and so he had no one, he sometimes visited with Mr. and Mrs. Reynolds and stayed quite a long time but he always spent a great deal of time alone in his room, and when he did come out he was very quiet, very gentle, all the judges were gentle, very gentle, they were all very gentle.

This cousin of Mr. Reynolds had a brother and a sister. The brother was a doctor who specialized in oriental diseases and he married a well-to-do and rather stout Greek woman and they had a number of children most of them twins. His sister was not completely a doctor but very nearly, she was a chemist too and not too young she married an engineer and when she was going to have a baby she began to stammer. She hoped her husband would be home in time to see the baby born and he was, it was a boy and they were pleased, naturally enough.

They had a cousin who was a doctor a very great doctor and very important.

His father and his mother had been important before him and his grandfather and his grandmother and even further back.

He himself had married well not exactly married but he had two children by a woman who drank, and later when his father and his mother and his grandfather and his grandmother were all

16

dead he married her and then she died, and there he was with his son and with his daughter.

The daughter was always with him or at least he was always with her, they travelled a great deal and nobody liked her, she had not liked what had happened to her she was liking what was happening to her but nobody liked her, not that that mattered because she liked what she had now, and having spent a great many years knowing that nobody liked her she now spent a few years knowing what she knew, and this was true.

The son could be liked by any one, not alone for he was never alone not drunk for he was always drunk not sober because he was quite often nearly sober, but just enough so that one day he was married. He said marrying was nobody's business but his own and his father never forgave him. Not that that made any difference to any one because if he wanted to, he and his wife could live with his father and sister, which they did.

His wife had been a friend of the wife of Mr. Reynolds' brother. Hope and her husband came to know the two of them very intimately and through them they all came to see a great deal more of Angel Harper.

Angel Harper later was a dictator.

Hope dreamed one night that very much later Angel Harper the dictator, said everything was all over, and she dreamed that she said to him and what are you going to do, and he said they will not go, they are all to be drowned but they will not go, and she dreamed she said to him and what will you do, and he said to her tell me what to do and she said to him you have invented so much invent a way to disappear that is to say to die and he said why, and she said why not die, and he said yes, I will die, and then she woke up.

In those early days she sometimes told her dreams to Angel Harper. He was not yet a dictator and he only said to her oh shut up.

The doctors now broke in and said, The deepest thing in any one is the conviction of the bad luck that follows boasting. That said Henry, that was his name, is something that dictators cannot get the best of.

What said Henry can they do about that.

Angel Harper was not yet a dictator nor sure yet that he would be one and so he did not answer.

Henry was the one who had found out that people like Americans who drink water and not wine, eat moist food, people like Italians and French who drink wine eat dry food, and people who drink beer eat soggy food.

Henry found out a lot and whatever he found out he said. He was now interested in dictators, naturally enough, Angel Harper was sure to be one and then there was Joseph Lane, well Joseph Lane never came where any one could see him not even Henry.

Easy enough said Henry.

Mr. Reynolds was a very nice man, he was polite and he was honest. He said, of any one who was polite, he is too polite to be honest. He never met anybody who knew his brother although they did live next door to one another.

Mr. and Mrs. Reynolds knew the district-attorney. He was a pleasant man. He wore a wedding-ring although as far as anybody knew he was not married.

He said he liked living in a country that was hilly and had marshes because one could find forget-me-nots growing any time all summer.

He liked to tell stories, so does any one, he liked to tell them rather than hear any one else tell them, so does any one.

He had a friend who was the youngest judge in the whole country. He was a judge and he had a very sweet smile and he studied the stars.

He made predictions and he wrote a little book which was never printed and which was called Intentions and Predictions.

In it he predicted that Mr. Reynolds would become a town-councillor, that he would give his town a new school and that he would have built in the town a new road which the town needed and which led directly to Mr. Reynolds' country property.

All these three predictions came true.

Mr. Reynolds' brother continued to see his friends. Each one of them continued to see their friends and each one of them made many new friends and they each one of them saw a good deal of their new friends. Nobody likes not to have new friends and to see a good deal of these new friends.

Give me new faces new faces new faces I have seen enough of the old ones today.

Neither Mr. Reynolds nor his brother ever said that but they each one of them did have a good many new friends and they each one of them did see these new friends of theirs very often and Mrs. Reynolds the wife of Mr. Reynolds did too have some new friends not as many as her husband Mr. Reynolds and he did not have as many new friends as his brother and his brother did not have as many new friends as his wife Hope Reynolds. She had more new friends than any of them and she saw these new friends more often.

She did sometimes meet the new friends of some of the other three, she did once see the young judge who had a very sweet smile and made predictions. He was not interested in Hope Reynolds but he said how do you do, and he predicted that she would come to know Angel Harper, but she knew him already so the judge's prediction did not mean anything to her, but all the same just like all true predictions it did mean something.

Among other things it meant that this man's name was Angel Harper which it was.

It gradually did mean that.

Mr. and Mrs. Reynolds when they met anybody always said how do you do and Mrs. Reynolds would say, after all how is it that anything is best left alone all alone. How is it said Mrs. Reynolds.

Mr. Reynolds for his part said that it was very likely that five hundred was as much as he liked to have at one time.

They were very good-looking and very pleasant and they were very comfortable and very restful as each one of them said what they said.

They neither of them ever said to any one be mine. They never did, neither Mrs. Reynolds nor Mr. Reynolds.

Mr. Reynolds' younger brother was always saying it is greed, greed, nothing but greed. His best friend was the widow of a tea-king, and she liked to wander in the rain in wooden shoes and carry an umbrella.

She felt she was a Chinese heroine.

Little by little the younger brother of Mr. Reynolds said it is greed greed nothing but greed. He often forgot in between, he was angry when he forgot and when he came to, he said to himself, it is greed greed nothing but greed, he never said this to any one else, he only said it to himself.

The widow of the tea-king had a friend, he was librarian of a legislative assembly. He and his wife had been married many years and had no children and then they had a little girl an unusually pretty one. The father always said nothing. He was a pleasant man and said pleasant things, he said he always said it is a pleasure to listen. His wife was very obedient and very active and often went in and out, and the little girl might have been a grandchild, only she was not she was their daughter.

He knew another librarian of a legislative family and he also had been married for twenty years and they never had had a child and then they had one, a little boy, he was not very good-looking, his mother was Swedish, and he did not look like her. Anyway the father was pleasant very pleasant and was always ready to answer when any one asked him about the future. It is very simple he said very simple there is nothing to look forward to except ruin. He said ruin, ruin when there are ruins it is a pleasant thought and ruin when it is ruin well anyway he was very quiet and he always said when anybody asked him, he always said there was nothing to look forward to except ruin. Ruin was inevitable.

He and his wife and the little boy went away and they could be met once in a while as it would happen.

Mrs. Reynolds and Mr. Reynolds knew that when summer was over winter would come but they did not really mind that, winter was cold and summer was warm and that was the only difference that was noticeable and even that was not always so, sometimes there would be warm days in winter and sometimes there would be cold days in summer.

Mrs. Reynolds said cold days in summer were not very agreeable but warm days in winter were not too bad.

If one did not see her for a whole week, it did not mean that there was anything the matter, it meant that she just did not happen to be about just then.

Angel Harper never passed in front of her house, he always happened to come the other way when he went to see Mr. Reynolds' younger brother.

Angel Harper stayed in hotels. In one hotel there was a wife who might have been very good-looking if she had been taller and her face not so flat. She did not like either her husband who was the hotel-keeper or the hotel. Not long after she went home to her father, who was a small contractor. He liked having her because she was very good at business, she hoped to marry an army officer but she never did at least she had not yet.

Angel Harper continued to know her.

She had a friend who was the wife of a photographer. The photographer had a sister who was born with only one arm.

He was very successful and had a great many children. Angel Harper went there and there he met a girl who was doing commercial painting. She had learned how in a correspondence school and always found plenty of work not very well paid but always plenty of it. Her people were dairy farmers and she went home to lunch and to dinner every day. Her mother was a very large stout woman and her father was an interesting medium-sized dark man. Her brother was a hard worker and very good-looking.

Angel Harper went there for dinner quite often.

Angel Harper had had a long youth and now as he grew older he grew fonder and fonder of potatoes. Besides eating them he liked to rub raw ones over his hands and arms and face.

He liked it better than soap.

He grew older.

If she is young and good-looking well if she is young and good-looking.

Angel Harper never answered that question.

One warm night in autumn when there was a low lying mist

alive with moonlight and there was thunder and lightning, he was quiet and he heard about Joseph Lane and he wondered if he knew many people.

Mrs. Reynolds the wife of Mr. Reynolds stayed at home and breathed out a sigh. She liked to prophesy. She said, purchase bye and bye will be not a matter of money but a matter of personality. If you are popular you can buy if you are not popular you can die.

Mrs. Reynolds stayed at home and breathed out a sigh.

She thought about butter and sugar and oil and coffee, she thought about meat and ham and hunger. She was never hungry but she always ate. She thought about noodles and cream. She was often thoughtful.

Life was that way. It was often thoughtful.

Mrs. Reynolds thought about days in the month. She thought about every day in the month. She thought she would prophesy for every day in every month not for herself but for everybody else. She knew she could if she would. Would she, she said she would.

To prophesy for years is more difficult than to prophesy for months. This she said is perfectly well known. She said spiders can exaggerate but never months and days. She was fairly fortunate because after all prophecies do come true yes they do.

She was the wife of Mr. Reynolds and that had been predicted to her before she knew Mr. Reynolds, and now she stayed at home and breathed out a sigh, of contentment.

Mr. Reynolds came in from a nice long cold walk, thank you said Mr. Reynolds thank you for having given me such a nice long walk. But I did not give you a long walk said Mrs. Reynolds. Oh yes said Mr. Reynolds you always give me everything so you did give me a nice long cold walk.

Mrs. Reynolds liked holiness but only holiness if it is accompanied by predictions. Holiness often is.

Mrs. Reynolds liked her cousins to be tall men. All four of them were, two of them were thin and tall and two of them were broad and tall. One of them had as a neighbor a little man quite shrunken who was nearly ninety. Every day he worked all day, he always said how do you do and he liked a dog but he always lost them and then he did not have one. He had a daughter and she was much younger, she also said how do you do and she also worked all day and every day and she also liked to have a dog and she also had one and she also lost him.

Mrs. Reynolds never met them but her cousin told her what they said. He told her that each one of them said that they had lost their dog. The daughter thought that their neighbor the cousin of Mrs. Reynolds had poisoned the dog but of course this was not so. It did make trouble though. One night there was screaming but nobody paid any attention and it never happened again.

None of Mrs. Reynolds' cousins were interested in either holiness or predictions. They were quiet, they mostly never talked, their father did, he drank a good deal and he liked to make jokes and he said don't give me money give me bank-notes, he had quite a few and he meant it when he said it, he said do not give me money give me bank-notes, money is no use, give me bank-notes.

His sons heard him, they always heard anybody who ever said anything. They all liked Mr. and Mrs. Reynolds but then who did not.

Please said Mrs. Reynolds please and sometimes when she said please there were tears in her eyes.

Please said Mrs. Reynolds.

She stood in front of her house and she said, yes now they are here and now they are there but well but perhaps they will have to join the dance.

Mrs. Reynolds liked holiness when it was related to predictions, she preferred that a man should be a holy man if he was to predict coming events, no matter how long he had been dead if he had been a holy man and he predicted coming events, well and Mrs. Reynolds was right, well the predictions would come to be true. Naturally he had to have been a holy man naturally yet and again.

Mrs. Reynolds was quiet, she was kind to all the beasts of the field and to domestic animals, nevertheless she liked food and potatoes and she liked houses, she did not really care so much about gardens.

In a little while she would sigh and at a distance Joseph Lane would hear her. He did not like women to be tall not at all he liked them to be round and pleasant and not small. He was careful of himself.

He never knew Mr. Reynolds and of course he did not know the brother of Mr. Reynolds nor his wife but he did see Mrs. Reynolds. He passed her house when he was thinking and all the time before he was old enough to do other things he was always thinking.

He said to himself, whether it is good weather or bad weather, and he said to himself, whether sunshine or rain is good weather or bad weather.

He said to himself, Very likely it will and he meant very likely it will rain or very likely there will be fog or very likely there will be sunshine. He had seen so much snow that he did not think about snow. Snow was not interesting.

He went back and forth every day, he was not where he belonged but he would be. He muttered to himself, whenever he muttered he muttered more or less the same thing.

Like that.

Sometimes people noticed him and sometimes they did not. Sometimes he noticed people and sometimes he did not.

If he went away, well if he went away. Nobody was there if he went away. For a long while he did not. He did not go away. Not like that.

Mrs. Reynolds was pleased to stay at home and so was Mr. Reynolds.

They had some visitors but not a great many. Mr. Reynolds liked to play cards but not Mrs. Reynolds, not at all.

Not as much.

Mr. Reynolds' brother did not care to play cards, not as much and neither did his wife Hope.

They did see Angel Harper from time to time.

Gloomy is when Angel Harper dreamed.

He knew anybody he loved was very beautiful, and one

night he dreamed that the one he loved was very ugly, he knew it was she and he knew he was he and he saw, oh dear he saw he saw her. Very ugly, and then he dreamed again.

There was no use in his dreaming again.

It is gloomy enough to dream again.

Calling out loud did not make him stop dreaming but Mr. Reynolds' brother came and woke him.

Perhaps well perhaps Angel Harper went away and they never saw him.

But ten years after, it made no difference because everybody knew about him and might he might be afraid enough.

You see I see
I see you see
Angel Harper
Once again.
I see you see
You see I see
Angel Harper.

Angel Harper looked just the same as he used to but Mr. Reynolds' brother and his wife Hope did not see him. They were alive all right but they did not see him.

All right.

Chapter II   The hoot-owl was hooting terrifically up the valley. Nobody knew just when or how Angel Harper was born. Not that it made any difference. It did not.

He talked to himself. He said, If you count forty-two you have forty-two, if forty-two are dead, and you count forty-two, you have forty-two.

He might have been worried about that word have, because of course there is the word halve, but he was not.

He did not have to say he was not, he just was not, not yet, he was not yet married, never yet.

So he began, being born did not interest him and being dead could not happen to him and being married was never a possibility for him and being older as yet was not happening to him and being younger had never happened to him, so what was the matter.

Sometimes nothing was the matter.

His name was Angel Harper and sometimes nothing was the matter.

He never said to any one, who are you, and really nobody ever said to him who are you.

Why, well why was he not interesting, he said as he said he said it, he said I am talking, and by god he was, he was talking.

Angel Harper was his name.

He met a man who was an officer, and the officer never liked anybody to do any business, he always said, dismiss all the people who work for you and close down your business.

This officer's name was Susan. Mr. Susan, and he had black eyes and white hair. He was obliged always to be present whenever anything happened and in this way Angel Harper gradually came to know him.

Sometimes in a hurry but often not at all. That was Angel Harper.

He did not like either day or night, anything made him nervous, and why not day and why not night.

He knew a custom house officer who raised everything he ate, corn for his chickens, cabbages for his rabbits, wine for his drinking, vegetables and potatoes, and peaches, he only bought meat and groceries, and milk and butter, everything else he grew himself.

He used to say to every one as he examined their baggage. It is better so.

And indeed it is.

He never had a chance to tell Angel Harper it was better so because Angel Harper did not care to eat rabbits or chickens.

Gradually it was very quiet, that was when Angel Harper heard his own heart beat and was scared. He knew he had a heart, and he loved himself for himself alone.

Never more than that, he told his friends, and they answered that they understood.

Every one understood Angel Harper, he was like that, they understood him, they heard what he said and they understood him.

By this time he had not forgotten, but he did not see Mr. Reynolds' brother and his wife Hope.

At the time he did see him he was not ready to be what he was. He was nervous and he was gloomy and he was earnest and he was older and he was silent and he was angry, he was all that then.

Mrs. Reynolds gently enough knew Joseph Lane. She said she thought that he was a foreigner, which he was.

Joseph Lane was strong and he did not drink, he came again and he went away and whichever he was doing, he did not startle any one and he did not cough, but, and this was true, nobody knew, no, nobody knew, what it was that he was going to do. Nobody.

Joseph Lane was ubiquitous. If he was not there then he was. Hours and hours there were hours and hours every day and hours and hours every night and he used them all he could use them all, he could call them hours and he knew what each hour had to do.

So many of them but not too many for Joseph Lane. He never thanked any one. Why should he. He had all those hours and if he had all those hours then he had them, such a lot of them.

Mrs. Reynolds was right when she thought that he was a foreigner.

Don't you know said Mrs. Reynolds that chickens are not sold.

She did not mean her own chickens or anybody else's chickens, she just meant what she said that chickens are not sold.

Mrs. Reynolds was like that.

Mr. Reynolds turned in his sleep, what is it you wanted me to do, he said. Nothing but be my angel said Mrs. Reynolds. Mr. Reynolds was still asleep, That is easy he said.

Hope the wife of the brother of Mr. Reynolds often murmured, I love my love with a *y* because she is often with us.

She knew Angel Harper but she thought Joseph Lane would

27

have been more interesting. She had heard of him but she had never seen him, never seen him.

He has had him.

He has had his help.

That is what Mrs. Reynolds said when she said thank you. She said it is a pleasure to be thanked, she said, she knew what the future would do.

Joseph Lane was not a neighbor, if he had been it would have been nice of him to say thank you Mrs. Reynolds when she did anything for him. Mrs. Reynolds was always ready to stand still. She liked bread and she liked food and she liked to be there. Bless me said Mrs. Reynolds, and then her husband came home. Her husband was Mr. Reynolds and even when he had something to do he came home.

Mrs. Reynolds said to any one, we would like to know what we could give you that would please you.

Some home-made brew is what they answered, and she made it very well and sometimes not always she gave some one a bottle. She once gave a bottle to Joseph Lane and he said thank you.

Joseph Lane was not of mixed blood although anybody might imagine anything about him and they did imagine that. But it was not true he was all of a piece and although it looked as if he were fierce and he was it was not awful not awful at all but it did, it did very well and as he grew older he grew stronger until at last he was strong enough and by that time he was not dead and nobody refused him.

But in the beginning well in the beginning very much in the beginning he said how do you do to Mrs. Reynolds and to Mr. Reynolds.

Mrs. Reynolds herself liked to cook, she also liked to say of those who could not cook, they have no time to cook. She never said of any one that they could not cook she just said they are very busy so busy that they have not time to cook.

This pleased Joseph Lane very much. He liked eating not potatoes but even potatoes. He was fond of celery soup and goose. He was also fond of ices and fried potatoes, but what he really liked was extra pieces of boiled mutton. Mutton boiled for

28

seven hours with all kinds of spices. He liked extra cold pieces of that.

He liked the same things all his life. Later on Mr. and Mrs. Reynolds never saw him. Mrs. Reynolds said she had never met him and in a way she never had. They had talked together that is she had said things to him and she had in a way known his name but all the rest was different from that and Mr. Reynolds had never said anything to him had never seen him and to be sure if Mr. Reynolds did not know his name then Mrs. Reynolds did not know his name.

Joseph Lane predicted that he would never see Mrs. Reynolds again and when he left he never did and she, she knew that it was not that. How could a prediction come true if she never had seen him. That is what Mrs. Reynolds said.

Not easily can older people not walk. Really older people walk more easily than younger people.

Mrs. Reynolds did not expect to be old enough to walk a great deal and easily and neither did Joseph Lane.

He said how old am I and nobody even answered him.

This is the way he lived.

He said how old am I and nobody ever answered him.

For which he joined neither in prayers nor in predictions nor in coughing.

He was older when he was young and then he was all the same.

They said, he is our father, they said it when he was young and he never smiled. He laughed but he never smiled.

Oh dear said Mrs. Reynolds I left the chickens at home and Roger will forget to feed them. Roger often did. He liked to sharpen axes and to whistle but chickens, no he said he would forget and even if he did not he went away and the chickens were all alone.

Poor chickens.

Some calves are very young and if they are they are given the same name they would have when they are older.

Mrs. Reynolds smiled almost tenderly when she said this.

Here and now said John, they had met John before but they

did not expect to see him. But there he was, he was saying here and now and everybody liked that.

John some people thought looked younger than he was and John some people thought looked older than he was and when he said here and now he knew that for the first time in his life he had written every day in his diary every day he had put down a thought. Here and now that was his thought.

John was never superfluous.

It was really John that saw Mr. and Mrs. Reynolds and then later saw Mr. Reynolds' younger brother and his wife Hope.

John saw Angel Harper and John saw Joseph Lane and John saw friends and relatives and next of kin. John saw them. Here and now. Nothing was extra, at one time he liked stones to be polished and at one time he liked stones to be rough. He liked celery and he liked honey, and he liked to make predictions but he did not care for other people's predictions. They were not here and now not to his feeling.

Almost all the time he was quite nervous and almost all the time he decided birds although they pick up grass and eat seeds do not graze. He really liked dogs to be upside down and he liked water-cress and best of all he liked money. Money was very useful he used to say and then he said it very slowly. And here and now. By the time Mrs. Reynolds saw him he had a quiet moment, he was not boisterous, he hid by himself more than most. And it was better that he should think than that he should eat.

He had a family he had a wife and children and he had an enthusiasm. It was for here and now. By this time he had decided to settle down in a house next door to Mr. and Mrs. Reynolds and quite near Mr. Reynolds' brother and his wife Hope. And so John did.

PART II

He was called John by his children and by every one. He always nodded to her brightly when he met Mrs. Reynolds.

John could have things happen to him. When he was walking with his dog, he had one, he would turn and then with him in place of his dog would be another one. Perhaps later his would be there again.

Mr. Reynolds liked to talk to John, they talked together as if they had been old soldiers. Well in a way they were, and that made them feel the same about things.

Mrs. Reynolds said how do you do when she saw him but she never talked to him. John liked women but he talked altogether with men.

It did not make any difference to any one that John was there, not yet or only not yet and yet he did say here and now. All of which was true.

John had a daughter he had three daughters but only one was not only old enough to get married but wanted to get married to a dark hairy man. She liked them like that. But really she was in love with a soldier small and round-faced and twice escaped from prison.

The first time he was caught and sent back and the second time after walking three hundred miles he did escape and did not have to go back.

He said he felt pretty weak. He was not interested in John's daughter. He was not thin but he felt rather weak. And later on he would go away.

Mrs. Reynolds told John that that was the way life was.

She said now suppose a man is a mayor of a town and mayors are suppressed there are not going to be mayors any more, now what would that man do. The chances are said Mrs. Reynolds that when he said good-bye he would cry, he would feel it so much that he would be choked and not able to talk at all not able to say good-bye at all but if he had to go he would have to go just the same. Now said Mrs. Reynolds, my husband is always ready to go home, he always has so much to do that it makes no difference to him if he is mayor or if he is not and if there are not going to be mayors any more so much the better, said Mrs. Reynolds. I do say she said it is just as well. That is the way it happens.

John nodded brightly to her and he went away.

John's daughter when she was young, young enough to go to school had seen Angel Harper. She had not looked at him and Angel Harper had looked at everybody so of course he had looked at her.

What is the use, everybody said, what is the use of Angel Harper being older and older.

Angel Harper knew that some time he would be old enough and after that he would never be any older.

Who heard him die.

Nobody.

John's daughter who had met Angel Harper when she was at school did not find him interesting, she said so later when everybody was talking about him. She said all she noticed about him was that he could not know what to say, later when everybody was telling the way Angel Harper talked and talked so everybody had to listen. Not at all said John's daughter, he just rubbed his fingers and said he could not say what he had to say.

John's daughter did marry a dark and hairy man who taught swimming and was quite old enough not to. But said Mrs. Reynolds to John, I never see your daughter, Mrs. Reynolds had never seen John's daughter. John nodded brightly whenever he saw Mrs. Reynolds, and he often did pass her.

He did not like seeing that a cat was dead but he did have to know it because it was put into his waste basket and a little dog found it. Of course then it had to be thrown away.

Mrs. Reynolds knew how to pray but she had not at that time any reason for prayer. Much later when Angel Harper had made everybody go to war and suffer Mrs. Reynolds every morning in her bath lying on her back and her hands pressed together prayed not against Angel Harper but she prayed for his opponent and she prayed against his friends. May they, she said, may they his friends be surrounded and surrender and may Angel Harper's opponents who are fighting win speedily and completely and may all others not be any bother to anybody.

This was then Mrs. Reynolds' prayer prayed every morning twice in her bath on her back with her hands folded together in prayer.

This she did in those days, days which had come to pass as had been predicted by Saint Odile, a saint of the seventh century.

Saint Odile had said, listen to me my brother, I have seen the terror in forests and mountains where the Germans shall be called the most war-like people of the earth.

It will happen that the time will come when a war the most terrible war in the world will happen and mothers will weep for their children and will not be consoled.

From the Danube the war will commence and will be a horrible war on earth, on the sea and even in the air, and warriors will rise in the air to seize stars to throw them down upon cities and make them the cities burst into flames.

Well that was what Saint Odile said would happen and it did. And Mrs. Reynolds every morning in her bath lying on her back with her hands pressed together prayed her prayer and prayed it twice every morning.

This was quite a while after, now John nodded brightly to her as he passed her.

There was the escaped prisoner. John's daughter was in love

33

with him but that did not matter and his face was round and so was his head and his name was Oliver. It does not make any difference whether Oliver was his first name or his last name. He hunted up Angel Harper and found him. Angel Harper was sitting alone and Oliver went up to him and said, Here I am.

Mrs. Reynolds always turned her back to the moon. On a winter's day she found the moon of an afternoon most objectionable.

Joseph Lane was the same. Later when he had gone away to his own country and forgotten everything, he always in the winter found the moon in the afternoon most objectionable.

When he saw a woman he looked at her. He was far away then back where he had come from.

Sooner or later he saw a woman named Claudia, she did not belong there. She walked with her feet sideways, her face was flat, her complexion was clear, her mother and her aunt was one woman and she did not like her, she thought she was her stepmother which she was, she thought she was her aunt which she was, she did not think she was her mother which she was, she had a half-brother, a whole brother and a father, the father died, which he did, the real brother was a prisoner and the half-brother helped his mother who was Claudia's aunt, mother and stepmother.

Enough said.

When there are lots of prisoners there are lots of prisoners.

Claudia said, it is a cold night, and it was.

Claudia also said, I am not going home, and she did not go home. Claudia also said that prisoners might just as well be dead and she was right they might just as well be dead.

Joseph Lane was never a prisoner neither was Claudia so they might not as well have been dead and they never were.

It is easy to live a long time if you are Claudia and Joseph, and they did, anyway everybody knew it was a long time and everybody gave up waiting for it to be over because it was not.

Claudia had a habit of always having with her a piece of cheese and a knife to cut it. Young or old she needed cheese and she al-

34

ways had it. Joseph Lane did not care for cheese it was a poison to him he could not eat it, so he never did eat it, young or old he never did eat it.

That is the way they went back to where they came from and were over every one and did what they liked and everybody knew it and stood around. Joseph Lane told them not to stand around and Claudia ate cheese with her knife and slowly it was enormous not the cheese but everything and they were all of it.

Enough said.

They did not have to begin anything. Nothing was begun. Enough said. To really do something that is to have something done you do not have to begin.

Mrs. Reynolds was far away and she heard every one say that Claudia and Joseph Lane were married in their way.

She would wonder if she ever had seen Claudia, Mr. Reynolds knew he had since Claudia had been there and if she had been there and Mr. Reynolds was very given to noticing everything he would have noticed Claudia. Mrs. Reynolds said yes, yes, yes said Mrs. Reynolds yes I do say yes, and she did.

She remembered that she had never heard the name Claudia, that she remembered.

She said yes I have never heard the name of Claudia. Mr. Reynolds said it was not the name Claudia, he said that if Claudia had been there and she had been there and if he had been there and he had been there, and as he always noticed everything he would have noticed her. Yes said Mrs. Reynolds. She said yes and after a while she said yes again. Yes she said.

Sometimes in her sleep Mrs. Reynolds would say She me I she, and then she would say yes we warm each other, She me I she. But she did not mean Claudia because she had never known anybody named Claudia. But Claudia was married to Joseph Lane everybody knew that, far away everybody knew that. Nobody knew that Joseph Lane was more wonderful than that. Nobody knew that. Not very likely that he said this or that. When he did it was what made them careful to be obedient. If not, well if not, there was no if not. Claudia never said if not. Claudia said nothing at all. Cheese was enough for Claudia, and being alone with a knife and cheese.

Mrs. Reynolds woke up one morning and she was so cold that she thought that she was dead and then she began to talk and then she knew she was not dead, that was the only way she knew it.

She knew that winters are just alike last winter was cold and so was this winter. She never said that, she only spoke of a day. She said it is cold today.

Hope Reynolds said to her husband the younger brother of Mr. Reynolds, the cold is over. Is it said her husband.

As she said it she sighed, she thought of Angel Harper and she said the cold is over. Is it, said her husband the younger brother of Mr. Reynolds. He was not interested in sighing, he was interested in Angel Harper even if Angel Harper was far away. It was always something to talk about. He had known Angel Harper when anybody who knew Angel Harper could know him and it was interesting to talk about even if Angel Harper was not interesting. Was he. Hope Reynolds did not sigh any more and her husband never had sighed.

Enough said.

That said Mr. Reynolds is one of the coldest spots in Europe and when he said it he meant it.

When he said that if it had gone on the way it had commenced he would have left home, he meant that too. He was often ready to like everything and he mostly did but when he did not like a thing he did not. He never liked what his sister-in-law told him about Angel Harper. He did not ask her to tell him, he was quiet and so she told him. His younger brother knew him better he could tell that his brother Mr. Reynolds did not like what he heard about Angel Harper.

They heard something then about him and later they heard a lot more about him and Mr. Reynolds said as for me I do not care about it, neither about him or what I hear about him. It is all right but I do not like the kind of person he is or what he looks like. I have never seen him but that is the way I feel about him. I do not like Joseph Lane. I have seen him, but that is different, I just don't like him that is all but Angel Harper is different. I

36

just can't see him, not that I ever have and I just cannot listen to any one about him not that I ever do. That is all said Mr. Reynolds and that was all.

Mrs. Reynolds said that as for her she did not think that stars were worlds, she thought that they were there just as they looked like particularly in the winter when they were the constellations with which she was familiar, she said they looked like that and they were like that and she was sure that Joseph Lane felt as she did about it. Now her sister-in-law Hope was sure that stars were worlds and that they were not just what they were, and she could persuade her husband of it, that is her own husband, the younger brother of Mr. Reynolds, of course Mr. Reynolds felt about the stars the way Mrs. Reynolds felt about the stars that they were just like that. Indeed said Mrs. Reynolds she had read in a newspaper that Angel Harper thought about stars the way her sister-in-law Hope thought about them.

Enough said.

Now how about it.

If the stars are just what they are then anybody knows about the future and if they are not what they are then how can anybody know about the future. Mrs. Reynolds never sighed.

If you break the bones in your right hand and have to have your hand put up in plaster, you are not very useful. Mrs. Reynolds made this observation but the fact did not annoy her. It was not her hand, of course not.

If whatever happens does happen then naturally enough Mr. Reynolds is always amiable, Mrs. Reynolds never told any one this but it was something which made her daily life what it was. And only this time Angel Harper and Joseph Lane had both gone away everywhere. Anybody could know that and Mrs. Reynolds never thought about either of them not then but she did recognize the stars in the heavens when she saw them. She did not often look up, she had rather small feet and when she walked she tended to look down to see where she was walking and when she stood still she met somebody and so she had to say something so naturally enough she did not often look up to see what stars were there but when she did look up she did see what stars were there and she did recognize them and she knew they were as they looked and she knew that they meant something.

Mrs. Reynolds sometimes talked about Turkey and sometimes she talked about Mexico. She even sometimes talked about Europe and Northern Africa. She did sometimes talk about generals and she often talked about chickens and who had not married George Irving. George Irving might get into trouble and even if he did he would never go away. Although George was no longer young neither his father nor his mother would let him go away and so the only thing he could do was to stay. He never knew either Angel Harper or Joseph Lane. Mrs. Reynolds always said so.

Mrs. Reynolds was drowsy and she turned and she murmured, I love my love with a *y* because he is useful.

Mrs. Reynolds was all of a sudden tired of winter. When she was asleep and turned around and some cold air came to her she murmured, it reminds me of the kitchen.

There was snow on the ground and it was very cold, only the birds and the trees knew spring had come and Mrs. Reynolds.

When she went to sleep she said thank you for the pillow. After that she slept and awoke in the morning.

In the meantime it was always in the meantime and if it was not it was exciting in the meantime.

Angel Harper knew when he was successful and when he was a failure, some thought he did not he thought he did not but he did. He knew.

Was he born in a church, was he born in a town, was he born brown.

He did not know and nobody else knew. If he had been different he might have cried but he never did cry he was nervous but he never did cry, not even when he said oh my, which he did.

It makes him nervous to know that yesterday is today and then and then there was no tomorrow because years were years but days were never days. For instance.

Just as much as he liked he did not go away.

To stay he said, but he never was able to ask any one again. Asking is nobody's pleasure. When he had it he thought he could measure that he sat. But just that. There he sat. They came around.

38

Darkness means night and daylight means light. They sat alone when they heard him say that.

It was frightening but nobody likes not to be frightened alone, when they did they saw him alone and he sneezed. Believe it or not he sneezed and almost like that it was an obligation.

Mrs. Reynolds had to know about predictions, she never wanted to know what was to happen to her but she just had to know what was going to happen to the century, had to know it in every way and in every way she did, come to know it.

And she was right, what she knew was what did happen to the century.

Angel Harper and Joseph Lane were in the century and so she knew what was going to happen to them. Mr. and Mrs. Reynolds were not in the century, they were Mr. and Mrs. Reynolds and so she did not know what was going to happen to them. When she was quite young she began to know what was going to happen to the century and then there came a time, there came a terrible time, all the time and she knew, she could know what was going to happen to the century, she knew because Saint Odile knew and she knew what the saints knew she knew what was going to happen to a century.

There was a saint named Saint Godfrey in 1853 and this is what he said.

He said that in the beginning of the ninth month of the year 1939 the Germans were going to be attacked by the French and the Anglo-Saxons.

Toward the beginning of the sixth month of the year 1940 the Germans were going to take possession of Lutece which is the latin name for Paris. The Latins, that is the Italians were going to help the Germans.

The French were then going to quit the fight.

In the tenth month of that same year, the Latins that is the Italians were going to suffer in the deserts of Egypt.

The Greeks and the Turks then joined themselves to the Anglo-Saxons.

In the second month of the year 1941, the eternal city that is Rome will burn, Avignon will see the pope. The Germans will then have to fight a new army that will come from across an ocean.

Perhaps this would be Australians and New Zealanders and Canadians.

There will be terrible distress and sickness in the German army.

Invaded from the South the Germans will want to give everything to the French.

In the fourth month the French led by an old man holding a sword and a cross in his hand once more are strong. Peace is once more all over the land.

The Latins that is the Italians stone each other and the whole country of the Romans goes to pieces at one time. Never again will Rome ever have any military strength.

In the fifth month the Anglo-Saxons will be masters of the Germans who will lay down their arms.

The French will once again disagree with the Anglo-Saxons because the Germans will ask the French to take care of them.

Peace in Europe will be restored in the sixth month.

Rome will be reduced to ashes, Germany will be governed for a time by the French.

The king will be once more king of France, this in the eleventh month and will bring peace and prosperity to France.

In 1948 there will be an appearance of revolution.

In 1980 an era of Anti-Christ will exist for sixty years.

Mrs. Reynolds read it all and showed it to every one and it was all true and she knew it was all true and it all would come to pass.

I do not said Mrs. Reynolds care about what happens in 1980, why would I, said Mrs. Reynolds.

When she dreamed again she dreamed of meat.

Once later on she dreamed that they were spending a whole day with a friend and they had three meats and then a cold supper. They had the largest oysters she had ever seen. They were as large as a large saucer.

This she did not dream at night, this she dreamed in the afternoon.

These dreams were very pleasant, as everything was to Mrs. Reynolds.

She was rather hoping that she would never see a boy named Roger again. He had fallen and broken his hand, not seriously, and actually he did go away and neither Mr. nor Mrs. Reynolds ever saw him again.

This was not quite so, Mr. Reynolds did see him again but that was of no importance to any one.

Sometimes a young married couple are very attentive to their parents and sometimes they are not.

Mr. and Mrs. Reynolds as is very well known never had any children so this was not a matter that was of great importance to them but nevertheless they knew it was true. Sometimes a young married couple were very attentive to their parents and then without any reason they were not attentive to their parents any more.

They might have a child afterwards or they might not. Mrs. Reynolds often talked about this. She naturally would talk about it because it is something that is interesting.

And so Mrs. Reynolds knew that centuries have their history and she might sigh and then again she might not sigh.

Neither she nor any one else really knew whether she would sigh or whether she would not sigh.

Mr. Reynolds came in, he did not meditate but he told Mrs. Reynolds what every one said. They said that suddenly in September 1940 the United States of America instead of being a part of a big flat land illimitably flat, the land against which Christopher Columbus bumped himself in 1492 became a part of the round world that goes around and around.

Mr. Reynolds said he had just seen Bob who was in America in 1917, and Bob said in 1939 that he said to an American, well and now America is just like anybody. Not at all, said the American. No said Bob well that is what I told the English forty years ago and they said no, they are separate and away, and Bob said to the American, you think you are separate and away but. Bob said and it only took a year for the American to know it and it took the English thirty years.

There are three stories that Mr. Reynolds always liked to

41

tell, Mrs. Reynolds always listened when he told them, some-times she did something else but doing something else did not stop her from hearing him tell them.

One story was about the romance of America about the cheap-est things being made of the best material and how Europe was very worried when they first knew about it, it seemed to them to be indecent and immoral and shocking and at the same time romantic. It was hard for Europe to understand that if things were to be sold by the million and be cheap they must be made of the very best material, in Europe it was expensive things that were made of the best material.

Well said Mrs. Reynolds that is what is.

The second story Mr. Reynolds liked to tell was that General Grant let all the Southern soldiers take their horses and their rifles with them, everybody is a farmer, that everybody knows and so it is necessary to have a horse and a gun. This everybody knows.

And then the other story that Mr. Reynolds always told was about how America that is how Admiral Perry had bombarded Japan so as to make them open their ports to strangers and do business with them and now in one short hundred years, because one hundred years is not very long the Americans are going to bombard Japan again to close Japan up again.

Mr. Reynolds liked to tell everybody that and Mrs. Reynolds, she often stood, she sometimes sat but she did quite often stand and she always stood and listened to him.

And then there was another story Mr. Reynolds liked to tell. He liked to tell how the Americans got rid of the gangsters, not by fighting, but by arresting them for not paying their income tax. That always surprised every one but Mrs. Reynolds did not listen much when he told that one.

Mr. Reynolds was a very quiet man.

Mrs. Reynolds did meditate.

She meditated about George Washington. She quite often meditated about George Washington.

Mr. Reynolds knew what freezing did to ground, how it made the earth higher so that gates would not open or close but that

42

you must not cut the rock down because when the earth was soft again the rock that held the gate closed would sink back into the earth again. He also knew how a wall made of cement would grow harder and harder for fifty years and then slowly grow softer and softer. He knew all these things and it was all right that he did know all these things and Mrs. Reynolds while she stood and meditated meditated quite often about George Washington.

She had when she was a little girl thought it would be wonderful it would have been wonderful to live in the time of George Washington, and now she stood and meditated and very likely it was a time of George Washington, first in peace first in war and first in the hearts of his countrymen, perhaps it was the time of George Washington. She stood and she meditated and perhaps it was the time of George Washington.

Perhaps it was religion, perhaps he had not been happy once like George Washington and when the holy water was passed to him perhaps he had refused to touch it because he was unhappy about it, but now now he was religious, he took holy water and it was a great thing to any one to pass it to him and to have him pass it on from them. First in war first in peace and first in the hearts of his countrymen.

And little boys who were disobedient and were not doing what they should what greater punishment could they have than not be allowed to salute when they saw his picture anywhere. What could be a greater punishment to any little boy than that, not being allowed to salute his picture when they saw it.

Mrs. Reynolds stood and meditated and she said how do you do and is the winter over.

She was not sure that she liked rain better than cold weather and rain was almost certain to follow after and here it was.

Enough said, here it was. She said, Mrs. Reynolds said that if Anti-Christ came in 1980 and her little niece in 1940 was nine years old how old would she be in 1980. Mr. Reynolds knew.

Well all the same, sometimes the rain would stop but would it. It is difficult to know about rain in a rainy country. Very difficult.

43

Her niece's name was Rose Table, little Rose Table although she was going to be very tall. At this time she often said not to her aunt but to her mother, it is strange but I am beginning to be very sad and sentimental.

It was not strange it was natural, little Rose Table a little sad and a little sentimental, although she had loved to climb trees eat snow and feed chickens and rabbits and cook on a cooking stove.

They went away to live in a desert, enough said.

If blonde people brush their hair, and make it curl they are called Gabriel. If dark people brush their hair and it does not curl, they are called Angel Harper.

Mrs. Reynolds liked to wear a beret, she was neither dark nor blonde, she was pretty with small features and very tall and quite heavy.

She knew that if you have any expression on your face your thoughts are different. Hers never were.

She said it again and again.

Claudia thought that she was married to Angel Harper. She was mistaken. Angel Harper was never married. He did not even have a brother.

Claudia had no expression on her face. She never had. That is what made her so certain that she was married to Angel Harper.

She scratched her nose which itched.

It looks like a bird said Claudia even if it is only a piece of wool. It has the eye of a bird. Claudia said this to herself. She was sawing wood and she said it to herself.

Wood to be burnt. She did not say this to herself. It was not necessary. Everybody who sees wood cut up and the weather cold knows that the wood will be burnt. Oh yes.

If in a fog a dog looks like a wolf it really does not. Mrs. Reynolds said that but she was not talking to Claudia.

In any sense all who were eating ate more than they wanted because would they no one asked but would they. Would they eat again. Primroses do not make salad nor cow food, nor even appetites eager.

Claudia was just as much unlike her mother as that. Her

44

mother said that Claudia had married a worthless man and everybody had warned her and now Claudia knew. Sulphur matches smell of sulphur, and dogs of dogs. Please said Claudia let us be nervous, and everybody was.

Once upon a time Claudia went away, she went away to stay and she stayed near Joseph Lane. He had gone home no more to roam and Claudia went away to where he was.

For this sight, she was grateful and so was he.

All who have gone away gave a groan.

So much for that.

And now weeks became years and years became days and days became longer. In a little while everybody ran. It was quiet and most of all, the truth was told. When it was Tuesday, Tuesday was the day, but only once in a while.

Nobody knows how easily they can forget the weather and whether it is better never to be better.

A soldier if he is not a prisoner is a Swiss.

That sounds funny but it is not. It is what makes them all sad, they said they were glad but they were all sad.

You do know, said Mrs. Reynolds she was not talking to Mr. Reynolds she was talking to a stranger, you do know how this is.

The full moon and the mountain, the mountain was a white mountain, and the moon was not.

This made Angel Harper see stars and when he did he knew that before he died he would be dead.

No one can add butter to roses he said. He liked to think like that. No one can add butter to roses. But after all they could and did and if they could and did he knew they would forget and if they forgot then he would be forgotten.

He acted as if he did as if he would be forgotten.

For most of the time, he would not be forgotten.

It was quiet, he said it very well, for most of the time he would not be forgotten.

It is difficult to make a great deal of noise all the time so difficult that nobody can rest. Whoever can rest best, can rest best. This is what Mrs. Reynolds said. She said whoever can rest can rest best.

45

She never knew Angel Harper which was just as well because she would have said of him that he would be drowned dead and he would not have liked that and really nobody ever did not like what Mrs. Reynolds said so it was just as well they never met. Just as well.

Wood to burn is very attractive, said Peter to Rene. I like it said Peter. And Rene who believed in making alcohol out of wood did not listen. Of course wood is attractive.

It is so much more delightful to saw wet wood than when it is dry said Rene. Let us moralize upon that said Peter. Rene was an inventor. Peter was a lover. Of himself. Was it a chance that they were brothers and one blond and the other brunette and was it a chance that they met Angel Harper and Angel Harper turned their way. Was it a chance said Peter. Was it a chance said Rene. Was it a chance said Peter and he turned away and then he turned back and called Rene. Was it a chance Rene, said Peter.

Did they think that they knew why Angel Harper was there. If they did they did.

They always called to each other even if other people were talking they called to each other Peter called Rene and Rene called Peter.

They did not listen to Angel Harper but that was easy enough that was before Angel Harper was a talker. When Angel Harper became a talker, Peter met him once but it was Peter who talked all the time not Angel Harper. Rene was not there.

That was a coincidence. It was extraordinary how Peter met Angel Harper and it was a coincidence that Rene met Joseph Lane and it was a coincidence that they both heard about Mrs. Reynolds and it was a coincidence that Hope the wife of Mr. Reynolds' brother said how do you do to them, and that her husband was in bed and that he was sure that Angel Harper was finished and that Joseph Lane would go on and that being in bed he Mr. Reynolds' brother was very likely to go on staying in bed. Which he did.

It was a coincidence not his being in bed because he often was but that his wife Hope should tell Peter to come again and that he did not come but that Rene did and that Rene left behind him

46

an electric lantern that could flash out lights of any color and be dim or bright or wide or narrow and that all this led to conversation.

Rene had curly black hair and thin hands and a high voice. Not so high as his brother Peter but high all the same. Angel Harper's voice was not high it broke very often which was why he talked all the time he had to repair the breaks in his voice and Peter, Peter's voice was so high it did not break. It was enough for Mr. Reynolds' brother that he was in bed quite enough and he never noticed coincidences even when they happened. He always said they were not coincidences. Just like that, he said they were not coincidences.

One day a woman her husband and a little girl were walking along and their dog and beside them there was a woman on a bicycle. She was quite good-looking and they were careful to know that she had a brother who was a seminary teacher who had disappeared although he was not drowned.

Mrs. Reynolds always turned away when there was snow and that day the snow was going to begin pretty soon. Mrs. Reynolds walked away. Her shoulders were higher and she walked away, quite away.

Beneath it all they knew that Angel Harper never stared and he never looked away, when everybody was afraid, afraid of Angel Harper he never stared and he never looked away, he did not have any way of looking, he mostly did not look at all not in any way. Everybody was afraid of him then very much afraid.

Mrs. Reynolds said what she had to say, she said he would not be drowned but everybody would be drowned and he well what difference does it make if everybody is afraid if they are all drowned, drowned dead. Mrs. Reynolds knew they would all be drowned and she turned away and walked away after she had had everything to say that she had to say.

Angel Harper was of course not then there.

Angel Harper will know tomorrow what he is going to do today.

When a little dog sticks himself on a needle on the floor he cries right away. When a little child falls down he does not cry

47

until he is picked up. This has a great deal to do with Angel Harper. A great deal.

When he was little and he fell down sometimes he cried and sometimes he did not. When he did not he remembered it and when he did he remembered it. He did not remember whether he was or whether he was not picked up. Anybody is picked up when they are little and if not they get up. Up is up.

Ten chickens out of twenty died. That is because they ate salt. The salt was in a sack and the sack was there and the chickens pecked at the sack and they swallowed the salt and they drank and they drank and they died.

Nobody could eat them because nobody knew why they died.

Angel Harper never listened to that but Joseph Lane did and that made Joseph Lane wait while Angel Harper died, did die.

But anyway he lived quite long enough for that.

And so not neglected not as much as they Mrs. Reynolds stood one road went into another and Mrs. Reynolds stood. Everybody had to pass by and Mrs. Reynolds stood. Angel Harper never passed nor did Joseph Lane. Not pass by.

After this painful event they heard about Angel Harper. Everybody did, everybody died and everybody did. Hear about Angel Harper just that much.

Once upon a time somebody prophesied. They prophesied that Angel Harper died. Once upon a time somebody prophesied, they prophesied about a horse and the horse of the prophecy was given away, this was not in the prophecy but it was not given for long because she to whom the horse was given could not feed the horse, he was that kind of a horse he had to be fed and she could not feed the horse that had to be fed so he went back again back again to bed where he always had been led to bed. And the horse he lived and he died there, but this was not the prophecy, the prophecy was that the horse was a horse and he was. The prophecy was right as are all prophecies, that horse was the horse. He was.

After that. Everybody believed in prophecies and everybody was right because the prophecies prophesied what was going to happen and what was going to happen did happen.

48

Mrs. Reynolds sighed, she said she was waiting and so was Mr. Reynolds and when the young man came they would be glad to see him and they would be glad to have him but as yet he had not come. Mrs. Reynolds said that she and Mr. Reynolds did not know whether they should go on waiting for the young man or not. They did not know.

When Mrs. Reynolds did not know, her teeth hurt her, and her teeth hurt her then. Some one told her that Angel Harper could be angry. Perhaps he will be drowned said Mrs. Reynolds hopefully. She often thought they would be drowned and lots of them were completely drowned in water, drowned dead in water.

Angel Harper, nobody likes to say Angel Harper and if they do like to say Angel Harper they do not say Angel Harper.

Who is angry.

More than that.

Who is angry.

Mrs. Reynolds was very patient and she was never angry but she did think that anybody who was angry should be drowned should be drowned dead in water. She did not say it of Angel Harper because she never mentioned Angel Harper.

Angry much anger very angry by being angry.

Angel Harper commenced by being angry.

Mrs. Reynolds stood and talked to three young girls.

They stood too.

They were at the corner the three young girls more or less together.

By the time they went on Mrs. Reynolds was left alone and then she went into her home.

Naturally they did not talk about Angel Harper.

Nobody did.

Mr. Reynolds' brother often used to think about how he could not remember what Angel Harper looked like. He did not only have that trouble with Angel Harper, he could not remember what most people whom he knew looked like. He knew what his brother looked like and he knew what Mrs. Reynolds looked like. When he had not seen his own wife for some time and that

49

did happen from time to time, he could not then remember well I suppose he could but he did not suppose that he could remember what she looked like.

But Angel Harper was completely like that, he would begin trying to remember his walk, or his nose or his mouth or his hair or his clothes and how tall he was and what he did with his hands and he just could not remember what Angel Harper did look like.

When eight come to lunch instead of seven it is all the same thing, it is like that.

The sister of Angel Harper went to school at a convent. The sisters taught her that when she was dressing she should be as discreet and modest as if an entire cavalry regiment should be passing in front of her. Now how could that be. She did not know but she hoped so and although he was her brother, she never saw him again, not ever. Not ever did she see Angel Harper again.

Mrs. Reynolds went to bed early. Mr. Reynolds did not go to bed quite so early, but actually it was not very much later. She had not more than been asleep before he came to bed and woke her, and then they both went to sleep and slept very well. They slept very well although before going to sleep they had talked about Angel Harper. They did always sleep very well.

Hay when it is growing can freeze. Oil when it is growing, clover when it is growing can freeze. Do not bother about the others, Angel Harper said it was he who said it first, do not when you bother about the others do not let oil and hay and clover when it is growing freeze. As soon as he said this it turned so cold that the hay which was growing and the oil which was growing and the clover which was growing did freeze. Everybody was just as much afraid as they were before.

When Angel Harper was a little boy he did not drill other little boys and make them march. Some do. He did not. He sat and when he sat, he sat. Enough said.

When he was a little boy he did not stand on a step and hold his hands up high over his head and throw down pieces of paper for other children to scramble for and pick up. Some do, but he did not.

50

He talked to himself and he said, all the same. And when he said all the same he meant it.

When Angel Harper was a little boy he never came again. They did not expect him. He did not very often find money lying on the road and when he did it was not very much but it was a great pleasure.

He once when he was a little boy saw a woman looking at a piece of tarred road, she said her husband the day before had fallen there and a woman had passed by and had been afraid to tell, her husband had bled not much but some but somebody else came along and now he was at home resting and she had gone out to see if some of his blood was still there and it was.

When Angel Harper came home and went to bed he did not sleep nor did he cry, he just said to himself, yes yesterday. And later he remembered having said yes yesterday and he said it again. Just again.

It was much later so much later and of course she never did know that is to say know how to meet Angel Harper that Mrs. Reynolds said, Have you caught cold. They had not. She said sticks and needles are not enough with which to make war. Perhaps yes perhaps no but she knew it was no.

Otherwise we would they said and they stopped reading the newspapers and stopped listening to the radio. Why. Because they were frightened. No not frightened but. Otherwise we would said Mrs. Reynolds. And otherwise. Well would they.

To Mrs. Reynolds all the same was never for them a name.

Mr. Reynolds' younger brother always led that kind of a life. Was that a light or was it not and if it was was it in any way peculiar. They sometimes called Mr. Reynolds' younger brother Mark although that was not his name.

Mark they said and he said well after all it was a bicycle lamp. And when he said that he turned away his head. No not to see the bicycle but not to see the reflection of the bicycle lamp upon the wall of a house. And why not. Well he always said I like to be called Mark, my wife's name is Hope and I like to be called Mark even if Mark is not my name which it is not.

Mrs. Reynolds never called Mr. Reynolds' younger brother Mark and she never called his wife Hope. As a matter of fact it was not necessary. Whenever Mr. Reynolds spoke of them and he did speak of them Mrs. Reynolds said yes. She always stood up and she always said yes. Sitting down said Mrs. Reynolds is comfortable but it is not necessary. So when Mr. Reynolds mentioned either his younger brother or his younger brother's wife she was not sitting she was standing. And just as slowly she mentioned that it was almost time to go to bed. She would eat two oranges as was her habit she would not be tempted by a banana, she would eat two oranges and then she would go to bed.

One day there was a priest sitting behind a rocky wall, he was sitting there not asleep and he saw Mrs. Reynolds, that is Hope Reynolds, he stood up, he was an old man and very thin and he said you are Mrs. Reynolds. Well yes that is I am Hope Reynolds yes I am Mrs. Reynolds she said. Well said the priest my nephew wants to know you. Know me said Hope Reynolds, perhaps he wants to know Mrs. Reynolds my husband's elder brother's wife. He wants to know Mrs. Reynolds said the priest stubbornly and if you are Mrs. Reynolds, yes I am Mrs. Reynolds well then he wants to know you. Where is he said Hope Reynolds. He is looking for wild mushrooms said the monk. So Hope sat down with the monk and pretty soon the nephew came along. He was a priest too and he had found mushrooms. You are Mrs. Reynolds he said. I am Hope Reynolds that is to say I am Mrs. Reynolds. Well it is Mrs. Reynolds I want to know. How do you do Mrs. Reynolds and Mrs. Reynolds said how do you do.

Bye and bye they separated, the nephew gave Mrs. Reynolds the mushrooms he had found, he gave her all of them. They were a kind she had never seen before, but she took them anyway and carried them home.

Enough said.

Hope Reynolds likes people who if they are sufficiently sad might hang themselves.

Angel Harper. Sometimes Hope Reynolds whispered Angel Harper, but if he was sufficiently sad they would not hang him. Not hang him, whispered Hope Reynolds. And as she walked along, she knew, not hang him, nor what she said. Hours and hours passed and that was what she said.

She did not see him, that is what she said.

If Angel Harper had a fortune there was nothing to hide away. Be by my side was not what he said. Not what he said.

All right. For them if they are fortunate all who are fortunate are all right. But they are not fortunate not how fortunate so they are not all right. All right not always all right.

All who are all right have a family home between two parks. Either or or carefully.

Need Angel Harper be bright.

Need Angel Harper be slight.

Need Angel Harper be white.

Need Angel Harper be all right.

All right with what.

With fire and heat, when all is said, fire and heat. And they all began to cry.

Angel Harper had not been there.

When Hope Reynolds was a very little girl their father and mother often went away all day, and all night too. There were four of them three girls and a boy and all little, and they did what they did. When they went to school their school teachers used to give them something to eat in the afternoon. Their father the one time that he was home wrote to the teacher and told her not to bother, his children had plenty to eat and better, and she just better had not bother. When the other children heard they said, oh ho and have they and that is why when they are thirsty they drink ink and when they are hungry they chew their pen-holder, and they are always thirsty and they are always hungry and they are always thirsty and they and always hungry and they are always drinking their ink and eating their pen-holders. At that time Hope Reynolds never saw Angel Harper, although he was only about twice as much older. And if she ever did see him she said she would not change places with him.

Not she.

Clothilde, Raymonde and Adele gave birth to Joseph.

When Angel Harper talked to himself about that, he shook his head. He talked to himself and said Clothilde, Raymonde and Adele gave birth to Joseph and once more he shook his head.

53

He was not interested in Clothilde, Raymonde and Adele he was only interested in Joseph having been born. He knew he would and then he cried, he cried quietly into his handkerchief, he knew he should.

After Joseph Lane was born it was no matter. Not then, but all right, not then did not matter.

Joseph Lane, nobody called him Joseph Lane. Even Clothilde, Raymonde and Adele who had given birth to him paid no attention to him. Not then. It did not matter.

A calf said Mrs. Reynolds has to have a calf so that she can become a cow.

Mrs. Reynolds wondered why Joseph Lane was rather timid about that. She had heard that he was not exactly ignorant but rather timid about that.

Mrs. Reynolds said that a crane flying over the marshes near a river was always alone. At least she supposed so because the only one she had ever seen flying was all alone. He went away.

Mrs. Reynolds was just a little amused by all this. She laughed. She did.

If a centipede climbs a wall of a room and even gets near the ceiling it cannot fall not at all. It is very interesting that it does so that it climbs the wall and then moves around as it will. There is no uneasiness because it cannot fall.

It is nice when there is no uneasiness because it cannot fall.

Any one can go to sleep and not dream because of it.

Moro, Nathaniel Moro, stayed in his room more than when he went out. He was quite stout, even when there was nothing to eat and he was quite hot even when there was no coal or wood to burn and he was quite tall and he was quite capable of saying when a lady arose come, and she said she was going to look for her dog, oh he would say I was about to ask you not to rise, thinking you were about to rise to say how do you do to me. He was also capable of saying when some one said they always were startled when they saw their name in print, oh yes I am too, every time I see my visiting card I am startled. This is what Nathaniel Moro said.

He was a friend of Joseph Lane, that is to say Joseph Lane always knew when Nathaniel Moro was there. When he was not there it did not matter but when he was there it did matter.

Joseph Lane was never happy or unhappy never had a door open or closed, never went to sleep or woke up suddenly.

It was not necessary that there would come a time for everything to commence. Not nearly very often. One might say not at all. And just then Nathaniel Moro came in. Nobody really noticed when he went out. He liked to have a cup of tea in the afternoon, that was quite definite, he really was indifferent if it was here or there. He was not Rosalind de Guy who always wanted her tea, always wanted her tea a small cup of tea and good and hot.

There were often enough together so that no one noticed it. They were mostly always apart and nobody noticed it. In a way it was fortunate that all who knew Joseph Lane were capable of being liked any day, very fortunate.

Away down in the town there was a very small one-armed man. Very small indeed. He had eight children, very small indeed, and he had lost his arm when he was five years old, at that time he had been very small indeed.

By great good fortune, Angel Harper was older and being older was angry. Why not when his name was Angel Harper and he did not love any one.

Why not indeed.

A little girl and her confirmation her name is Mary Louise, and being confirmed makes her very happy. Happier than when later she is married, says her mother because there is no anxiety mixed up with confirmation but there always is with matrimony, always is with matrimony.

Mary Louise went to school and at school she heard them talk of Angel Harper. It made her shiver. She had blue eyes and she did not shiver very often but now and then. Shiver.

She liked Saints, one saint every day, she liked saints, her own saint and other saints, she had never heard of Joseph Lane, and even if she had, he would not have made her shiver. Shiver.

X y z, made her shiver, and when she heard the name of Angel Harper it made her shiver. Nothing else ever made her shiver.

She was quite young and she lived to be old older than her grandfather who might have lived to be older if he had not broken his leg when he was old.

Later on when she heard the name of Angel Harper it did not make her shiver, because he was dead then and anyhow, nothing lived after, nothing but the saints so she said and they they had never made her shiver.

Clouds were here and there and certain kinds of clouds bring rain. If it rains on one day there will be no hay, if it rains the next day there will be no wheat, and if it rains the next day there will be no wine. But all the same there is hay and wheat and wine, all the time.

Angel Harper could do nothing about that he could do nothing about that and Mary Louise knew it, and so well after all it was all very well, when they said Angel Harper she hardly noticed it and if she did not notice it she did not shiver and she did not.

Mary Louise had a little cousin, she had not seen her since the little cousin was baptized, and yet when they met they had a great deal to say, they even sighed together.

Mrs. Reynolds said it is awkward to sigh.

For then it is, she said.

And then she said, strawberries can get wet. Mrs. Reynolds had more time to dry strawberries than most people, she said they were called strawberries because you put straw under them to keep them dry.

By this time Angel Harper was there again and when they said there they meant everywhere. That is just where he was.

Mrs. Reynolds said oh and she meant it.

Mrs. Reynolds could climb a ladder.

Mr. Reynolds liked gravel. Some men do. Mr. Reynolds did.

Mrs. Reynolds said that anything made him sad. He was not sad he was quiet. He said he understood about predictions. He said they were right, in what they said was going to happen. But it did not happen that way, but it did happen. Now said Mr. Reynolds take Angel Harper, they all say that he will come to an end. He certainly will, and pretty soon, he certainly will and then they all say how he will come to an end and when. Well when might be right but how never could be right, it would said Mr. Reynolds not be natural if what they thought was going to happen would happen. No said Mr. Reynolds that would not be natural.

Yes said Mr. Reynolds one knows that there is going to be spring and summer and fall and winter, yes everybody is right about that there will be but just what will happen any day in spring summer and fall and winter well that is not so easy to know.

So said Mr. Reynolds they are right when they predict that Angel Harper will come to an end and that he will come to a bad end, but what is that bad end and how it is going to happen that said Mr. Reynolds that will be a surprise, well to Angel Harper and to everybody who predicts about him, but and that they will know he will come to an end and to a bad end so of course they will say they do predict right and perhaps they do.

Mr. Reynolds never sighed, he was too quiet to sigh, and he never talked he was too quiet to talk and he never predicted, he was too quiet to predict, but he knew about predictions and he knew about sighing and he knew about talking. What really interested him was gravel, particularly wet gravel. He liked gravel wet rather than dry, it gave him a satisfaction, and he liked it not to be too regular in size, he liked the pebbles to be small and larger, it was more satisfactory like that.

It is not always easy to get gravel and it is not always easy to have it wet, and it is not always easy to have it irregular but Mr. Reynolds always had it like that.

Once in a while some one asked him about his gravel. He always answered about it, and explained just how heavy it was when it was bought, he preferred it to be wet when it was bought and he said so.

Mr. and Mrs. Reynolds had a quiet life.

PART III

She had a grandchild she had had a son-in-law and four months ago coming home in the dark he fell into a little river and he was drowned and she had a younger daughter and she wanted to shake hands with me.

Not at all a dream although there was a dream a dream of their all coming to a housewarming and he going away to look at a Ford car which looked funny and everybody being lost and birds little birds being very optimistic because they sang in the rain.

This was what happened on Saturday and Angel Harper, all of a sudden was older. If he was really older it was not so exciting and he was really older.

When this you see remember me sang a little bird. But what was the use if he was a little older and it was not any longer exciting.

If he was dead and defeated, if guns shot and clouds fell and water rose and tunnels swelled was it not at all exciting.

Mrs. Reynolds said she preferred potatoes.

And she was right.

Francis Holstein was an old man, they made him the head of the local legion and he said a few words. When that happened he mentioned that he had said a few words.

Nelly Winsome came to see him, she said I dreamed that Angel Harper had never been married.

58

Oh yes he hasn't, said Holstein.

And if he has never been married I would like to see him said Nelly.

But I do not know him said Holstein.

You do not know him said Nelly, well she said if you do not know him how could I have dreamed that he had never been married.

Holstein began to laugh and then he began to cry well not exactly cry but he began to look funny.

Nelly was most anxious. Bye and bye she had eaten her dinner.

No one she knew knew Angel Harper.

She saw Mrs. Reynolds and she asked her. Mrs. Reynolds said I am telling just as I told you before I do prefer potatoes and I do not need butter, lard will do it. Now if you have anything to say she said to Nelly say it to my husband. And if you want to wait until He comes in you had better not go away.

Nelly made up her mind to stay.

When Mr. Reynolds came in he said he would not change his time to summer time, he would just eat an hour later or earlier, well he did not care.

But is Angel Harper married persisted Nelly.

Angel Harper said Mr. Reynolds, dear me.

By this time Nelly Winsome was desperate she decided to go home eat something indigestible and dream again and she did.

Mrs. Reynolds said she could not remember how Angel Harper wore his hair. She said she did not know the color of his hair. She did not say she did not remember because perhaps she had never seen his hair. Perhaps not.

He was not bald well anyway when she had seen him he was young young enough to have all his hair. But had she ever seen his hair, even if she had she would not know the color of his hair or the color of his eyes, as she never had spoken to him she would not know the color of his eyes, and how tall he was, she had never noticed him even if he had passed her house, anyway she did not remember anything about him. Of course she knew his name was Angel Harper. That was just enough. Mr. Reynolds said that if the weather was set to be fair all the signs that look like rain do not count and if the weather is set for rain all the signs that look like clearing do not count. And he was right. It was the same about war and about victories. His brother said that when he was with Mr. Reynolds and Mr. Reynolds said what he had to say.

There was a Miss Goodman, she was almost a dwarf and she looked as if she limped, perhaps she did not and she had a flat face and her father was a major in the army and her brother wanted to be an officer too. She said that she herself liked winter sports. It was hard to believe but she always meant just what she said. She also said that when she lived anywhere for five years she preferred it to any other place. She was very interested when she heard that Mrs. Reynolds and Mr. Reynolds lived where they did. She wanted to know how often they or either of them had seen Joseph Lane. They did not know, and so they could not tell her. Mrs. Reynolds said she was used to that.

Mrs. Reynolds said that the barometer was falling. She said it to two women with whom she was talking, one of them was tall and her name was Ida, the other one had a hoarse voice which was loud and her father had once killed a man in a fit of anger.

They said, when you ring nobody answers and when you do not ring nobody answers.

After a while it was a little later and the dog was given away. He was a black dog with curly hair and when he was little he had been very very timid and then later he had a violent nature. Not alone that but it was a bother.

Bother said Mrs. Reynolds, if it rains every day and every night too, that is a bother.

All right.

Angel Harper was half as fat as he had been.

What said Mrs. Reynolds.

Half as fat as he had been was the answer.

By the time Angel Harper was well known it was just begun.

Mr. Reynolds woke up about three in the morning. He looked out and saw the moon shining. He woke up Mrs. Reynolds and told her the moon was shining. By the time she was awake and had looked out it was raining.

It had rained for twenty-eight days in the daytime and in the evening and at night and now it was raining again.

By this time Angel Harper was very well known, so well known that everybody knew about him.

Mrs. Reynolds meditated, she was sitting and she said she was thinking, she was thinking whether if now somehow somebody gave her a piece of juicy beefsteak, well would she could she swallow it, would it go down.

She was meditating.

Of course it was either that or not at all, and since it was not at all it must very certainly be either that.

After there had been a very long silence somebody mentioned they mentioned Joseph Lane, they said nobody has forgotten him. They were busy. They were busy remembering Angel Harper, and if they were busy remembering Angel Harper, they did not forget Joseph Lane but it was there all the same.

Once in a while every once in a while, the sun was shining and the sun could shine so that it could come to be very hot. Some were used to it and some were not. Joseph Lane felt that nothing that was climate could make any difference, not to him.

Angel Harper was hidden away from climate.

There.

Mrs. Reynolds said it was too bad that roses did not last longer. Mrs. Reynolds said it was too bad that roses changed color.

The neighbors said it was too bad that the Reynolds had no children. Mr. Reynolds had no nephews, Mrs. Reynolds had two nephews. When there were a great many people who lunched with the Reynolds everybody said Mrs. Reynolds did it all very well.

Very well.

At no time had Angel Harper or Joseph Lane or a third one whose name began with a B, not any one of the three of them had ever lunched with the Reynolds. They had never seen each other nor the Reynolds. By this time, it was time for the flowers to be arranged according to color size kind and wild and tame. Late at night everybody went to bed.

By this time darkness was disturbed by moon-light and day-light was disturbed by thunder.

By leaving it alone Angel Harper could wait. Not patiently but long.

As we have the material said Mrs. Reynolds we might as well build an addition to our house. Building this addition pleased Mr. Reynolds. It exhilarated him.

If you are nervous any news makes one nervous, said the wife of Mrs. Reynolds' nephew. They were afraid that like a great many he was going to be a bachelor and remain unmarried but he did marry, not a pretty girl a long thin one and he was very fond of her. They had a little girl who always remembered anybody's name. She visited Mrs. Reynolds who liked to have her but did not know what to do with her. But it was not necessary to do anything, anything at all.

This little girl never said what she thought about Joseph Lane and Angel Harper. When she cried she rarely cried but when she did cry she did say What was their name, oh dear what was their name. And nobody answered because nobody listened, they just gave her something to please her and she naturally did not cry often.

When she was photographed for the first time, she cried but then when they told her not to she stopped crying. Her father and mother said she cried so seldom you could count the number of times she had cried.

She was named after Mrs. Reynolds but nobody called her by that name. Mrs. Reynolds preferred it to be like that. Mr. Reynolds did sometimes call her by this name but he spoke to her so seldom it did not matter very much.

Why should two men sit in a meadow with one horse. Joseph Lane asked this question. Why said his brother-in-law's cousin does the color of that distant mountain remind me of pearly girlie.

It does said Mrs. Reynolds, everybody sitting with their hats on on top of a half finished building, it does look like a scene in a theatre. But said Mr. Reynolds it has not that gayety.

For this they think of everything.

Mrs. Reynolds was astonished that her heart went out to the sorrows of Joseph Lane and it did not go out to the troubles of English pigeons. English pigeons do not alone coo like a dove they fly like a magpie.

All of which made Joseph Lane be one at a time.

For this for them.

Now earnestly to take to task a dog a cow a calf a very young pig and imitation silk.

And to remember that all of it is forbidden.

Angel Harper changed from letting them not dance to letting them dance and this is the reason why.

Why.

It is easy to not have a calf suck its mother's milk said Mrs. Reynolds only sometimes the knot comes unfastened.

Angel Harper never observes whose cow is outside when it is a cow, now.

And then it is never too late when the sun never sets that is to say when there is always a light.

Angel Harper said he never did it just the same but how difficult to do it on the same day and not to do it the same. If he felt as he felt he felt he would feel like crying and if he felt like crying he would feel very funny.

By the time that this happened it was nearly all over but now, and now is now, now it is only just begun.

There came a time when retired school-teachers fished in the lakes and the streams to get a little fish to feed their cats, that was all.

It is very strange that Angel Harper resembles himself. At first he did not, he did not change but at first he did not. No said Mr. Reynolds, I do not like him, not that I ever met him, not that he ever met me, not that but I do not like him.

Not liking him said Mr. Reynolds, not liking him I do not like him.

Angel Harper knew that sooner or later, Joseph Lane did not know that sooner or later and that was natural enough because for Joseph Lane there was no sooner or later, for Angel Harper as soon as, there was sooner or later.

Mr. Reynolds said when somebody said this to him, I will take mine sooner.

Mrs. Reynolds dreamed that she was followed by a wild rabbit who wanted to become tame and Mrs. Reynolds was willing that he should come and be tame and he came.

There was an end of Angel Harper but was there a beginning. Those who know knew. That is they knew when he was through but oh dear there was all in between. This was not so for Joseph Lane not so.

For him there was no beginning or ending of Angel Harper, he would destroy Angel Harper destroy him. How could you destroy anything that had a beginning and ending. Joseph Lane knew better than that better than that.

So not enough Mrs. Reynolds but more Angel Harper, more Angel Harper.

Angel Harper was not born, to be born, means to be born along and though he followed after he was not born along.

He followed after and after he followed after it was as if he had come and come he did and when he came he remembered his name.

All this sounded very well but he never told it. He could not think in that way, he could not remember, he only remembered what he left. Little by little he tried to remember what he had but he never could, he could only remember what he left.

One day, it was not very late in the day he began to speak, he said, when I speak I speak and I speak once in a day twice in a day three times in a day I speak and then I speak on the day and on that day I speak.

This was the first speech he ever made.

It was not dark by the time he went to bed but he was very tired and so he sat and as he sat he saw, he never saw when he spoke or when he ate or when he walked, he did sometimes see when he sat but not that day not the day that he made the first speech he ever made. No not on that day.

Mrs. Reynolds did think that she changed her mind with the circumstances. She did think that she often heard about one doctor who was not on good terms with two other doctors. The

64

wife of that doctor so Mrs. Reynolds thought looked like a foreigner but and that was undoubtedly true she was of no importance.

Doctors lawyers sailors airmen and Indian chiefs they all made Angel Harper shiver not when he was awake and not when he was asleep but they did make Angel Harper shiver.

Two by two makes him through.

Angel Harper if he was a boy did it to annoy but it is doubtful if he ever was a boy. So much for that.

If he ever had a sister he never had had a brother and if he had had a brother he would not care to have a sister. But really Angel Harper was not interested in there being a family, if he could anyhow and he did that was enough. Enough said.

So his life began and he never prayed although he believed in what they said. He always did even when everybody thought he did not. He believed in it a lot, so much so that it would have been much better not so.

Mrs. Reynolds never had the habit of sighing. She knew that she and Mr. Reynolds would go on just as comfortably as not.

She said, I think that it is better to be in bed than sleepy, but I am sleepy said Mrs. Reynolds and she was.

Mrs. Reynolds saw two little girls and a little boy playing in the dust, she thought at first that they were playing marbles but then she saw they were making a little mound of dust. What is it, said Mrs. Reynolds and then she saw that there was a terrible big beetle underneath and he worked his way out and the more they covered him with dust the more he worked his way out.

Oh yes said Mrs. Reynolds.

Mrs. Reynolds remembered well she did not remember it but some one told her about it, a man was going along with a hunting dog who was deaf, hunting dogs need to see and smell they do not need to hear, so they said, anyway he was walking along with the hunting dog that was deaf and suddenly an automobile came along and the man jumped into the road and saved the dog, he had a hunting knife at his side and a gun on his shoulder and he stumbled and fell and the gun went off and the knife went into his side. A woman came along she had been scared by the gun and she saw the man was bleeding but it was from the knife and he said it is nothing at all and he went on but by next day he had lost so much blood he had to go to the hospital and he was never very well after, so Mrs. Reynolds said.

Mrs. Reynolds dreamed, she dreamed that Angel Harper was all over and she said in her dream I dreamed that Angel Harper was all over, and she dreamed in her dream that she said it is so many years later and Angel Harper is all over and she dreamed that she dreamed that Angel Harper was all over.

Oh yes she said. I do dream. Yes she said I do.

Once more it was not just yet. Joseph Lane never wanted to know how many months make six months, he never wanted to know how many days make twenty days, he never wanted to know how many hours make two hours and he never wanted to know how many minutes make thirty minutes. This is what made Joseph Lane live longer which he did.

A miller had two sons, one died and the other would die, the miller was a small man with very blue eyes, he said he had no luck.

All this was when Angel Harper was heavy and eating and when Angel Harper was heavy and eating, he ate.

Well next to eating he liked ham and next to ham he liked chocolate and next to chocolate he liked cake and then, then he was silent, he was all alone and he was dead and he was quiet and every day there were pages and pages of how to have happy days.

Angel Harper knew that white dogs are white, he did not know anything about black dogs being black. He did not shake his head but he acted as if he was very angry very very angry.

Mrs. Reynolds remembered the first time she ever ate crawfish. It was in the hills, the car was making a strange noise, they were nervous about it, she and Mr. Reynolds, very nervous and they stopped somewhere to have lunch and they were given crawfish. She knew what they were and Mr. Reynolds had eaten them before so she ate them too and she liked them. Now she was eating them again, they did not have much else to eat that day, that is they had potatoes and beets and water ice, but then after all well after all they had crawfish and she liked them. She liked them red and she liked them now. She laughed when she said that and Mr. Reynolds smiled.

Mrs. Reynolds was quite occupied and so was Mr. Reynolds.

They wanted to know what the news was, but after all, it would do just as well to know the news tomorrow as today. In every way the news was the news of yesterday, and yesterday was another day and so was tomorrow.

They might be just as occupied tomorrow as today but then again they might not be.

Mrs. Reynolds said it did not make as much difference as it might. She said how do you do, and after all, she laughed and said how do you do is just as much news as anything, and as she said it she laughed.

Mr. Reynolds was not there he was occupied and he was quiet. It was very restful to be Mr. Reynolds and Mrs. Reynolds, that is what Mrs. Reynolds did say, and she went into the house to stay.

Mr. Reynolds said that he had never liked Angel Harper. He said that he had never had any such feeling about Joseph Lane. He said, Joseph Lane, well Joseph Lane, anyhow he said and he meant what he said, he said he had never liked Angel Harper, not in any kind of a way and he had never changed about that and it was not very likely that he would change about that. Mrs. Reynolds felt that way about it too, she had never liked Angel Harper and now she knew that it was more than that, she knew she would like not only that Angel Harper would be dead but that he would always have been dead. That is what she said and she said, she meant what she said.

The only thing said Mrs. Reynolds about which I cannot make up my mind is just what way he should be dead as dead. She could think about it but she could not make up her mind about it. Mr. Reynolds said don't think about it. But she said yes she said yes I do think about it but I cannot make up my mind about it how dead Angel Harper can be dead, all dead.

Yes said Mr. Reynolds.

Mrs. Reynolds saw everybody give each child a peach, there were three girls and a boy, the boy liked to play a toy piano and work a Punch and Judy show, two girls liked to sit in the dirt, and the third was very strong, and some one gave each one of them a peach, and Mrs. Reynolds saw it. She said, said Mrs. Reynolds, I saw it as I went along.

It was yesterday and nobody was anxious about that nobody was anxious about Joseph Lane, and nobody was at all worried about his name. Why should they have been. Mr. Reynolds always knew when there was a new or old and a middle moon and he said, not that it was very important but it was a necessity for him to know it. And Joseph Lane, coughed when there was a moon, and as there always is a moon he coughed all the time. It was not his health, it was his stomach that made him cough so Mr. Reynolds said and Mr. Reynolds also said of course he did not know him, he had never seen Joseph Lane, and it was not a necessity for him to have seen him, and very likely he would never see him.

Oh said Mrs. Reynolds, if we all have less to eat we can get thin and tighten our belts, and if we have still less to eat and have to die of it then if we have to die of it we can all die together. Yes yes said Mr. Reynolds and it was true he said yes yes and he meant it, it might all come to be true as true as that.

It was a long way to wait and in the meantime every day there was a dark cloud, a very dark one. An Angel Harper cloud said Mrs. Reynolds and she said as long as Angel Harper lived there would be every afternoon and sometimes even in the morning and quite likely at noon a very big dark cloud in the sky even if it did not make any lightning nor any hail.

Yes said Mrs. Reynolds I do know that you yourself do not care for wine, that you prefer butter. Mrs. Reynolds stood and felt very well, she was talking to Mr. Reynolds' cousin who had come part of the way with her. Yes said Mrs. Reynolds, it is that way, you begin to feel a longing a real longing for a city, for buildings for small country and pretty gardens and for streets and for things in them, yes you do. And indeed she did, the cousin said she did, she had had enough of hills and distant mountains and stone houses and strange cows and children, and stone walls and up and down and rocks and trees and bare spaces.

68

Just now.

Angel Harper was bitter he was where he was and he was bitter, he ate what he ate and he was bitter, nobody saw him just then and he was bitter and little by little it was as much worse and he was bitter. By the time he had finished standing he was bitter, by the time he had finished sitting he was bitter. Bed did not interest him. He was bitter.

Joseph Lane was far away and as far away as he was there he was, there were no cuckoos there and there were no sea-gulls and there were fields and fields and there was darkness and every little while everybody did everything and Joseph Lane thought he would whisper but he found himself to be very comfortable and so he thought out loud and as he thought out loud, he knew it was regular and that he would win. Oh yes said Mrs. Reynolds, she was not there of course oh yes said Mrs. Reynolds the time has come. Has it said Mr. Reynolds.

By that time it had and everybody suffered. Thank you for not being ready said Mrs. Reynolds and laughed, she said the masons were building walls and the painters were putting in windows and the carpenters were building doors and her husband would bring it all back.

That is what Mrs. Reynolds said.

Mrs. Reynolds liked to know what was happening so she asked everybody as they were passing. They each told her what was happening and there was a great deal happening. One told her that for the first time in his life he was out with an umbrella when there was thunder and lightning and it made him feel as if the lightning was hitting the umbrella. I suppose said he that an umbrella could be a lightning conductor. Mrs. Reynolds said she never went out when there was thunder and lightning, she did not go out when there was sun shining or moon shining or indeed when there was wind or when there was rain or when there was hail or when there was snow nor indeed when it was cloudy. No said Mrs. Reynolds no. And she meant no. She was amiable about it but she meant no.

Her husband lost thirty bottles of olive oil, well he was sorry and so was she.

So as it was a time when so much was happening, so much did happen. Every day was so much nearer the end than the day before and as for a year well there was really no looking back a whole year. A year dear me a year said Mrs. Reynolds just as if it was a year or as if it had been a year.

So much as it was it was just as much as it was or more.

As much as it was said Mrs. Reynolds remembering Angel Harper. So much, she said, as much, she said, as much as it was, she said. In conclusion she made all ages be quiet, quiet and useful. Yes said Mrs. Reynolds quiet if not useful. Useful if not quiet. Quiet and useful, useful and quiet.

Fed and unfed who is dead, said Angel Harper and his nose turned red, not with drink nor cold nor fear but with indigestion.

I knew how lucky he was said Mrs. Reynolds and she remembered all the sad things she had seen. There were two of them. And there was nothing in between.

Mr. Redfern was ill and with his hands behind his back he walked up and down and his wife working at her wash watched him. It was sad.

Mrs. Reynolds talked about everything and she knew that Joseph Lane was very well. He is very well I thank you said Mrs. Reynolds although she did not know him but she said it because she wished him well and because she wished that Angel Harper was more dead than he was. To be sure said Mrs. Reynolds he will be dead. Very likely said Mr. Reynolds. And said Mrs. Reynolds they were both right, as indeed they were.

Mrs. Reynolds wanted their tiles to have flowers on them but Mr. Reynolds preferred them a simple grey. As they could only get grey ones, as there were no others it was just as well said Mrs. Reynolds that they were agreed. Just as well said Mr. Reynolds and smiled.

It is always a kindness said Mr. Reynolds to relieve them when they are there. And said Mrs. Reynolds they are always there. Not always said Mr. Reynolds and they like to eat. So do we said Mrs. Reynolds. She also remarked that when men had no tobacco to smoke they ate more.

Mrs. Reynolds' brother-in-law, Mr. Reynolds' younger brother said that the weather was so changeable that you could not say whether there was going to be rain or dry weather.

He never said this to Angel Harper, he had not said it when he knew Angel Harper because then it was not true, the weather then was not so changeable, and now when the weather was so changeable he did not see Angel Harper at all. Not only was Angel Harper far away but Angel Harper naturally did not see him and so he did not see him. Naturally not.

Some dogs like walking in the dark and some do not, it may have something to do with their color or with the light in their eyes, green red or silver or it might be that nothing makes any difference. It might be that.

For this many thanks was never said by Angel Harper.

Do be careful right along was never said by Angel Harper.

Eat while you can was never said by Angel Harper.

Hear when they speak was never said by Angel Harper.

Lift a chair up before you sit down was never said by Angel Harper.

Joseph Lane practised what he preached, he recited poetry. He liked the Elegy in the Churchyard, he said and leave the world to darkness and to me. Just so said Joseph Lane just so, and as he said it, he was wise, he said for this which is mine, there is no reason that this which is mine is left to me. Left to me means nothing said Joseph Lane and he was wise, as naturally wise as that.

These two men Angel Harper and Joseph Lane were not alone and separately and together and as they approached.

And then well then for which it is mighty easy to be anxious.

I am anxious said Angel Harper but I am not.

And Joseph Lane knew that it did not matter, hours are clouds and there are more than if they do not matter.

And so quite as easily as fathers and feathers.

Angel Harper and Joseph Lane met and never met.

But which, said Joseph Lane.

Angel Harper was destroyed.

But which said Joseph Lane. But all that was a long time after.

In the beginning Angel Harper was Angel Harper.

Mrs. Reynolds never laughed but she said who and when she said who she was making fun of Angel Harper.

By that time a great many knew him and a great many were able to withdraw when they were afraid of him.

Afraid of him said Mrs. Reynolds.

By that time it was more than ever that every one knew his name. They did not say fie fie for shame everybody knows his name.

But they might have said Mr. Reynolds as he sat down to turn away.

Orders when given can be given again said Joseph Lane but when he said it he knew that he was slow slow slow as cold molasses is slow and slow as growing pumpkins are slow slow as meadow grass is slow that is when cows are chewing. Oh yes said Joseph Lane and there was a choke in his voice. I am to blame if I am not slowly to gain, everything being the same. Joseph Lane was narrowly near to sneezes and tears but he ate all the same. It is necessary to eat in order that no one is to blame and Joseph Lane never finds anything necessary.

For this he was famous.

But said Mrs. Reynolds cows can run. And indeed cows can, they have a way of running away, not for better food nor even from anxiety but cows do run away.

This said Mrs. Reynolds is not a strain upon me to say. And she said it. Mr. Reynolds said it is not necessary that when I reply my nephew will die. But the nephew of Mr. Reynolds was dead. He had been killed in the war and Angel Harper well of course nobody can tell but all the same it would be all the same even if vegetables do grow more easily than meat.

Mrs. Reynolds never said that she thought meat was sweet but she did say that she did find that carrots and ice were both sweet.

Oh said she and it was not often but she did pray, oh she said when I pray and they go away then I say they have gone away.

And now after all Mr. Reynolds remembered Angel Harper and how much Angel Harper had annoyed him. Yes said Mr. Reynolds make no mistake about that Angel Harper is annoysome, he is dangerous, he is painful, he is owned and he is annoysome and I would be just as well pleased if they killed him. If not he might just as well be dead. This is what Mr. Reynolds said. His wife Mrs. Reynolds was easy going and she liked to gossip but she agreed with him. They both had the same opinion of Angel Harper. I know what my husband meant by what he said, said Mrs. Reynolds.

Mr. Reynolds' younger brother and his wife Hope had two friends staying with them, Mr. and Mrs. Madden-Henry. They had never met either Angel Harper or Joseph Lane but might as well have. That is to say they knew so many who had who had, that is to say seen and heard and felt and told, and they were always ready, Mr. and Mrs. Madden-Henry to go there when they were to go there and it always was almost true of them that they would go there. If they did they would see and hear and feel and tell all about Angel Harper. They were not so likely to go where Joseph Lane was not so likely not at all likely not even the least bit likely nor did they really want to, they did want to that is they might very easily pretty nearly want to go where they would hear and feel and see and tell all about Angel Harper and they said Angel Harper and they knew very well what they had to tell when they said, Angel Harper, and they did oh quite as often as ever they did say yes very much, as much as, with them, Angel Harper.

Mr. and Mrs. Madden-Henry admired Angel Harper because he never coughed. They knew that of him. He never could or would or did cough. Joseph Lane might cough did cough would cough but and this Mr. and Mrs. Madden-Henry knew Angel Harper never had and never would cough. For this they did very much admire him.

Bat said Hope Reynolds, the wife of Mr. Reynolds' younger brother, Bat is a word that has two meanings, one that flies by night and one that hits a ball.

By this she meant to express her admiration, her very great admiration for Angel Harper.

Her husband Mr. Reynolds' younger brother listened and said after a little hesitation, Yes I know it.

Mrs. Coates was a widow. She had had a son and he died, he

was a soldier but he did not die of wounds or being killed or exposure, he just died at home like his uncle his cousin and his grandmother. Mrs. Coates had greatly respected Mr. and Mrs. Madden-Henry, but when she heard them say that they admired Angel Harper because he never coughed, she began to think badly of them, and gradually she came to despise them.

She said she had been mistaken in them, she said a great many people began by respecting them and came gradually to despise them. Mrs. Coates said that she herself was interested in what any one said but nevertheless she herself was certain that Mr. and Mrs. Madden-Henry were mistaken.

Gradually everybody came to know what they thought about everything some because they expressed their opinions and some because they were afraid to say anything, so one way or another way every one came to know how they felt. Felt, said Mrs. Coates, eighty percent of the people are afraid and of the remaining twenty percent half are imbeciles and the other half fanatics. Felt said Mrs. Coates and she went away slowly and very well in order to do what she intended to do which was what she did.

It was midnight and Angel Harper fell asleep as he slept he knew he was not through and as he slept he knew he was no Jew and as he slept he knew that he was blue, blue with care and white with hair and afraid at night which was his share. Thank you said Angel Harper who was asleep and he thought it was a hoodoo.

Just then it was true that the window was open and as it was open he was away because Angel Harper never could stay either awake or away and yet in a kind of a way he never slept and if he ever slept he was nervous. All this was when it grew colder and colder.

Leave us is what Angel Harper shouted and he did not mean it. He never wanted to be alone and it was not really necessary that he ever was not even when he was asleep.

I know one at a time said Mrs. Reynolds. They come and ask me to give them money to help school-teachers and sisters and babies and prisoners and evergreens, and bright boys and anything else they see, and they say they will send the money I give

74

them away right away. But no, said Mrs. Reynolds although I do give them the money I am very tired of it. Very much very tired of it and pretty soon when anybody wants anything well I will tell them wait until they are older wait wait, and by that time well by that time it will be all over, just well all over.

Not again said Mr. Reynolds.

So it was very much what they needed when there was a little chill in the air and summer was over, not all over but just over.

How can Angel Harper be all here said Mrs. Coates and when she said it she did not know whether she should have her mouth open or her mouth closed.

In either case fifteen was of more value than twelve and thirty-three than twenty-four. All of Mrs. Coates' friends explained all these things.

Yes said Mrs. Reynolds, when white is white and black is black, even when in very bright sunlight a man in blue looks as if he had on a white suit, even then, when the nights are cool and the sun is warm even then well even then Angel Harper will not come to a good end. August chickens are very little on the first of September and even then, and Mrs. Reynolds turned away even then well when I never think of them, then I know that he will die and not bye and bye but just die. And said Mr. Reynolds that will be a good riddance to bad rubbish.

It is very likely that nobody knew anything about what Angel Harper was. What was he. He was just as he was when eggs are eggs and potatoes are cold potatoes. He even was as he was when chickens were scarce and there were no pigeons. He was what he was when cold was cold and ice was ice and all the rest was just the same as all the rest. And by that time he was not forgotten but nobody was interested to know whether he was anxious or not.

What do you care what do I care said Mrs. Reynolds if nobody has any day to say that Angel Harper is there.

Better leave it alone said Mr. Reynolds.

All of us are older, said Mrs. Reynolds. Not twenty years older said Mr. Reynolds. Well anyway not twenty years younger said Mrs. Reynolds.

Every once in a while she and he shrugged their shoulders. They remembered Joseph Lane and they sneezed and they remembered Joseph Lane and then they went to bed and just before they went to bed they remembered Joseph Lane.

Who has been here said Mrs. Reynolds. And nobody said who had been there, but Mrs. Reynolds knew that Mr. Reynolds' younger brother and his wife Hope and their friend Mrs. Coates had been there.

Mr. Reynolds said it is better to go to bed than to be dead. Mrs. Reynolds shrugged her shoulder and said good night.

Once in a while Angel Harper ate. He never remembered that once upon a time he had been eight. Leave out what it is all about. That is what Mrs. Reynolds said in her sleep. But she was not asleep. She sighed but she was not asleep. And then the moon had a ring around it and she was asleep. She and Mr. Reynolds both slept. They slept pretty well.

I love my love with a v because he is virtuous said Mrs. Coates and I love my love with a k because he is kindly said Mrs. Coates. She was the kind who would think of Angel Harper just that kind.

Angel Harper when he was ten was gentle then and liked to think of the theatre. He liked to play the voices in Punch and Judy he borrowed a little one from a boy neighbor. He was not so gentle then. He liked to play on a child's piano with five keys, he borrowed that from a little girl who lived near them, and he liked to cover his face with a black veil, and put transparent paper over one leg and to hang something behind to be a tail and he liked to be alone so he could not fail. He also liked to be with two or three and have the littlest of them tell him what to do. He did. He was gentle enough then and he was neither small nor tall he was ten.

Mrs. Coates sighed. She said she would like to meet Mrs. Reynolds but and this was not necessary she would never hope to have time.

Mrs. Reynolds said that she often thought about having a doctor but she really did not prefer one to another and so it was just as well not to have any. Mr. Reynolds tried to persuade her but she Mrs. Reynolds said that she was very sensitive and if you were as she was very sensitive it was as well not to see a doctor. And it was left unsettled just like that.

When he was eleven Angel Harper liked to sit with his back to a tree trunk and have next to him a little boy and a little girl and each one of them would have a newspaper with pictures and each one would read the one they had. Angel Harper liked to do this of a summer evening. He also liked to wear black, he preferred black to any other color, he did not like white or blue or brown he preferred black. He never mentioned black but he preferred it.

Once when he was twelve he ate twenty macaroons and an apple. He liked it although he never said it. He said that he preferred macaroons to fruit, he said he preferred coffee to potatoes, that is he never said this but he thought that if he said anything about coffee or macaroons or fruit or potatoes he would say that. Just then when he was twelve he knew that what he thought he said and what he said was not what he said. He said that it was just as often as not dark early but he preferred it to be dark early only when it was dark early he might not like it, and if he might not like it he might change it. This is what he felt when he said how do you do or good-bye. Nobody knew when he was thirteen whether he was very silent or whether he talked a great deal, neither he nor anybody else knew, they just did not know.

And so.

When he was thirteen his voice was hoarse and he was angry that he was so old and very angry that his voice was hoarse.

By the time he was fourteen he felt better about having been thirteen.

When this you see remember me said Mrs. Reynolds and she smiled, she naturally smiled because naturally she would naturally not again mention Angel Harper, so she said, and she knew what she said.

It was all so far away, indeed it had never been, she had never not ever seen Angel Harper but she did oh yes she did and how she did oh yes she knew his name not when he was fourteen but when he was forty.

Dear me she said, I do get homesick. For what said Mr. Reynolds, for lying on a couch and seeing a wall opposite and not trees and fields. You should said Mr. Reynolds be pleased that you see what you do see. And why not said Mrs. Reynolds when I know so well the difference between eight o'clock and five minutes of. Mr. Reynolds laughed he liked to smile and when he smiled he liked to smile. There is no use in so many people being killed said Mrs. Reynolds if it always will be eight o'clock. Oh yes said Mr. Reynolds, and they both knew that that time had come.

PART IV

Feel fell and far. Mrs. Reynolds never liked the letter f. She said it made her feel afraid. Just then she hated boils and soils. Boils were dangerous and soils were a bother.

She liked to count eleven.

After a little while Mr. Reynolds said he would wait. Well he would wait for the clock to strike eleven again or even twelve.

He would wait.

I heard it said Mrs. Reynolds. I understand why they did it said Mr. Reynolds but it would be preferable that they did not do it.

One at a time never happens with bombs said Mr. Reynolds' younger brother William, it is always two at a time, and said Hope his wife I do not like hare to be too far gone before they cook it. I, said Mr. Coates, I.

Angel Harper when he was fourteen began to feel pale. He wondered whether it was this that made him feel pale or whether it was that.

I wonder said Angel Harper when he was sixteen, I wonder if there is a bear there. There was no bear there. There never had been bears there.

It is wonderful said Mrs. Reynolds now when there is no way to go anywhere except on foot or on bicycles that I never had so many people to whom I could say how do you do. And there is so much to say, said Mrs. Reynolds. Yes said Mr. Reynolds yes there is so much to say.

When Angel Harper was sixteen, he was not seen. Not that he had gone away not that he did not have anything to say, but, and it was at this time that he did not come along and when anybody looked for him they did not find him. So much for that.

I said Mrs. Reynolds I have not helped to put a rose in with dahlias, but I can see said Mrs. Reynolds, John Jones does admire that it was done. I am here said Mr. Reynolds and indeed he had come home to dinner although it was very late. But then they had the habit, sometimes it is a habit and sometimes it has to be of having only soup an apple and a piece of cake for dinner. What do we call it said Mrs. Reynolds and she was very careful to go in first. Mr. Reynolds came in almost at once and then they both waited.

Mrs. Reynolds knew that she did not like to eat and if she did it tended to make her feel flushed. Oh yes she said yesterday was the day when my brother went away. Of course he never came back. There are those that never come back.

Mrs. Reynolds knew what was needed every week. Mr. Reynolds listened to her, and then he smiled, by himself. He was not tired, although the day was long and not too warm.

Nobody in the Reynolds' family ever said thank you. It was not necessary.

The white dahlias with the little pink rose and jasmine are lovely said a friend of the family. And she was right they were. They were just right.

When Angel Harper was eighteen, there were hours and hours and he might have been dead.

When he was nineteen he remembered that when he had been nine years old he had made a swing of a piece of board and string too small even for the smallest child and he loved sitting with his back against a tree and swinging this swing. When he was nineteen he remembered this thing.

When he was twenty he knew that if a branch of a tree touched a wire the light went out. How about it, said Angel Harper.

When Joseph Lane was a baby he just was a baby. He had a grandfather an old man with a short beard and blue eyes and considerable hair both beard and hair were white and he sat not in the sun and not in the shade and he said whenever he saw any one, he is not a hot number, he is half baked, and he meant the mayor and he said he meant the mayor.

When Joseph Lane was five he looked like a doll, sometimes like a black doll and sometimes like a white doll but he always looked like a doll. He made noises like a doll he stood like a doll.

When he was eight he was nervous, and when he was nervous he was black and when he was not nervous he was white, and half the time he was nervous and half the time he was not nervous.

When he was eleven, he was fat, and when he was fat he was careful and when he was careful he was quick and when he was quick he was successful.

Then when he was fifteen he suddenly grew thin, he was so thin he could not swim because he shivered so much and he did not like anybody or anything to touch him. He remained thin until he was twenty-seven and when he was twenty-seven he was fat again.

When Angel Harper was twenty-two he gloomed and when he gloomed he remembered that when he was seven he had hung a bell on a string and he had hung a doll on a string and he had hung a hat on a string. He remembered this thing when he was twenty-two and he was glooming.

When he was twenty-three, he knew the difference between wood ashes that stain clothing and wood ashes that clean clothing and he sighed and he cried and he was old too old to do what he was told but it did happen.

And then he was twenty-three and then he was twenty-four and then there was war and he was a soldier and he heard firing.

Mrs. Reynolds sighed when she was tired but after all what was the use of a castle if there were no sheep cows or horses, please believe me said Mrs. Reynolds but all this was not at the same time. That is naturally enough then she had not heard any mention of Angel Harper she had not heard any mention of Joseph Lane.

She said oh so much later, what did he mean.

That was what she said.

At this time Mrs. Reynolds met a friend, she said how do you do, and even if it hurts said Mrs. Reynolds even then, how do you do.

It is easy to prepare to the advantage of everybody. And all at once well said Mrs. Reynolds not all at once.

Well all at once and a little at a time, Mrs. Reynolds had said that what a saint that is if a saint saw what she said, then a saint was right to say what she said.

All at once said Mrs. Reynolds and she sighed. A boil said Mrs. Reynolds is painful and when it is followed by another and smaller one then the smaller one is not painful said Mrs. Reynolds.

Mrs. Reynolds was not careful of what she said but as she did not speak quickly and she always waited well not for an answer but for something it was all right that she said whatever she did say.

Once upon a time there was plenty of time and when there was plenty of time it was after Angel Harper and Joseph Lane were very well known. Not everybody knew that there was plenty of time but there was plenty of time. By this time Angel Harper was fifty years old and Joseph Lane was even older, not that any one did remember just when Joseph Lane had been born. There was nothing exceptional about that.

In memory of pleasant days that were and were not sad days said Mrs. Coates and sighed and Hope the wife of Mr. Reynolds' younger brother William sighed too.

By the time everybody had been a bride Rose hoped too. Rose hoped that George would say yes. Rose lost herself among the trees of George's home in the hopes that he would say yes. But George just looked the way he looked and there was always another day. George was not eager to know anybody else by name.

One day he said, Angel Harper and as he said Angel Harper the world was all aflame and nobody was to blame.

That was George. He was tall and thin and his face was round and his hands were long and he carried a shot gun. By the time this happened everything might have been over but it was not everything had only just begun. George had been a soldier and now he was a civilian. There were lots of them.

Mrs. Reynolds said that distilling sometimes lasted until the new year and if it did well her husband was always patient and he was always rich even if he was not rich enough.

Mrs. Reynolds said they had potatoes to eat they had wood to burn so there they were eat heat and wait.

When Angel Harper was twenty-five he was just as much alive. That is to say, he was a soldier that is to say he was a corporal that is to say he was not dead nor wounded nor anywhere. Very likely neither he nor they made it be any different and when it was over, there were no crowds of hours.

Sometimes it is over and sometimes it is not over and when it is over Angel Harper could sit and when it is not over Angel Harper could sit. Not a horse. Just sit.

There is a difference between twenty-nine and thirty. When you are twenty-nine it can be the beginning of everything. When you are thirty it can be the end of everything. Mrs. Reynolds had nothing to say about that. She was not looking when there was anything to say about that.

When Angel Harper was twenty-five twenty-six twenty-seven and twenty-eight, it was so busy that he forgot all about it, forgot it while and after it. Joseph Lane was considerably older and he forgot it.

Mr. Reynolds did not forget he said he said he did not like their kind of mind. He often said he minded their kind of mind. He said he remembered that a lot.

Mr. Reynolds liked potatoes that is he said they were useful and necessary and should be bought in large quantities. Small quantities of potatoes were not useless but they were annoying. When he said this Mr. Reynolds thought about it and having thought about it he did not repeat. Mr. Reynolds never repeated it, his wife Mrs. Reynolds did but he did not, he said well he did say good night again but only when it had been said to him.

Angel Harper was not yet forty-one, he was only twenty-five and he was still more alive, more alive than he had been at twenty-five and more alive than he had been at thirty-one, but and this he did not say to any one he was not no he was not so alive at thirty-five that wishing was anything. He neither wished nor was well, he neither sat nor fell but he could fall. Luckily he was not tall so it did not hurt him. Believe him, said some one, believe him when he says it did not hurt him, and they did believe him.

Mrs. Reynolds dreamed all night about frogs. She herself in her dream did not swallow one but a friend who had not swallowed had one inside her and the doctor had to get it out of her. When Mrs. Reynolds woke up she wondered what her dream meant.

Mr. Reynolds said that he was accustomed to little bits. He said he was accustomed to little bits at a time. He made fun of her, gently made fun of her.

At this time once very likely very likely Angel Harper was left. At this time twice very likely very likely twice he was left.

At this time three times very likely, very likely three times he was left.

At this time four times very likely four times he was left.

As much as ever Angel Harper was left.

Mr. Reynolds said left left left right left, he had a good job and he left.

Left right left.

Mr. Reynolds said he himself always ate well when he was hungry and he was very regularly hungry.

And then.

If you are looking down while you are walking it is better to walk up hill the ground is nearer.

Angel Harper was now thirty-eight and it was not at all too late.

Listen here.

A little star hung out of the full moon like a balloon.

Angel Harper did say one day, I have caught a flea on me. He was then forty-three.

Mrs. Reynolds murmured if a dog has worms. She was not then at all of course she was not there where Angel Harper said his say about the flea. He was very far away.

When Angel Harper was forty-three, he might have met some

84

people on the road when the road was empty but he did not go out to see.

When this you see remember me was not said when he was forty-three.

When he was forty-three he remembered that when he was thirteen he would sit by a drain and whisper in it to some one on the other side of it.

He would whisper through it sometimes call through it even if at the other end of it there was only a very very little girl. Once when he was sitting there talking through the pipe that led to the other side of the road, he saw passing a very heavy little boy harnessed to a little wagon and on the little wagon there was a chain a heavy chain. The heavy little boy made a noise as if he was an ox.

When Angel Harper was forty-three he remembered all that.

It was very often once in a while and there was snow once in a while.

Whenever there was snow Mrs. Reynolds had a habit of saying, Better not.

All this time Joseph Lane was naturally older, if you are dark and sit and have a black beard that has grey hair in it, and you are short and heavy and not careful of what you drink if you are older always older than you were it is not necessary that in the end you do not win. It is not you that does win but win you do. Do do said Joseph Lane, he liked to imitate an owl and a frog and a bat and a circle.

Just my age said Joseph Lane. He never laughed, he never slept he never shook himself and he never talked or walked. And then well then was not at that time.

When Angel Harper was forty-three it was not at all at that time.

Not at all said Mrs. Reynolds, Mrs. Reynolds was calling to some one to come. Not at all said Mrs. Reynolds.

Mrs. Reynolds liked grapes, not so very much. She liked grapes she liked bread, she liked coffee and sugar, she liked that and this and she liked more than enough of silk. Yes said Mrs. Reynolds.

By this time nobody knew the age of Mrs. Reynolds and the age of Mr. Reynolds.

There was no of course about anything when they were met.

I like fish said Mrs. Reynolds, but just now there is no trout about. I do said Mr. Reynolds and he almost laughed although he only smiled.

Thank you for cutting trees down said Mr. Reynolds' brother William's wife Hope. Hope was to have a little girl or if not a little boy. Or if not a little of both. She liked walnuts. Walnuts were almost a necessity.

Hope Reynolds knew that there was a clue to Angel Harper. And she used to stare not at him because he was not there, he was never there but she used to stare and stare, and her husband not only went out he went away with a friend and he stayed away until he came back again.

It is easy said Mrs. William Reynolds.

Mrs. Reynolds never said anything. She just said easy, and that was all she said. They never met and if they did they did not say anything.

In a little while Angel Harper was forty-four, and this did make him shut a door.

Believe it or not he did.

And then at forty-four he remembered when he was five, and not very much alive he knew a little boy of three, who was a foundling and very well taken care of all the same and very large in size and was dragged in a cart when he did not want to walk. Angel Harper was five and not very much alive and the foundling of three was bigger than he all this was so and everybody told him so.

When he was forty-four he remembered this not at all suddenly but when somebody sent him queens which they did when he was forty-four.

He liked queens.

In a little while he was still forty-four and he was awake about that he was awake about being forty-four.

So much was more than that and Mrs. Reynolds cried. She did

not often cry but she did cry. Perhaps it was too much and perhaps it was not too much.

That is the way it was.

Mr. Reynolds did not mention that she cried, he was not only there but then she had not cried. By that time it was half past six and dinner was eaten very late. It was almost nine o'clock when they ate dinner in summer even when the time was not changed.

It is so easy to be grateful for anything. Mrs. Reynolds never said that. She stood or sat as it pleased her.

And then suddenly that is to say unexpectedly something was taken away, not from Mr. Reynolds and not from Mrs. Reynolds, something was taken away.

Mr. Golden was a doctor. He said he was a surgeon. He said he specialized in everything and he was there.

Strange as he was it was that that he was.

And he said he knew Angel Harper, that is that he had known him when Angel Harper was forty-three. He said Angel Harper remembered that when he was twelve he liked to sit and swing a string and on the string was a swing and in the swing suspended from the string were two dolls and he liked to sit and swing the string which made the swing swing and in the swing were two dolls and Angel Harper liked to sit and swing the string that swung the swing.

Doctor Golden told this well he told it when he met any one at a jewelers. He never told it otherwise. Something about a jewelry store made him tell it as if he had never told it before.

Angel Harper went on being forty-three and it was not sooner or later and it was not over, later on it was all over that is it was over being forty-three but for a considerable time a very considerable time it was not over.

Over they used to call and a ferry came and took you over. Very much later it came to be that but by that time Angel Harper was fifty and over, and then there were no bridges and if anybody wanted to cross over they had to call out Over and the ferry came to take them over.

But when Angel Harper was forty-three there were plenty

of bridges everywhere and he kept on being forty-three. It was not yet all over.

Mrs. Reynolds said, under or over, and her husband Mr. Reynolds said let us go to bed.

It is natural that if any one has an employee they should worry if he was run over.

My husband Mr. Reynolds, said Mrs. Reynolds turned as pale as a lemon.

After all said Mrs. Reynolds I like to see people I know well dressed and I like to know where they are going and what they do when they are there and how they come home again.

I tell them I know said Mrs. Reynolds and when I tell them what I know then they tell me if it is so. And it is very nice to know said Mrs. Reynolds. Mr. Reynolds was a little tired after his shock. But he did not go to bed any earlier than was his custom.

Angel Harper continued to be forty-three and forty-three was not for him any younger than forty-four. Not for him.

Are you ready yet not yet, this was not said to or by Angel Harper, it was never said by or to Angel Harper.

Angel Harper was not tired of being forty-three. He never really wore out being forty-three.

And nobody had it to say and nobody knew what day he would have to have it be another day. Not once in all the time that he was forty-three did he have it be another day.

It was often neither very late nor very soon in the morning that Mrs. Reynolds opened the window and closed it again. And then.

Mrs. Reynolds said that for them there was no excuse. She preferred that they should be well dressed even if they did intend to eat as well as pick grapes. As well repeated Mrs. Reynolds and then she turned away. As well when she said as well it was one of the few times that she felt that something else was very necessary. It was not as if hours and hours had passed not as much as if it was two o'clock. She chose that time because it was almost that when they were ready she and Mr. Reynolds. She and Mr. Reynolds.

88

There was then not any pain when Angel Harper changed from forty-three to forty-four. There was not any pain for him to be forty-four. He remembered when he was forty-four that when he had been twenty-three he had done his peepee under a walnut tree.

Under a throne that is under a moan Joseph Lane was not alone.

Who when he awoke was dead, not only after but before he said and then his hair was on his head and his name was Joseph Lane, steal him. Steal him or not he did and did not forget that there was no need not to have him. So they had him. Not one at a time but him.

All this time Mrs. Reynolds had not said thank you as no one had loaned her anything. She did not want anything, she had everything, she was more often than ever not sitting but standing.

Leave carrots out put salads in were the words with which Mrs. Reynolds greeted some one. That some one said not at all I would rather not than not at all. Mrs. Reynolds began to laugh and then a little more and she laughed again. Then once in a while Mr. Reynolds came and he smiled when he went away and when he came again he was still smiling.

That was a happy day, at any rate it was a happy evening.

By the time winter had come it was not any longer a summer evening. Mrs. Reynolds said that she said that patches of dark green grass were agreeable to the eye and that she had a dog and that dog did not die. Another dog had but not this one. And once again she said and not this one. Mr. Reynolds said that she was right, he added and not this one.

At once something happened, they were not cold but they shivered and they said, close the door, and the door was closed and then they both felt warmer. It is early to feel warmer said Mrs. Reynolds and Mr. Reynolds answered, not at night. And then they were ready to hear anything that was said. They were always ready.

Please said Mr. Reynolds, do not hesitate if you want to come in.

They were almost as ready to get up as they were to go to bed.

And then once in a while they were not able to leave the house.

But when they did they were always welcome. But this was not often. They always stayed at home.

Mr. Reynolds preferred to hear any one say anything if they mentioned a name. Somebody said Joseph Lane. Mr. Reynolds did not hear him. Mrs. Reynolds did but she was just about to go in.

After that there was quite some time when they talked about whether they preferred dates or figs or raisins. Mrs. Reynolds said she preferred walnuts, and Mr. Reynolds said that he did not care very much for any of them he liked cheese.

Angel Harper was a name if you knew the name. Forty-four was his age if you knew his age.

Bye and bye was not what mattered not to him not to them. Once in a while Angel Harper felt like tears, tears in his throat but not in his eyes.

By that time he was waiting to be forty-four. He remembered that if he saw any one come racing down hill, he was not to blame. Because as he never spoke, he never said, because, for them it is not quiet to be left out loud. Come in said Angel Harper and they were not welcome. By that time he was forty-four and it was very different, very very different.

The house used to feel like ours said Mrs. Reynolds, and now, Well now perhaps it feels like theirs. Mr. Reynolds was too busy to answer.

As the nights grew colder Mrs. Reynolds went to bed earlier. Not because she was cold because the house was warm but because the nights were long. Thanks for coming again, said Mrs. Reynolds and she said she was surprised when they came. In these ways one day was not like another. Stars were not and houses were not and moons were not. And Mrs. Reynolds never woke softly. When she was awake she was awake.

There might be a sigh when she heard of Angel Harper. She could hear now of Angel Harper. Some one said to her, Mrs. Reynolds have you ever heard of Angel Harper. Yes said Mrs. Reynolds and she smiled a little yes said Mrs. Reynolds. Mr. Reynolds has a brother and that brother well, said Mrs. Reynolds you know what brothers of your husband are, well he was a brother of my husband and oh long ago very long ago, ever so long ago he had heard of Angel Harper, my husband never said that he had heard of Angel Harper but there was no doubt about it his brother William long ago had heard of Angel Harper.

Anybody then began again to say is Joseph Lane Joseph Lane. By that time he was or he was not. If he was then it was not necessary to wish him well and if he was not then it was necessary to wish him well. Wish him well said Mrs. Reynolds and then she remembered bye and bye and so she changed her mind and said it again she said wish him well. Of course this was a long time after Angel Harper was forty-four. When Angel Harper was forty-four wish him well was out of fashion wish anybody well was out of fashion, wishing was out of fashion.

Mrs. Reynolds was not out of fashion, she wore a beret in the winter and in the summer nothing on her head at all. It had always been so, she was never out of fashion because it had always been so.

Once in a while she took out a new blotter to put on Mr. Reynolds' desk. She preferred blue but if she could not find blue she would put up with rose, and when she put up with rose she liked it very well. Mr. Reynolds liked what he had. It was not Mr. Reynolds who remembered or forgot that Angel Harper was forty-four. Mr. Reynolds knew that in another year everybody would be older. Well said Mr. Reynolds to Mrs. Reynolds well and is it not so. And Mrs. Reynolds never turned away but she did not answer, she said she was too busy to remember any year certainly too busy to remember this year. Mr. Reynolds' brother William could remember for all of them and as for his wife Hope it was just as well that there was no one there to go away because certainly it might be said of her that they did go away. Alas said Mrs. Reynolds but this was much later and when Angel Harper was older and Mrs. Reynolds knew all about Angel Harper. Alas said Mrs. Reynolds that William's wife Hope did not still know Angel Harper because Angel Harper might then go away, go away, said Mrs. Reynolds, Yes go away.

Of course he was not there but that was the way Mrs. Reynolds felt about it and when she said it to Mr. Reynolds he said

91

yes well yes, but what is the use of saying it as she does not know Angel Harper, indeed said Mr. Reynolds I am not sure that she ever did know him, at least said Mr. Reynolds I am not sure that he ever knew her.

Mrs. Reynolds sighed and said it was cold in winter, which was undoubtedly true there where they were.

And so Angel Harper was forty-four and Joseph Lane was Joseph Lane or he was not Joseph Lane. In any case at that time Mrs. Reynolds sometimes read about them in a newspaper but she never talked about them to any one let alone to Mr. Reynolds or Mr. Reynolds' brother William or Mr. Reynolds' brother William's wife Hope.

Angel Harper was forty-four and he had not yet shut a door. The door was not open but any way if he had come to stay the door was not closed not at all closed and Angel Harper was not ready for more. When he was forty-four he was not yet ready for more. But more was there. Not more but anyway it was there.

Angel Harper was forty-four. Joseph Lane was more than forty-four. It did not really matter how much more than forty-four Joseph Lane was, it did not matter to him and it did not matter to Angel Harper and in a way nothing that was did matter to him and in a way it did happen to matter, to Angel Harper when Angel Harper was forty-four.

So he was forty-four. The moon and the sun knew that he was forty-four, forty and four.

Mrs. Reynolds dreamed that Mr. Reynolds said to her My love my love, I love my love. And Mrs. Reynolds dreamed that Mr. Reynolds said this to her and she told him that is she woke him up to tell him that she had dreamed that he had said this to her, and he said, if you dreamed it then I did say it, and he went to sleep and she dreamed it again and she woke and she was not certain whether dreaming it was satisfying or not satisfying.

Anyway when she heard she read it just as well that Angel Harper was forty-four, she said first to herself and then to Mr. Reynolds well anyway it was just as well that I dreamed what I dreamed and that I woke you to tell you about it. It is just as well. Mr. Reynolds answered her, yes just as well. And indeed it was just as well.

Angel Harper was forty-four, it was not thunder at the door, but when he was forty-four he remembered that when he had been fourteen, he played a game and each one, not he but each one around him had a knife, and each one came up to him and whispered something to him and he did not whisper anything, but each one and then over again came up close to him and whispered something to him and each one of them had a knife and he did not have a knife and he never whispered anything. When he was forty-four he remembered about this that it had been happening when he was fourteen.

Enough said, Angel Harper was forty-four and if he did not knock they did knock at a door and he was forty-four. To know that he was forty-four did not stop his being forty-four. Not.

When he was forty-four there was no either or, there was so much not to do, Angel Harper never did that not even when he was forty-four. Forty-four his forty-four was a long time and all that long time there was more. Forty-four.

Mrs. Reynolds was quick to tell again that she did not dream, she said she did not like to dream and when she did dream she liked to know if the dream meant anything. She asked a friend who had a book that told all about the meaning of dreams but if you did not remember what you had dreamed, How about that. She said to Mr. Reynolds how about that and Mr. Reynolds said make it up, but Mrs. Reynolds was not like that, if she dreamed and if she did not remember what she dreamed even if she wanted and she did want to know what the dream meant, she would not make it up, even if she could think of something she might have dreamed but actually she could not. Why not said Mr. Reynolds, but said Mrs. Reynolds you do not under-stand, but Mr. Reynolds did, at least so he said.

Mrs. Reynolds knew Mr. and Mrs. Oxner who had two chil-dren, they were very patriotic and very excited, they always were, the two children not so much but Mr. and Mrs. Oxner, and they might dream every night, but it would always have to do with something patriotic.

Yes said Mrs. Reynolds, Mrs. Reynolds did not say yes just to say yes, she said yes because she doubted very much if she knew how she felt about anything and if she did not know how she felt about anything she said yes.

By the time Angel Harper made forty-four sound more, everybody knew what he was before he was forty-four. It came about that there was no doubt that he was forty-four and everybody would have to know more. Everybody and there was no everybody any more, everybody was just beginning to know that Angel Harper was forty-four. By that time cows were cowards. Angel Harper might have been one too if he had not been two. He was two, he was Angel Harper and Angel Harper was not one he was two. That is what is meant for him to be forty-four. It was more than merely two it was two. Such was Angel Harper at forty-four.

Just then there was no reason why Joseph Lane should be neglecting or neglected, none at all. He was quite not mightily, and not all in vain. Joseph Lane when he was sounded as if he was was not vain. He was not nervous he was not cured, he was not any more later than ever before. He knew that there was more present than past, and more well he knew all about forty-four. And that was more than Angel Harper did, Angel Harper never really did, he never really did know all about being forty-four. If he did nobody was startled and as they were startled he did not. But anyway he was forty-five and he was still alive.

Mrs. Reynolds never gave a dinner party but there were very often people eating dinner. She liked eating not so much, she did not eat so much but she liked eating and having others eat so much. And so as often as not others stayed to dinner and ate their dinner with Mr. and Mrs. Reynolds. One evening even Mr. Reynolds' brother William and his wife Hope and a friend of theirs who was a sculptor but Mrs. Reynolds laughed and said her nose was too small for sculpture and Mr. Reynolds' patience was too short for sculpture but anyway there they were and they stayed for dinner and Valerie Harland stayed for dinner and then as they were all eating their dinner Valerie Harland said To

94

be or not to be Angel Harper and everybody laughed. And then when they were laughing the sculptor said laugh but do not forget that Angel Harper is living yet, and that reminded them all of the joke about your father-in-law is your father-in-law living yet and the answer no not yet. And they all laughed and Mrs. Reynolds laughed and she said I'll tell you about Angel Harper. Mrs. Reynolds' brother William knows all about Angel Harper, and his wife Hope knows all about Angel Harper but I said Mrs. Reynolds I do not know anything about Angel Harper but I will tell you all all about Angel Harper.

Angel Harper said Mrs. Reynolds is a stranger and a stranger can do things nobody born in a country can do. They let a stranger do what he has to do. And what will Angel Harper do, he will finish so that everybody in that country will be through through fear with everything. You'll see said Mrs. Reynolds you'll see. What I say is true. Mr. Reynolds said nothing but he said he liked to mix cheese with his sweet dish. He thinks cheese and milk and eggs as a pudding together or so closely following one another is everything. And the sculptor muttered something about Joseph Lane and he went on eating and Mrs. Reynolds' brother William and his wife Hope wanted to speak but what was the use of saying anything when everybody was asking Mrs. Reynolds if she liked cooking and she said she did not but she liked to see people eat and that was the end of that.

And besides said the sculptor I love to wander around the countryside.

It is said Mrs. Reynolds just as well not to remember as to forget.

By the time Angel Harper was forty-five, edges were as near to being edges as anything and when there were not anything Angel Harper coughed. He was not only nervous but he coughed and then all of a sudden he stopped coughing. He saw her and she was blonde and stout and he loved to go about. For them he said and when he said for them he knew nothing was at stake. He sat down at a table and there was no one standing. He sat down at a table and the table was painted green and white and after that he knew that he was right.

95

Right right.

Angel Harper was forty-five and he was not stout but his head was more around than it would be if it was different. Angel Harper did not have a different head and that was the reason he was not dead when he was forty-five instead of which he was alive.

Far away and not at all at play was Joseph Lane and that was not at all what anybody had to say.

Dear me.

If they commence dear me and if they stop and commence dear me.

Mrs. Reynolds knew that she was of use yesterday. She said yesterday made her nervous. She said she felt like that.

And then once again she had a feeling that yesterday made her nervous again. She said nervous again. Not really nearly nervous. Mr. Reynolds knew she was not nervous not nervous at all. He knew that when she said she was nervous she meant that she was nervous.

Butter by weight said Mr. Reynolds. Butter we ate said Mrs. Reynolds and they both laughed and Mr. Reynolds shook his head and so did Mrs. Reynolds. Mrs. Reynolds shook her head, and then she said she would go in. They were really not outside when she said she would go in.

When the judge said that he was going to leave Mrs. Reynolds said that she had known three judges and they were very different but they still had something in common. One was quiet and wrote poetry, the other was not so quiet, but was pretty quick and ate a great deal and liked his clothes, the third was quiet and read a great deal and finally had cataracts in his eyes and could not read any more.

Mrs. Reynolds had known them all more or less at the same time and she had not felt that it made any difference to herself or to Mr. Reynolds. Mr. Reynolds was very pleased with the time as it went by. He knew when to like snow and when to like rain. Mrs. Reynolds did not care for snow and did not care for rain.

Oh dear said some one Angel Harper is forty-five. Oh dear. And there was just this to do and it was done. Oh dear.

Much that was necessary was dressed in its best. That was what Mrs. Reynolds said when she saw any one pass by that is not any one but some one.

By the time that a truck was loaded, there was no more reason to wonder which way it was going. Mrs. Reynolds did not wonder. When after a while there was a difference between turning to the right and turning to the left Mrs. Reynolds said that she had seen which way they went but it had not made any difference to her. Mr. Reynolds said he would stay at home while she went out and he did.

Forty-five, it might not be necessary that Angel Harper ever was forty-five but if it was not necessary it was nevertheless a success.

Please said some one and when some one said please they meant if you please but in the way that Angel Harper wondered if when forty-five was over it would be forty-six there was no intention to please. Please said every one, and what they meant was if you please.

Angel Harper remembered then when he was forty-five that when he had been five he had liked to tease. He had liked to tease for walnuts and for rubber goats. He also liked to tease for butter and for pieces of cake. And then once he remembered that he had intended to give away a half of a walnut and when he came back the walnut was gone. He had eaten the walnut all the walnut and the walnut was gone. Why not, said Angel Harper he was six then and he began to cry and very quickly then he said to himself bye and bye and when he said to himself bye and bye he did not cry and then and when he was forty-five he was remembering and then never again did any one of them see him cry. They had not seen him cry even then, not even then.

And so it was a well known fact that Angel Harper was forty-five and still alive. Still murmured Angel Harper, yes still and alive murmured Angel Harper yes alive and he was forty-five. Believe it or not just as you like he was still alive at forty-five.

Mrs. Reynolds was never speechless with joy. She could be surprised and a little open her mouth and not say anything. Why not she said. She meant why not not say anything. Mr. Reynolds smiled, he was not tired, not easily tired, not at all tired and he smiled.

Angel Harper minded if they made a noise, not exactly like that but he minded if they made a noise, not if they made a big noise but a little noise. A little noise startled him but not a big noise. Oh yes when he was forty-five he was forty-five.

When he was forty-five he remembered that when he had been fifteen he had wondered if any apples had been seen. By the time he was forty-five he knew that apples would thrive in cold climates as well as warm ones and he knew that he had some years at least to live and when he would live he would see to it that he would have whatever it was necessary that there should be. A loud noise came when he was forty-five and that loud noise was should be. It was almost as tall as a call, and that call that was there was a terrible noise and it was a noise like should be.

That was when he was forty-five and he knew that even if it made a shade he would need a noise as loud as should be. So this was what made when he was forty-five such a loud noise.

Mrs. Reynolds had very nearly lost her way and as she was trying to find her way she said that it was very nice not to hear a noise. If she was not certain which way was the way she had to go it was better so that there was not any loud noise.

Let it alone, she said and she did not like to be alone, she did not have to let it alone because it did not make any difference, not exactly any difference and very shortly she was home. She said to Mr. Reynolds that she had almost lost her way. You did said Mr. Reynolds not really. No not really said Mrs. Reynolds but I might have lost my way if I had not happened to find the way to come home this way. Then they went in to dinner and they had a pleasant dinner and Mr. Reynolds asked Mrs. Reynolds if she was tired at all and she said no not at all, but really she was a little tired and she went to bed early and Mr. Reynolds had not intended to but he went to bed early too.

It was when Angel Harper was forty-five that Valery Hopkins began to think of dice. It was easy for him to think of combinations of making additions of knowing that two and two make four and that four and four make eight, and it was easy for him sooner or later to think that everything he did added up to something. Little by little Valery Hopkins grew stouter and as he grew stouter and his neck grew stouter and his feet and hands in proportion grew smaller well just then was the time when somebody said to him and he answered I am the same age as Angel Harper. That is the first time that the age of Angel Harper was something to compare with something.

That is the way it was Angel Harper was forty-five and if he was forty-five four more was going to be four more but now he was forty-five.

Mrs. Reynolds said that if she said what a shame she did not really mean that anybody was to blame. She said what a shame and when she said what a shame she meant that it was a shame that so many people knew his name. Dear me said Mrs. Reynolds now I know his name. She meant that she was not frightened but there it was she said to Mr. Reynolds does it make you uneasy to know his name. Well said Mr. Reynolds it might if I thought about it but I do not remember to think about it and said Mr. Reynolds it is always best to be happy while you can And he said to Mrs. Reynolds we are going away for a while. And Mrs. Reynolds said yes and Mr. Reynolds said no and it was so they did and then they did not go for a while. They decided to stay at home. They always liked to decide to stay at home and there was no use in their arranging to go away because they never did go away. They always decided to stay. And so said Mr. Reynolds why worry about everybody hearing his name Angel Harper's name and that he is forty-five as long as we stay at home. And Mrs. Reynolds said as long as we stay at home. And she felt a little uneasy but she said very well very well she said and they decided to stay at home they decided not to go away.

PART V

Angel Harper was forty-six.

Exactly forty-six.

Really when Angel Harper was forty-six he was in a fix. And so was any one. And every one. Believe it or not it is true and it made every one pretty blue.

Come quickly and come easily and come softly is not the same thing said Mrs. Reynolds and she was tired. Mrs. Reynolds was not very often tired but she was tired.

She would like to have had a pony carriage. Why not an automobile. Why not an automobile said Mrs. Reynolds but really she would like to have a pony carriage. Mr. Reynolds said he felt that way too, not that Mr. and Mrs. Reynolds were blue not at all but each one in her or in his way felt that they would have liked to have a pony and a carriage today. Well yes rather than an automobile. Quite a bit rather.

Angel Harper was forty-six and as he was forty-six he was not further than bye and bye. How said Angel Harper and that was the beginning of a very long thing, How now said Angel Harper and by the time he went on he was not ending, How now and how. By that time there were more rocks than windows and he was well he was anxiously well he was, he was well, yes he was well, Angel Harper was forty-six and he was very well.

Much said somebody and when they said much they trembled. Tremble not said William Wallace and William Wallace was warm and as he was warm he was warmer and as he was warmer he was warm in winter.

Oh how said William Wallace how can Angel Harper be forty-six. But he is said William Wallace, he Angel Harper is certainly now forty-six, and he does not any longer need to remember. Tears come easily to William Wallace and they came as he said that Angel Harper who certainly was now forty-six did not any longer need to remember.

It is not only in August that anybody is forty-six but also in November. Beware said some one to Angel Harper beware of August and beware of November. Angel Harper was not so busy being forty-six that he could not hear this warning but what can a warning do. A warning cannot help him through neither through August nor through November nor through forty-six. Not in any way. And there are so many around, if there are millions or forty millions or five millions or any millions around what can a warning do, just what can a warning do. Much as there is need for it what can a warning do. Angel Harper heard William Wallace say that they can mix up a morning with a warning. Angel Harper did not sleep very well then but he was forty-six. How is it to be well at forty-six. Nobody asked him and nobody answered him.

Forty-six.

Far away and every day Joseph Lane made hay. He likes to make hay in a beard and in time, and in more than appalling sickness. But little by little fire goes away. That is what Joseph Lane says to his son but he never sees his son so he cannot say to him what he does say to him. That is the way Joseph Lane comes to be ready to get up when he has not yet been in bed. Like it or not he is not tired and he is not wet and he is not ready yet. Like it or not he is not ready yet.

All this time Mrs. Reynolds was ready to come home. She and Mr. Reynolds had not been away but she was ready to come home. When I come home said Mrs. Reynolds I am home. And that is what she meant and she said Besides when I am home I am home. When Mr. Reynolds heard her he knew that he was busy as he had a great deal to do and although he always did it he had quite a bit to do. He was at home and so was she so there they were they were at home in their house which was their home and their dog muttered in his sleep and soon they were all asleep, Mrs. Reynolds, Mr. Reynolds, their servant and the dog.

Angel Harper was never interested in a hunter or in huntsmen nor in their dogs. He had seen them close by and at a distance in a piece of woods or two or three together and he knew that if he flew he would fly away from them but actually he walked away from them and muttered to himself that he was a vegetarian which he was. At forty-six and still a vegetarian. Eat drink and be merry but he was very nervous yesterday as well as today. When he was forty-six he remembered having seen in an automobile a doctor a priest the doctor's wife and daughter and a horticulturist, and they had all made him just as angry. Might he have been just as angry, he might and he was. He had also seen a hunchback in another automobile and that had made him angry too just as angry. He counted one two three up to a hundred and he was not quite as angry but quite angry enough. He was forty-six and he was quite angry enough.

He did not like the stars when they said not angry enough. Stars do say not angry enough and when the stars said not angry enough then Angel Harper was not angry enough. Once in a while when he was forty-six he was angry enough. Once in a while.

I know said Mrs. Reynolds I know that a young man does not know the difference between the sixteenth of November and the twenty-sixth and then she sighed. Why said she why should any young man know the difference between the sixteenth of November and the twenty-sixth. When Mrs. Reynolds sighed it did not make any difference to her and it did not make any difference to Mr. Reynolds. She did not exactly like to sigh but when she did sigh she did sigh. And then she remembered her mother. Her mother had never sighed. She was very content was her mother and she even had grandsons who were soldiers and aviators but she never did sigh not really sigh.

Mrs. Reynolds was very careful of what she had and she had enough for every one, when she had enough for every one she did not give anything away although she was generous and she sighed and why not if when it was why not she still sighed. And then laughing a little she met the sister of her uncle's brother. Not a real uncle of course and she said well, and the sister of her uncle's brother said well and they both laughed together. It was quite dark and the evening was dusky and they did both laugh together.

Did said Mrs. Reynolds did Angela Haynes come back after she left so beautifully dressed that it might easily be understood that she would never come back. Angela Haynes was a neighbor and all of a sudden Mrs. Reynolds remembered that she had the same initials as Angel Harper. What of it, said Mrs. Reynolds and she said to Mr. Reynolds what of it and he answered my dear that is for you to say and Mrs. Reynolds said, she does have the same initials and she was so beautifully dressed that she might very easily never come back. And Mr. Reynolds laughed and he said and what of it and Mrs. Reynolds laughed and then they went in to their dinner. It was a rainy day and the evening came to be dark early and some friends telephoned and then they sat quite quietly and they heard Angela Haynes come home and Mrs. Reynolds said and what of it and Mr. Reynolds laughed and he said what of it and he said it is bedtime and they both went to bed. And what of it.

Angel Harper when he was almost forty-six was almost old enough to be alone but he never was, not only that he never was but there was no way that he ever would be alone. Not any way in which he could or would be alone. Not when he was forty-six.

Mrs. Reynolds said that she had heard that Angel Harper never could be and never would be alone. And she was right about it, she said to Mr. Reynolds that she was right about it and he said of course she was right about that.

Angel Harper was forty-six and being forty-six it came about that he was all of forty-six and the whole year that he was forty-six was not day by day but month by month, and each month was all of that. It might almost terrify Angel Harper to be all of forty-six and just as soon as all around him were certain that he was terrified they were terrified and as soon as all around him were terrified he was and he was not terrified and there was never anything that happened suddenly and it was partly that and partly that it was all there just as if everybody was standing. Angel Harper never sat, if he sat he was nervous but if he stood he was not nervous and as he stood suddenly there was silence and in the silence Angel Harper was forty-six. Forty-six was there and all of it was on the edge. Edge of what, nobody asked but it was an edge. It was the edge of forty-seven Angel Harper was forty-seven.

When he was forty-seven he remembered about wood, he was not certain that it was wood it might have been coal, and he remembered about his mother. He did not remember whether she had been strong or whether she had been weak. He did not remember. He remembered about his mother and wood for a fire and he remembered about his mother and coal for a fire but he did not remember whether his mother had been very strong or whether his mother had been very weak in the way he remembered her in connection with wood or was it coal.

Then he was forty-seven and forty-seven was very occupying so occupying that there were not whole stretches of days one after the other, there were no days at all, there never had been any nights and forty-seven was not really so nearly being ready as Angel Harper had even been before. Nervous or not believe it or not, day and night or not, day after day or not, Angel Harper was forty-seven, not beginning forty-seven not ending forty-seven, just forty-seven. Let said Angel Harper let forty-seven alone, but he knew that he was not ready for forty-seven so because he was not ready for forty-seven forty-seven was not ready for him. But if he was forty-seven and he was forty-seven then he was forty-seven. Angel Harper was forty-seven. It ended in that, that is just then it ended in that, it ended in that Angel Harper was forty-seven.

Mrs. Reynolds was anxious to see some one who had been a witness of hours of coming home. Mrs. Reynolds said it took them hours and hours to come home. And it had. Mr. Reynolds was glad to be at home and so was Mrs. Reynolds. She said so and so did he. After they had come in some one rang them up on

104

the telephone. Mrs. Reynolds answered the telephone. Are you home asked Mildred, yes said Mrs. Reynolds and it took us hours and hours to get in, yes said Mildred and as I have not seen or heard from you for two days I wanted to know, yes said Mrs. Reynolds it did take hours, and said Mrs. Reynolds I did have a witness of it taking hours and hours to get in. You mean said Mildred Mr. Reynolds oh no said Mrs. Reynolds he was with me no I mean all those who were taking hours and hours to get in. Oh yes said Mildred and now what is happening. Well said Mrs. Reynolds what is it that is happening. Don't you know said Mildred don't you know that Angel Harper is forty-seven. Who said Mrs. Reynolds. Angel Harper said Mildred, Oh that said Mrs. Reynolds, well good night said Mrs. Reynolds and then went into the other room and she said to Mr. Reynolds, Mildred says that Angel Harper is forty-seven. Is he said Mr. Reynolds that is very interesting. Is it said Mrs. Reynolds and then they had their evening meal and then they went to bed when all is said they went to bed. Yesterday and today.

How many hours can Joseph Lane count. That is what Angel Harper said when he shouted out loud. Shout said somebody that is shout when you are stout, but neither Angel Harper nor Joseph Lane were stout and Mrs. Reynolds did not remember that she had even seen them. She remembered about wood and about coal and she remembered about her mother but she did not remember about Angel Harper not even when they said that he was forty-seven, she did not even then remember about him.

Do you said Mrs. Reynolds, and then she stopped. Well said Mr. Reynolds. Do you said Mrs. Reynolds, do you like what you are used to, and Mr. Reynolds said Well yes and well well no. Yes said Mrs. Reynolds. And then they went to bed. Well yes said Mrs. Reynolds and then they did go to bed. It was almost noon of the next day and on that day some friends came to stay. And Mrs. Reynolds said to each one of them one of them was Herbert and the other one was Carrie and she said to each one of them How do you like or do you do you like what you are used to. Herbert said he was beginning to and Carrie said that she used to and they each said to Mrs. Reynolds and you and Mrs. Reynolds said oh yes. By the time evening had come Mrs. Reynolds had not forgotten anything, she was used to not forgetting anything certainly never in the evening and even very likely not in the morning or in the afternoon. She never liked any one either to stay or not to stay. When it was fairly early at night she liked to say good night.

After all said Mrs. Reynolds a change is not everything. She liked apples but not to eat. She liked apples to be there and she hoped although she never expected that they would keep. Will they keep said Mrs. Reynolds and Mr. Reynolds said yes very likely. And Mrs. Reynolds said she had no feeling about very likely. Mrs. Reynolds was certain that bye and bye she would be at home and she always was.

Mrs. Reynolds said she was not interested in far away and yet far away might come very near. And if it does said Mrs. Reynolds. Mr. Reynolds did not answer.

There was no reason why if Angel Harper was forty-seven Joseph Lane should be older. No reason at all. It made everybody just a little nervous to know that there was no reason.

Angel Harper when he was forty-seven did remember that when he had been twelve, bread was or was not interesting, he could not remember whether bread had been or whether bread had not been interesting. When he was forty-seven.

Bread and then he sat down and stopped thinking. Bread and then he got up and stopped thinking. Twelve years old and then he said when and where were the men who ate anything and indeed where were they, when he was forty-seven they were neither here nor there, by that time in between he had commenced thinking, and as he commenced thinking he was forty-seven and at forty-seven so he said when he was talking thinking is something nothing or everything. He was not easily tired when he was forty-seven. And this made him forty-seven. Which was what he was. When Angel Harper was forty-seven, wide was wide and he was there beside. To be closed is not the same and yet perhaps that was his game. Who can say what forty-seven is when very likely it is forty-seven. Angel Harper was forty-seven and it was not a year later, not one year later.

Eats and oats said Mrs. Reynolds can easily be confounded in printing, and she laughed again. Mr. Reynolds laughed. They liked laughing not loud laughing. Mrs. Reynolds was very ready to see anybody who either passed or who came in. She said would they not like to say how do you do and any one of them did like to say how do you do. Some without being at all disagreeable did not say how do you do. Yes said Mrs. Reynolds.

And now said Mrs. Reynolds, well and why not said Mr. Reynolds. And now said Mrs. Reynolds, if I have heard everything I have heard it all. And then they went to bed.

By the time Angel Harper was saying his prayers Joseph Lane was saying his prayers. This had happened this would happen, this could begin this could be sin, and therefore Angel Harper was forty-seven. They were far apart and news is far apart and so is remembering. Shall I tell you what I am doing, said Angel Harper angrily. He was not angry and if he was he was still as ready to be angry and if he was ready to be angry, adding sitting down to waiting is not anything. He sighed about forty-seven, he knew it was useful, he knew he would not remember being forty-seven but as he was forty-seven and he was forty-seven, by which it was of just as much use to him as if he had a use for it. A use for it. Well nobody said that it was just as well not to laugh at that.

Laugh at that said Mrs. Reynolds and she was very ready to talk to Herbert or Carrie or Helena or Joan or Paul or Charlotte or Francis or Abel or Cain or even Andrew Soutar. Why not when it is just as well to talk or not to talk. And she did talk. If you come by again said Mrs. Reynolds perhaps you will see me and if you do thank the others for me. For what, said Mr. Reynolds. Well why not said Mrs. Reynolds and then they went in. They knew that Angel Harper was forty-seven and it did worry them not really but just enough, it was almost like sneezing or like taking snuff. An old habit that might begin again.

Good night said Mrs. Reynolds and then she went in.

Do you think said Mrs. Reynolds, that it is frightening. She did not say this to Mr. Reynolds but to Mr. Reynolds' younger brother William. She knew that he had known what was going to happen or what had been happening that is he had known it all when she had not found it interesting nor frightening and so now she said to him do you think that it is frightening. He looked around and said that he had found that he had beautiful hands. Who has beautiful hands said Mrs. Reynolds and he said the mason had beautiful hands, and indeed the mason did have beautiful hands which was what made him a good working mason. Mrs. Reynolds was impatient and then she did remember how when William had gone to see his mother who had been very ill the sight of William had made her well and William had told his mother she must never worry because there were everywhere good and kind people so his mother should never worry. Mrs. Reynolds remembered all this as she went away but she did say that she really never wanted to see or hear William again. She said it to herself and then later she said it to Mr. Reynolds and Mr. Reynolds said all right, it did not interest him whether he or Mrs. Reynolds did or did not ever see or hear his younger brother William again.

Oh dear Angel Harper was forty-seven. Is anybody dead yet said some one and some one answered him, not yet.

When Angel Harper was forty-seven he remembered when he had been only eight, some boys threw stones at him and one hit him but did not hurt him and he cried like anything, he cried all along the road until somebody stopped him and then he stopped crying. When he was forty-seven he remembered that one time an old woman told him that in a city a little dog always had a coat put on him to go out but not in the country. In the country no kind of a dog ever had a coat put on him but in the city yes, it was a city habit. He remembered when he was forty-seven that this had at one time been told to him by an old woman sitting on the side of the road in the country. It was not cold yet when she told it to him.

And so being forty-seven was not completely everything but it was what was going to be forty-eight. Forty-eight might be all hate or all late. Which is which.

Mrs. Reynolds said something about which was which. She said she was just standing and talking she said now for us and

we are here and as we are here we are as we are and as we are
and we are which is which and which was which. She said too that
it was not very likely that it was all finished and done and not
very likely that it was only just begun. Which if it is said Mrs.
Reynolds would make it more than ever unlikely that it is which
it is. There is said Mrs. Reynolds no escaping hearing his name.

And indeed it was then just as true. There was no mistaking
and there was no escaping hearing his name. It would said Mrs.
Reynolds make my teeth hurt to hear his name. What said Mr.
Reynolds. Yes said Mrs. Reynolds you know what I mean. And
indeed he did he did know what she did mean.

Forty-seven, Angel Harper was forty-seven and he knew he
was not near tears, so sure was he that he was not near tears tears
that could come into his eyes that he knew that no tears could
come into his eyes whatever he tries. Whatever he tries.

Forty-seven and gracious me said Mrs. Reynolds gracious me.
She knew exactly what she meant and how to do exactly what
she meant to do. She went suddenly into the house and there
suddenly she began to cry. I do not know why said Mrs. Reynolds
and Mr. Reynolds said he knew why but it was not yet time to
cry not yet and perhaps it would be better to wait until it was
wet. Yes said Mrs. Reynolds and she began to laugh and she said
she would have half and he could have half. But it was really
Angel Harper being forty-seven that made her cry and she could
only try and hope that he would never be forty-eight. But he
was forty-eight and all her hoping was just too late. Yes said
Mrs. Reynolds and Mr. Reynolds said yes too. And then they
decided to go to bed as was their habit every night and they did
to-night although undoubtedly they did have a little fright. This
was what it was. Mrs. Reynolds knew that forty-seven for Angel
Harper to be forty-seven was safer for them than for Angel
Harper to be forty-eight, and she knew too that it was too late.
Mr. Reynolds said they had better not think about anything but
just go to bed and they did.

Mrs. Reynolds knew that it was raining that day. It rained all
day. It made no difference she knew that it made no difference
but it did rain all day. As it was raining all day she had a good

deal to say, and she was ready to say that there was Angel Harper and there was Joseph Lane and there was well why not when they were. And if they were and they were what difference did it make if it rained all day or if it did not rain all day. What difference does it make any day if it rains all day. Well she said and as she said Well she looked out of the window and there it was it was raining all day. It made it certain that Angel Harper was going to be well he was he was forty-seven and even that was happening that it was raining all day. Why not said Mr. Reynolds. Just why not said Mrs. Reynolds and Mr. Reynolds laughed, and then Mrs. Reynolds laughed too.

Well it was certainly certain that Angel Harper was forty-seven and it did not make everybody shiver because they all changed their minds. Everybody changed their minds.

It was getting very serious and very solemn his being forty-seven.

Men said Mrs. Reynolds always think that they can make the whole world bigger but they can't said Mrs. Reynolds. Well they think they can said Mr. Reynolds. Yes but they cannot said Mrs. Reynolds.

This was in the afternoon, it was not yet evening or night so Mr. and Mrs. Reynolds had still some time before them before it was time for them to go to bed.

It being afternoon Mr. and Mrs. Reynolds stayed for tea, and just then some one came in and he had once seen Angel Harper and he said do not believe what I say, but anyway believe it or not, some day he will go away. Who will go away said Mrs. Reynolds. Angel Harper said the man, well certainly said Mrs. Reynolds he has to stay before he can go away, anybody does. And everybody laughed but all the same Mrs. Reynolds was right, if anybody is to go away he has to stay before he can go away and this was to prove true of Angel Harper. If Joseph Lane did or did not Mrs. Reynolds said she did not care, he could be anywhere but Angel Harper, well what is the use of his having that name. No use said Mr. Reynolds.

Every day is another day when Angel Harper is forty-seven, even cake gets to have another meaning and as to candy and milk and cream and oatmeal, dear me said Mrs. Reynolds looking forward, I do wish I did not have to say so.

There is said Mrs. Reynolds no use in trying to stop Angel Harper from being forty-eight, he was forty-four and he is now forty-eight and each one of them is a date. Date rhymes with hate, murmured a man. Yes said Mrs. Reynolds it does and so does cloud rhyme with outloud. Oh yes said Mr. Reynolds it is getting late, and he was right it was getting late so they went home to dinner and after that they went as their habit was to bed.

Angel Harper was forty-eight and it looked mighty nearly as if it was too late.

Too late for him to be forty-eight or too late to have him be forty-eight.

It looked as if it was going to be too late that he was forty-eight.

And why not said Mrs. Reynolds why not have it be too late. Why not said Mr. Reynolds because when it smells like snow it really means fog. Why not said Mrs. Reynolds and she said she did feel a little nervous a little as if she might like to cry.

And now Angel Harper was forty-eight and that was a date. Any day might have been could have been would have been a date not for him but for any one.

Like it or not I will forget it said Mrs. Reynolds and she remembered that it was later than it had been.

Once a day somebody came in and when they came in they sat down and when they sat down they drank something and they ate something. Mrs. Reynolds was very hospitable and so was Mr. Reynolds and they were well to do and they liked giving anybody something to drink and something to eat and to eat with them and to drink with them. Everybody moves around somewhat but Mrs. Reynolds and Mr. Reynolds mostly stayed at home.

There were hours when they did not see Mr. Reynolds' younger brother William and his wife Hope. Mrs. Reynolds usually mentioned these hours as hours and Mr. Reynolds said why not call it days. Or even years if you like said Mrs. Reynolds.

But if it was really years that would mean that Angel Harper was older and older and that said Mrs. Reynolds would be catastrophic. She liked that word after she said it and Mr. Reynolds laughed.

But indeed it was nearly there not yesterday not today but next year.

Mrs. Reynolds had always said that she was not interested in years. Not much in months. Weeks were not so bad and days would do. Indeed days did do, they did very well indeed, said Mr. Reynolds and then he added and if it is night tonight let us go to bed, and then they did. They went to bed.

Forty-eight who is forty-eight. And it was a weight a kind of dead weight that Angel Harper was forty-eight, Hope who had known him many years ago told everybody so and really it was not necessary for her to tell everybody so, everybody kind of knew that it was so.

Was it so. Well yes it was so.

When Angel Harper was forty-eight, he remembered that when he had been twelve he had never liked any word that began with F. There was father and feather and fever and forever, he had not liked any word that had begun with f and here he was he was still there, and forty-eight, well forty-eight did begin with f, and here he was what he was. He did remember that when he was twelve he had not liked any word that began with f. When he was forty-eight he also remembered that when he was seven he could walk backwards completely on the edge of his heels, his heels had metal on them that is on the back of them so that they would not wear out, and he could walk quickly backwards on the edge of the heels of his shoes. When he was forty-eight he could remember when he was seven, but when he was forty-eight well f means forward, and f means faster and f means farther and f means means, he said said Angel Harper f means and as he said f means well then he said he did not remember. He did not say he did not remember and then everything stood still and as it stood still well nothing stood still, and after all stood and still were not together.

Let me be not after but before, said Angel Harper and he did not hesitate about f the letter f not at all.

112

Mrs. Reynolds said that after all what was the difference between sawing wood and sawn wood, she said that it could be very clearly seen that she meant what she said. She said that the days did not change but she was expecting something and she said if she was expecting something she did not know what it was that she did expect. Mr. Reynolds looked up and listened and as it was not afternoon, he thought he would wait awhile, and Mrs. Reynolds said why do you not answer and Mr. Reynolds smiled and said but I do.

Mrs. Reynolds was very patient all that year the year that Angel Harper was forty-eight. Why not, it is never too late not to be impatient and also not to be patient and all that year the year that Angel Harper was forty-eight. It did not bother Mr. Reynolds to be patient or not, and Mrs. Reynolds said to him or not and he answered well if not or not. They were very well both of them very well and very well satisfied both of them in that year that Angel Harper was forty-eight.

When anybody came and somebody always came they all sat down together and Mrs. Reynolds explained that as she was patient it was just as well that she was patient, even if her being patient did not bother Mr. Reynolds, and Mr. Reynolds always said that her being patient did not at all bother him.

They talked a great deal all that year that Angel Harper was forty-eight, everybody did and so did they even Mr. Reynolds talked quite almost all the time that he was talking all of that year.

Have you ever heard of Joseph Lane said Mrs. Reynolds and everybody said of course they had. Nobody not even Mrs. Reynolds asked any one if they had ever heard of Angel Harper. Everybody had and everybody knew that this year he was forty-eight. There was no use in insisting said Mrs. Reynolds but if I did wish said Mrs. Reynolds I would wish that Angel Harper would break a dish. A dish of what said Mr. Reynolds. A dish which would make him late. Late for what said Mr. Reynolds late for being forty-eight, said Mrs. Reynolds and they both laughed a little and as it was late they said it was so late that they would go to bed and they did. And sighed Mrs. Reynolds even if it is late Angel Harper is still forty-eight. And it was true he was, he was still forty-eight.

The last battle yes the last battle will be a battle of a mountain. Mrs. Reynolds did not know why she said that but she had. She had said that, not that it was her idea because it was not but because she had heard it and she did not know where she heard it but she had heard it just as she had heard linger longer Lucy. You do said Mrs. Reynolds that is I do said Mrs. Reynolds I do hear things. Why not said Mr. Reynolds. Well why not, said Mrs. Reynolds some do not, and well well said Mrs. Reynolds and if I do well I do always tell you. Yes you do said Mr. Reynolds and they were very careful to be pleased with what they had to say, today just as they were pleased with what they had to say every day.

Some one perhaps it was a cousin told Mrs. Reynolds about two sisters they were daughters of a farmer and they had both had children, that is to say the oldest had a baby in secret and the younger sister helped her to kill it, yes kill it, and then the younger sister had a baby in secret and the older helped her younger sister to kill it. And then somebody found it out and the police came and they took both of the sisters to prison and the oldest began to cry and tell everything and the younger did not cry but she told everything and when everything had been told she said and now you know everything let us go home so we can milk the cows, cows have to be milked and she could not see why they did not let her. Cows have to be milked when milking time comes. Cows do.

Well anyway that is true said Mrs. Reynolds but and she hesitated to sit down, she said if you like to stand up better than you like to sit down, yes said Mrs. Reynolds everything is puzzling if it is not troubling. And that said Mrs. Reynolds to her cousin reminds me did I ever tell you that I do not know whether I was awake or just not asleep anyway I was not in bed yet and the last thing I said was the last battle will be a battle of a mountain. The cousin was naturally not interested in that and she went away. Mrs. Reynolds went in and told Mr. Reynolds

114

the story of the two sisters and he said yes yes I was there. And indeed he had been there and he had not told Mrs. Reynolds because he thought it would worry her and she said very likely it would have if he had told her but not at all when her cousin told her. And Mr. Reynolds said yes and he laughed and he did understand her.

Little by little every night was every night and every morning was every morning and though it did take a very long time Angel Harper was still forty-eight.

Mrs. Reynolds said that William's wife's cousin's son had a murmur in his heart. And what of it said Mr. Reynolds, well they found it out when he was being examined for gymnastics, and what of it said Mr. Reynolds it is not dangerous, no said Mrs. Reynolds and they all know that but it worries them all a lot. And then she said she had just been hearing that Angel Harper was forty-eight and he wanted to go to war before he was fifty. What for said Mr. Reynolds, yes said Mrs. Reynolds with a sigh what for.

It was dark one night very dark, sometimes it was very dark at night and sometimes it was light at night, but whether it was dark at night or whether it was very light at night before it was very late Mr. and Mrs. Reynolds went to bed.

Who said it was easy said Mrs. Reynolds and she meant what she said.

When Angel Harper was forty-eight, there began not exactly began but there almost began to be days when Mrs. Reynolds said that she wondered perhaps when she went to bed, she would not sleep well that night. Mr. Reynolds laughed and said not at all but all the same Mrs. Reynolds did say that it was not so of course she did sleep all right but perhaps the next night and anyway was it all right. Well said Mr. Reynolds if it is not all right what can you do about it. And Mrs. Reynolds said it was not so, whatever happened well whatever happened well then whatever happened and Mr. Reynolds laughed and said I told you so.

All the same Angel Harper did continue to be forty-eight and Mrs. Reynolds did continue to say that it was too late for him to be forty-eight and would he continue to be forty-eight. Yes said Mr. Reynolds until it is too late and indeed it was so Angel Harper continued to be forty-eight until it was too late.

Mr. and Mrs. Reynolds said to one another that they hoped he would go on being forty-eight but said Mrs. Reynolds now it is too late and Mr. Reynolds said nothing at all.

Once in a while somebody said Joseph Lane. Mrs. Reynolds said she was not interested in that as a name and Mr. Reynolds was otherwise occupied and besides it was Friday night and regularly every Friday night they went out at night.

That time they went to Mr. and Mrs. William not their brother and brother-in-law they never went to see them but Mr. and Mrs. Simon William.

Naturally they all talked about how Angel Harper was still forty-eight. Why not if that was so and it was so and they all knew it was so and they all knew that they had nothing to do about it, they could not stop it, not stop Angel Harper being forty-eight and perhaps later not being forty-eight but forty-nine. Mr. and Mrs. Simon William sighed and Mr. and Mrs. Reynolds sighed and Jenny William sighed and they all said well there is no use in spending the night in sighs let us go home and go to bed. That is what they all said and that is what they all did. Anyway that is what Mr. and Mrs. Reynolds did. It was a bright night that Friday night and it was not very late at night.

All of which made somebody anxious but not really quite yet either Mr. and Mrs. Reynolds. They went to bed and slept.

Since Angel Harper was forty-eight it was easy for him to remember the date. He said not today not yesterday and he did not hesitate to say that he was forty-eight. He was angry that there was any doubt that he was forty-eight angry and angry again he said it was clear that there was no doubt that he was forty-eight. He said that days made him angry but not years, he said that weeks and months did not exist for him that days were days and each day made him angry but that a year was white and green and yellow and perhaps it made him mellow that years were years. Who says days said Angel Harper and he was angrier again angrier than ever.

116

It was true that he was forty-eight and that it was not yet too late not too late for him to be forty-eight but just in general not too late.

Believe it or not it was not too late.

By the time that Mrs. Reynolds was asleep, she had a neighbor who could not sleep, and his wife could not sleep and his son could not sleep and the servant could not sleep, nevertheless they were all asleep. Mrs. Reynolds laughed when she heard it. She said some one who is apt to be wonderful when Angel Harper is forty-eight is not so wonderful when it is too late for Angel Harper to be forty-eight. In this way said Mrs. Reynolds whether we stay here or not and we always stay here we never do not in this case said Mrs. Reynolds there is never any use in wondering. If I wonder said Mrs. Reynolds nobody ever says to me are you disappointed and I am not, no not either disappointed or not disappointed and she sighed. I never tried said Mrs. Reynolds. And Mr. Reynolds said no. And she said I said no I never tried. Well said Mr. Reynolds if at first you don't succeed try try again. And Mrs. Reynolds said it was time it always was time to go to bed and it was time.

Angel Harper was very careful when he was forty-eight never to state that he had ever heard well not that he had never heard but all the same that he had not come to hate, whom said Angel Harper, not when he was alone because then he was never alone, but all the same he did say that when he was forty-eight it was not the date to hate, he hesitated again to say whom, but he knew it was Joseph Lane. Just then he refused to say what he ate not Joseph Lane but himself, and yet it was necessary to state what he ate when he was forty-eight meaning for Angel Harper to state what he ate when he was forty-eight.

Silence followed, all those around him were not silent but they were silenced and when he was silent and he was silent sometimes silent even when he was forty-eight, well when he was and when they were, then there was not any silence, because every one listened when he had it to say and he did say all he did say.

It makes one groan in one's sleep said Mrs. Reynolds. And Mr. Reynolds woke up and asked why, and Mrs. Reynolds said because he does not die, and Mr. Reynolds said who does not deny, and Mrs. Reynolds answered oh my, go to sleep, do not listen to me go to sleep, and Mr. Reynolds said I will.

It was late when they woke up and had a cup of coffee and all and Mrs. Reynolds did remember that she did groan in her sleep, and she said she was right to groan in her sleep and Mr. Reynolds said why not. And indeed Mrs. Reynolds had been right to groan in her sleep and to say with all her might, I wish he was dead.

Right, well said Mrs. Reynolds different things are different. And they are.

Mrs. Reynolds was not late, she never was because she was always waiting. She knew it was not necessary not only to know but she knew that it was true that to wait now might make her wait then and to wait then might make her come again to wait now. Wait for what she said to herself but really she knew she knew that it was not only watchful to wait but careless to wait and pleasant to wait and ready to wait. She was ready to wait and indeed if Angel Harper was forty-eight there was nothing to do but wait. Mrs. Reynolds knew that this was so although nobody told her so. She did not tell anybody so, it was not even just so, it was not even a thing to know. Wait said Mrs. Reynolds and she knew that it was not too late to wait.

Angel Harper was forty-eight and any day not any week not any month not any year but any day he would be forty-nine and if he were forty-nine, nobody knows just why, but everybody began to cry, well not really but to be ready to cry. Just like that to be ready to cry. Angel Harper was not forty-eight he was forty-nine. Forty and nine makes forty-nine. Be ready said Mrs. Reynolds and in a way she was and in a way she was not. No said Mr. Reynolds in a way she was not.

PART VI

When Angel Harper was forty-nine, the very first day that he was forty-nine and the sun did not shine, on the very first day that he was forty-nine he remembered that when he had been eleven, he had been going up a hill and still he had a little girl she was seven leaning on his arm and it was a very straight hill and when they were half way up another little girl came along and they all did not go on going up the hill, they turned away into a place where there was nothing to see but they did go there because it was only half way up the hill and then Angel Harper did not remember what happened there, he just did not remember.

When Angel Harper was forty-nine, Mrs. Reynolds did not stop to say no or yes or even I guess, she did not stop at all and when Mrs. Reynolds did not stop at all and did not stand still and did not join herself at the gate and did not come again well then Mrs. Reynolds knew that what she would have to do might if she had it to do might be very terrifying might be well might it be that Mr. Reynolds would have to go away and if he did, indeed if he did what would Mrs. Reynolds say. She would say that that is not what she meant. Not. She might even cry, but then Mr. Reynolds would not be away long at his age he would not be away long, and besides he had to have very special things to eat, and besides, well besides said Mrs. Reynolds and Mr. Reynolds said do not worry it is not yet yesterday.

And indeed Mr. Reynolds was right, it was not yet yesterday although it was certainly very near to being it.

And so Angel Harper was forty-nine, and Mrs. Reynolds knew that she was going to know that it was so.

Mrs. Reynolds said that when there was great difficulty in finding food and when found it was not very abundant that was the time to buy very expensive and detailed and complete cook books. And which is it now said Mr. Reynolds. This said Mrs. Reynolds I do not know yet.

But said Mrs. Reynolds whether and then she stopped, whether, she said and she knew something was coming, whether said Mrs. Reynolds and indeed it was not only whether but weather and who would be where. Mrs. Reynolds did not know but she did know that nobody no not anybody could tell her so.

Mr. Reynolds sighed it was quiet at night and then they both went to bed.

There is no great difference said Mrs. Reynolds between seeing a lot of people and not seeing a lot of people because if you do see a lot of people well then you do see a lot of people and if you do not see a lot of people well then any people you do see are a lot of people and so you always do see a lot of people.

Even she said Angel Harper who is forty-nine. And then she stopped well said Mr. Reynolds and Mrs. Reynolds said and then she stopped.

For a proof of forty-nine being washed in winter and sold in summer. You mean cold said Mr. Reynolds. No said Mrs. Reynolds I mean sold.

Sold was a good word and being washed was a good word a little by little anybody knew that there was no way to break through to break through the fact that Angel Harper was forty-nine.

It makes me feel kind of sick said Mrs. Reynolds, what said Mr. Reynolds, well what said Mrs. Reynolds and she said if she was not so good-natured she would be angry. But said Mr. Reynolds it does no good to be angry. And that said Mrs. Reynolds is why even if I were not so good-natured I would not be angry. But perhaps said Mrs. Reynolds I will be angry and indeed perhaps. Mr. Reynolds smiled and they knew that the cold weather would last longer than the warm weather but not this year.

Do you call it the year forty-nine or the year Angel Harper is forty-nine, and Mrs. Reynolds knew that nobody would change their name and so that year was begun.

Begun and gun and a son of a gun and the sun, Mrs. Reynolds heard some one who had come to drink water say all these things and she went into her house. Why not when she knew that if it came to it horses would come to water led by a halter.

It makes it difficult, that if wishes were horses beggars would ride. It makes it difficult. In some funny way Mrs. Reynolds felt rather choky and there were almost tears in her eyes.

It is very sad that it does happen that Angel Harper is forty-nine. If said Mrs. Reynolds he never could be forty-nine well that said Mrs. Reynolds that would be just fine but alas, said like alas, said Mrs. Reynolds, alas Angel Harper is forty-nine.

Mrs. Reynolds knew and Mr. Reynolds too that it was true Angel Harper was forty-nine.

Now forty-nine is only of use if some one wants to do something before they are fifty.

Mr. Reynolds' younger brother William was much younger than fifty or forty-nine and he asked everybody to come to see and see what they could do to keep Angel Harper from being forty-nine. William Reynolds was like that, he said let us all say what we have to say and then in some way we will manage to keep Angel Harper from being forty-nine.

Mrs. Reynolds sighed she said she was tired, she said she had had a good deal to do and if it was true that William Reynolds was going to try, well said Mrs. Reynolds then they would all die. Perhaps not said Mr. Reynolds, perhaps not what, said Mrs. Reynolds, perhaps not yet said Mr. Reynolds.

It was very useful to have lists, but William Reynolds' wife Hope never had lists. None of her friends had lists and none of her uncles had lists and none of her aunts.

Mrs. Reynolds had lists, she had lists of linen, and possessions, and days and ways. Mr. Reynolds liked her to have lists.

Mrs. Reynolds even had lists of saints. Mr. Reynolds liked her to have lists.

Every day they expected Wednesday to be the first day that

Angel Harper was forty-nine but was it. Angel Harper would have preferred Tuesdays or Sundays. Angel Harper the day he was forty-nine came murmuring the word oats, but nobody knew what he meant. Naturally it frightened them but nobody knew what it meant.

The second day that he was forty-nine he said that he had not said oats the first day that he was forty-nine and when they all heard him say that he had not said oats the first day that he was forty-nine they were all of them pretty well frightened all the time.

I know a bag of oats said Mrs. Reynolds and Mr. Reynolds said yes. Oats were easy at least they were then. But nobody smiled. It is almost easy not to smile. Saints do not smile said Mrs. Reynolds and Mr. Reynolds smiled and they therefore although it was not late it was early enough on that date to go to bed so they went to bed.

That was the second day that Angel Harper was forty-nine.

Guinea hens roost in trees, they are mysterious birds, in the noise they make and the ways they take. The only thing that Angel Harper said was old enough to frighten him was a guinea hen and if it did frighten him, the time would come, all of which was true, the time would come.

By the time nobody was frightened of him the time would come to frighten him and he did remember then that a guinea hen could frighten him. It is a religion of the guinea hen to frighten Angel Harper. Angel Harper was forty-nine not for the third time but for the third day at that time.

Mrs. Reynolds felt cautious and as she felt cautious she was ready to go to bed. It is easy to go to bed if you feel cautious said Mrs. Reynolds, and Mr. Reynolds laughed, he did not have to feel cautious he was cautious, quite another thing.

Angel Harper dreamed of wooden houses on the fourth day when he was forty-nine, and he looked the other way, wooden houses have windows and windows are frightening particularly when there is the fifth day of being forty-nine.

My gracious said Mrs. Reynolds if nobody felt at home would a home be far away. Mrs. Reynolds began to think of very queer things after Angel Harper had had his forty-ninth birthday.

Naturally she knew that it was true and she knew about him. Well said Mr. Reynolds think of Joseph Lane, not I said Mrs. Reynolds not I it is all the same but I am not thinking about Joseph Lane. Oh dear said Mrs. Reynolds and naturally she went to bed, it was evening and she went to bed. Mr. Reynolds said he would be up later, he would wait to put out lights. Lights said Mrs. Reynolds I have a funny feeling about lights. Perhaps said Mr. Reynolds we will all have a funny feeling about lights. But said Mrs. Reynolds we can always go to bed. Perhaps said Mr. Reynolds and then Mr. and Mrs. Reynolds went to bed.

Mrs. Reynolds when she went out liked to see the Oxners because they were so excitable, there was Mr. Oxner and Mrs. Oxner and a girl about seventeen who had just not passed an examination and a boy who was a boy scout and a very large mother-in-law who had a great deal to say and it was always all about the foreign situation, any foreign situation excited the Oxners, to be sure he was a jeweler and sold wireless and so but even if he had only sold dusters and artificial flowers they would all have been excitable and interested only really interested in the foreign situation any foreign situation and naturally Angel Harper being forty-nine was a foreign situation a most continuous foreign situation. And so said Mr. Oxner and I feel so low said Mrs. Oxner and I told all the girls said Miss Oxner and when I heard said the mother-in-law and the boy scout waited to have foreign stamps given to him and he just said I like them and then they all went on, there was a foreign situation and it excited them the whole family of the Oxners. Mrs. Reynolds always went home and told Mr. Reynolds all that they had told her, sometimes there was something that Mr. Reynolds had not yet heard and so he always listened well he always listened anyway, why not when Mrs. Reynolds had anything to say, why not.

And Mrs. Reynolds was never tired when she came home from listening to the Oxners' foreign news even when it was bad news it was refreshing news and made her feel not restless but almost excited, not as excited as the Oxners but pleasantly excited and if you want to talk to Mr. Reynolds all the time it is pleasant to come home with something that she had not yet said to him so whenever Mrs. Reynolds went out she always went in to see the Oxners.

Oh dear said Mrs. Reynolds, it is kind of sad not to be glad but foreign news can be like that, it can be something which makes it sad not to be glad.

Angel Harper forty-nine, might almost come to be a crime, not a crime in a crime story but a crime like a crime, a crime that does not rhyme. How do you like what you have to do, they say and they feel kind of queer. Who does. Why anybody does.

It does not seem so but it is true. Angel Harper was forty-nine, five days, not five days at a time, but for that time he was forty-nine. It is easy to be nervous and it is easy to be happy and it is easy to be late and it is easy not to begin and it is easy to have nothing happen. But when it does. Dear me when it does.

Mrs. Reynolds almost began talking in the morning. It was not her habit but she almost began talking in the morning.

She pronounced Manitoba delightfully, it is a word said in any country because Manitoba wheat can be planted anywhere. Where said Mrs. Reynolds and she answered herself, and said anywhere.

It was February and not yet August and each day was coming nearer. If they do it startles if they do not it scares and if they do and if they do not then it settles.

Mrs. Reynolds knew about eggs, eggs when they are beaten settle that is if you leave them and do not use them. Use what said Mr. Reynolds, use eggs said Mrs. Reynolds, and Mrs. Reynolds knew that she was very handsome and so did Mr. Reynolds. It was not August yet and both Mr. and Mrs. Reynolds were good-looking and they went on knowing it quite comfortably any day or any evening.

Mrs. Reynolds knew that saints were not mistaken. This never came out in her conversation at least not yet but she did have the feeling. Mr. Reynolds did not say anything.

August if it is hot is welcome and if it is not hot it is welcome. And what about Angel Harper said Mr. Reynolds I have heard enough about him said Mrs. Reynolds. What said Mr. Reynolds, heard enough about him said Mrs. Reynolds. And it was what was meant by teaching said some one. Teaching said Mrs. Reynolds, teach him said Mrs. Reynolds. Teach whom, said some one, and Mrs. Reynolds turned away she did not want to mention his name nor did she want to hear his name. Angel Harper was forty-nine and if everybody knew his name Mrs. Reynolds remembered shame shame fie for shame everybody knew his name. And he was forty-nine, Angel Harper was forty-nine, and everybody knew his name. He remembered then he was really forty-nine he remembered that when he had been twelve that there was a doorway in which he sat while he wondered why he was that.

When Mrs. Reynolds was really troubled she would talk to anybody even somebody who might be dangerous, and when Angel Harper was really completely forty-nine she was really completely troubled and she really and completely then talked to anybody and when she talked to anybody she told them what she thought and what she thought was that she was right to be just as completely and entirely troubled as she was. It was not enough then to tell it to Mr. Reynolds or to anybody but she just had to tell it to everybody. She knew when people were dangerous, dangerous to themselves and dangerous to anybody dangerous to life and limb. She liked to say to life and limb and she knew that when Angel Harper was really forty-nine that it was not really that, it was not that he was dangerous to life and limb, but life and limb, oh dear life and limb and Mrs. Reynolds knew and she said it too there was too much to say to do anything, oh dear she said life and limb, and she just did say that thing she just did say life and limb.

Forty-nine she knew all the time that it was meant to be forty-nine. Angel Harper was meant to be forty-nine. Oh dear said Mrs. Reynolds, and she knew that when she said oh dear she meant oh dear and there was a reason for it. She was not one to say oh dear when there was no reason to say oh dear and she said to Mr. Reynolds that when she said oh dear, and he said yes you said oh dear, yes she said and when I said oh dear there was a reason for it. And Mr. Reynolds said yes and now and Mrs.

Reynolds said oh dear yes let us go to bed, and as they went to bed she did say oh dear.

This was the year that Angel Harper was forty-nine and Mrs. Reynolds knew she was right and she was right to say oh dear that year.

It was just about then that a funny thing was happening, there was a young man and she never did know his name he told her but she never remembered his name and he told he was studying to be a clergyman and that he knew Latin, and Mrs. Reynolds said yes. And he told her about some saints and then he told her about Saint Odile and what she had said in Latin and Mrs. Reynolds said yes and what did she say, and the young man said he would bring it to her translated some day, and it was almost five months later just when Angel Harper was almost through with being forty-nine that he brought it to her, and this was it.

Mr. Reynolds said oh yes, but she said yes not oh yes but yes and she was right so it turned out but just then it seemed more like oh yes than like yes. But anyway this was what the young man brought to her. And when he brought it to her he said today is Saint Odile's day and Mrs. Reynolds did say yes.

And it certainly did turn out yes, but it was a very very long yes very long and a long mess before it was all yes.

Listen to it said Mrs. Reynolds to Mr. Reynolds and he did listen to it.

The prophecy of Saint Odile and she did it in the seventh century said Mrs. Reynolds.

Listen listen to me my brother, that said Mrs. Reynolds is the way she commenced, listen to me my brother because I have seen frightfulness and terror in the forests and in the mountains where the Germans shall be called the Nation the most violent the most aggressive in all the world.

She that is Germany will have a moment when there will arise in her midst a warrior, the most horrific the most terrible, and he will make a complete an entire a universal war and all the peoples the mothers not only of sons but of daughters who resist will curse, and they will weep like Rachel they will weep for their dead children and nothing will console them.

From the Danube will come this horrible war, from that country will come the man who will undertake the most appalling war that the human race has ever endured, twenty different nationalities will go to war, the arms they will use will be made of flame, and their helmets will be covered with points from which will shoot lightning while their hands will be throwing bombs and fire.

They these terrible people will achieve victories upon the earth upon the sea and even in the air because there will be warriors winged warriors who will fly and rise up into the firmament and they will seize burning stars and throw them down upon cities and villages and will set them on fire, and start terrible conflagrations everywhere.

All the nations of the earth will stand paralyzed and will all cry out where oh where, from whence comes all their strength. The earth will be shaken by the force of the struggle the rivers will be reddened with blood and the monsters of the ocean will have taken themselves in fear and trembling into the depths of the sea.

All the peoples will be astonished that all the opponents together are unable to stem the tide of their victories and then literally torrents of blood will flow around the mountain, and this will be their last battle.

And so the conqueror will have attained the summit of his success.

Thus toward the middle of the sixth month of the second year of fighting there will be thus the end of the first period that can be called the period of bloody victories. He will then think that he can dictate his own terms.

The second part of the war will equal in length the half of the first part, it will be a period of decline, it will be full of surprises which will make everybody shiver.

About the middle of this second part the conquered people will be crying for peace peace. This will not be the end but only the beginning of the end when the fight will begin in the city of cities. At this moment his own people will want to stone him and extraordinary happenings will take place in the far East.

The third period of short duration will be called the period of invasion because by a just judgment the land of the conqueror will be invaded from all sides, his armies will be decimated by strange happenings and every one will say, this is the finger of God.

All the peoples will believe that the end is near, the scepter will change hands and all of his people will rejoice.

All the despoiled people will have back what has been taken from them and indeed will have something added to them.

The region of Lutece will be saved because of its blessed mountains and by the prayers of its good women although every one will have thought that all was lost.

But all the people will congregate upon the mountain and thank God because every one will have seen such horrors in these days that future generations will never want to see its like again.

But really the era of peace without iron will really have come and we will the two horns of the moon unite with the cross, for in these days all who have been terrified will adore God in truth and the sun will burn with a brilliance hitherto unknown.

And when said Mr. Reynolds will it begin.

Oh dear said Mrs. Reynolds and when she said oh dear she meant that it was very nearly begun.

When a husband dies and leaves his wife alive, she does not attend the funeral not in some places, when the son dies, the mother attends the funeral but not the father, not in some places, and when Mrs. Reynolds thought about this she tried to explain it but she could not and so said she it does just happen that way, that is the way it is.

It is very often said Mrs. Reynolds that some one is affectionate and if they are well then tears come into her eyes. You always say eyes not eye, said Mr. Reynolds and he laughed gently at her. All the same it was part of the way of the day on which Angel Harper was forty-nine.

So then. Everybody began to cough not because they had a cold but because they did not want to say that on that day, Angel

128

Harper was forty-nine, and if he was forty-nine and he was what would happen it was just like living over a mine.

Oh dear they said and they coughed instead and everybody gathered together. They gathered away as they gathered together.

To gather away, well how about it.

Edith Eleanor Jane Augusta Fairweather had married and had three daughters, the oldest was Joan the second was Elizabeth and the third was Katherine. The father's name was Benedict and there was no brother.

Where should they live, well they might as well live anywhere as when and since Angel Harper was forty-nine sooner or later they would have to go away. Mrs. Reynolds said when she met them how do you do are you still here, and they were.

That is one way to stay. The second family that was still there were friends of William the younger brother of Mr. Reynolds, they did not care about Hope the wife of William, they were amused by Mrs. Reynolds and they forgot Mr. Reynolds. They were a husband and wife both unusually small and they were old enough to do better but they still did very well. They liked mountains and they were aggressive and they were always ready to look as if they were not going to run away. They would if they knew it they would predict that Angel Harper would fill them with horror, but anyway it was very useful to suppose so, and they had this to do.

They are not annoying said Mrs. Reynolds and it looks as if we might do something to help them. They do not need help said Mr. Reynolds. No said Mrs. Reynolds no they do not need help, and as it was late in the evening and summer was coming and Angel Harper was getting to be more and more and more forty-nine. Mr. and Mrs. Reynolds went to bed.

Mrs. Reynolds said to Mr. Reynolds that she did listen to anybody talking about death-beds, perhaps said Mrs. Reynolds it is because that Angel Harper is forty-nine all the time, well anyway William Red is dead, his wife loved him and admired him and said the house was always filled full by him and that she had prayed and prayed that until he drew his last breath that he could always take nourishment and her prayer had been answered and he had taken nourishment until his last breath when he opened his arms and said good-bye all.

And is that all said Mr. Reynolds yes that is all said Mrs. Reynolds.

They had both known William Red and now he was dead. Well that has nothing to do with Angel Harper said Mr. Reynolds, no said Mrs. Reynolds no but all the same. All the same what said Mr. Reynolds, well all the same said Mrs. Reynolds anyway Angel Harper is forty-nine and it does make me think of death-beds and it did.

It is not in beds that they will die said Mr. Reynolds and Mrs. Reynolds began to cry and then she stopped and said well said she what is there to say when everybody will be gone away. Mr. Reynolds said well I will go too, yes said Mrs. Reynolds I know but she was sure and it was true that it was not better so. Anyway not yet said Mrs. Reynolds anyway he that is Angel Harper is only forty-nine perhaps there will yet be time. Let us go to bed said Mr. Reynolds and they did so.

All this time Angel Harper knew he was forty-nine he knew it all the time and it was so and he knew later on there would be snow. How did he know that later on there would be snow. Well forty-nine, forty-nine was the year they discovered gold so he was old and forty-nine was the year when he would not need gold, so he told, and they heard him say so and so nobody had to go. Believe it or not and they all had to believe what he decreed.

Mrs. Reynolds said I told you so and Mr. Reynolds did not say no.

Mrs. Reynolds did like the wind in the trees, she liked wind in the trees very much especially when it was very cold in the winter and there were no leaves upon the trees and she could know and she did know just how cold it was. Not now, she said, and when she said not now, she thought about it being later and when she thought about it being later, she just did remember all about not now.

It is so easy said Mrs. Reynolds to give it away, what said Mr.

130

Reynolds, what you say, I mean said Mrs. Reynolds it is so easy to give away what you say. And said Mrs. Reynolds, I mean that well but let us go to bed said Mrs. Reynolds.

Pretty soon it was tomorrow and every day Angel Harper would have another day and the day did come well there is no use not saying the day did come when Angel Harper had had enough of being forty-nine, he was not yet fifty but he had had enough of being forty-nine and on that day, Mrs. Reynolds said well I knew it was too good to be true and she said she meant to say that just every day and going to bed every night was just too good to be true. Just too good to be true. And Mr. Reynolds did not say that he thought so too, he just had nothing to say, and just then nothing to do.

It was so easy for Mrs. Reynolds to stand there, she did not stare she just had to share what she had to say with anybody who passed that way and this is what she had to say.

She said that Mr. Reynolds said do not pity them, and she said, he said no do not in any way whatever happens to them do not pity them.

Mrs. Reynolds sighed she did not pity them and as she sighed she did not pity them.

Understand this thing, this was when Angel Harper was fifty-one that she did not pity them, Mr. Reynolds said and no one should pity them.

But now Angel Harper was forty-nine and Mrs. Reynolds sighed and she knew as she sighed that when Angel Harper was fifty-one that no one that not any one would pity them, would pity Angel Harper or any one of all of them.

Let let her guess, she said Mrs. Reynolds said it was not a guess it was that a real saint could tell what was real and what was well.

And would a real saint pity them pity Angel Harper then, and Mrs. Reynolds knew very well that not any saint would pity them, not any one would pity them. Hell.

And so it is so it is not only that they say so it is so, when they are bad really bad everybody is glad really glad that the really bad cannot succeed, cannot live long, cannot get along cannot come to anything, they must end and everybody must be glad

131

and this is so even though everybody always has said that it is so. It is so. And by being bad it means doing what they know they should not do, being afraid because it is true that they should not do what they know they should not do.

Angel Harper said Mrs. Reynolds is forty-nine and this is the time he will shine. But said Mrs. Reynolds he may drink champagne now but later on he will drink water, he will drown and water will weigh him down and down will go his crown, Mrs. Reynolds said it and she knew but all the same she trembled all through and she believed that Saint Odile knew and all the same she trembled all through and Mr. Reynolds did not know but he was calm and clear and it did show although as he said he did not know.

And now Angel Harper was completely forty-nine, and for him it was very fine.

Let us think, said Mrs. Reynolds, let us not drink let us think said Mrs. Reynolds and she looked around her and as she looked around she saw a robin-red-breast and as she looked around her she saw what she liked best, she saw everything just as she liked best.

Who knows who is here said Mrs. Reynolds and indeed nobody was there who was not always there. Nobody.

Surely and it was not too late to be early, surely said Mrs. Reynolds early to bed and early to rise makes a man and a woman healthy wealthy and wise, and tonight said she to Mr. Reynolds, tonight we will not go to bed early. Why not said Mr. Reynolds, why not said Mrs. Reynolds well why not said Mrs. Reynolds and all the time she knew why not, she knew she was expecting why not, and she was right, there was a why not, somebody said over the radio why not and the why not was that Angel Harper was forty-nine and that was a crime. There was no why not, it was just not. Mrs. Reynolds did not begin to cry but she knew why why she might begin to cry. Might Mr. Reynolds go away oh dear might Mr. Reynolds go away oh dear.

Well this is clear, Angel Harper was forty-nine and if it was fine for him it was not fine for Mrs. Reynolds and Mr. Reynolds not at all fine, not fine at any time. Oh dear.

This is the way Angel Harper had his birthday. He was forty-nine he was going to be fifty and in the meantime there was Joseph Lane. Not startling not sparkling and not preparing and not filling but killing. How are you. This was not a beginning. There was no such thing as beginning in Joseph Lane. Beginning has an entirely different meaning.

Do not said Mrs. Reynolds do not mention Joseph Lane unless you have to and Mr. Reynolds said he did not have to.

They knew of course they knew, the Reynolds knew two brothers both short and fair and stocky one whose eyes were blue and one whose eyes were yellow, and one was simple-minded and made toy houses and the other was an owner and raised cattle. Many of his cattle had something the matter with them but that did not interfere with his raising them and selling them.

They both liked Christmas and little villages and green trees, and they both bored Mr. and Mrs. Reynolds when they came to see them. When they came they were helpful they did finally go away. They had one advantage, they would not look as if they knew that Angel Harper was forty-nine and they would not look as if they knew that Joseph Lane was never through.

This in its way was a comfort to Mrs. Reynolds and when she saw them she said not at all and she meant it.

Besides a bride, at this time there was no bride, well of course they did marry but that is not the same thing. Of course said Mrs. Reynolds it is not the same thing. And now the year had come the year that Angel Harper was forty-nine and dear me well not for long but dear me they called Mr. Reynolds to go away, not to go away and play and luckily said Mrs. Reynolds luckily not to go away and stay. I have to see that he eats what agrees with him said Mrs. Reynolds and if he is away dear me said Mrs. Reynolds.

Of course there had been a war and Mr. Reynolds had been there and so naturally he could only eat what would agree with him. This is a natural thing anybody knows that about a war that after a war you have to be very careful about your eating. Very careful said Mrs. Reynolds and she meant what she said when she said very careful and she was very careful of Mr. Reynolds and dear me and now he had to go again. But not for long said Mrs.

133

Reynolds. Mr. Reynolds did not say anything but actually it was not very long and he was home again and that was because he had to be so careful about what he ate. A great many who had to be very careful about what they ate were home again. Were home again said Mrs. Reynolds and Mr. Reynolds was home again.

Not to be afraid to be home again is something said Caesar Rivers and he always said things like that. Mrs. Reynolds liked to talk to Caesar Rivers, she had never known him before but now she knew him. His wife was Celestine and now she knew him and his wife. Dear me said Mrs. Reynolds and she meant dear me. Caesar Rivers was a refugee. Anybody was a refugee who had to go away. To go away said Mrs. Reynolds is what they do. But some come said Mrs. Reynolds and in a way more came than went away and here was Caesar Rivers and his wife Celestine Rivers and his daughter Anabel Rivers. All three of them passed by and stopped to talk to Mrs. Reynolds. How do you do said Mrs. Reynolds when she saw them and the daughter Anabel Rivers answered for all of them, Very well I thank you, and then they went on their way.

Going on their way well Angel Harper was not only forty-nine, he was fifty and nobody said hello fifty, why not, because he was not that kind.

There was a boy and even then there was a Christmas party and Mrs. Reynolds gave the boy a fountain pen and some other boy took it from him before he could put it into his pocket and the boy who had been afraid that somebody would take his coat or his scarf or his cap made a mistake and instead they took his fountain pen before he had it. Mrs. Reynolds told him he had made a mistake and she was right.

Now said Mrs. Reynolds and she remembered Saint Odile now said Mrs. Reynolds when Angel Harper is still forty-nine now said Mrs. Reynolds and she never burst into tears but she stood still, now said Mrs. Reynolds supposing everybody made a mistake and they did not take their hat or their coat or their scarf which they thought they might take but their fountain pen which they did not know they were going to have and it was taken away before it was put into their pocket.

Alas said Mrs. Reynolds she knew that it was true she knew that alas was true, not for her and not for him, not for Mr. Reynolds but she knew that alas was true.

Read four for refugees said Mrs. Reynolds and she remembered that a colonel who was later to become a great man when at the club they all were talking about wanting war, he said, said the colonel, and do you think said the colonel, that wars are always funny. And perhaps said Mrs. Reynolds perhaps, lead kindly light, perhaps said Mr. Reynolds remembering another great general when they were all talking about their specialties he said and he was a general he said I specialize in general ideas, and more than ever Mrs. Reynolds did not sigh but she said alas, and now Angel Harper was still forty-nine and Joseph Lane, Angel Harper did not know the age of Joseph Lane, did not know said Mrs. Reynolds the age of Joseph Lane. And she said and there was a kind of triumph in it, she said to Mr. Reynolds, and Angel Harper does not know the age of Joseph Lane, and Mr. Reynolds said nothing, because for him there was nothing to say but Mrs. Reynolds had something to say, she said he does not know Angel Harper does not know the age of Joseph Lane, Angel Harper is forty-nine, he knows everybody knows he is forty-nine, said Mrs. Reynolds and she sighed and she said alas, and as she said alas, she knew it was nearer Christmas than it was Monday.

Christmas said Mr. Reynolds, yes said Mrs. Reynolds Christmas and then it was time and Mrs. Reynolds and Mr. Reynolds went to bed as was their habit, even then they went to bed as was their habit and so there is no peace on earth when Angel Harper is forty-nine and when Angel Harper and it is a fearful thought that and it makes Angel Harper not shiver not cough but quaver, it is a dreadful thought that he does not know no he does not know how old is Joseph Lane. He is forty-nine and that is fine said Angel Harper, said Angel Harper just said Angel Harper.

And now night makes Saint Odile and Angel Harper did not know that a saint was so, but Mrs. Reynolds did and she began to believe, for which there is no question and no answer, it is enough for which she and Mr. Reynolds are in bed when all is said are in bed.

Ducks are easy to surprise said Mrs. Reynolds and indeed they are. If they are easy to surprise if it is easy to surprise ducks then how about men, said Mrs. Reynolds.

And now Angel Harper was forty-nine, and war well war, what is war said Mrs. Reynolds and Mr. Reynolds who had been to war and now there was another war Mr. Reynolds said, well war is not funny, it seems funny it seems almost nice and funny when there is no war but when there is a war said Mr. Reynolds then war is not funny.

And so there was coming to be a war and Mr. Reynolds was right, he undoubtedly was right, war when there is a war the kind of war that war is, war is not funny.

Angel Harper was not so sure, he did not know what war was, he had been in a war and having been in a war he thought another war would be funny. Angel Harper was like that, Mr. Reynolds was not like that that is the difference between a man who was in a war and is now making a war he thinks the first war was not funny but since he is making a war then the war he is ordering is going to be funny, going to be that kind of a war. Mr. Reynolds knew better, he had been in every war, he had not wanted to be in any war, and he did not think any war would be funny. He did not.

And Joseph Lane, well he had a way of thinking about that, only he did not think about that he did not think about a war if it was a war then it was not a war and if it was not a war then it was a war, that is what a war is when it is but Joseph Lane never had to think about a war because war was not what there was to think about, and so a war being funny or not, a war was not that. It was not a war. But and wait a bit, but, and wait a little or a longer bit.

And so Angel Harper was forty-nine and nobody can deny that he did not die when he was forty-nine.

Leave let us rest, said Mrs. Reynolds and by that she meant what she said. Leave let us rest, from then on if they rest, well they do not rest best.

One at a time said Mrs. Reynolds and she meant what she said, because she meant that one at a time was the way they would go away and any who came back would come back one at a time.

It was funny that Mrs. Reynolds felt that it would be like that because never before had it been like that, never before.

Angel Harper was forty-nine, and war was there, where well pretty well everywhere, not really everywhere yet and not yet was there what is known as wet, not yet.

Mrs. Reynolds sighed, she said it was not as bad as it might be, pretty bad but not as bad as it might be, and Mr. Reynolds who was not there did not hear her say it, but he would come back pretty soon and he did and he said it was pretty bad but it would be worse and it was. Please be sure that it was. Neither Mr. nor Mrs. Reynolds said that but they heard that it was true that it was said. Please be sure that it could be worse and it was.

All this time Angels and axes and butter and blisters were very frequent. Half of the time not out loud but very frequent.

Think said Mrs. Reynolds how many neighbors we have and Mr. Reynolds who had come back, said yes. It was nice for Mrs. Reynolds that Mr. Reynolds was back. Angel Harper was not yet fifty he was only forty-nine and Mr. Reynolds was back.

Lead kindly light. Mrs. Reynolds never sang but she knew words and words were these, lead kindly light, when she met Mr. and Mrs. Arundel, she said to them where have you been. They said that their lives had been upset, why not said Mrs. Reynolds and she did not turn away but she looked after them, they were not yet at any distance but at any rate she looked in the direction in which they were going. Lead kindly light.

By this time it was getting darker in the morning and in the evening and as it was getting darker, sometimes more people passed by and sometimes nobody came by. Mrs. Reynolds said that there was no use wishing, and she meant it, she said it was quieter when there was no use wishing, ever so much quieter, and Mr. Reynolds said yes it was ever so much quieter.

You would have thought said Mr. Reynolds' younger brother William, they never saw him any more but somebody told them what he was saying, you would have thought said William that what was happening was exciting. Mrs. Reynolds said yes William would have thought that what was happening was exciting, that would be just like him, but everybody knows said Mrs. Reynolds that excitement, and then Mrs. Reynolds looked the other way, looked in another direction. Every day she did that. It was no use looking only in one direction, well in a way there was no use in looking in another direction. Lead kindly light was not mentioned either by Mrs. Reynolds or by Mr. Reynolds at least not that night. Good night said Mrs. Reynolds and then their friends went away and Mr. Reynolds looked up and Mrs. Reynolds looked up and they all went to bed, each one in the place where they went to bed.

Angel Harper was forty-nine and it was all happening, it happened like that almost exactly like that.

Mrs. Reynolds said she did not mind contradiction, and it was true, she did not, most people do but she did not, it was true, and Mr. Reynolds said it was true when she asked him.

One day, it was New Year's day one day said Mrs. Reynolds it is not a new day. If said Mrs. Reynolds if Angel Harper could stay forty-nine that would be bad enough just as bad as bad enough, but said Mrs. Reynolds if he does not always stay forty-nine will the sun ever shine. Mr. Reynolds smiled a little and he said well not at all, and he meant just that he meant not at all. Little by little it was diminishing that is to say the time when Angel Harper was forty-nine was diminishing and if it were going to happen that he would be fifty, well said Mrs. Reynolds, and when she said well she did not mean well, not at all did she mean well.

She said well the year Angel Harper is forty-nine is the year thirty-nine, by that she meant, that thirty-seven the temperature is under normal, that thirty-eight the temperature is all right, but at thirty-nine well a little more would be a bore, at forty it is more and when Angel Harper would be fifty it would be the year forty, and then forty-one, oh dear forty-one is a dangerous one, and forty-two, well there would be the end of everything.

Believe it or not said Mrs. Reynolds and she added but I believe it.

So then here they were then and everybody knew then that Angel Harper was forty-nine, and everything was going to happen and that Mrs. Reynolds would not go to anybody's wedding, neither would Mr. Reynolds. The only baby they knew who was born just then was not born in wedlock. Its name was Jenny Christine, and they laughed aloud. Mrs. Reynolds laughed out loud, she said it had never happened to her before that the only baby that she knew of as born just then should have been born out of wedlock.

Do said Mrs. Reynolds do they build homes much now, and Mr. Reynolds said not now.

It was strange believe it or not it was strange strange enough to make Mrs. Reynolds open her eyes and open her mouth strange that when they were all worried they were not afraid. Angel Harper is said Mrs. Reynolds only he does not know it and we none of us are and we think we are said Mrs. Reynolds. Mr. Reynolds said that he was anxious that Mrs. Reynolds should be right, and she said she was right, and Mr. Reynolds said then it was all right. He said it made him feel ready to go to bed and she said well then all right let us go to bed and they went to bed.

It is very easy to watch other people moving about, when Angel Harper was forty-nine they all began to have to move about, some even came past the house of Mr. and Mrs. Reynolds, and when Mrs. Reynolds saw them she said she was sorry for them and she was.

No said Mrs. Reynolds forty-nine is not a good age, sixty is a good age, even seventy is a good age, I am said Mrs. Reynolds not so old but I have seen my mother and my father and I have seen my husband's mother and his father and sixty was a good age, they liked living then and what they did pleased them and seventy was a good age they liked what they did then they could slowly realize every minute of it, and they liked every minute of it, and eighty was a good age, but forty-nine and she said what she knew was true, forty-nine is not a good age, it is not said she it is not young enough and it is not old enough and said she Angel Harper will never be sixty and he will never be seventy and he will never be eighty, he will be forty-nine and fifty and fifty-one and fifty-two and those are not good ages not good ages at all. Mr. Reynolds said he was going to be those ages soon, yes said Mrs. Reynolds but that is different that is in between, but Angel Harper well he thinks forty-nine is a good age, but and Mrs. Reynolds sighed again but well it is all very well, oh so very well that he is all wrong, all wrong, and that makes a very good song said Mrs. Reynolds the song of how Angel Harper is all wrong. Oh come to bed said Mr. Reynolds, when all is said then come to bed, and that said Mr. Reynolds makes a good song.

What happened one winter evening, the snow was falling and the snow was very white. While it was very white, there was no light. While Angel Harper is forty-nine, said Mrs. Reynolds there never is any light, that is in the street, and it must not shine out. But anyway whatever Mrs. Reynolds had to say, it was snowing and the snow was white and there was a light. Well it was moonlight and it was so light that Mrs. Reynolds said what is the use of there not being any light, and she was right there is no use in there not being any light.

On that night, somebody came along, it might have been in a storm but actually it was not a storm, there was only snow and a light, but anyway he came along and he was singing a song, it might begin said the song, it might begin and he might win, and then again he might not he might just not, that was the song that went on and Mrs. Reynolds said to Mr. Reynolds did you hear him, and Mr. Reynolds said yes I heard him, and said Mrs. Reynolds he means Angel Harper, and Mr. Reynolds said perhaps why not and said Mrs. Reynolds I do hope that he will not, and Mr. Reynolds said perhaps and why not. And so they went to bed again, it looked late and indeed it was quite late because they had been talking quite late and as late as it was it was very light and they went to bed while it was still moonlight that night.

And so every day made it come that Angel Harper was no longer forty-nine, any day and when the day did come he would be fifty and then he would be fifty-one, and dear me how dreadful for every one how very dreadful, really dreadful for every one. But now he was just forty-nine and a good many did hope that

140

that would be his decline, but not at all, not yet, is your father living yet not yet, Mrs. Reynolds laughed a lot when she heard that one.

But formerly, Angel Harper had said there is no use in being fifty, before being forty-nine, he had thought he really had thought of being fifty before being forty-nine and then he thought again, he said he would be forty-nine and begin again, in other words he thought that being fifty would be really the time of beginning although actually beginning when he was forty-nine.

He had never heard Mrs. Reynolds say that fifty as well as forty-nine was too old and too young, to really begin, he had never heard of Mrs. Reynolds nor of Mr. Reynolds why should he have heard of them, one might say truly say that he had never heard of any one, and after he was forty-nine he never again remembered when he had been seven or ten or even when he had been twenty-one. He did not even remember about snow and if you walked about in it you did not walk as fast as when there was no snow. No snow. He never even dreamed of no snow not he. If you dream then when you dream you dream that in that dream you mean something which is not a dream. This might be the way any one could dream. But Angel Harper never had dreamed, that is to say if he did dream he did not remember his dream and really on principle he did not dream at all.

Mrs. Reynolds never mentioned that Angel Harper did not dream. She said she had enough to do to know that he was forty-nine and was going to be fifty and that was enough without bothering about his dreaming. She could dream of course she could dream and Mr. Reynolds could dream not so much but he could dream not dream a dream Angel Harper was forty-nine and he was going to be fifty and that was no dream not any-body's dream not at all said Mrs. Reynolds and Mr. Reynolds listened to her and the snow was not very white that night and they went to bed again although it was only ten.

A man shooting or threatening to shoot with a gun, a man carrying a lamb, a dog looking at a major, the dog black and large and the major small, a guinea-hen looking at the dog and a woman very cautious, Mrs. Reynolds did not only dream of all these but when she did dream of them it did not make her nervous but she knew what it meant. Well what said Mr. Reynolds but Mrs. Reynolds did not answer and when she did she said she thought she had better just try to dream again which she did. Naturally when they went to bed she did dream again but this time she dreamed a singular disaster, she dreamed that she saw a half of a beef pass by and after that there were soldiers and after that they went away. So said she to Mr. Reynolds you see, and Mr. Reynolds said yes he did see and he laughed. But said Mrs. Reynolds there is nothing to laugh at nothing at all, remember said Mrs. Reynolds every time I dream well in between every time I dream they will choose not me but them. Well said Mr. Reynolds patiently if I understand you right you mean that soon Angel Harper will be fifty. And Mrs. Reynolds did mean that but she did not like to say so, it was too much like being threatening, and being threatening is just what it was.

And so think again about how they could come to be not only one but one one one which is three. Angel Harper could not be three, Joseph Lane perhaps, Saint Odile very possibly but Mr. and Mrs. Reynolds remained just the two of them and when it was late enough and sometimes late enough was quite early and sometimes not but anyway when they did go to bed Mr. Reynolds was very apt to say and now there is no more to be said, but Mrs. Reynolds did not agree with him, of course not, there was a great deal to be said. Supposing said Mrs. Reynolds as they were going to bed supposing something happened and we were not going to bed. Mr. Reynolds laughed and said all right, and she said sleep tight, and together they said well that is all right. But what she really meant and on the whole she preferred to say it in the morning was that the time had not come that Angel Harper was not forty-nine but fifty. Oh dear me.

PART VII

Angel Harper was fifty and so then did begin did really begin the struggle between Saint Odile and him. Mrs. Reynolds said she knew it but that she never said it.

When Angel Harper was fifty, oh dear, Mrs. Reynolds had been saying oh dear and now she did not go on saying oh dear but from time to time she said, oh dear.

Everybody around began to say oh dear, Mr. Reynolds did not say oh dear but he smiled a little sadly when Mrs. Reynolds said Oh dear.

And now Angel Harper was fifty and it was getting pretty serious, nobody saw anybody they used to see and it was getting pretty serious, oh dear me said Mrs. Reynolds and when she said oh dear me she wanted to say to Mr. Reynolds that it was getting pretty serious but she did not say that it was getting pretty serious she did not say it just then she only said that she was not seeing any one she used to see no not any one, and Mr. Reynolds said and what then but what he really meant to say was that he still saw her and she still saw him, so what then.

One day Mrs. Reynolds came home and as she came home she met some one, he was a man she often talked to and she asked him what was the news and he said oh dear me, Angel Harper is fifty but said the man I don't care if Angel Harper is fifty as long as Joseph Lane is older, I, said the man, I like them older. Mrs. Reynolds went home and told Mr. Reynolds and Mr.

143

Reynolds said yes, so Mrs. Reynolds went to bed that night just a little better satisfied that it might be all right. But said she all the same Angel Harper is fifty and that is a shame because he will just go on with his game, and oh dear me said Mrs. Reynolds and in a way she was right. She might just as well say oh dear me as not. Why not said Mr. Reynolds and laughed at her so then they both went to bed feeling a little strange.

The next day she heard that John the cousin of Mr. Reynolds' brother William's wife Hope was drowned with his wife and one or two of his daughters. It was very cold weather and it did upset Mrs. Reynolds. She knew that it could happen did happen would happen. How could it not happen, Angel Harper was fifty years old and so it did happen.

Mrs. Reynolds said that it did not keep her awake all night but she could not help knowing all night that this was what happened that it was very cold weather and that they were all drowned, perhaps one of them was saved but which one, well anyway said Mrs. Reynolds and Mr. Reynolds was upset too, well anyway said Mrs. Reynolds. And then the next day their dog was frightened by soldiers playing at being scouts and firing off their guns and her dog was frightened well if it was not her dog it was a dog that was frightened and ran away. He was very frightened said Mrs. Reynolds but even so he did come home again, and Mr. Reynolds was pleased because he liked dogs. And said Mrs. Reynolds there is no use blinding oneself to it all these things are happening, Angel Harper is fifty years old and all these things are happening, dear me said Mrs. Reynolds and Mr. Reynolds sighed, he did not often sigh but he sighed, it was in the morning and he sighed, if it had been in the evening it would have been different but it was in the morning and Mrs. Reynolds knew that it was not natural for Mr. Reynolds to sigh in the morning so Mrs. Reynolds said she wished she had not said it, but now it was too late because after all Mr. Reynolds had had to sigh in the morning.

Everybody said Mrs. Reynolds everybody hates Angel Harper and his fifty years, and she was right, she said she was right and she knew she was right, but it was not all right, and Mr. Reynolds laughed a little when she said that and he forgot that he had sighed in the morning but she did not and she said that she did not.

After all said Mrs. Reynolds after all John, the cousin of your brother William's wife and his two daughters were not drowned, he had just left them he had gone off with another woman and they had to go home alone, no said Mrs. Reynolds reflectively they were not drowned, and Mr. Reynolds said yes it was true they were not drowned.

And so said Mrs. Reynolds and she laughed it had nothing to do with Angel Harper being fifty, and then she said well and Mr. Reynolds laughed and said well and by that time it was evening and they went to bed, it was early to go to bed but why not go to bed and they went to bed.

Every day it was getting more so and Mrs. Reynolds said it was getting more so and Mr. Reynolds did not contradict, he went off alone to hear the news and then he came home and told her and then they had supper and it was quite cold and first she went to bed and then he went to bed, every evening and every night.

And then one day Mrs. Reynolds saw a great many people coming who did not come to stay they were passing that way and she did not say anything when she saw them because there was nothing to say and when Mr. Reynolds came home she told him and he said all right there is nothing to say, not any way today, and Mrs. Reynolds said perhaps there will be nothing to say any day and he said perhaps not and they were both right and there was the next day and there was nothing to say, Angel Harper was fifty and there was nothing to say completely fifty and there was nothing to say.

And then said Mrs. Reynolds a lamb has died of hunger. What said Mr. Reynolds did I not tell you said Mrs. Reynolds the lamb of the Davilles' has died of hunger. Why said Mr. Reynolds did they not give it something to eat, because said Mrs. Reynolds they had nothing to feed it, and said Mrs. Reynolds they said, and Mrs. Reynolds felt a little queer as she said they say and Mr. Reynolds felt a little queer when she said they say, and they did not go on saying what she was going to say, they went in to dinner and that night just a little earlier than they usually did they went to bed and she did not go before he was ready, they went up to bed together.

Angel Harper was really fifty then certainly fifty then and that meant that thing.

While Mrs. Reynolds was sleeping she heard herself saying, why did the lamb die, and she heard a voice that answered because he was hungry and then she heard herself asking and why was he hungry and she heard the voice answer because he had nothing to eat. And she woke up and she woke up Mr. Reynolds and she said to him is it so, and he said is what so and she told him and he said well perhaps not now but perhaps later and then she let him go to sleep and she went to sleep to sleep herself. And when she woke up she said to Mr. Reynolds and I did dream it and he said you did and she said and you said perhaps not now but perhaps later did you mean it and Mr. Reynolds said yes perhaps he meant it. And then there was another day a quite cold day and they did not go away but a good many others came their way.

One of them was a cousin of one who was their neighbor. It was a funny family. A sister and a brother were married the sister to a nice man but later than her brother, her brother had been married and in trying to save a horse from drowning he caught cold and then he got typhoid and then he died they had one little boy named Gabriel and that was that. Then the boy's aunt married a nice man and she had first a boy and then a girl, the boy's name was William and the girl's name was Claudine, and then their mother in going out walking got her feet wet caught cold and died. And then the mother and the father of the three cousins married and then well then there was a great deal of trouble because the mother of Gabriel wanted everything for him and William and Claudine wanted it for them. Dear me, and now they had all gone away, married or not money or not they had all gone away and they were passing that way and as Mrs. Reynolds had nothing to say she went in. She did not want to see them passing and Mrs. Reynolds never knew whether they passed or no and she told Mr. Reynolds so.

146

Angel Harper was still fifty and nobody thought that he could be fifty so long, so long and so strong.

Fifty said Mrs. Reynolds fifty so strong and so long and Mr. Reynolds did not answer.

Monks said Mrs. Reynolds dreamily do not sleep long at a time in their beds. Nobody knew what had put that into her head. Nor she either.

It was cold weather when he was fifty, it would be colder when he was fifty-one, Mrs. Reynolds said it was true, even if the sun shone.

And now Mrs. Reynolds said that she did not really care whether there were curtains at the windows or not and Mr. Reynolds said and what do you care and Mrs. Reynolds said that curtains are a sign of the times. And she was right they are.

And now she began to wonder how many different nationalities she knew, and when she began to count, she turned to somebody who was passing and she said to him and you. Well naturally he did not know what she was talking about, he said his name used to be William and now it was Henry and it used to be Vandermeulen and now it was Anderson and when he told her all this Mrs. Reynolds said to him and why do you tell it to me and he answered her he did it because she looked so trustworthy. Mrs. Reynolds did not know whether she liked it or not and when Mr. Reynolds came home she told him and he said and she said she did not know whether she liked it or not and Mr. Reynolds said and what did you say to him and she said she did not say anything but she thought about something and when Mr. Reynolds did not say she said she thought about Saint Odile and Mr. Reynolds said and why what has she to do with this and Mrs. Reynolds said you wait and see and she was right they did wait and they did see but by then by the time she had said wait and see it was very cold in the evening and they went to bed.

Angel Harper was fifty and it was quite cold in the evening and so Mr. and Mrs. Reynolds went to bed, they put hot water bottles in the bed and they went to bed. Which was right enough.

Angel Harper was not more impressed by the cold than he had been by the heat he thought he was more impressed by heat than

by cold but was he. All who stood around thought that he was
more impressed by heat than by cold but was he. The only thing
Angel Harper ever heard was the word, was he. It is funny about
these two words was he, Angel Harper knew that he did not
remember was he, indeed he never heard was he, but there it was,
was he, was he more impressed by the heat than by the cold, he
thought he was more impressed by the heat than by the cold but
was he. He never said he was impressed, he never did, the only
thing he said was that heat was hot, he never said cold was cold.
He never said it.

Anyway said Mrs. Reynolds anyway, and when she said anyway it was another day, she of course never would see Angel
Harper although she did say anyway and when she said anyway
it was just another day.

Angel Harper was fifty and all eggs broke. When eggs broke
and dogs left there was no change. Mrs. Reynolds was still there
and so was Mr. Reynolds and they were not delighted, they were
there which after all was enough to make Mrs. Reynolds say that
she almost forgot that there was day after day.

I did almost forget said Mrs. Reynolds and Mr. Reynolds said
there was time enough and Mrs. Reynolds felt better because if
Mr. Reynolds said there was time enough then in the morning
she could look about and in the afternoon she could see what
there was to see and in the evening she could hear what there was
to hear and then they would go to bed.

How many left today said Mrs. Reynolds and Mr. Reynolds
said he could not say.

Just then somebody came along, leave it to me he said just as
if it was a song. Leave it to him said Mrs. Reynolds and why
not said Mr. Reynolds. Well said Mrs. Reynolds now I have to
know that Angel Harper is really fifty, well said Mrs. Reynolds
now I am ready. Ready for what said Mr. Reynolds, ready for
Saint Odile said Mrs. Reynolds. Mr. Reynolds sighed, he wished
he could hear something but really he was not anxious, how could
anybody be anxious in a time like that just how could they. Mrs.
Reynolds said she hoped something. What said some one, and Mrs.
Reynolds was not any worse off than she had been, so she said.

148

At this time, gardens were very much more occupied than they ever had been, sometimes three were busy in a garden where only one had been, and sometimes six or eight were busy in a garden where only two had been. Mrs. Reynolds went to look at them and then she came back and told Mr. Reynolds what she had seen.

Later on he said why not, but just then he was busy enough, quite busy enough.

Little by little every day Angel Harper was more fifty than he had been and as he became every day more fifty than he had been what did Mrs. Reynolds think of him. Nobody asked her but what did she think of him. She thought that he was not as useful as a plumber and more dangerous, she thought that he was not as useful as an electrician but more violent, she thought that he was not as regular as a gardener but more destructive, she thought that he was more solemn than a baker but more fiery, and she thought he was not as bloody as a butcher but more deceitful, and then she burst out into hysterical laughter and Mr. Reynolds said what is it, and she said it is Angel Harper and he is fifty just fifty going on being fifty, and if, and she gave a deep sigh if he only never came to be fifty-one. But he will said Mr. Reynolds and Mrs. Reynolds sighed and said yes he was right, he will. And if he will said Mrs. Reynolds what will we do and Mr. Reynolds said we will do what we always do, and what is that said Mrs. Reynolds, just that said Mr. Reynolds just what we always do, and Mrs. Reynolds sighed and she said yes, and Mr. Reynolds said it is not time to go to bed yet and Mrs. Reynolds sighed again and she said no not yet.

One day she came home in a great hurry, what do you think she said to Mr. Reynolds what do you think I met some one, he is a captain in the army and he said he had heard that Angel Harper was afraid. Afraid of what, said Mr. Reynolds, afraid of Joseph Lane said Mrs. Reynolds, well what if he is said Mr. Reynolds what difference will that make and Mrs. Reynolds sighed well perhaps not any she said, and Mr. Reynolds patted her back and he said think of Saint Odile, why do you not, and she said yes I will, and that was that.

And now to tell a story.

Once upon a time Mrs. Reynolds, she was dreaming this of course once upon a time Mrs. Reynolds began to think that everything was extra. Whatever she had was extra, not regular but extra, even Mr. Reynolds was extra and as she was thinking that everything was extra she suddenly turned and as she turned she saw somebody come in. And as he came in she said to herself what is his name and then she suddenly decided that nobody had a name, and then she woke up, and that frightened her not the waking up but that nobody had a name and she told Mr. Reynolds her dream and he said perhaps it will come to that that nobody will have a name and Mrs. Reynolds said she would not like that at all, and Mr. Reynolds said her liking it or not would not stop it. And she knew he was right it would not.

Anyway her neighbor's daughter Amy was going to marry, after all why not, if he goes away well why not and if he does not go away well why not and later on when Angel Harper is fifty-one perhaps if Amy were to marry she could not marry in white she would have to marry in color or in black and that well anyway said Mrs. Reynolds I always know what is going to happen. Like Saint Odile said Mr. Reynolds, and yes said Mrs. Reynolds and yes. And she was right it was yes and yes.

It is funny said Mrs. Reynolds it is funny, when anybody marries it is funny and when anybody does not marry it is funny, the only thing said Mrs. Reynolds that is not funny is that Angel Harper is fifty, and said Mrs. Reynolds and saying it made it sound awful and said Mrs. Reynolds he will later be fifty-one. Well said Mr. Reynolds, there is no use said Mrs. Reynolds in saying well, you know very well there is no use in saying well.

Well there was no use in saying well and there was no use. There was only one comfort, and that was Saint Odile. Who, said any one, and Mrs. Reynolds always said Saint Odile. They looked at her as if she was a little strange but said Mrs. Reynolds I am not strange at all of course it is Saint Odile. Saint Odile says that when Angel Harper is fifty it will be awfuller and awfuller and it is awfuller and awfuller and everybody knows it is aw-fuller and awfuller and Saint Odile says that when Angel Harper is fifty-one, well then it will be awfuller for him awfuller and awfuller and when Mrs. Reynolds said awfuller and awfuller she meant awfuller and awfuller and she meant it for him.

Little by little Mrs. Reynolds continued to stand and not sit, she did sit sometimes, mostly in the evening but during the day she did mostly stand, and little by little she began to talk about Joseph Lane, not that she knew anything about him or about any one who knew anything about him but said Mrs. Reynolds, somebody has to do something and perhaps said Mrs. Reynolds it will be Joseph Lane. Mr. Reynolds did not say perhaps he did not say anything. Sometimes he did not say anything and then it was bedtime. Tonight he did not say anything and it was bedtime, at least he acted as if it was bedtime and Mrs. Reynolds said it was bedtime and she knew if she said it it would please him and so she said it and it was bedtime and then they went to bed because it was bedtime.

One day Mrs. Reynolds did not have anything to say, they had invited Mr. Reynolds to go to a wedding and they said would she come some other time and Mrs. Reynolds said why not and then they had nothing to say but really it had something to do with Saint Odile and Mrs. Reynolds began to know something about how they felt about that and she was sure and they were not.

If not why not said Mrs. Reynolds and she was right. And she talked about it to Mathilda Drexel and Mathilda Drexel felt the same way, she knew what Saint Odile had to say and Mrs. Reynolds did not say to her not at all and Mathilda Drexel said I believe, and Mrs. Reynolds gave a sigh and did not ask why.

She knew so she did not ask why.

What is a boat said Mathilda Drexel and when she said that Mrs. Reynolds was a little impatient and said Mathilda when you said boat you meant to say goat, and Mathilda really could not say that she had not. But all the same they did agree about Saint Odile, and Mrs. Reynolds told Mr. Reynolds what they each had had to say. And then said Mr. Reynolds she had to go away. And Mrs. Reynolds laughed. She was serious and sure about Saint Odile but all the same Mr. Reynolds could make her laugh.

And now every day Angel Harper was fifty if he was a day and there was no way to make that go away. And Mrs. Reynolds said there is no way and she did not laugh at all that day, no matter what Mr. Reynolds had to say. Mr. Reynolds had nothing to say.

Did said Mrs. Reynolds did anybody like a military man. Well said Mrs. Reynolds if they do are they not mistaken, and said Mrs. Reynolds if they do not are they not right.

Mrs. Reynolds meant what she said.

It is funny said Mrs. Reynolds and she remembered all the military men that she had seen and known, she had seen more than she had known but she had known some military men, it is funny said Mrs. Reynolds and she said she did not mean that military men were funny oh dear no they were not funny and besides that they all had wives and besides that well besides that they were military men.

When Mrs. Reynolds was there she saw them, she knew that when there was a war she had to see them and she knew when she had to see them there was a war.

Oh dear said Mrs. Reynolds, and when she said oh dear she meant oh dear. She knew that from now on she would only have new friends, why not Angel Harper was fifty and if Angel Harper was fifty then most certainly most regularly certainly she would have friends but they would all be new friends.

What are friends said Mrs. Reynolds and before Mr. Reynolds could answer she answered, friends are the ones you know and the ones you just then see all the time. Are they friends said Mr. Reynolds and Mrs. Reynolds said yes they are friends, the ones you know and the ones you see all the time they are your friends and Mrs. Reynolds said oh dear me and now they are all ones I did not know before and there are so many of them.

Of course Mrs. Reynolds did not say so but of course no one of them was a military man nor the wife of a military man not any of them. And so said Mr. Reynolds those you see and know are not friends. No said Mrs. Reynolds not when they are military men, and so of course they were not and that was all there was to that.

152

Angel Harper was fifty, Joseph Lane was the age he was and it did not matter, and the days were either longer or shorter and that did not matter and every day was part of that year and dear me said Mrs. Reynolds yes dear me yes that does matter.

There was a man who raised fish for the government, he had a long moustache and he was often about, but when he was not he was bitter, he was bitter about all the men who were killed, he who raised so many fish felt very strongly about how bitter it was that so many should be dead dead dead, dead because of Angel Harper of the fifty years of Angel Harper, dead dead dead, because of the fifty years of Angel Harper. When Mrs. Reynolds heard him she stopped to hear him. Mrs. Reynolds was never bitter and when she heard him being so bitter she said he was right, he was certainly right to be so bitter and he said he was bitter and he was.

When Mr. Reynolds came home that evening Mrs. Reynolds told him how bitter the man raising fish for the government had been and Mr. Reynolds said yes, and Mrs. Reynolds said he does raise fish millions of fish and Mr. Reynolds said yes, and Mrs. Reynolds said and I told him I agreed with him, he was right to be so bitter and Mr. Reynolds said and did you agree with him, that is do you agree with him, are you bitter and Mrs. Reynolds said she had not agreed with him that she would be bitter but that she agreed with him that he was right to be bitter, and Mr. Reynolds laughed and then they went to bed feeling just a little bit bitter.

Undoubtedly nobody can tell what is the matter when everybody is right to feel bitter. Bitter. Bitter.

Little by little Angel Harper was fifty always fifty and little by little he might come to know that as he was fifty, he was fifty. He had a fright, he saw with all his might that he was fifty and he had a fright.

Joseph Lane had no fright, he was all right, whatever age he was it was all right, he did not come to feel that a fright was a fright, but if it was it was all right. He was as far away as that, and being far away even if anybody knew he knew that he was not through, not through at all. Joseph Lane was never peculiar, there was no one there to be peculiar, no one. Any one and any one was no one.

And Mrs. Reynolds had a fright that night, it was not a dream, it was some one who came knocking, and she told Mr. Reynolds and he said it was too late to knock and anyway they would not knock they would ring. And he was right they would not knock they would ring, but all the same Mrs. Reynolds had a fright that night.

Every day Mrs. Reynolds remembered yesterday. She said she did and she did, she told Mr. Reynolds that every day she remembered yesterday. Well said Mrs. Reynolds I never did before, I used to just remember today but now said she I always remember yesterday. And said Mrs. Reynolds whenever I do, well she said, I just do, every day I do. There is no use in being queer said Mr. Reynolds and Mrs. Reynolds said yes there is no use in being queer, but it is queer every day now I remember yesterday, I used only before Angel Harper was fifty, I used only to remember today but now every day I remember yesterday.

That day there were no children there. All the children had commenced marching by and Mrs. Reynolds had begun to cry. She was not very fond of children and she never had had one but she did begin to cry. And when Mr. Reynolds came home she told him that she had begun to cry but that she did not know why that there was no reason why. And Mr. Reynolds said well if you feel like it it always is better to cry and then Mrs. Reynolds said but you know I never do cry, and Mr. Reynolds laughed and said not even if you try, and she said she felt funny and he said all right let us go to bed and they went to bed and Mrs. Reynolds slept very well and that day she did not think about yesterday.

Mr. Reynolds came in one day and said that his brother William with his wife Hope had gone away, they had gone away because they had known Angel Harper long before he was fifty and they thought that on that account they had better not stay, so they had gone away. Where to said Mrs. Reynolds, this said Mr. Reynolds I do not know, they did not say they only said that they had better go away and so they had gone away. Yes

154

said Mrs. Reynolds they had better have gone away, after all so they say they did know Angel Harper but in what way and Mrs. Reynolds shook her head as if she had a great deal to say but not today.

And so Mr. Reynolds' brother William and his wife Hope went away, going away meant something before Angel Harper was fifty, but now that Angel Harper was fifty there was no difference no difference at all between going away and not going away. Mrs. Reynolds said that as for her and Mr. Reynolds they would not go away and since they would not go away, they might come to make a difference between going away and not going away. Mrs. Reynolds said that she when she said that it made her think of Saint Odile and thinking of Saint Odile. And Mr. Reynolds interrupted and said that he was going to stay and she was going to stay because after all if they went away there was no place to go, and so, there was no difference between going away and not going away. And Mrs. Reynolds said yes and Saint Odile.

Well said Mrs. Reynolds, she was talking to herself now she did not often talk to herself, but she was talking to herself now, Saint Odile and she did not sigh and she did not cry nor did she try. Saint Odile said Mrs. Reynolds and then she began to sigh. Pretty soon Mr. Reynolds came home and she said and Angel Harper, is he still fifty, and Mr. Reynolds said you do not need to bother, yes he is, and Mrs. Reynolds began to sigh and said yes I know he was and is, he is fifty and there is no use in going up and down or forward or back or across, one might just as well wait here. Well said Mr. Reynolds what do you think we are doing. And Mrs. Reynolds acted as if she were just waking up. Sometimes she said there will be no meat and no fish and no eggs, well said Mr. Reynolds what of that, well said Mrs. Reynolds we will then do without, even if we are not so stout. And Mr. Reynolds laughed and they went to bed. He was never cross and she was never cross and they went to bed. Angel Harper was still fifty, and every day there was less and there was more about his being fifty. Do shut the door said Mrs. Reynolds, and she was right, do shut the door even when there was no door to shut. That was what Mrs. Reynolds felt might happen but she was not afraid, neither she nor Mr. Reynolds was afraid, although she did not like to go out at night. He did not mind but she did.

Today said Mrs. Reynolds Angel Harper is still being fifty and it did seem long.

Life said Mrs. Reynolds life is strife, dear life, said Mrs. Reynolds and she sighed a little.

She remembered that when she went to a wedding with her husband they both enjoyed their lunch and they wished the young married couple a happy life and she also remembered that at a wedding the young couple take a rosy view of life, not that Mrs. Reynolds had ever had any views, but still after all a husband even a nice quiet gentle husband when he is no longer so young is older and he likes a wife and he likes his way and his way is his way and her way is her way and anyway, well said Mrs. Reynolds perhaps the husband who married today does not smoke a pipe, but anyway he has well anyway he will have his way or he will not and Mrs. Reynolds sighed again and said it did not matter and Mr. Reynolds laughed and said it certainly did not matter and anyway. Well they had eaten a great deal and that made them tired, they were not used to eating so much and they went to bed early and after all they did sleep very well, they thought they would not but they did. Yes said Mrs. Reynolds waking up not early but late, yes life is strife, dear life, dear life. And she sighed a little. She had almost forgotten that Angel Harper was fifty, it is difficult to forget that Angel Harper is fifty, in the Bible it says that the poor are always with you but that said Mrs. Reynolds oh dear me that is nothing compared to Angel Harper being fifty. And is he fifty, said Mrs. Reynolds, she was almost talking to herself, is he fifty, and everybody heard her say is he fifty, and everybody said, it was awful but he was fifty Angel Harper was fifty, and how many people were suffering in summer and suffering in winter because he was fifty, how many, and Mrs. Reynolds said how many, and nobody answered. It is difficult to count when so many means more than everybody, and Mrs. Reynolds murmured Saint Odile, and just then she began to count, and she began to count out loud, and she said the one she would count, count and count was Saint Odile. And said Mrs. Reynolds wait and see, Angel Harper he is fifty, he will be fifty-one, wait and see said Mrs. Reynolds and she meant wait and see, when she said wait and see, she really meant it.

Light kind of light, and she said she would love every kind of light, and Mrs. Reynolds when she heard her say it said but if she was not married, and said Mrs. Reynolds even now yes even now it does make a difference. Of course when Mrs. Reynolds said even now she meant what she said. Even now, Angel Harper was fifty and even now whether she was married did make a difference. Mrs. Reynolds did not make use of any argument, she knew that if you were not married and did not love religion even now it did make a difference. Once again Mrs. Reynolds said even now and when Mr. Reynolds came in she told him that even now it did make a difference.

Every little while said Mrs. Reynolds you forget everything and when you do then there is no use in not being careful, because when everything is forgotten and then Mrs. Reynolds stopped to think, when she stopped to think everything was forgotten. It was just at that time that there was as much noise as before and as much noise as before is very terrifying. But said Mrs. Reynolds it is not necessary as much noise as before is not necessary and so she was just about to be careful and then once again there was just as much noise as before.

It is strange said Mrs. Reynolds that there is no noise, and indeed it was strange but there was no noise. Angel Harper was fifty but there was no noise and Mrs. Reynolds took this occasion to think about Joseph Lane, she knew that by his name there would be no noise at all, it is very often neither warm nor hot when there is no noise at all and nobody knew whether Joseph Lane was ought to be or was there at all.

Mrs. Reynolds wished that Mr. Reynolds had been at home and that he would be at home and when he came home she said to him that she was glad he was home and he said he was glad she was glad and they both laughed a little and she said all the same and when she said all the same she meant it. Every time she said

157

all the same it was quieter and then they went to bed and as they went to bed she said well all the same I am glad we are going to bed.

Mrs. Reynolds knew that in winter the days get longer. It is still winter and the days get longer, and she said, when it is winter and the days get longer instead of knowing that Angel Harper is fifty I keep thinking that he will be fifty-one, and if he is, and Mrs. Reynolds was almost a little pale when she said and if he is, and she knew that when he was well anyway the days being longer and it being winter would not really be any comfort to her. If it snows in winter said Mrs. Reynolds and it does and Angel Harper is still fifty well said Mrs. Reynolds in that case I can go on waiting a little longer. And said Mr. Reynolds what happens if you do not wait a little longer, well said Mrs. Reynolds and she knew it was true in that case it will be true that there is nothing to do.

Mrs. Reynolds was right in that case then it would be true there would be nothing else to do. Mr. Reynolds was never mournful, if he had been he said he would be then but as he was never mournful he was not mournful then. Mrs. Reynolds said she was not then, but she really was she was really a little mournful then. Why not, if Angel Harper was fifty and everything was that and it was not all over, not his being fifty, not his surely going to be fifty-one, if it was not all over, not at all over, sometimes Mrs. Reynolds did not know if it was not only just begun, well anyway, one and one, well do one and one make two. Mrs. Reynolds was not at all sure, not if Angel Harper was fifty, which he was and was going to be fifty-one, which he was. There were times when Mrs. Reynolds said she did not know any one, and in a way it was true because she did not know any one that she had known the year before, to be sure she did know these things did happen she knew some whom she had not seen for years and years, they came by not because she was there but because there was not anywhere where they could go without coming to where Mrs. Reynolds was then. Oh dear said Mrs. Reynolds it did not use to be like that, but and then Mrs. Reynolds well she did not begin to laugh but she might well anyway said Mrs. Reynolds as long as we stay it is not better this way but any way it is a change from any other way. Yes said Mr. Reynolds it is time to go to bed and it was.

Mrs. Reynolds suddenly woke up she heard herself saying if he is fifty and he is how old is everybody, and Mr. Reynolds woke up too and said he did not know. How could he know how old everybody is, even Mrs. Reynolds now that she was really awake knew that she could not know how old anybody is and anyway said Mrs. Reynolds what difference does it make to anybody but themselves how old everybody is. Why then said Mr. Reynolds do you bother and Mrs. Reynolds began to laugh and cry and said it was all because of Angel Harper how could anybody forget that Angel Harper was fifty, perhaps said Mrs. Reynolds he is beginning to get absent-minded and does not know how old he is. But said Mrs. Reynolds not yet, and Mr. Reynolds said go to sleep and they went to sleep and Mrs. Reynolds dreamed about not yet dreamed that Angel Harper would get absent-minded but not yet, and she woke up and told Mr. Reynolds and he said very likely it was not yet. Indeed very likely it was not yet but said Mrs. Reynolds it will happen, Angel Harper will get absent-minded and he will not know how old he is and when that does happen said Mrs. Reynolds, and she sat down and began to think and she remembered, well she tried to do the arithmetic and he remembered what Saint Odile had said, she had not said about how old Angel Harper was but she had said how long it would take him to be successful and to be worried and he had to be a certain age, yes a certain age, Mrs. Reynolds knew how to do arithmetic and she did arithmetic and she said not yet, and she told Mr. Reynolds that it was not yet, and Mr. Reynolds said of course she had already told him and Mrs. Reynolds said yes but when I said it I had not yet done the arithmetic and now the arithmetic says not yet. Not yet what said Mr. Reynolds, why Angel Harper said Mrs. Reynolds oh Hell Angel Harper said Mr. Reynolds and he meant what he said, and as he went away Mrs. Reynolds began to regret that it was not yet, and yet it was too soon for it to be yet. Angel Harper was fifty and there was everything the matter and as there was everything the mat-

159

ter but Angel Harper was not yet absent-minded enough to forget how old he was then of course it was not yet.

As Mrs. Reynolds was very careful, she did not think that it was necessary to go out to dinner. As she was very careful she did not think that it was necessary to ask them to come to dinner, but if they came in and they looked as if they would like it she asked them to sit down with them and take dinner with them. Naturally they began to talk about Angel Harper, and as soon as they got talking about Angel Harper, Mrs. Reynolds began explaining about not yet, about Angel Harper being fifty but not being yet absent-minded enough to forget how old he was. And when said one of them one night while he was dining when do you think Mrs. Reynolds that Angel Harper will be old enough and absent-minded enough to forget how old he is and Mrs. Reynolds said not yet, and they all laughed and she laughed too. And then they talked about it and as they left Mrs. Reynolds said not yet. And then after they left Mr. Reynolds said shall we go to bed and Mrs. Reynolds said not yet, but all the same she said they would and they did, they went to bed.

PART VIII

Spring had come and Angel Harper was fifty-one. Mrs. Reynolds knew that Saint Odile did say that then would begin that Angel Harper would go under every one but had it begun. Mrs. Reynolds did not sigh and she did not say but still she did see that perhaps it had not begun. Perhaps but still she did say perhaps it had begun. And Mr. Reynolds said well anyway they would not go away and indeed they did not go away, all the same they stayed where they were, Mrs. Reynolds said they did and they did.

Yes said Mrs. Reynolds it snows every Saturday and so on Sunday there is snow on the ground and almost now Angel Harper is fifty-one and said Mrs. Reynolds and she did not sigh but she felt a little dreary when she said that there are worse things than snow. Mrs. Reynolds felt a little funny when she said Saint Odile out loud, she knew she believed in what Saint Odile said but when she said it and every one kind of acted as if they did not quite want to hear her say it, not that they minded her saying it but all the same well there was not any shame, but all the same, after all Saint Odile did say that it would end in that way that the last battle was to be the battle of the mountain and then there would be fighting in the streets of the holy city and it was all true that is it would be all true but all the same she did feel a little queer when she said it out loud not because it was queer if Mrs. Reynolds was sure that what Saint Odile had said would come to be true and that then Angel Harper would be through, that he would come perhaps come to be fifty-two, but certainly not any more, and even if and she was sure Mrs. Reynolds said Saint Odile, you see Saint Odile was right and I was right to believe in Saint Odile, then she did feel a little funny because they felt a little funny. Not Mr. Reynolds believe it or not Mr. Reynolds did not feel funny and Mrs. Reynolds did not feel funny when Mr. Reynolds heard her say Saint Odile but with every one else well she did feel a little funny. It had snowed every Saturday for quite a little while now it had snowed every Saturday but sooner or later there would be a Saturday without snow and then sooner or later the end would be begun. Would said Mrs. Reynolds would that be fun, some things said Mr. Reynolds are funny that are not fun, and Mrs. Reynolds went up to him and said that was a good thing. Of course it was said Mrs. Reynolds and after all and it was Saturday and there was no snow there was rain but that is not the same. Said Mrs. Reynolds, no it is not the same.

And then well then like a bolt out of the blue it was true everybody knew that Joseph Lane was still living. Mrs. Reynolds almost forgot the rain it was so exciting almost but not quite and she said that she would tell what she had to say to a husband and wife and four children. He was a captain in the army she had a mother who was crazy, he the captain was a little queer and the four children were funny, not the little girl but the three little boys. Mrs. Reynolds saw them quite often and though she felt that way about them she could not help telling them about Joseph Lane.

Mrs. Reynolds made it necessary that the name of Joseph Lane should be mentioned all the same. She did not know why, she said that as for herself she did not know whether he did or whether he did not exist, she said she had heard that since there were forty who looked just like him, perhaps he was not living any more, perhaps one is the same as none and perhaps none is the same as one, but and she had a feeling she said she had a feeling that if Joseph Lane was none, and he might he certainly might be nevertheless the time would come when Angel Harper was fifty-one and he would have to be afraid he would certainly have to be afraid and very likely it would be of Joseph Lane whether there was a Joseph Lane or whether there was none. And when Mrs. Reynolds said all this she felt that she had said something and she had a great deal of satisfaction. She did not tell it to any particular person, she told it to any one who was listening at such a time, a time when Angel Harper was fifty-one anybody could stop and listen.

That is the way it is just then, and Mrs. Reynolds in a way had more to say than any one because she had all day to say what she had to say and all day any day there was always some one who stopped and stood or sat while she had something to say. And then when Mr. Reynolds came home she told him and he listened about what she had said and what they had said as they stood or sat any time during the day.

One day they were beginning to think about getting in the hay, a great many people who had never thought anything about hay or about anything growing now that Angel Harper was fifty-one began to find it all very interesting. After all you have to eat, and when Angel Harper is fifty-one it is almost harder to have anything to eat almost harder, and so when they were beginning to think about getting in the hay, Mrs. Reynolds had a great deal to say. And she said it in the afternoon, not that she could not have said it in the morning or in the evening but as a matter of fact she did say it in the afternoon. That afternoon, she saw so many people pass by. One was a mother of a little boy, her name was Mrs. Ellen and she had no time to spare but she did stay to hear all that Mrs. Reynolds had to say. What said Mrs. Reynolds what do you think is going to happen. Mrs. Ellen did not know and she said so. Mrs. Reynolds said that if it were not for Saint Odile she could not have courage to go on, and what said Mrs. Ellen does Saint Odile say, and Mrs. Reynolds told her, she told her about the way it would happen that slowly the strength in Angel Harper would pass away and then it would be all over, and Mrs. Ellen who had no time to stay listened to her and listened to her and then she said she had to go away her little boy was waiting for her but before she went away she

163

asked Mrs. Reynolds if she thought it would really be that way, and Mrs. Reynolds said yes she thought so, and said Mrs. Ellen what does Mr. Reynolds say, and Mrs. Reynolds said, pooh, you know what men say, they scare each other so none of them can say what they want to say, but when I say what I want to say then Mr. Reynolds does not say no he just says that I say so. Well said Mrs. Ellen I hope it is so, and Mrs. Reynolds saw her go away. Any afternoon Mrs. Reynolds could say all she had to say, and every afternoon, it was getting warmer and as it was getting warmer she could stand longer and say more of what she had to say. And then she laughed and went home and then she sighed and went home and then sometimes she felt as if she might cry and she went home and sometimes she was sure that it was all so and she went home and told Mr. Reynolds so and he said he was sure that if she felt that way that it was what she ought to say and she was pleased that he felt about it that way.

Angel Harper was fifty-one and water could run and oh dear it was rather horrible yes it was.

She knew she said it too she knew that staying where you were was something but never going away that was something too, and she was not sure, and she knew that going away all the time going on going away was something and not having any place to stay was something. Naturally she never said anything about this something because if she did well she would change it to something else that was the only way not to be frightened all day and as a matter of fact and it was true, Mrs. Reynolds was not frightened at all not at all frightened. When Mr. Reynolds came home she said she had seen a boy and a woman talking to a quite young soldier, and Mr. Reynolds said and what did they say and Mrs. Reynolds said she had not been near enough to hear but she just wanted to tell Mr. Reynolds what she had seen. Every day was nearer summer and if it was nearer summer how much nearer was it to summer. When Mrs. Reynolds said that she said she did not care whether she said it to a fat old man or to a thin one. Mr. Reynolds laughed and said if things would go on longer the way they were going there would not be any fat old men or fat young men or anything fat everybody would be

164

thin. Mrs. Reynolds said she did not care to hear him say that, was she not quite plump and Mr. Reynolds said yes she was and he said he himself was quite a little fat and perhaps well perhaps they could continue to keep a little of their fat on them. Well said Mrs. Reynolds and Mr. Reynolds laughed and said to begin not getting thin perhaps they had better go to bed and they did they went to bed and as yet they were not thin, not at all thin. And so the day that is every day made it come nearer to be summer, the time came when the summer was so near it might be frightening if anything could frighten them but as Mrs. Reynolds said they were staying where they had been and they were going on staying. Dear leave me not was a poem that Mrs. Reynolds was saying over and over again and as she explained what she meant was that leave me not, was a dear thing, and not that she meant that dear should not leave because of course well of course there was Mr. Reynolds and of course he was not leaving. How dear leave me not is said Mrs. Reynolds she said she liked the poem better that way.

They said at least somebody said, he was a sergeant and the husband of a school-teacher, and was soon to be killed, well killed in war of course and he said that he had heard that when Angel Harper could not sleep he put himself to sleep by spelling out keep awake keep awake keep awake, and so well not always but sometimes it did put him to sleep. I have heard said Mrs. Reynolds that Joseph Lane never knows when he is awake or when he is asleep and so he does not have to spell keep awake to put himself to sleep, and the sergeant said well perhaps and then he went away to get killed. His wife the school-teacher did not know for a long time whether he was dead or not and then she remembered what he had said and she tried to put herself to sleep by spelling keep awake over and over again but it did not work very well and her face was swollen with crying but she had a little boy and although he was only three years old he was a comfort to her and she had a mother who was the widow of a garage-keeper and she too was a comfort to her. She lived in a little place and taught school there and just around her there were among them all fourteen widows and only one widower, well said Mrs. Reynolds and she went home to Mr. Reynolds and told him all about it and he said well too and that was all there was to that.

Mrs. Reynolds said to Mr. Reynolds that there was no difference between slowly and quickly, if anything was done slowly then they were impatient that it was not happening more quickly and when it was being done quickly then they were impatient because it was being done too quickly. Yes said Mrs. Reynolds perhaps Joseph Lane is right in not knowing the difference between being awake and asleep and if he is, Mr. Reynolds grunted. Yes said Mrs. Reynolds when I was young and I read that a man gave a grunt when somebody said something to him I did not believe that he did really grunt, but now said Mrs. Reynolds I do, and Mr. Reynolds gave a grunt and said it was time to go to bed and he was right it was time to go to bed.

If in every way it was a day in which Angel Harper was more fifty-one than he had been then it was time that trains stopped puffing and that chairs were not there to sit in and that hens when they saw snow stopped laying eggs and when cows saw snow it excited them and they jumped around and perhaps some of them broke their leg. Angel Harper was fifty-one and there was no longing no longing for anything.

Mrs. Reynolds said that no one seemed to be longing for anything and she said she knew she was right, and she said it to a garage-keeper who was worried and when she saw he was worried she said to him he might just as well not worry. His foreman had a son who was a dwarf and the foreman died, but this did not worry the garage-keeper, what really worried him was that Angel Harper was fifty-one. That he said did really worry him. Well said Mrs. Reynolds and supposing he gets to be fifty-two. He had better not said the garage-keeper. And then he began to laugh. He said he always laughed when he was nervous. Mrs. Reynolds said that he was like the cows when the snow blinded them and the garage-keeper said why not. But anyway anybody might feel that way. If said Mrs. Reynolds they did not feel that way they might feel that way tomorrow. The garage-keeper reminded her of the old song what's the use of smoking if you blow the smoke away, what's the use. And Mrs. Reynolds said she would tell Mr. Reynolds what he had to say and when she got home she did tell Mr. Reynolds, and he smiled and said well and what is the use. Mrs. Reynolds was very pleased that he had said that.

Mrs. Reynolds knew that eyes are a surprise. She said that she liked to see everything but her eyes did turn away from some things. They turned away from a funeral they turned away from soldiers making believe firing, they turned away and she thought she wanted to go on looking but as she said eyes are a surprise. She listened to everything, she even listened to a young girl who was going to marry a soldier because her mother drank having lost her husband in one war and her son in another war and now her daughter was to marry a soldier so there would be some one to defend her from her mother, and Mrs. Reynolds said she hoped that some one would go to church with her and the girl said yes she thought so because the soldier was buying champagne and there he was and he had four bottles and they were going to be married in church. Mrs. Reynolds told Mr. Reynolds when he came home, Mrs. Reynolds told him that she was worried about the landscape, she said it used to be such a pretty landscape and now it was such a sad one, and said Mrs. Reynolds it has nothing to do with my eyes being a surprise not at all, William's wife Hope always had said that it was a sad landscape and I knew it was but after all it was not and now it is. Do you think said Mrs. Reynolds that Angel Harper being fifty-one has anything to do with anything, to be sure said Mrs. Reynolds, your brother William's wife Hope knew something about Angel Harper before any of us knew that some day he would be fifty-one. Well anyway said Mrs. Reynolds and she meant what she said well anyway we have enough apples to eat and they had and she said that they must be very well satisfied with that and they were. Dear apples said Mrs. Reynolds and she began to laugh and then cry a little and Mr. Reynolds said now don't worry and Mrs. Reynolds said she never did and it was true she never did.

Would and there was a sudden sound not a loud sound but a long sound would Angel Harper be fifty-one when he was

167

fifty-one or would he be fifty or would he be fifty-two. There were so many people surrounding him just then that he did not hear the sound that was not a loud sound but was a long sound. And by that time if it was not over at any rate it had died away and he was fifty-one.

Mrs. Reynolds wondered was it only begun or was it almost done, he was fifty-one, Angel Harper was fifty-one and Mrs. Reynolds knew that they used to throw away their stockings when there was a hole and now they had to mend them and they used to have anything they wanted to cook with and now, well said Mrs. Reynolds well and in a way she knew that it was not well but she said and she meant what she said, she said well.

Mrs. Reynolds knew that a captain's wife was in love with a colonel that is to say she knew that a colonel was in love with a captain's wife at any rate she knew that when she saw them together they looked as if they were in love with one another and said Mrs. Reynolds to Mr. Reynolds if Angel Harper had not been fifty-one they would never have been together. Never, never, said Mrs. Reynolds and Mr. Reynolds told her not to bother. Well said Mrs. Reynolds if I do not bother then I will have to bother about Saint Odile. Well then bother about Saint Odile he said and then he said well let us bother to go to bed, and she said it was no bother and she was right it was no bother. Anything said Mrs. Reynolds can be a bother and she was right anything can be a bother and then she thought that it would be better to bother about Saint Odile so she began to bother about Saint Odile. Sometimes it was a worry to her to bother about Saint Odile but on the other hand if she could really bother about Saint Odile then it would not be such a bother that Angel Harper was fifty-one. Oh dear me said Mrs. Reynolds and Mr. Reynolds had already gone to bed and so she went to bed too, usually she went to bed first but tonight he went to bed first but that was not any bother, not at all any bother. When she went to bed she told him that it was not any bother and he laughed and said that was all right, she was right it was not any bother.

Do please said Mrs. Reynolds she said it to everybody do please be sure that the way to endure is to be really sure, yes said Mrs.

Reynolds do please be sure. And you said anybody and Mrs. Reynolds was pretty nearly sure that she was sure just as pretty nearly sure as you can be sure and then suddenly well not suddenly but once in a while it was a long time but she was sure that Angel Harper was fifty-one and then, well anyway Angel Harper was fifty-one and Mrs. Reynolds turned that way that is to say she was looking that way and as she looked that way she had a very great deal to say. Do believe me she said to Mr. Reynolds and he said of course I do and that was true it really was true.

And now it was the morning of every day and Mrs. Reynolds felt that way she really did. Well she said he is fifty-one, well just wait she said, he is fifty-one and then she suddenly well not suddenly but she did hear again of Joseph Lane and her mouth opened with astonishment. Is it true, she said and Mr. Reynolds said it was true.

Mrs. Reynolds heard William Ross say that anyway those that did not believe in war any more would come out best out of all their troubles, she said she heard him say that anyway, she said to Mr. Reynolds that at first she had paid no attention to what he said because his name was William and she had never believed anything that Mr. Reynolds' brother William had said but all the same perhaps it was true that life was hard if you did not weaken, perhaps it was true that those who did not believe in war might go as far as those who did believe in war, even if William Ross' name was William perhaps he was right. Anyway said Mrs. Reynolds she had dreamed that night that she had been taken to ride on a motorcycle and Mr. Reynolds said she did well to dream it because he thought very soon the only way to move around would be by walking and said he since his name was not William perhaps Mrs. Reynolds would believe him. And Mrs. Reynolds sighed and said she was beginning to believe him and she really did not care for walking but anyway she could stay home and others would come by walking and that would come to the same thing and by that time it was evening and they had their dinner and they went to bed again.

Well said Mrs. Reynolds and she did not go in or out she just stood, and as she stood she felt better. She knew that her stomach felt softer and that there were no pains in her arms or in her hands, she felt even tender and then she knew that she was very comfortable and she heard herself say with a sigh, I do not want to cry. It was just that that made her feel careful. She felt that everything she felt made her know that she knew. I do, she said. All this was to herself and then having said it to herself she said she would say it to any neighbor. She felt that any neighbor might be very well satisfied to hear her say it. Well she said he is fifty-one, and well she said he is that one and well she said there is another one and well she said and then she did not wait for an answer. She knew that the neighbor might begin to try to cry and Mrs. Reynolds waited to go home so she went home. It is not easy not very easy to be satisfied to say what she was going to say just before she went away. When she was home Mr. Reynolds was there and she told him and he said let me alone, I do not want to know why they tell you so, and then when he saw that she looked troubled he said well yes all right, but anyway you might just as well be just as glad tonight as you could be any night. Mrs. Reynolds knew very well what she meant and she never meant to say that it was not so but was it so. Anyway it was foolish just to expect that it would ever finish. What she said to herself, well his being Angel Harper being fifty-one, and there being Joseph Lane. Oh dear she said let us go to bed and they did.

Mrs. Reynolds said that she had her ups and downs, and when she had her ups and downs she had her ups and when she had her ups she had her downs. Well she said and anybody knew that when anybody felt hopeful everybody felt hopeful and it was true when everybody felt hopeful then anybody felt hopeful. Some said Mrs. Reynolds went up first and some said Mrs. Reynolds went down first but either way and in every way everybody felt the same way. Now there was that about Angel Harper being fifty-one. At that time everybody was so sad that nobody could be sadder and yet all the same said Mrs. Reynolds nobody is to blame and if they are said Mrs. Reynolds then nobody ought to blame them. Yes said Mrs. Reynolds and she felt that way yes, and if there was nothing to do well then we would not do anything and if there was something to do, Mrs. Reynolds asked every one she saw, a soldier without his uniform who had just been married and was buying his wife a radio, a young man who was just coming to be a clergyman, a husband and wife and their daughter who were either very hopeful or not hopeful at all, Mrs. Reynolds asked every one she saw is there anything to do and in a way she knew that they were right there was not anything to do. There was not even time to wait not time even for that said Mrs. Reynolds and when she knew there was no time to wait she looked around to see whether Mr. Reynolds was coming back, and he was, he was coming back. Well then when he had come back it might be just as if it had been at any time as if Angel Harper had not had any age and as if when they had not heard of Joseph Lane they did not know he was there. And yet said Mrs. Reynolds and she did shake just a little bit nevertheless said Mrs. Reynolds he was there. Which he, said Mr. Reynolds, and Mrs. Reynolds did not answer because she knew very well that Mr. Reynolds knew which he, which two he she meant, why not, how could anybody not. Angel Harper was fifty-one. Oh dear me said Mrs. Reynolds when it was later. She did not remember anybody she had known, well of course Mr. Reynolds, but that was the same as nothing that is to say the same as everything and she could of course not really forget that Mr. Reynolds had a brother William who had a wife Hope but all the same Mrs. Reynolds knew very well that just now and everybody was like that, that just now not anybody knew any one except every one that they did not know before. But of course said Mrs. Reynolds and then Mr. Reynolds said it was late and it was, the time changed, well said Mrs. Reynolds it can change in the middle of the night, the time can, well said Mr. Reynolds let us be asleep first and they were.

The next day Mrs. Reynolds stopped and spoke to a total stranger. They say nowadays, she said, that they think they can, well said the total stranger can they, and Mrs. Reynolds said they do what they can. Mrs. Reynolds then asked the total stranger where he came from. Oh said the total stranger my name is Hudson from Hudson's Bay, and he said that is very far away and I am staying here. Oh are you said Mrs. Reynolds and then she went away.

Mrs. Reynolds felt restless that day, she came in and she went out and sometimes she felt as if it was all going to end well oh very well and sometimes she felt that it was not going to end at all and sometimes she remembered Angel Harper being fifty-one and sometimes she felt that he never had been and sometimes she felt that she was foolish to believe in Saint Odile and sometimes she felt in spite of everything what Saint Odile said was going to happen was going to happen and sometimes she wanted to only talk to total strangers and sometimes she felt she did not want to see any one and then she was a little tired and she sat down and she began to read a novel and she knew that she never could read a novel that did not end well and so. Just then it was not easy for her not to see any one because after all it was spring-time and in spring-time well everybody she had not seen was coming past just then and if they were coming past just then she had to listen to them and she had to tell them something and though of course they all knew all about it she had to tell them that dear me Angel Harper was fifty-one and she was tired of his being fifty-one and any one of them had to say the same thing and Mrs. Reynolds had to ask each one of them what they really thought about Joseph Lane and each one of them had to say that they were not feeling just like that that day and Mrs. Reynolds said she was not feeling like that either and evening was coming and it was commencing to be cold again and perhaps she had better light a fire. Shall you said she to herself shall you light your fire and she knew she meant a great many things when she said anything and she always said something so of course she meant a great many things and so she did light a fire and Mr. Reynolds came in and then it was later in the evening and she had told him everything that everybody had said and that she had said, and Mr. Reynolds said that he had said all that too and everybody else had said all that to him and now they would go to bed and she said yes they would go to bed and they did they put out the lights after they went to bed.

And as she put out the lights Mrs. Reynolds said that Angel Harper was certainly fifty-one and Mr. Reynolds said do not begin again and Mrs. Reynolds said she was not beginning again she was just going on and then they went to sleep and that was comforting.

It was very nearly morning and there was a noise, oh dear me said Mrs. Reynolds that is that awful Angel Harper just going on being fifty-one and she woke up Mr. Reynolds and asked him what he thought it was and Mr. Reynolds said he thought it was something and he wanted to go to sleep again and he did. Mrs. Reynolds knew, she said she knew and she knew that Angel Harper was frightened too, he would not know because he did frighten every one he would not know but any dog knows what it knows and does Angel Harper, Mrs. Reynolds was half asleep and the noise had wakened her and she knew that Angel Harper being fifty-one had frightened her and she also knew that, and there was a noise again and she thought she had better go to sleep again, because if she did not she would have to wake Mr. Reynolds again and if she did wake Mr. Reynolds again then well then anyway what was the use if you were frightened well after all if Angel Harper was fifty-one and just then she remembered Joseph Lane. Thank God she said I can remember something and why not, she said to herself, and just then just before the noise came again she fell asleep and this time it did not wake her. When it was morning it was morning again and if it was morning again then they would both be awake and if they were both awake well anyway only once in a while would there be anything really frightening in the morning.

One day Mrs. Reynolds remembered Lydia. She did not care about Lydia. Lydia was always having children and Lydia was always complaining and Lydia was always rich enough and Lydia was very blonde and her eyes were blue, and Lydia was mistaken, she really was mistaken, she said Angel Harper was fifty-two, but Lydia was mistaken, Angel Harper was fifty-one. Mrs. Reynolds was hoping that Lydia would go away and that she would never see her again and when she said that to Mr. Reynolds he said well why not not see her and Mrs. Reynolds said she would not and she did not but she did remember her and when she remembered her she remembered that Lydia had said that Angel Harper was fifty-two and that was annoying because Angel Harper was fifty-one. That he was fifty-one was all that Mrs. Reynolds felt that she could endure and anyway she said she was going gradually to have Joseph Lane be more important than Angel Harper, and besides she did not know how old Joseph Lane was and of course that did make everything easier. Well said Mrs. Reynolds and she wished that chickens were commoner that is to say more abundant and likewise eggs and butter and meat, and even potatoes, not that she did not have enough because she did but she did wish that they were more abundant.

Let us help ourselves said Mrs. Reynolds.

It is wonderful said Mrs. Reynolds how you feel what you feel and Mrs. Reynolds did feel what she felt. Who would not when, and just then Mrs. Reynolds felt that it was happening and as there was not much left, not much left she knew that it was time to begin again. Beginning again was to believe to really believe to have no doubt that Saint Odile was right, that the last battle was to be the battle of the mountain and then there would be the invasion of the country of Angel Harper, and such invasion, dear me not contrary to my hopes said Mrs. Reynolds and when she said not contrary to my hopes she felt she could almost think about it in detail. She did not like to talk about it in detail not yet but she did think that she could almost really almost think about it in detail. And when she did there was hope, I arouse hope in myself she said and she meant what she said. As she went out she saw some friends come in and as they came in she said to them and what is the news, and they said there is none, and Mrs. Reynolds did not listen to them, she knew that there was news and as there was news she did not expect them to give any other answer than the answer they gave. When Mr. Reynolds came home she told him and he said yes there was none. All the same Mrs. Reynolds did have a contented feeling, she might not have had but she did have a contented feeling just then.

Mrs. Reynolds met a very large stout lady who complained of rheumatism. She had a very handsome daughter dark and tall and slender with long hands. She did not complain of rheumatism, she smiled when her mother did a slow smile and a very capably pleasant one, and Mrs. Reynolds wanted to know if they liked their daily life, and they said well yes they did. There was more to it than that. There was a young sister and the older sister said that the younger sister might be married before she was. She said, it did quite frequently happen like that. The mother thought that they had better all wait a little longer. And she did not want to know what Mrs. Reynolds thought but anyway, she had a tall son and two younger girls and one of them was a little simple-minded and they all were quite busy, each in their own way and her husband was a very capable man and when he was younger when they were in bed it was warmer than it was now when he was older which of course was natural enough every age has its own way of being warmer and colder, and rheumatism could be a thing to be avoided if there was warmth enough. It is strange said Mrs. Reynolds that sometimes the winter is one way and sometimes another, they seem alike winter and winter but they are not said Mrs. Reynolds and the same thing is true of sum-mers and there is no doubt about it. The large stout lady said yes, and Mrs. Reynolds said yes, and although nobody went away at least not just then they never did see each other again.

It was very likely that Mrs. Reynolds dreamed at night and when she did and she forgot what she had dreamed she wished very much that she might have remembered what it was that she had dreamed. She never dreamed of Angel Harper never. She never said why not and Mr. Reynolds never said why not and she never said that she did not dream of Angel Harper but it was a fact she never had dreamed of Angel Harper. In a way it was very necessary but she never had. By the time it was getting longer and longer that Angel Harper was fifty-one, she knew he knew, nobody knew what was the fun, and indeed there was no fun no fun at all for any one that Angel Harper was fifty-one. And now it was coming to be serious that Joseph Lane was not fifty-one, very serious. I like it said Mrs. Reynolds and like it or not Mrs. Reynolds did like it. She was full of hope at least she hoped that there was hope and in a way yes in a way she was full of a hope. Yes she said Saint Odile yes she said full of hope yes she said, and Mr. Reynolds laughed and said he would remind her. By that time it was eight o'clock but not yet dark, but then then when Angel Harper was fifty-one time was very funny, it was always changing changing whether they need it or not. Mostly said Mrs. Reynolds not, and Mr. Reynolds laughed and said if not then not, and Mrs. Reynolds said she wished that she was a cow and then she would only know now, and not about the clock going back and Mr. Reynolds laughed again and said that a cow had to go to bed and so did a hen and what then, and they had dinner and they went to bed feeling quite tired but quite cheerful. That did happen now and then when Angel Harper was fifty-one.

Listen to me said Mrs. Reynolds to Mr. Reynolds the time has come to listen so you must listen to me. And what I say said Mrs. Reynolds is that it is sure, Saint Odile knows she knows and she says that the last battle they will fight, will be the battle of the mountain and they are fighting it now and then then wonderful things will happen in the Orient, Christians will become Christians, and everything will become everything and it is commencing and listen said Mrs. Reynolds the time has come to listen so listen to me. Mr. Reynolds said yes, he did not mean yes but he said yes and yet he did not not mean yes when he said yes, he did and he did not mean yes, and he did not and he did mean yes and Mrs. Reynolds said she was not satisfied the way that he did and did not mean but she was, she was quite satisfied. She said everybody walked when they have to go anywhere and she was right everybody did have to walk when they had to go anywhere, and Mr. Reynolds said did Saint Odile say that everybody would have to walk, and Mrs. Reynolds she did not want to make fun, and he said he did not he really wanted to know and she said no, and he said no not no but know and she said oh come it is time to go to bed and he said he liked to go to bed, and she said was it too early and he said no not even too late and she said she thought he was silly and he said she liked him to be silly, and she said not as silly as he was and she said all right and he said all right it is night and then they went to bed, as he said, he said they went to bed

and she said of course he said they went to bed, but said she it
is time to listen now and you listen to me, Angel Harper is fifty-
one and Saint Odile says the end is begun and it will not be a
long one, and Mr. Reynolds said all right but night is night, and
so good night and they went to bed and slept tight.

It was then the morning and it was storming it did not make
any difference what they were going to do what were they going
to do dear me what were they going to do. They were surprised
that is what they were going to do, no matter what they expected
they were surprised, like it or not they were surprised and one
at a time they were surprised and both together they were surprised and still Angel Harper was still fifty-one, and though
they felt that it was all over was it all over or was it just begun.
Certainly there was nothing to say more than that, they did not
only not recognize him when they saw him but they wished that
he would go away. Angel Harper was still fifty-one that day
and Mrs. Reynolds was getting ready to say that she had something to say. She knew what it was and it was just that, and really
almost really she had had enough she felt that way and she wanted
to say that she had enough and that Mr. Reynolds had had
enough, enough and enough of Angel Harper being fifty-one,
more than enough, always more than enough. And so she said
if well begun is almost done, I want to be done with well begun.
Done done she said and she was almost angry when Mr. Reynolds said that she might just as well wait, it was not too late to
wait. That is the way Mr. Reynolds felt about it at least so he
said, and Mrs. Reynolds said she was beginning to think that she
almost began to feel that she was quite pink with pleasure when
she thought about Joseph Lane. What said Mr. Reynolds. Well
said Mrs. Reynolds it is not only his name but all the same I am
feeling like that and Mrs. Reynolds did feel like that. Oh dear
she said she did feel like that. And tomorrow said Mr. Reynolds,
well said Mrs. Reynolds why not tomorrow but perhaps after
all there will be no more allowed tomorrow perhaps not Mrs.
Reynolds said she was beginning to think pretty well that it was
perhaps not, perhaps not she said. Well anyway Mrs. Reynolds
did say that she was beginning to be fed up, not with food said

177

Mr. Reynolds and Mrs. Reynolds began to laugh, no she said not with food, and she was right that was what she was not fed up with just not, not with food. Wood said she, well yes wood, and good said she well it is not all to the good, and just then she decided to go out and not to stay at home and she did.

In the spring a young man's fancy lightly turns to thoughts of love but said Mrs. Reynolds no not now, it turns to spring offensives and spring offensives, well said Mrs. Reynolds he is fifty-one and it will be done it certainly will be done at the end of fifty-one and as she said it Mr. Reynolds looked at her to be sure that she was certain, and to his surprise she was and so well he said if it is so it is so, and you do know and Mrs. Reynolds said she did know and that it was so. Well said Mrs. Reynolds it is a great relief to me even if I do not believe it it is a great relief to me, and Mrs. Reynolds felt quiet again and said she was going out and she did. As she went out, she said it was funny that some people did continue to be stout. It really was funny and as she looked about well there were not a great many that were stout, not a great many, and said Mrs. Reynolds the few there are seem to be so because they have that the matter with them and she was right that was the reason. And so little by little she began to look around and she felt that she had to tell them all to go home and she did and she did not go home because just then she felt that she just had to be out. When she was out she was out for all day, she had gone out not to stay out but because there was no time to go in she stayed out and that is what she thought, she said there was no difference between thought and fought, and it made her feel funny, that was all, she said, it just made her feel funny. That was what she said.

And then it happened she knew it was true, it was all going to be over as if it had not been begun. She knew that it was just as Saint Odile said, she knew that although it did not feel the same it was the same and she knew that the name Angel Harper was the name was one everybody knew too well and so it was all over and there was nothing to tell, she knew she knew but she knew that perhaps tomorrow she might doubt if it was true but it was true all the same all the same and she knew even though

178

she had a certain shame when she said it was true and that she believed what Saint Odile had to say even so she knew well she did not know that would be true tomorrow because after all tomorrow was not yesterday it was not even today but all the same Saint Odile did say it was true and now she knew that it was true and although she was frightened all the same all the same she was not frightened, oh yes she was she said oh yes she was, and she knew oh yes she was and it was true oh yes she was, she said oh yes she was but all the same it was not all the same, well she said it was not Joseph Lane that had made it not be the same because after all she did not really know his name, but anyway she would go home. She said to Mr. Reynolds when he came in that she had thought to tell him that she would never be ever frightened again but really although she knew that that was not true nevertheless perhaps nevertheless she might not be frightened again. And Mr. Reynolds after listening did not say anything, nothing ever did frighten him not because it was not frightening but because being frightened was not what he was doing and whenever he was awake he was doing something. Mrs. Reynolds said yes, yes was not just agreeing it was saying something, yes she said and when she said yes Mr. Reynolds liked to hear her say yes because when she said yes he knew she was saying something and whatever she said made it pleasant for him and so that day was ending and after dinner there would not anybody come in, more and more although they saw everybody more and more it seemed not that, not like that, not like that at all, that is what Mrs. Reynolds said perhaps not like that at all is what she said and Mr. Reynolds said it was time to go to bed and it was and they went to bed.

The next day Mrs. Reynolds said something was a puzzle to her. It was why Mr. Raymond was not polite to her not considerate toward her not willing that she should have her way. She wondered whether it was because Mr. Raymond suddenly realized that his name commenced with R as did Mrs. Reynolds' and he suddenly had had a feeling that he wanted to be the only one there just then whose name began with R. These things do happen said Mrs. Reynolds when she was telling about it to a friend Mrs. Chambers who happened to be walking in the same direction, they do not make you nervous said Mrs. Reynolds but they do not make you a little uneasy. But said Mrs. Chambers, well I know said Mrs. Reynolds but it does happen that is it did happen and that is the only explanation, after all, said Mrs. Reynolds, here we are, there is no doubt she went on that here we are, we have no automobiles and cannot buy shoes, and have not too much to eat and so it can happen said Mrs. Reynolds and she meant what she said, it can happen that Mr. Raymond might feel that way about the letter R and the beginning of his name. I do mean that he might feel that way about it said Mrs. Reynolds, and then she said good-bye to Mrs. Chambers and she went on feeling a little puzzled not really puzzled because after all said Mrs. Reynolds since well there is no doubt about it since when when Angel Harper is just still going on being fifty-one, not anything might happen because a good deal of the time nothing does happen but anyway said Mrs. Reynolds just then she saw Mr. Reynolds and she hurried a little to join him, but anyway she said, there has not been anything happening and so we might just as well go home, and they did, they did just as well go home and going home was not puzzling not at all puzzling.

Mrs. Reynolds said that she had been upset, had been said Mr. Reynolds, well said Mrs. Reynolds if I am upset then I have been, and she meant what she was saying. She meant that just at first she had been upset and then she was upset and then she was not upset and anyway what was the difference, it might be just as well to live by day just as well as not. If you did not how did you live said Mrs. Reynolds upset or not. She was quite excited, she said she knew how it was, it was like that, now supposing said Mrs. Reynolds and she was quite excited supposing well of course Saint Odile is right said Mrs. Reynolds the time will come and it is almost time for it to come when all this will be over just over, but said Mrs. Reynolds and she was very excited supposing well there is no question Saint Odile is not mistaken, like it or not said Mrs. Reynolds well of course we do like it said Mrs. Reynolds but like it or not Angel Harper will be all over, all said Mrs. Reynolds I can spell all, and over said

Mrs. Reynolds I can spell over, and so said Mrs. Reynolds Angel Harper will be can be will be all over. And Mrs. Reynolds sighed a little and sat down. And Mr. Reynolds said it was exciting but tomorrow was another day to be excited in so that they might just as well go to bed now and they carefully did they carefully went to bed.

It is not very likely that just then Angel Harper could remember that when he had been a boy he could write in a note book and nobody could annoy him. It might easily be that he could remember this thing. And gradually Angel Harper gradually began to try to cry. He felt that it would make a difference to him if he could gradually begin to cry and every day he was hoping that gradually he would begin to cry that gradually he would begin to try to cry and that then gradually he would begin to cry. He had a feeling that if he could gradually begin to cry, Joseph Lane would be disappearing and if Joseph Lane would be disappearing then snow would be blue and everything would be through and that he Angel Harper having gradually begun to cry could spend his time all his time in crying. That would be a nice thing to do a nice quiet pleasant thing to do to spend all the time in crying. Angel Harper was hoping that this might happen to him that he would come some time to spend his time pleasantly spend his time all his time in crying.

But always just then somebody would tell him that Joseph Lane was not disappearing and Angel Harper heard what they had to say. He did not hear anything about Saint Odile. Why not because praying is just as pleasant as crying but Angel Harper had nothing to say nobody heard him say anything, how could they when he was hoping that gradually he could begin to cry.

Oh dear said Mrs. Reynolds I am not mistaken when I say oh dear and she was right of course she was right, she was not mistaken not at all mistaken when she said oh dear.

And now said Mrs. Reynolds just to be solemn, there is nothing mistaken there is no mistake about Saint Odile and there is no hesitation and no leaning in Joseph Lane, and said Mrs. Reynolds and she was firm and there was fire in her eye there is no gradually coming to spend the time in crying in Angel Harper, none at all none at all, and she looked at the weather and she said it was not going to snow because it was too warm, the snow was over, the grass had not yet begun, and it was an unwelcome thought that the more they grew the more they slew each other. She said this to a blacksmith and she said it to a carpenter and then she came home and said it to Mr. Reynolds, she said just for fun she was going to say how do you do to him and then she would explain everything to him, and he laughed and said he had heard it before, and Mrs. Reynolds said yes but not this time you have not heard it this time and she said if he would only wait she would have her watch regulated and then she would come back and tell him what the watchmaker had said. What did he say said Mr. Reynolds when she came back and Mrs. Reynolds said that she had not been mistaken, the watchmaker had told her everything and in no way had Mrs. Reynolds been mistaken because it was just as she knew it was going to happen and as Saint Odile had said, it was going to be all over. It is never necessary to say what was going to be all over because everybody knows and that is what Mrs. Reynolds said when she came back from the watchmaker and she was very right everybody knows, of course everybody knows what it is that is going to be all over.

It has been a long day said Mr. Reynolds let us go to bed and they did they did as he said they did go to bed.

I forgot to tell you said Mrs. Reynolds to Mr. Reynolds the next day, I forgot to tell you that when I saw Mr. Arnold today and I did see him, he was not very busy nobody is very busy just now because there is nothing to do so I said to him something about a farmer and he said to me do not mention farmers to me I hate them all. And then I know what he meant, after all there is not very much to eat just now and farmers grow all the food anybody can eat, and so of course anybody can hate them all, I do not know said Mrs. Reynolds that I do that I do hate them all but I do understand what Mr. Arnold meant when he said he did, that he did not want to hear any one mention a farmer because he did hate them all. I wonder said Mrs. Reynolds and she sighed a little, I wonder about eating, of course we all do eat, and little by little we eat less and when we eat less little by little we begin to get impatient, impatient sighed Mrs. Reynolds with Angel Harper being fifty-one, of course said Mrs. Reynolds men mind too about wine and about tobacco some women mind too said Mrs. Reynolds and she looked at Mr. Reynolds she knew that he did not mind not mind awfully too, he just did not mind too, it was not necessary for him to mind he just went on living, and just going on living was occupying, yes said Mrs. Reynolds looking at Mr. Reynolds and smiling yes indeed it is and she knew what she meant and she knew that Mr. Reynolds was there and oh dear me yes it is not necessary to be impatient if you are patient, Mr. Reynolds did not say anything and he had a pleasant expression. Oh said Mrs. Reynolds, I thought it was the end of Angel Harper being fifty-one but was it. Mrs. Reynolds did not say that she was going out and when she went out it looked just the same. She came in and said it was not the same and Mr. Reynolds said that was right it was not the same. The only thing said Mr. Reynolds that is the same is at night because then they were asleep and even if they dreamed well it was all right, because dreams go by contraries or else they do not and so the night was all right. Good night said Mr. Reynolds although it was not yet night.

PART IX

Mrs. Reynolds for which she came to see that she was a little puzzled again. She knew that if a woman was crazy and had a lover and the lover was the colonel and the colonel had lots of funny ways, he thought he was very attractive but was he and the wife of the captain who was crazy and had four children did not think she was very attractive but she was and said Mrs. Reynolds they moved away, everybody moved and they moved away. What said Mr. Reynolds and Mrs. Reynolds said everybody moved away.

Mrs. Reynolds woke up early in the morning and Mr. Reynolds was or was not listening and she was saying Saint Odile knew that when Angel Harper was fifty-two he was through. And it was early in the morning and Mrs. Reynolds wanted to go to sleep again so she said it over and over again and then when she was not sleeping she began to spell it, it seemed different to her when she spelled it without saying each word before she spelt it, and she hoped in this way that sleep would come, sometimes it does and sometimes it does not and Mrs. Reynolds really never knew whether she had fallen asleep or whether she had not.

I wonder said Mrs. Reynolds why they want to be a mayor why they want to be a general why they want to be a governor, I wonder said Mrs. Reynolds and she thought if she had time she would sit down to wonder, but actually she did wonder even although she did not sit down to wonder. Saints that she could understand and even other things she could understand but a mayor a general or a governor, why said Mrs. Reynolds why, and she was very careful not to say anything about that because after all if any one did want to be that it would not do to discourage them, no that would not do Mrs. Reynolds knew that if they wanted it it would not do to discourage them. It was all right about Mr. Reynolds he did not want that, when they made him an alderman he was not sure that he did want that and if it had not happened that he had happened to have a coat with a fur collar he would never even have accepted that.

And so even when Angel Harper was getting on in fifty-one getting on so much that even Mr. Reynolds had a slightly nervous feeling still even then some did think they wanted to be a mayor or a general or a governor and Mrs. Reynolds said she did find it a little surprising. Day by day she found it a little surprising day by day she found it all a little surprising and that day she met some one and she told them that day by day she did find it a little surprising, but they were in a hurry to get home because anything might be dangerous just then anything and so they were in too much of a hurry to get home to stop to listen, even although it was always pleasant and in a way surprising to know what Mrs. Reynolds found day by day to be surprising.

Let well enough alone said Mrs. Reynolds and she meant what she said. Irons in the fire said Mrs. Reynolds and she meant what she said, three feet forward and two back said Mrs. Reynolds and once more and yet again she meant what she said, and little by little she began to be acquainted with wondering was it going to happen. It meant all that to her and by the time it was time she said to Mr. Reynolds that she would not bother him again but she said to Mr. Reynolds and she meant what she said actually she would be doing nothing but bothering him bothering him all the time, why not she said and she told him she meant what she said. If said she and she said she meant what she said, and then when she said if she said she might just as well keep quiet.

One day she decided that she would not wear gloves, it was a little warmer and gloves were scarce anything could be scarce why not said Mrs. Reynolds when so much was destroyed and

perhaps well anyway although it looked like it Angel Harper
was still fifty-one and so on. Mrs. Reynolds said she really did
not care for so on. One day she said that she did believe in what
Saint Odile said and when she made a copy of it she believed it
all again. Not again and again but just again. She told Mr.
Reynolds that there was a difference and he said that there was
no reason why he should not agree with her.

The day had gone she felt better again she told Mr. Reynolds
that she felt better again and that everything was all right and
that she was very bright and that she felt better again.

Mrs. Reynolds was standing at her door and she saw a colonel
coming toward her dressed in his very best clothes. It is natural
said Mrs. Reynolds to him that you do, well of course I mean
that you do dress in your very best clothes because pretty soon
you will have no use for them, yes said Mrs. Reynolds pretty
soon you will have no use for them. Yes said Mrs. Reynolds when
so much is happening there is no news day by day no news at all
day by day. The colonel in his best clothes did not care to hear
what she had to say, he saluted very delicately with a very pretty
motion and he went on his way. Mrs. Reynolds had this to say, she
said she liked to see him, she liked to see him moving and bowing
and saluting, she told a soldier who was passing that he might as
well rest, any soldier might as well rest said Mrs. Reynolds.

By the time that Mr. Reynolds came home Mrs. Reynolds was
ready to say that she was wondering all day if Angel Harper
was going to have a fifty-second birthday, she said she just wondered and wondered about this all day. She said she had plenty to
do and plenty to see and plenty to hear, and she said she talked to
everybody and she always heard everything about everything
and nothing much was happening, there was so much going on
that it was just as if nothing at all was happening nothing at all
but all the same all day she was wondering and wondering and
wondering would Angel Harper have his fifty-second birthday.
Mr. Reynolds said that if it was not so warm and the air was not
so heavy he might listen to her wondering but after all what was
it after all was it Joseph Lane who sat and thought or not. You
do said Mrs. Reynolds make me feel better and she laughed or

186

not, she said, and if you are warm and if you are tired and if you sit down then you are not worried. I am never worried said Mr. Reynolds and it was true he never was worried.

Rainbow and Saint Odile and War and Revolution, these said Mrs. Reynolds are four things to think about and I do said Mrs. Reynolds I do think about them just now. She did not know whether it was early or late but she was thinking about them. How do you do she said not to anybody but just to a rainbow and to Saint Odile and to war or revolution and as she said how do you do to them she felt better she felt quieter, she felt stronger, she felt more contented and she was ready to sit down and be quiet.

If said Mrs. Reynolds for some reason we have to leave our house could we find another. I think so said Mr. Reynolds. You have to be right these days said Mrs. Reynolds you have to be right about everything just now. And I am said Mr. Reynolds, you said Mrs. Reynolds sooner or later and it does not make any difference what you think you have to be right and it does not make any difference whether it is sooner or later you have to be right about everything said Mrs. Reynolds about Angel Harper about Joseph Lane, and said Mr. Reynolds about Saint Odile and about a rainbow, he always looked a little uncomfortable when he said this to Mrs. Reynolds yes she said you have to be right about everything and the greatest thing it is easy to be wrong about is quicker or slower, it is always either quicker or slower then when you are right you know it is going to be, it is not what you think it is what you know oh dear said Mrs. Reynolds it is so slow. It is quick enough said Mr. Reynolds and then he had to go away for the day.

Mrs. Reynolds saw so many that day that she forgot some of the things they had to say. She met one woman who was very thin, she tended to be very thin whenever she became strange and left her four children without paying any attention and would not talk to her husband who was a captain and wanted to go away in a boat although she was afraid she would be drowned and perhaps afterwards she would never know where she had been. When Mrs. Reynolds saw her she said how do you do but she would not let her speak to her so of course she did not remember what she had been saying. Another woman she met was some one who would not listen but just went on talking and she knew that she would not let any one take anything away from her but nevertheless well said Mrs. Reynolds it will be taken away, but the woman did not hear, nobody went away but the woman did not hear her and it did not make any difference whether it was evening or whether it was morning she just went on talking and nobody listened to her. And Mrs. Reynolds met a man whose father was a colonel and whose mother was deaf and whose sister was married and they all hoped to know somebody and if they did or if they did not they said so. Mrs. Reynolds talked a while with that young man and hoped that he was too well to have anything happen but said Mrs. Reynolds if it does or if it does not, what said the young man his name was James Early what he said but Mrs. Reynolds said it was of no importance and she had forgotten what she did say, well of course said Mrs. Reynolds later when she was telling the story to Mr. Reynolds of course she had not but what was the use if she had or if she had not James Early was destined to go away, they all did, what was the reason that Angel Harper was fifty-one, well said Mrs. Reynolds a little triumphantly that is, that is the reason. And then she met a Doctor who was kind, doctors are kind when they are that kind but he had been married almost all his life to his wife and he had five girls and two boys and the youngest girl who was still a baby was every inch a lady. Dear me said Mrs. Reynolds after all said Mrs. Reynolds, it is very likely said Mrs. Reynolds that there will not be any mistake. After all Angel Harper might never come to be fifty-two and then what a happy hullabaloo, when everybody says to everybody how do you do, and everybody answers everybody very well I thank you. Mrs. Reynolds felt very strange she knew it was a day when she would see every one either coming or going and she did and it made her feel funny just as funny as that. If anybody knew that there was going to be trouble everybody was in a hurry but when there was so much trouble then nobody was in any hurry. Mrs. Reynolds walked slowly and she stopped quite often she knew that anyway well once very quietly she said she was hoping that Joseph Lane was happy. Not said Mrs. Reynolds that it makes any difference to him whether he is or whether he is not, but anyway it is very nice and quiet of him to go on very nice and quiet of Joseph Lane to go on and Mrs. Reynolds gave a sigh of relief, whether or not it was useful she did give a sigh of relief. And pretty soon she was home and Mr. Reynolds came home and they talked about it and then considerably later they went to bed, not that Mrs. Reynolds was sleepy no not that night but anyway considerably later they did go to bed.

Mrs. Reynolds said that she had enough it had not happened because she had had enough. Not having happened because she had had enough she said was a reasonable thing.

Angel Harper remembered, he was so afraid of fifty-two as afraid of fifty-two as anybody had ever been of sixteen, he remembered that really he had been too old to play being a driver and having other children harnessed in front of him as horses far too old and still yes he had been far too old to do it and still he had been doing it when he was far too old to do it, and suddenly well not suddenly but underneath, he was afraid that that was what made him afraid of being fifty-two, afraid and afraid, he was afraid of fifty-two, it was frightening, fifty-two being fifty-two was frightening and he was afraid.

Mrs. Reynolds had not heard of that, she knew everything but she had not heard of that, she did not say that she had heard of that but how could she say she had not heard it when she did not hear it, which was quite enough.

She was a little uneasy, she said she was a little uneasy but she said she was not no she was not never again would she think about what was going to happen, she had given it up given up thinking what was going to happen and whenever she did it was a mistake it made her go wrong it made everything go wrong. No said Mrs. Reynolds never again no never again would she think would she let herself think about anything that was going to be happening. Let it alone she said and she meant what she said and Mr. Reynolds said why say it, and Mrs. Reynolds said she said it so that she would that is to say that she would not do it. And Mr. Reynolds was satisfied and so was every one.

Mrs. Reynolds began to wish that she had been able to help Joseph Lane to read out loud. That was a funny idea she had, read out loud. She just began to think about Joseph Lane and wished she knew how true it was that he did not know how to read out loud. Let him alone said Mr. Reynolds, yes said Mrs. Reynolds of course I will let him alone, of course of course I will let him alone. Of course said Mrs. Reynolds I will let him alone, it is silly said Mrs. Reynolds because of course not alone I never knew him but even when I heard about him I never thought about him, and all the same said Mrs. Reynolds and she sighed all the same I wish I could help him could help Joseph Lane to read out loud.

There is a difference said Mrs. Reynolds and she meant what she said there is a difference between winter and spring and spring and summer, even and she began to feel a little funny even when it looks as if Angel Harper might come to be fifty-two. Might so come. Never mind feeling ashamed said Mrs. Reynolds and she really did not when she was talking even mind said Mrs. Reynolds being ashamed of feeling ashamed and she felt very funny. She did not know what it was but she told Mr. Reynolds that it was because well she felt that way and he said he would comfort her and he did, and so she said perhaps if they went to bed they would sleep and Mr. Reynolds said of course and so they went to bed and they fell asleep and it was all right. The next morning, there was a little less every day there was a little less and Mrs. Reynolds said yes every day there was a little less to trouble them. And Mr. Reynolds laughed and was quiet and that was all right.

Mrs. Reynolds said that life was just one spring offensive one after the other, she giggled, it sounds funny said Mrs. Reynolds but is it, anyway since Angel Harper was born in the spring what else can he do than have a spring offensive too, Mrs. Reynolds giggled but really she said she had enough she could do with a spring where only the spring was doing a spring offensive, she thought she said she thought that that would be a nice change oh dear she said, excitement and hope and calm, oh dear, she said, in the spring oh dear she said oh dear and she said she knew it sounded funny and it made her giggle but it was not funny at all, oh dear said Mrs. Reynolds and she meant it, oh dear a spring offensive, and if Mr. Reynolds had been asleep she would have woke him up to tell him so but he was not asleep and he was not there so after having said all she had to say about the spring offensive to the air she went out to see if she could not see some one and tell them about the spring offensive and how she did hope that there never would be another one.

While she was out she saw that everybody was going home, she stopped one of them and she said to him why are you all going home, don't you know he said he was young and tallish and fair and walked with a little lurch don't you know he said it is because we are all tired. Tired of what said Mrs. Reynolds well he said we don't know just what we are tired of but we are tired, yes said Mrs. Reynolds I know, the spring offensive, well said the young man call it that if you want to be busy about it but anyway we are all going home. And where said Mrs. Reynolds interestedly where is your home. Well said the young man that is what we are just too tired to find out. And so Mrs. Reynolds went home, she knew where her home was but she did know that the spring offensive another spring offensive might make her too too tired, to know where her home was. She went home and she told Mr. Reynolds, and he said don't worry, and so she said she would not. She did though want to know when Joseph Lane was born because he never talked about a spring offensive so perhaps he was not like Angel Harper born in the spring, she thought said Mrs. Reynolds that summer or winter offensives were pleasanter, they were warmer or colder well anyway they did not make you so tired but dear me said Mrs. Reynolds spring offensives dear me they were tired, too tired, and Mrs. Reynolds began to droop a little but she said and she meant what she said she said she would not worry.

Angel Harper was fifty-one would he ever be fifty-two, rainbows and Saint Odile tell the truth said Mrs. Reynolds and she went to bed not happy but pretty happy and Mr. Reynolds said he was glad she was.

The next day she saw running away well not exactly running but running across a lawn the captain's wife who was in love with the colonel and the colonel was in love with her. As Mrs. Reynolds saw her running across the lawn Mrs. Reynolds felt funny, Mrs. Reynolds did from time to time feel funny, in the distance she saw a man he was not in uniform but officers never are and she did not know at that distance whether it was the colonel or the captain but very likely if it was the captain his wife would not have run across the lawn so it must have been the colonel. Mrs. Reynolds met some one and told them and then she said you could tell by the way she was running how courageous she is, but said Mrs. Reynolds if she is courageous then she can easily not be which said Mrs. Reynolds is sure to happen she is sure not to be. And then the day began to cloud over and Mr. Reynolds said he thought it was going to rain and if it did it would not be too bad, not at all said Mr. Reynolds not at all bad. Mrs. Reynolds said she was getting tired she said she did not know whether it was worry or the weather or the kind of food they had or perhaps said Mrs. Reynolds what makes me tired is that after all Angel Harper might come to be fifty-two and not all through. Oh dear said Mrs. Reynolds I am young enough to know better not so young but young enough to know better and Angel Harper he is old enough never to know better, oh dear said Mrs. Reynolds, do you know said Mrs. Reynolds night and morning I am thinking good better best, and sometimes I say good better best so much that I do not get any rest. Better go easy said Mr. Reynolds what is good enough is never too good. And just then they heard a noise. All noises either get old or better said Mrs. Reynolds and she felt very anxious to say more but just then she could not think of anything to say. After all said Mrs. Reynolds although I seem to forget about it I do believe in Saint Odile. Better go to bed said Mr. Reynolds since you have nothing more to say better go to bed. I think I will said Mrs. Reynolds and she yawned a little I think I will go to bed said Mrs. Reynolds and she did. Mr. Reynolds waited a little he listened a little he put out the light a little and then he went to bed. Mrs. Reynolds was already asleep when Mr. Reynolds went to bed.

It was early in the morning when the moon was still shining, the moon can shine when the day is dawning and Mrs. Reynolds did not wake up and she did not wake up Mr. Reynolds but she might have but they were both tired and so they went on sleeping. Every day might be the day when Angel Harper was fifty-two and any day might be a day for Joseph Lane and any day might be the day that Saint Odile meant by what she said and Mrs. Reynolds and Mr. Reynolds went on sleeping although the moon was still shining quite brightly although the day was breaking.

Mr. and Mrs. Reynolds going on sleeping was discussed from time to time by quite a number of people, some thought that they would and some thought that perhaps they would but anyway they did.

It is said Mrs. Reynolds just as strange as that, there are funerals some people even live over a cemetery, and there are weddings and there are births and all the time well they do not wonder but they do not know no they do not know whether ever Angel Harper will have a fifty-second birthday or not and if not, well said Mrs. Reynolds if not there is no cause to sigh, there has been cause for him to die of course of course that said Mrs. Reynolds and she was looking back and as she looked back she saw such a very large bird's nest in a tree that it frightened her, and when she was frightened she did not sit she just stood and when she just stood it was very natural that she knew exactly what she did know. It is so said Mrs. Reynolds to Mr. Reynolds and that was a comfort to her it was a comfort to her that it was so. Mr. and Mrs. and Miss Bowen were comforts to her, Mrs. Bowen because although she did not look at all as if she could believe in Saint Odile did believe in her when Mrs. Reynolds believed in her and Mrs. Bowen always wanted to know exactly what it was that was to happen and Mrs. Reynolds always told her, and Mr. Bowen was a comfort to her because although he did not believe in Mrs. Bowen or Mrs. Reynolds or Saint Odile nevertheless he liked just as well as not not to know that it was not so because after all if it was so well then he would not know but nevertheless it would be so and Miss Bowen was never to be married her sister was married and went on having children but each one that came was a girl and that was something that made no difference to Miss Bowen but it might and anyway in that sense Saint Odile was different she really was different but Miss Bowen did manage to be indifferent she really did manage to be indifferent, so Mr. and Mrs. and Miss Bowen were really a comfort to Mrs. Reynolds and she often went in to visit them but she did not stay very long. Really Mrs. Reynolds did not stay anywhere very long, but she did stay long enough for it to be necessary, very necessary.

Can I said Mrs. Reynolds and she remembered Joseph Lane, she did not know if he was there but she did find herself saying can I and when she found herself saying can I she felt hopeful not really hopeful but not hopeless so from time to time she found herself saying can I, and when she did she felt that she was nearly home. By that time, she had forgotten the very large bird's nest she said that one of the nice things about springtime was that the birds were small and so she and Mr. Reynolds sat down to dinner and they were really pleased Mrs. Reynolds said that they knew best and Mr. Reynolds said that it was just as late at night, and as there was nothing else to do. Well said Mrs. Reynolds shall we go to bed, and Mr. Reynolds said why not and they did.

He is tired, who said, said Mrs. Reynolds that who was tired. He is tired, said a woman who was bow-legged and fat and accompanied by a thin husband who looked as if he had just escaped, he is tired she said, I know he is tired. Do you mean your husband said Mrs. Reynolds, no said the woman I mean Angel Harper, he is tired. Really tired said Mrs. Reynolds how do you know he is tired, because he is tired said the woman.

Well said Mrs. Reynolds if he is really tired then we can forget him, and they all said not yet and then they went away.

Anybody can go away said Mrs. Reynolds to Mr. Reynolds but we never go away, well said Mr. Reynolds, I said said Mrs. Reynolds that Angel Harper is tired, yes said Mr. Reynolds and if he is tired then those who go away will stay and those who stay will go away, I would like said Mrs. Reynolds to have a roast chicken roasted with lots of butter and I would like to see a city

said Mrs. Reynolds and Mr. Reynolds said let us go to bed and he
meant what he said and they went to bed.

It was like that said Mrs. Reynolds, it was not hardly every day
or every week or every month, it was said Mrs. Reynolds hardly
that. But said Mrs. Reynolds I think I think Joseph Lane might
mean not in between but he might mean, and just then Mrs.
Reynolds remembered that she did not mean not really mean in
between, Mrs. Reynolds said that in a kind of a way everybody
had forgotten to mean in between. As Mrs. Reynolds was looking
far away, she saw a lame woman who began to cry, she said she
did not cry because she had a sick husband or a hard life but she
began to cry because a woman who had chickens, not for sale
but to keep had been rough to her, Mrs. Reynolds said that she
did not understand anybody these days who had chickens who
had even one chicken would naturally be rough to any one.
Why not said Mrs. Reynolds and Mrs. Reynolds said she understood it very well and when she went home and told Mr. Reynolds about it she said she understood it very well and she asked
Mr. Reynolds if he did not think that she understood it very
well and he said he thought she did understand it very well.

Sometimes said Mrs. Reynolds a registered letter is upsetting,
but not said Mr. Reynolds if you are not upset, yes said Mrs.
Reynolds and she knew he was right, she said she knew he was
right, and she said she did know that he was right.

The next morning although they did not get up very early
they were both very busy, not tired but just very busy.

A dog can have rheumatism said Mrs. Reynolds which makes
me so very sorry for him. But dogs, well dogs, said Mrs. Reynolds and she knew she said she knew that they were lying down,
not easily said Mrs. Reynolds when they had rheumatism. And
so said Mrs. Reynolds women think they can do something when
men cannot do it, some women feel like that said Mrs. Reynolds
and then they act, well said Mrs. Reynolds and she smiled a little
and Mr. Reynolds looked quite peaceful well said Mrs. Reynolds that is what women can never do they cannot cook for the
day after tomorrow, they do not said Mrs. Reynolds they never
do like the day after tomorrow, anybody said Mrs. Reynolds

can understand that and then said Mrs. Reynolds I will be very careful.

It was a little later in the day and first there was a windstorm and then a very little rain and Mrs. Reynolds said it did not worry her at all, and indeed it did not worry her because she was not in a hurry. As she was not in a hurry she stopped to talk to Alexander Master, a man who was not a very old man but was not very likable. After they had said how do you do Mrs. Reynolds asked him what he thought about it, and he said he thought that it would rain tomorrow but probably not day after tomorrow. Do not said Mrs. Reynolds tell me about day after tomorrow tell me said Mrs. Reynolds what is going to happen now. Well said Alexander Master what is going to happen now is what is happening now. Oh said Mrs. Reynolds I do not mean that I mean everything, and she said you know everything, and Alexander Master sighed a little he said Mrs. Reynolds why not sigh. And Mrs. Reynolds said she did not care to sigh. Why not said Master why not, because said Mrs. Reynolds there is no way to begin to sigh without a sigh and oh dear said Mrs. Reynolds I know that you know that everybody just does know that, tell me Mr. Master said Mrs. Reynolds tell me what is going to happen. Just then an airplane flew over them, oh dear said Mrs. Reynolds and now you will be looking up and you will not tell me anything about what is going to happen, and she went away and felt that Alexander Master was very irritating and she went home and told Mr. Reynolds that Alexander Master was very irritating. Dear me said Mrs. Reynolds it is so tiresome not to know what is going to be happening, well anyway said Mrs. Reynolds perhaps Angel Harper is not going to have his fifty-second birthday or if he does perhaps he will not be a year older and if he is not then that will be the end of that. Perhaps said Mr. Reynolds and then they went to eat something. They liked to know what everybody was eating but all the same they Mr. and Mrs. Reynolds went in to their house and they ate something.

It was the month when if Angel Harper was going to be fifty-two the month had two full moons in it, the first day of the month was a full moon and the last day of the month was a full moon, and said Mrs. Reynolds I never knew that it is rare, that it happens very seldom said Mrs. Reynolds and I always thought there were thirteen full moons in every year and I looked up last year's calendar and it is not so, a month for the moon is not twenty-eight days, it is twenty-nine or it is thirty very often. Dear me said Mr. Reynolds is that so, yes said Mrs. Reynolds very excited it is so, it is most exciting but it is so and perhaps said Mrs. Reynolds Angel Harper will die between full moons and then he never will be fifty-two, don't said Mr. Reynolds don't get too excited, you had better stick to Saint Odile, else said Mr. Reynolds you will not go to sleep and then you will wake me to tell you so, all right, a full moon does not take twenty-eight days all right this month has two full moons in it, all right everything is going to happen all right, all right, but do not get excited or else you will not go to sleep right and sleep tight and Mr. Reynolds put out the light, and Mrs. Reynolds was so puzzled about the full moon not being twenty-eight days and there being two full moons in the month Angel Harper was to be fifty-two and wondering whether Joseph Lane knew about it and being pretty certain that he was not there to care and she was asleep and so was Mr. Reynolds both of them tightly asleep until the next day. The next day Mrs. Reynolds met a woman who was bow-legged and looked poor but not forsaken and her husband was in prison, well not in prison but a prisoner, and Mrs. Reynolds said to her, it is warm today and she said yes, some one had offered to send her brother money from another country and her brother said he did not need any, and this man's daughter was engaged to be married to a young doctor there in that country and the young doctor accidentally stuck himself with a needle and he died and the young girl who was only twenty-one was not married. It is a sad story said Mrs. Reynolds and then she went home. She was tired she had slept well but she was tired, two full moons in one month and the month in which Angel Harper was going to be fifty-two was tiring, Mrs. Reynolds knew it was tiring, it was not tiring to Mr. Reynolds but it was tiring to her and she went home to rest, and she did not and when Mr. Reynolds came home she was not tired any more and she told him and he said he was not tired and Mrs. Reynolds said she knew that he would not be tired and then they had their dinner and then they were tired and then they went to bed.

Mr. Miner says, said Mrs. Reynolds to Mr. Reynolds that there is a great difference between there was an army and there is an army and a great difference between there is an army and there was an army, and said Mrs. Reynolds when I heard him saying that it made me nervous. Mr. Reynolds did not say that when Mrs. Reynolds told him this that it made him nervous but Mrs. Reynolds knew from the movement of his upper lip that it did make him nervous.

Mrs. Reynolds said that what she was most anxious about was sugar, she said that she herself as was well known did not care very much to eat jam indeed there did not seem any time of the day when it was really for her a suitable moment to eat jam but she did not like there being an abundance of fruit and no sugar with which to make jam and besides Mr. Reynolds did eat a great deal of jam and as Mrs. Reynolds repeated it was her one anxiety, would there and there was certainly some question of it would there be any way of getting enough sugar to make as much jam as she wished to make. Dear me said Mrs. Reynolds I never did think there would come a time when everybody would know that nothing was easily obtained, nothing at all and just then Mrs. Reynolds heard a call and she went out and there in front of her door there were more and more, more soldiers and more soldiers and Mrs. Reynolds for a moment forgot just how old she was forgot just how old Mr. Reynolds was, forgot just how long she had taken everything for granted and then she said well I am glad to see them and she waved to them and they waved back, not all of them but some of them did wave back. Mrs. Reynolds said that she would have liked to have said oh dear me, but she knew that it was not the time to say oh dear me, there had been times when it was all right to say oh dear me and there would well perhaps there would come again a time when it would be all right to say oh dear me but not just now, so she put on her hat and took her umbrella and went out walking, she said she believed in walking, as a matter of fact she preferred standing to walking but she did say that she believed in walking.

It was almost dark and she wondered if it was going to rain, whether it did or whether it did not, it and she began to laugh a little whether it did or whether it did not it would not melt sugar. Rain said Mrs. Reynolds never did melt sugar and then she went home again and Mr. Reynolds came home and they had dinner and a little later not very much later they went to bed and they slept very well although Mrs. Reynolds did wake up earlier than was her habit. Mr. Reynolds did not.

After all said Mrs. Reynolds and as she said after all she sighed, she wondered she was sure that she knew but all the same she wondered would Angel Harper have his fifty-second birthday, no of course he would not but would he Mrs. Reynolds kept on sighing until she heard herself sigh and then she stopped sighing. She knew that she stopped sighing and little by little she was really awake and then it was morning and really time to get up and she and Mr. Reynolds did get up.

Dear me said Mrs. Reynolds every day, well said Mrs. Reynolds you might say every day brings it nearer to his birthday to the birthday of Angel Harper and said Mrs. Reynolds I wish said Mrs. Reynolds that my birthday did not come just ten days after. Not said Mrs. Reynolds that it makes any difference, any difference to what said Mrs. Reynolds any difference to him to me to any anything, but said Mrs. Reynolds it does make me hysterical, like it or not said Mrs. Reynolds it does make me hysterical, it would said Mrs. Reynolds make anybody hysterical to have Angel Harper have his birthday, his fifty-second birthday, oh dear oh dear said Mrs. Reynolds and she certainly meant what she said she meant oh oh dear. I know said Mrs. Reynolds that a couple who are not married have a baby and her name the baby's name is Mary Christine, I know it said Mrs. Reynolds and it has something to do with Angel Harper's birthday said Mrs. Reynolds I know it and, well said Mrs. Reynolds and she felt suddenly very calm, well said Mrs. Reynolds everything is going to happen now, and she sat down and began to read Saint Odile's prophecy and she said to Mr. Reynolds well that is that, and then they went in to lunch. It was Sunday and they were both at home and the sun was shining and the snow was melting, and said Mrs. Reynolds it might be rather horrible. And Mr. Reynolds said well not today and that was really all he had to say.

One day Mrs. Reynolds went to see a friend, it was just a few days now and Angel Harper would be fifty-two that is if he was not through before his birthday and Mrs. Reynolds knew well she did not know but she was quite sure and there was no reason why not or rather no reason why he should be through before the birthday that made him fifty-two. So she went to see a friend and they went into the vegetable garden and there under the raspberry bushes there ran a mouse a brown mouse and behind her three little grey mice. The friend sat and said what and Mrs. Reynolds called to the man who was working in the garden to come and catch them. He was an old man and all his sons and his sons-in-law except one who was a dentist were soldiers, and he had not been one and he came quickly and he caught two of the little mice and killed them by squeezing them between his thumb and forefinger and Mrs. Reynolds pointed out the third little mouse which he did not see and he caught that one and killed it in that way but he did not catch the brown mouse and then he went away and Mrs. Reynolds did not know how she felt about it. She did not think about it but she did not know how she felt about it. Then they went into the house and her friend killed some flies that were buzzing inside in the window and Mrs. Reynolds did not know how she felt about it. Then she walked slowly home and when she was home Mr. Reynolds was there already and they went in to dinner and Mrs. Reynolds said to Mr. Reynolds that she had heard a great many stories all day and that they were true but that she did not believe them and Mr. Reynolds said yes, and Mrs. Reynolds did not start to tell any stories, she said that anyway any day Angel Harper would have his fifty-second birthday and said Mrs. Reynolds I do not know whether I shall cry or whether I shall not cry. Well said Mr. Reynolds you are not crying now. No said Mrs. Reynolds no she was not crying now, she knew she said she knew that it was too late to sigh but she did not know whether she would

200

or whether she would not cry. Anyway said Mrs. Reynolds there are still three days to stay and any day although Saint Odile and she looked a little ashamed and a little sure anyway said Mrs. Reynolds not today. It is said Mrs. Reynolds a very nice day today neither too hot nor too cold and tonight said Mrs. Reynolds it is a very nice night, it is not too hot and it is not too cold. In which case said Mr. Reynolds we might as well go to bed, and they did, just as he said.

Some one said that one of the neighbors had been run over, Mrs. Reynolds went to see, the three daughters were fooling with their brother and another and they were locking each other up in the cellar. And said Mrs. Reynolds how is your father. He has to stay in bed for ten days and not go out for three weeks said the oldest daughter whose name was Nelly and she used to be very pretty but now she was not so pretty but all the same she seemed quite pretty. Mrs. Reynolds went home, today Angel Harper had his birthday and he was fifty-two and so said Mrs. Reynolds what difference does it make to them and indeed it was true it did not make any difference to them because they were just like any one and it did not make any difference to them. Angel Harper was fifty-two and it might be well it might be that he would remember that when he was fourteen some one walking along was eating candy and perhaps Angel Harper could not remember but perhaps she offered him some and if she did did he accept a piece or did he not, did he eat a piece or did he not. He did not know whether he did or whether he did not, and not knowing not being able to think if it was true he was not able to know what he would do. When he said and he felt funny, now he said and he felt funny, he knew that now made him feel as funny as he felt then about the candy and he knew that now he did not know what he would do just as he did not know what he had done then. Now he was fifty-two, it was his birthday that he knew. He had to know that because a birthday is a celebration, whether it or he is celebrated or not. And so and he began to know there was no not, knot, he said, there was or there was not not. Dear me he said and he felt as if he might fall down in a fit. But he said if I am fit. But and that is what a birthday of fifty-two can do he was not to know if he was or if he was not.

Dear me said Mrs. Reynolds I wish I knew said Mrs. Reynolds I wish I knew that after all it is Joseph Lane, I wish I knew and ordinarily she walked very slowly but this time she almost ran. Dear me said Mrs. Reynolds and she was out of breath and she sat down. She wished Mr. Reynolds was home but he was not so she just sat. It was the day that Angel Harper was fifty-two so Mrs. Reynolds just sat.

PART X

I thought said Mrs. Reynolds that I would be very depressed, why said Mr. Reynolds because said Mrs. Reynolds Angel Harper has had his fifty-second birthday but not at all said Mrs. Reynolds I am not at all depressed, I am feeling very peaceful, and calm, and content, and not at all depressed, I am very surprised said Mrs. Reynolds but I am not feeling not at all feeling depressed. Well said Mr. Reynolds, yes I know said Mrs. Reynolds but if he has had this birthday well he can never have this birthday again and if he can never have this birthday again, then can he have any birthday, and Mrs. Reynolds gave a happy sigh and she said she had just met a man quite a young man who said this country around here did not produce very much, you worked very hard and you produced very little, not said Mrs. Reynolds that I really thought he did work very hard. Oh dear said Mrs. Reynolds if everybody had as much meat and potatoes and butter as they asked for, would they said Mrs. Reynolds worry if it stopped. And just then she heard something go by, and so she said perhaps they had better go to bed, and they did.

Why should they said Mrs. Reynolds why indeed should they when after all everybody wants what they have. Mrs. Reynolds thought about this she did not talk about this because it might frighten her, she did not talk about it even to Mr. Reynolds but she did know that it was true they did all want what they have and when they have it they want it and when it is not what they have they want it. Want is a funny word said Mrs. Reynolds and she meant what she said want is a funny word, it means to want that is to be going to have or to be going to be without and either way said Mrs. Reynolds and now she did begin to talk either way you do see people again even if it is not so very likely and when you do you do say oh Therese and then the servant you have now knows that the oh Therese is an old servant who has married and has two children and most unexpectedly comes to say how do you do and is it not very pleasant weather.

Some people are difficult to satisfy about weather said Mrs. Reynolds and I said Mrs. Reynolds find it very difficult to remember whether Angel Harper has just had his fifty-second birthday or his fifty-third birthday, I find it very difficult said Mrs. Reynolds to remember and said Mrs. Reynolds if I am mistaken it means either that he is a year older or a year younger or that the time has not passed altogether. If the time does not pass, dear me said Mrs. Reynolds it is just as well not to know about January and winter and February and summer and April and altogether.

I know said Mrs. Reynolds I do feel like that and she went out to meet all her friends and they were all together and they all said sit down and she sat down.

It is not confusing to be mistaken said Mrs. Reynolds, it is not difficult to find it difficult said Mrs. Reynolds and here we all are and every day we find it difficult and every day we are mistaken and we all sit down. They all laughed naturally they all laughed although they did not feel like laughing. Naturally not said Mrs. Reynolds when Angel Harper is fifty-two and in spite of everything bye and bye he will be fifty-three. Bye and bye said Mrs. Harnese, well said Mrs. Reynolds and if I am mistaken. They were all very polite, they said she was not mistaken but Mrs. Reynolds knew better she knew she was mistaken and as she knew she was mistaken she decided to leave them and to go home which she did.

There is plenty of allowance made for those who do not change their mind and plenty of allowance made for those who do not change their mind, Mrs. Reynolds was saying this as she was walking home and then she met a stranger, she was startled, she thought he was walking behind her, perhaps he was, she thought he was following her and perhaps he was but at any rate she said that although she was startled she was not frightened and that after all everything could be agreeable as well as disagree-able and so she was not going to think about it, so she began to walk slowly and he was a quiet young man and he said to her are you Mrs. Reynolds and she said yes but I would rather you would speak to Mr. Reynolds and the young man said it is my duty to speak to Mrs. Reynolds and I always do my duty. In which case said Mrs. Reynolds I will leave you and she did and then it was all over and she did not know what to do but as she was at home she felt at home and she thought she would wait until Mr. Reynolds came home which she did. It was almost dark by that time but she felt quite calm and she knew that she must not get agitated and so she did not. When Mr. Reynolds came home she told him all that had happened and he said dinner first and then to bed, and so they did, they had dinner first and then a little while after they went to bed.

The next day Mr. Reynolds' younger brother William came to see them, they had not met for a very long time, and William's wife Hope did not come because she was going to have a baby. I am wondering said Mrs. Reynolds to Mr. Reynolds after Wil-liam was gone and Mr. Reynolds said well perhaps William was full of information, he told about how Angel Harper had such a funny feeling about Joseph Lane that he was all black and blue from the way he pinched himself to make himself say his name when he had to mention him. William was full of information, he naturally did not listen when Mrs. Reynolds tried to remind him of Saint Odile and what she had to say, William had enough information about everything and after he left, Mrs. Reyn-olds said I wonder if he is coming again and Mr. Reynolds said well yes perhaps and William had stayed for dinner and now it was quite late in the evening and they closed up the house and went to bed and Mrs. Reynolds dreamed about two very large

205

slices of ham upon a silver salver, and there was nothing else to the dream and Mr. Reynolds slept very long and the next day the sun was shining.

The next day Mrs. Reynolds met a man he said his name was William Williams and he was a friend of William Reynolds, he said he was looking for a widow who lived somewhere near and whose name was Andrew and she was living with a family named Rogers and and this he said was the most exciting part of the story nobody knew anything about her and nobody had ever heard of her and yet he had a letter to her from her cousin who was in hospital and whose brother-in-law was a tailor. Mrs. Reynolds wanted very much to know why he wanted to find this widow but he did not tell and she did not find any way to ask him. All she could say to him was and does it make a difference to you if you do not find her and he answered that there is no difference one way or the other and even if there is a difference even if it makes a difference it is not really different. Oh dear said Mrs. Reynolds it all makes me think of Angel Harper getting older and William Williams answered, I refuse to think of Angel Harper, I think of Joseph Lane. Oh do you said Mrs. Reynolds and she added, do you know I wish I could be disagreeable but I am not able to be. Just at that moment William Williams walked away and so Mrs. Reynolds could not introduce him to Mr. Reynolds who was coming that way. Later on they talked about it together but even if William Williams did have an overcoat over his arm and he did it would not make it all seem more natural. Not at all. It is very disagreeable that nothing is natural said Mrs. Reynolds and she began to cry and Mr. Reynolds comforted her and said that he was natural, and she laughed, and said he certainly was and she said she would go on forgetting about what everybody was saying and they went home to dinner and then they listened to some music and then they went to bed and they hoped that the weather would be warmer. Every day it was just a little bit.

It is no doubt not useless said Mrs. Reynolds not to have it happen, and she wondered why Mrs. Andrews who used always to be out in her garden was never out in her garden. She used

to be so energetic not alone about her gardening but about Angel
Harper and that had been for Mrs. Reynolds a great pleasure
and now she was never out in her garden, to be sure she had
married again, a prisoner of war had run away and had come to
see her and to everybody's astonishment she had married him
but even so that did not seem to be any reason why she should
not be out in her garden, and everybody said that there was
nothing the matter with her that she was quite all right and as
gay as ever and really as much occupied with the life and well
perhaps the death of Angel Harper as ever but she was never
out in her garden and Mrs. Reynolds never saw her. And if
Mrs. Reynolds never saw her they could not talk together and
if they could not talk together they could naturally not know
how each other felt about Angel Harper having had his fifty-
second birthday and so little by little Mrs. Reynolds prepared
to ask somebody else and she did and every day she and somebody said what they had to say. Nobody said Mrs. Reynolds
ever gets tired of saying what they have to say. You might think
they do said Mrs. Reynolds and sometimes they almost do said
Mrs. Reynolds but really not said Mrs. Reynolds nobody really
gets tired of saying what they do say.

It was dark in the evening but somehow it was not frightening and Mrs. Reynolds knew very well that every day the dark
came later and then later on every day the dark came earlier and
she also knew that it was very important so that she could do
all she had to do, and she said to herself really and truly I have
not very much to do and she meant what she said although really
and truly she always had to say a good deal every day and if
she did not say it all every day perhaps and it was true perhaps
it would not be true that Angel Harper was fifty-two.

Angel Harper knew that when he was fourteen he first knew
that there was an enormous moon a cold moon that came up not
too soon but not at noon but at night, and it was an enormous
moon and a cold moon although spring had come, and the moon
was called a red moon a rough moon a Russian moon and Angel
Harper knew that when he had been fourteen he had first seen
this moon to know it as such a moon and now Angel Harper

was fifty-two and spring was come and it was true, the big moon the enormous moon the cold moon the red moon the rough moon the Russian moon was a moon, Angel Harper hoped it might be noon, but was it noon, no said Angel Harper and he hoped it was yesterday but no it was not yesterday it was today, and Angel Harper could not go away.

Mrs. Reynolds was feeling funny, she said she still felt that Saint Odile was all for her money, well of course said Mrs. Reynolds I know money has nothing to do with it even if a man I met who had four children who had been taken away from him and he offered to get them back again did offer to sell me money that was two hundred years old that he said that he had found while he was working. But did he said Mrs. Reynolds and Mr. Reynolds said more likely he has not got it, and Mrs. Reynolds said that she had never thought of that. And indeed she had not. The man wanted to come to see her but she had said no she would go to see him. Well said Mr. Reynolds and Mrs. Reynolds said of course not, she would not. But said Mrs. Reynolds Saint Odile said it would happen not about the money but about Angel Harper feeling funny. To be sure said Mrs. Reynolds she never said anything about Joseph Lane except that Angel Harper would find that he was a mountain and a mountain at last a mountain would stop him. I know too said Mrs. Reynolds and then she said to Mr. Reynolds let us not stay at home, no do not let us stay at home let us go out, she got quite excited. I know she said that a stout man is going to come and bring us a rabbit and said Mrs. Reynolds I do not like rabbit, and so she said to Mr. Reynolds let us go out, and they did and they took their dinner out and they only came home in time to go to bed, and Mrs. Reynolds said she was sure the rabbit had not come but when she came in there it was the rabbit it was in a basket, it was a grey rabbit and as they that is Mr. and Mrs. Reynolds had not gone to bed yet they had to dispose of it, in some way and they did, they put straw down and they put the basket with the rabbit in it on the straw, and Mrs. Reynolds sighed a little and then they went to bed but she did say just before they went to bed that she did not care for rabbit.

208

One day well said Mrs. Reynolds any day can be one day, and just now said Mrs. Reynolds it is easy to see that if she is bow-legged and very dirty and has run away from her husband and keeps goats and her husband from time to time is three months in prison for stealing wood and water and apples, well said Mrs. Reynolds it is easy to see that she was born in a very nice house and was a colonel's daughter. Oh dear said Mrs. Reynolds every day there is a new way to be satisfied. What said Mrs. Reynolds can satisfy Angel Harper, and she said if at first you don't succeed try try again, but said Mrs. Reynolds he does succeed at first, and that is all the trouble with him and so, and just then Mrs. Reynolds felt as if some one had called out in a loud and heavy tone, Joseph Lane Joseph Lane and she felt she knew she felt as if this was a revelation and she went home and told Mr. Reynolds and he told her that she had much better stick to Saint Odile. Not said Mrs. Reynolds that I have forgotten her, not at all, I know said Mrs. Reynolds that it will have to come out that way, the way Saint Odile says it will but said Mrs. Reynolds there is no use in not pleasing oneself if it is just once in a while. Indeed said Mrs. Reynolds I met Henry Harrison today and he said that whether we knew it or not it was all going to happen. What said Mr. Reynolds well said Mrs. Reynolds what he meant was that whatever happened later on you had to wonder if it was not what was not expected, and then he went on to say, that any day either one or the other would not know what to do next. Who did he mean said Mr. Reynolds. Well said Mrs. Reynolds he could not have meant Saint Odile so he must have meant Angel Harper and said Mrs. Reynolds and she gave a sigh, may be he is right and may be he is, and if he is, oh not now said Mrs. Reynolds and she was quite excited not now because Saint Odile said not now, and then she smiled very happily and kissed Mr. Reynolds good night and she said she really was very happy because after all Saint Odile was right. After all said Mrs. Reynolds every day it is useless to worry, so said Mrs. Reynolds now when I meet any one I ask them if they like what they bought when they were out shopping and they all say there is nothing to buy and it all costs so much money, today I saw Henrietta

Dudley and her basket was so heavy she could hardly carry it into the house, but and she was quite right she said there was nothing to buy and it all costs so much money, and said Mrs. Reynolds they are right and said Mr. Reynolds it is time to go to bed and it was and they did go to bed.

While they were in bed, Angel Harper made up his mind and as he made up his mind he remembered that when he was sixteen years old he had for the first time had a heavily decorated belt and that he had worn it but he had not wanted any one to see it and as he had not wanted any one to see it he covered it over but nevertheless he was always uneasy lest any one did see it and would ask him about it, nobody did, and now when he had made up his mind he remembered about that belt, and he felt to see if he still had it, of course he did not have it now, now that he was fifty-two years old of course he did not have it, but and that was what made him feel for it, if he had had it would he have made up his mind.

Just then Mrs. Reynolds turned over in her sleep and said she wondered how long something was and the next morning she could not remember whether it was that she had dreamed and but she did know that it was a beautiful day and that she liked beautiful days. Sometimes said Mrs. Reynolds Sundays are beautiful days but not always said Mrs. Reynolds and then she went to sleep again and by the time she woke up again it was still beautiful weather and she and Mr. Reynolds decided to enjoy it. It is said Mrs. Reynolds not easy just now to enjoy it but we might as well said Mrs. Reynolds and they did, they did thoroughly enjoy it, and by evening they were very tired and they had dinner and then they went to bed.

By the time it was really necessary Mrs. Reynolds knew that she had not been that she was not mistaken. She had not hoped that her friend's granddaughter should be a princess after two first unfortunate marriages, that is to say the first was unfortunate the second was dead before he was married and now she was a princess well well said Mrs. Reynolds and I know they all like it. Any doctor said Mrs. Reynolds would like to have his daughter be a princess and any woman would like her granddaughter to be a princess and there it was she was a princess and not even far away, that was the remarkable part of it that she was not even far away. It is easy said Mrs. Reynolds to accept what you have and it is easy said Mrs. Reynolds to be kind to some one who has not been very obliging but above all said Mrs. Reynolds it is very convenient to like what you have. And said Mrs. Reynolds it is very inconvenient to know that Angel Harper is going to be fifty-three and Mrs. Reynolds began to cry not that she was nervous but she really had thought that Angel Harper never would be fifty-three and if he were to be fifty-three would he go. Mrs. Reynolds stopped to speak to Edmund and she asked him what he thought. I said Edmund am only thinking about rabbits. I wonder said Edmund why rabbits die. Well said Mrs. Reynolds I understand that if you are really worried about why rabbits die, I cannot ask you to try to think about whether Angel Harper will be fifty-three, but said Mrs. Reynolds if you should find out why rabbits die then perhaps you can commence to think about whether Angel Harper has to be fifty-three and if it is so, how do you know. Well Edmund began to laugh, he was quite blonde and his face was red and his eyes were prominent and he was very easily disappointed and he was very easily patient and he did quite like Mrs. Reynolds so he told her he thought by Saturday, he would know why rabbits die and then he would tell her about the birthdays of Angel Harper, and she said she would tell him about Saint Odile and that they neither would have to tell about Joseph Lane and Edmund laughed again and said it might just as well be pleasant and Mrs. Reynolds went home very cheered, and after dinner she told Mr. Reynolds just what Edmund had said and then they went to bed.

In the meanwhile said Mrs. Reynolds, and she said that she meant in the meanwhile because in the meanwhile, well everything that happens or does not happen happens then. And said Mrs. Reynolds she met a man who had given up all hope, and so said Mrs. Reynolds in the meanwhile having given up all hope he had no hope, and so he said he would go too, as he had no hope he just would go too, and if he were dead well anyway that would be one less who had no hope, so said Mrs. Reynolds in the meanwhile summer has come, and in the summer there is no rain and no snow. So Mrs. Reynolds went out every day and when she went out every day she met a man and she asked him what his name was, she said she easily forgot names and that is the reason she always asked every one what their name was, you see said Mrs. Reynolds in the meantime I know that you have a name, and said the man is that any pleasure and Mrs. Reynolds said yes it was a pleasure. She said she understood very well how for a great many people what was a pleasure was not a pleasure, she understood that very well, she could not say that she understood it too well but nevertheless there it was and said she as she was going away in the meantime I will really try to remember your name and tell Mr. Reynolds your name and that I know will be for him a pleasure.

And so she went home and she did remember the man's name and she told the name to Mr. Reynolds and she was right it did give him a certain amount of pleasure to know that Mrs. Reynolds had met him.

So it was not dark very early and little dogs that had bells on them made a pleasant tinkling and there was this that was the matter with every one that the more they waited for any day to pass the more every day did pass and the more every day was there and Mrs. Reynolds said to Mr. Reynolds that she herself did not intend to go on waiting for every day to pass because after all little as it was for all of them to wait she herself had really decided from now on not to wait for every day to pass. I am not said Mrs. Reynolds interested in Angel Harper I know that he is fifty-two but said Mrs. Reynolds I do not find it interesting not as interesting, no said Mrs. Reynolds not as interesting that he is fifty-two, although said Mrs. Reynolds I am sure I will find it well it will be exciting when he is fifty-three said Mrs. Reynolds and Mr. Reynolds said anyway even if it was not dark enough it was late enough to go to bed and so they did they did go to bed, and a bird was singing but they did go to bed, it did not feel like midnight but it might have been and so they did go to bed.

212

The next day although it was summer it was raining and it was Sunday and Mrs. Reynolds said she did not feel like talking nor like walking nor like standing, she said she did not feel like sitting, well then what said Mr. Reynolds I might said Mrs. Reynolds kneel in the garden and she did and she thought about what she felt was going to happen. Just then four people passed they were all dirty and they were all forlorn and they were all crowding up against each other and by that time Mrs. Reynolds had gotten up and went out to talk to them, she asked them where they came from and they all four said that they did not come from the same place so what was the use of talking about it. It was decided said one of them that we would walk together and so we will go on and they said good-bye to Mrs. Reynolds and they went on. Mrs. Reynolds as she looked after them began to wonder if it had been more interesting before than it was now and she began to wonder if she was later up on Sunday than on any other day, and she hoped that they would not be disappointed and she was very careful to shut the gate and she went in and she sat down and she took to reading a book which did not very often happen, she was usually far too occupied to read a book but she did read a book today although she very soon was thinking of Saint Odile and could she have been mistaken, and she knew that of course not Saint Odile could not have been mistaken.

Mrs. Reynolds said to Philip Leroy who was passing, it is very hard to believe that winter has changed into summer, it is much easier to believe that summer has changed into winter. Philip Leroy was a man who had been poor, he was one of four brothers and four sisters, and he had managed so that they did not become rich but in a way they had become important and he had become important and his brothers and his sisters had gotten tired of him, and he was always talking and everybody had to listen, that is to say they had to stay while he was talking and nobody no not anybody ever did compare him to Angel Harper, not he himself or any one else compared him to Angel Harper. How old is Angel Harper Mrs. Reynolds asked him and he said that Angel Harper was fifty-two, he himself Philip Leroy was forty-two, but there was nothing to make any one compare Angel Harper and Philip Leroy, nothing at all.

Little by little there was less of every day and Mrs. Reynolds said it was not discouraging. She said and she felt that they might laugh at her but all the same she did say that Saint Odile had had to say that there would be less of every day.

And so there would tomorrow, it was very warm but, and that was more than certain the cold would come and when it came well when it came then Angel Harper after that would be fifty-three and then everybody would be free. Oh yes oh no said Mrs. Reynolds and she did say that she would be able to say I told you so. Not at night, at night, said Mrs. Reynolds well of course it was all right, but all the same, at night she just could not remember his name, whose name said Mr. Reynolds, and Mrs. Reynolds said well if she could remember his name she would not have had to say that she could not remember his name, and anyway she said nobody says that his name is Joseph Lane and if it is Mrs. Reynolds said if it was she could remember that she never did forget. Forget what said Mr. Reynolds who was quite sleepy yet, and Mrs. Reynolds said well anyway she did not forget Saint Odile and Mr. Reynolds said then they really had better go to bed and they did.

It was nearly right of them to know as much as they did, Mrs. Reynolds said that it was really very right of them to know as much as they did and Mr. Reynolds laughed, and he said good night and he hoped they would sleep well and they did.

I am said Mrs. Reynolds getting more certain that Saint Odile will win, I have always been certain said Mrs. Reynolds but now I am more certain that Saint Odile will win, I think said Mrs. Reynolds I think about menus about what we will have to eat and all the time, well said Mrs. Reynolds I am always more excited because I am getting now said Mrs. Reynolds I am getting now to be perfectly certain that Saint Odile is right right really right and said Mrs. Reynolds and she was talking to Miss Harper who had stopped in passing, what said Mrs. Reynolds did you have for dinner last Sunday, I find it very difficult to vary my menus and so I ask everybody in passing what they had for dinner last Sunday. Miss Harper who was going to visit a friend who had a sick cow, well cows, are very important said Mrs. Reynolds milk is very important said Mrs. Reynolds and so is cheese, and said Mrs. Reynolds will you ask your friends what they had for dinner last Sunday and tell me when you come by. No said Miss Harper, no I do not think I will, it is all right said Miss Harper when you ask people what they had for dinner last Sunday but if I asked well said Miss Harper it just would not do. Yes said Mrs. Reynolds with a sigh and then she smiled pleasantly yes she said I do quite see that.

Angel Harper was well into fifty-two and the air was growing colder and he did not know whether or not he was growing older. He remembered when he had been thirteen that he had seen an airplane and when he had seen an airplane he wondered if he was about to shiver and there had been other children there much younger and their mothers were very busy just then and the airplane had gone away and now that Angel Harper was fifty-two and the air was growing colder he remembered that but he could not remember whether he did or whether he did not shiver, he just could not remember that. Little by little he was always fifty-two and little by little he would not be fifty-two and now if the air was growing to be colder and if he was going to be older would he or would he not shiver. He never said no, he never said no and no and he never said go, and he never sat and he never no never heard a rat and at last nearly at last as not he knew that it was just as well to go to bed early as late.

When Mrs. Reynolds heard about that she said to Mr. Reynolds let us go to bed early and they did.

It was necessary for Angel Harper to remember that when he had been fourteen he still had a grandmother and when he remembered that he said he did not remember and he was right he did not remember that.

When Angel Harper was fifty-two somebody who asked him if he was through did not have any answer and when he did not have any answer he did not ask again and when he did not ask again he thought that he was almost overwhelming and when he thought he was almost overwhelming, Angel Harper did not go away, he said to himself he might have but that he had decided to stay and he did he did decide to stay.

Long and at once they came to go away and Angel Harper said not and yet nobody spoke about him. Mrs. Reynolds said to Mr. Reynolds it is all the same but nobody says any more about him, about which one said Mr. Reynolds about John's father, no said Mrs. Reynolds about Angel Harper and Mrs. Reynolds was right, she said that it was true and it was true they were beginning not to forget about him but they were beginning not to mention him and that made Angel Harper and in a way he could remember any day just then that maybe it was true it could make Angel Harper just then feel like any one, which said Mrs. Reynolds was not a mistake but might be if it was true make him be mistaken for any one. Which said Mrs. Reynolds could not be a pleasure, to whom said Mr. Reynolds well why anyway said Mrs. Reynolds it does not make any difference if they do forget him, no said Mr. Reynolds only it does, and Mrs. Reynolds knew that he was right because of course it did, it did make a difference if not any one was remembering to mention Angel Harper. Mrs. Reynolds laughed she said you do tease me about John's father but I never saw him and she meant that when she began talking how could Mr. Reynolds know who it was and it might be John's father and which John said Mrs. Reynolds it is funny but I never did know a John and Mr. Reynolds said well all the same it is a common name and he was right all the same it is a common name and all the same any John can have a father so there it was no one just then was mentioning Angel Harper.

It was different about Joseph Lane, nobody was mentioning Joseph Lane but that was different of course it was different and any one knew it was different and Mrs. Reynolds did not say anything it was so evident that it was not interesting so she did not talk about it, instead she talked about a poor young man whose father worked in a post-office and he had been very much thought of the poor young man and he was now thirty-two and it was very nice but he was a poor young man and everything was all right and it was just as well, of course said Mrs. Reynolds and of course it was not just as well but it was all right and she felt very comfortable and tomorrow was another day and Mr. Reynolds said well if tomorrow was another day they might just as well go to bed and they did.

Not said Mrs. Reynolds I do not mean in between. And said Mrs. Reynolds and she knew that when it was all through that is to say finished it would be so very difficult to interest anybody in what Saint Odile had had to say, it would all seem so very far away and so Mrs. Reynolds felt that every day she would have to say well not really say because if you say what you have to say then some one has to hear you say what you have to say and as every one would then be far away that is that they would not be far away but they would be far away from what Mrs. Reynolds had to say about what Saint Odile had had to say and so well just then anyway it had not all yet finished as Saint Odile had said it would but then that was natural enough because it was not yet finished at all indeed as Saint Odile had said it was not yet to be finished and so one at a time that is once at a time that is every once in a while once Mrs. Reynolds had to say and she brought out not as if they would hear what she had to say about what Saint Odile had had to say but as if Mrs. Reynolds did not want not to have to say what she had to say about what Saint Odile had had to say. There said Mrs. Reynolds and now I am going anywhere, and when she went anywhere sometimes she met more women than she met men and sometimes she met many more men than she met women and Mrs. Reynolds said he was a pretty little soldier he was carrying two bottles for his friends to drink and there they were his friends were only they were not in sight and there he was very tired but holding the bottles very tight, and he was said Mrs. Reynolds such a pretty little soldier and I said how do you do to him but a soldier must never answer how do you do because if he does he is not a soldier, and said Mrs. Reynolds he was such a pretty little soldier, and she was right, he was a pretty little soldier.

When Mrs. Reynolds went home she knew that it was not yet late at night and she said it was not going to storm and she was right there was no storm and when Mr. Reynolds came home and they had their dinner she said either the summer had just commenced or the summer was almost over, anyway she said and she said she had to be very careful about the light, well anyway at night and Mr. Reynolds said do not bother and she said all right she would not bother and it was getting later and it was time to go to bed and so their light would be out and it was true their light was out and they were in bed and nothing disturbed them and they slept all night.

If said Mrs. Reynolds a winter is long how long is it.

Well said Mrs. Reynolds I met a man and he told me about how long a winter is, because you have to know how long a winter is because of bees, you have to leave them enough to eat of honey for every day of winter so said Mrs. Reynolds the man said the winter so he thought was to be sixty days but not at all the winter was seventy-five days and so all the bees were dead, he was a nice-looking man said Mrs. Reynolds he was on a bicycle and he was walking up hill and he had just bought a new hive for his bees, and said Mrs. Reynolds I have never seen him before although he told me where he lived. So said Mrs. Reynolds and indeed said Mrs. Reynolds the winter is as long as that or if the winter is over the winter was as long as that, oh dear said Mrs. Reynolds there is no use forgetting that Angel Harper is still only fifty-two only fifty-two said Mrs. Reynolds and when she said fifty-two she said that she had been noticing that although anybody would know if you asked them all the same in a kind of way everybody was beginning to forget. It is funny said Mrs. Reynolds very funny that what is not forgotten there is still some time in which to forget. Are you said Mrs. Reynolds to Mr. Reynolds are you ready yet and he was and they had dinner and in a kind of way it was winter and in a kind of way it was time to go to bed although Mrs. Reynolds said if they went to bed too early they would wake up too early, and anyway, well said Mrs. Reynolds and Mr. Reynolds said he felt very well and they both did so they went to bed early and slept very well although they did wake up a little too early. Because said Mrs. Reynolds if you wake up too early the day is too long, too long for what said Mr. Reynolds, and Mrs. Reynolds said that

218

it was perfectly true if a day was too long it was too long and that was all there was to that.

That day Mrs. Reynolds met some one who was up very much earlier he looked like a very young man but he was not as young as he looked and when he was up so very early it was to see how it looked so very early and then it was a habit and he was always up so very early. This said Mrs. Reynolds had nothing to do with that, and Mrs. Reynolds explained to Mr. Reynolds that when she had said with that, she of course meant Angel Harper. Oh dear eight is plenty early enough to have enough of Angel Harper being fifty-two but, and Mrs. Reynolds was firm he might become fifty-three but he will never become fifty-eight, and Mrs. Reynolds meant what she said and she was not too late.

Angel Harper was going to be fifty-three and he remembered that when he was sixteen he was sitting and beside him was an alcohol lamp and he wanted to light it but he had no alcohol with which to fill it and around him were sitting several very little girls and when he sat he was sitting, this was all when he had been sixteen and an older man a large man with his hands hanging down in front of him and a little low yellow dog following behind him came past him and Angel Harper knew he was a doctor and that he performed operations and that when he wanted to light an alcohol lamp there was alcohol in the lamp and it would burn and Angel Harper when he was fifty-three remembered that this had happened when he was sixteen and it had been in the afternoon not very late and a quite pleasant evening and later on the rain had come and later on the sun had come again and later on he went away home and his mother and his grandmother were there and he went to bed and he was sixteen and now he was fifty-three and it was Wednesday morning.

Oh dear said Mrs. Reynolds but Saint Odile said we will not have to wait long and she and Mr. Reynolds went to bed as was their habit every evening.

PART XI

Mrs. Reynolds met a very nice woman very nicely dressed and she was carrying a very pretty bunch of flowers. Mrs. Reynolds said how do you do to her she often said how do you do and she said what a very pretty bunch of flowers. Yes it is a very pretty bouquet, was the answer and then they talked a little about the weather and then Mrs. Reynolds said and it is a very very pretty bunch of flowers, yes was the answer I walked out into the country to see some friends and I did hope to find there some eggs or perhaps a chicken and they were very kind and they gave me these very pretty flowers. Well said Mrs. Reynolds and then they said good-bye and when Mrs. Reynolds told the story to Mr. Reynolds she said and you see it is kind of sad she did want eggs or perhaps a chicken and they were very kind they gave her a very pretty bunch of flowers and said Mrs. Reynolds there is no doubt about it it must be all over soon it just must be all over soon, now Angel Harper is fifty-three and Saint Odile said it would be all over soon and anybody can see that it must be all over soon. Mr. Reynolds said something funny happened to him, he was standing in the garden and he thought he heard Mrs. Reynolds talking and she was not there, and where was she well she was somewhere, and anyway he not only heard her talking but he heard somebody answering and it was about a bunch of very pretty flowers and about flowers not being either eggs or chickens and Mrs. Reynolds said perhaps there was an echo and Mr. Reynolds said yes perhaps but he had never noticed it before and Mrs. Reynolds said that was perhaps because he was not standing just in the same place and Mr. Reynolds said perhaps.

Mr. Reynolds said they must not get uneasy because it might be all over soon, as well as not, and perhaps there was no not. Mrs. Reynolds said it was a pleasure and anyway perhaps Angel Harper was not well he was fifty-three, there was no doubt about that but all the same perhaps he was as well as not. It has got to come said Mrs. Reynolds and she took off her hat and they sat down and Mrs. Reynolds said that even when she was thirty she did not like water, she liked her water hot, she did not like cold water, and she said if it was not all over soon perhaps there would not be any hot water and that she would not like and Mr. Reynolds said well anyway the water is hot tonight and it was and they went to bed all right.

When Angel Harper was fifty-three, he remembered that when he had been nine he asked the others to build him a little room that would be like a prison and in that he sat and he knew that it was true, that he was too old to cry and too young to feel excited and so he would rather be there even if he did care he would rather be there. And when he was fifty-three he remembered that when he was fifteen he asked them to make a very small inclosure of stone and in that in a chair he sat alone and sometimes he let another boy sit in there with him and near him he let a little girl make a little park with flowers and when he was fifty-three he remembered all that. He might not have remembered all that, because when he was fifty-three there was not much to remember at, because he often felt very different from any day to any day. What shall I do he said if I am or if I am not a Jew, what shall I do he said, he was fifty-three and he was not lonesome and he was not subdued, he was very rude, not rude to himself because although he was afraid he went away to go ahead and he never never went to bed. So one at a time there was no time.

Good night said Mrs. Reynolds to Mr. Reynolds when they went to bed, let us sleep well said Mrs. Reynolds to Mr. Reynolds and they did.

It came about slowly that it was morning, Mrs. Reynolds said it was often like that and if it was often like that she did wonder if dogs found anything to be astonishing. Very likely said Mr. Reynolds and he said he would be working late and might not be at home very early. Just then Mrs. Reynolds felt nervous and said so. She said she knew that every day would be something and if it was she was full of hope. It is easy said Mrs. Reynolds to be full of hope when you are sure that there is reason for being hopeful. Mrs. Reynolds said she felt very complicated this morning and so she would calm herself by reading the predictions of Saint Odile. Mr. Reynolds smiled pleasantly and went away which was his daily habit.

Mrs. Reynolds knew exactly what to do, she went out and when she went out she looked to left and to right and she thought she heard somebody say something. Naturally enough she heard them say oh dear, there were so many who said oh dear just then. Mrs. Reynolds went on a little farther and she met three women and a boy who said he was an orphan. But said every one is he, and the boy said what is an orphan. They explained it to him they said an orphan is a boy whose father is dead and whose mother is dead, then said the boy I am not an orphan because my mother is living and my father has gone away but all the same said the boy I am an orphan, I have three sisters said the boy but all the same and he had a stubborn expression all the same he said he was an orphan. Mrs. Reynolds and the three ladies looked at him and the boy burst out crying and they all walked away and each one of them in a different direction and when Mrs. Reynolds was all alone she went back again but the boy was gone. Bye and bye she knew that she would not see him again and she went away.

A little at a time she went on her way and she met Edmund, Edmund was the adopted son of her cousin who was a widow and had lost her own son and she had not really adopted Edmund but she had raised him and Edmund although he was very good-humored was not pleased when he had not enough to eat, and said Mrs. Reynolds to her cousin, it does happen, yes said her cousin it does happen and now that Edmund is earning his own living and has a wife and no children it does happen. Naturally it does happen and Edmund at one time complained but now he thought that after all he had less indigestion and it was just as well. Mrs. Reynolds said she was going home and Edmund said he would go with her part of the way and they talked about the weather. Pretty soon Mrs. Reynolds stopped and said Edmund will Angel Harper ever be fifty-four. No said Edmund and then he looked very earnest and then he shouted a little, no he said Angel Harper will not ever be fifty-four, and Mrs. Reynolds said yes Edmund I thank you then she went away.

It was not dark early that day and when she went home Mr. Reynolds was there after all he had come home early, he usually did and they had their dinner and they talked a little and Mrs. Reynolds said that she had seen Edmund and Mr. Reynolds did not say anything further about Edmund and Mrs. Reynolds said yes and Mrs. Reynolds said she was tired and Mr. Reynolds said let us go to bed and they did.

When Angel Harper was fifty-three and he began to wonder a little if perhaps he would never be fifty-four he remembered that a long time before when he was twelve he was in a very strange costume, a hat of a girl and an apron of his mother and he was playing with water, he remembered the water was coming out of a faucet and he had on a strange costume and he was playing with the water.

Oh dear me said Mrs. Reynolds and she was not thinking because she did not know that, but she did say when this you see then think of me and she went out and it was a warm hot morning and she met a nineteen-year-old boy whose name was Andrew and she said to him how do you do you look very tired, you are always very healthy I have never seen you tired before and Andrew said yes because in the last two days he had walked fifty miles twenty-five a day, and Mrs. Reynolds said and were you all alone and he said no I was with my third sister and she said is she tired too and Andrew said I do not know I never noticed and Mrs. Reynolds said you had better rest and he said yes but I do not think I will and then they said good-bye and each of them went home that is they went toward their home,

Mrs. Reynolds and Andrew, and Mrs. Reynolds saw a man with a beard standing and looking and she remembered well it was almost fifteen years now and they had just come into that neighborhood she and Mr. Reynolds and she had seen the same man stand and look and really well anyway it was just like that and Mrs. Reynolds went home and Mr. Reynolds was there and she told him that some one had told her that Joseph Lane felt very strong and Mr. Reynolds said he was very glad to hear it. He repeated I am very glad to hear it and then they sat down to dinner and it was still quite daylight and it was too early to go to bed, and Mrs. Reynolds said even if I am very sleepy I do want to know about civilians being dead. Civilians said Mr. Reynolds, I met a girl today her name was Ruth and I asked her just what you asked me and she said, one woman makes four soldiers, so what is a civilian, and I said what is a civilian and now you ask me what is a civilian, let us said Mr. Reynolds let us go to bed it is still daylight but let us go to bed and it was still daylight and they did go to bed and they slept very well and very long.

Mrs. Reynolds woke up wondering whether it was better to dress warmly in summer, and should a straw hat be trimmed with velvet ribbon. All that day she was troubled, she met a man whose name was Fred Vincent and his wife was slowly going crazy and did not keep house for him and he had nothing to eat so he was going out to buy cheese and he had just bought three cheeses and was going home with them to his brother and his wife and each one of them would have one cheese although cheeses were smaller now than they used to be. And he met another man Fred Vincent met another man whose son had gone off to be a soldier and there they had given him injections against all sorts of diseases and that had preyed on his mind and he had gone a little crazy, he was not dangerous but he talked a funny language that no one could understand but now he was home again and he had had a big abscess on his leg and he was better and was almost quite well again. Don't you think said Mrs. Reynolds that he always had a tendency to be queer, Mrs. Reynolds herself knew some strange dialects and she asked Fred Vincent which one of them the boy talked but Fred Vincent did not

224

know. I used said Mrs. Reynolds to know his mother her name was Frances and then Mrs. Reynolds went away, on her way she met a tall man very warmly dressed who walked very quickly and he said how do you do to her and she said how do you to him and she knew who he was although she did not know his name and she knew he was queer and she was a little afraid of him and she went home and she told Mr. Reynolds that she was sure that Angel Harper would not live long and then they sat down to dinner and then they both went out together and then they both came in together, Mr. and Mrs. Reynolds and then they went to bed and it took Mrs. Reynolds quite a while to fall asleep but she finally did and she slept well but not as long as she was accustomed to sleep because she always was accustomed to sleep very long.

Mrs. Reynolds said she did not know what to say when she woke at break of day except that she would like very well to go to sleep again and with some little difficulty she did. She said while she was going to sleep again that if with some little difficulty she was not frightened, it reminded her of a young woman who was to have a fortune if she married a soldier within the month and she got pneumonia and all the same she did marry him and she lived happily ever after, it is said Mrs. Reynolds just like that going to sleep again with a certain difficulty. When she woke up she said that she knew everything was better and she said to Mr. Reynolds even if he were to say is it, all the same it was and it was not yet too late for Saint Odile to be right, and patiently waiting, well said Mrs. Reynolds patiently waiting, and Mr. Reynolds said who was up first, and Mrs. Reynolds said that that did not matter and anyway said Mrs. Reynolds nothing does matter because it is everything is going so well. It depends said Mr. Reynolds what side you are on, oh of course said Mrs. Reynolds naturally of course and then they sat down to breakfast and they were quite happy.

There is nothing said Mrs. Reynolds so frightening as a watch dog who is with you to protect you when he gets frightened because he thinks he hears something, but anyway Mr. Reynolds had gone and Mrs. Reynolds was alone well she would not be alone long, because either she would go out or she would stay in but she would not be alone long. Mrs. Reynolds did say that anyway in these days a dog could walk on a highway without much danger of being run over. It is said Mrs. Reynolds one of the reasons why things are not what they were, and when she said this she did not heave a sigh and she did not feel that she might ever have to cry because after all Angel Harper had been all the ages he had been and now he was fifty-three. All the same said Mrs. Reynolds I do say oh dear me, all the same I do say it said Mrs. Reynolds and she wondered if she really felt the way she did. It is said Mrs. Reynolds not easy to know whether you do feel the way you do. She asked a young officer to listen to her and he said he was glad to and she said what is your name and he said that it was all very well to have a name like his but why tell it and Mrs. Reynolds said she would like to know it and he said his name was Jack Sweeney and Mrs. Reynolds said thank you and she said good-day and she asked him if he was going to stay and he said very likely, well she said if very likely you are going to stay I am not very likely to see you again because there are so many of you and the young officer said he was being hot after all it was very hot weather and Mrs. Reynolds said why certainly and as she had to attend to several matters she said good-bye and went away.

Mrs. Reynolds did know that Angel Harper had not entirely made her sad, but she remembered Saint Odile and then she knew that Angel Harper did make her have to be entirely sad.

Angel Harper was fifty-three and he remembered that when he was thirteen he sat in a chair and counted leaves and ate cherries and he remembered that it tired him to count leaves and that nevertheless he did make a note of the number of them. When he was fifty-three he knew that he was fifty-three and added addresses were not for him, there were no added addresses for him. We said Angel Harper, and we said Angel Harper it was not dark because the days were long and it was not early because the nights were short.

Mrs. Reynolds never said we, she did not need to because she and Mr. Reynolds were one and everybody else was some other one so Mrs. Reynolds did not have to do more than ask any one how old they were in order to know their age. Naturally enough she had never asked Angel Harper how old he was because she had never met him, and besides that, any one, hardly any one, well it was any one any one knew that Angel Harper was fifty-three and it might be a short time and seem long or it might be a long time and seem a short one. Yes said Mrs. Reynolds when she met Herbert Armor, yes I have just heard that Lydia has gone away to have her second baby in an airplane. Really said Herbert Armor, yes said Mrs. Reynolds yes she is going to have her second baby in an airplane and she is going to call him Philip, the first one and she called him John the first one was born in a bed but the second one and she is going to call him Philip, she is going to have born in an airplane. But said Herbert suppose it is a girl well said Mrs. Reynolds in that case she will call it Philippa, but anyway said Mrs. Reynolds, airplanes go up and they come down so really perhaps the little Philip will be born in a bed like his brother John. Good night said Mrs. Reynolds and left him. It was almost evening and nobody was careless because little by little everybody had learned to be careful. Good night said Mrs. Reynolds and she went home to dinner, and after dinner she and Mr. Reynolds sat for a while and she told him about Lydia and then it was time to go to bed although it was not yet dark and they went to bed and Mrs. Reynolds tossed about a little and coughed a little and then she slept and Mr. Reynolds slept and they did not wake up early and it was a little cloudy and said Mrs. Reynolds that is better than too much sunshine. I said Mrs. Reynolds prefer winter to summer, summer is full of the anxiety of having things grow. And said Mrs. Reynolds if I wait, well said Mrs. Reynolds if I wait it is not too late. And so Mrs. Reynolds went out, she felt lonesome, it was not often that Mrs. Reynolds felt lonesome, but she went out and she felt lonesome. There was time to feel lonesome, she met Mrs. Vincent and she told Mrs. Vincent, that she felt lonesome. Mrs. Vincent said that she herself did not feel lonesome but that she felt strange. And Mrs. Reynolds said that she did not feel strange but that she did feel lonesome and then they said good-bye and each one of them went away. Bye the bye said Mrs. Reynolds to Miss Harden as she met her, bye the bye said Miss Harden and they both began to laugh and they began to talk about Mrs. Vincent, Mrs. Reynolds said it is strange that Mrs. Vincent does not feel lonesome but that she does feel strange and Miss Harden said that Mrs. Vincent was a little strange, Mr. Vincent knew that Mrs. Vincent was strange that she was not lonesome but that she was strange and that Mr. Vincent had told Mr. Harden and Miss Harden that he wondered if Mrs. Vincent would go on feeling strange and Mrs. Reynolds told Mr. Reynolds what Mrs. Vincent had said and Mr. Reynolds said that Mr. Vincent had told him that his wife did not feel lonesome but she did feel strange, and Mrs. Reynolds said well and they went in to dinner, and there was a storm a windstorm they hoped it would rain but it did not, it was only the wind that blew, and Mrs. Reynolds said it was strange that it had been so hot and now it was so cold and they went to bed and they slept very well.

When Monday follows Sunday said Mrs. Reynolds then something else happens, and what she meant what she said she meant was this, even if it was enough anybody could feel that everybody had had more than enough of it. Mr. Reynolds said yes, a man had just told him that his wife had had enough and so thought it was all about ready to stop, and in a way yes in a way they were all reasonable about it, enough is enough. Mrs. Reynolds said that when Tuesday followed Monday it was almost enough and everybody knew that enough was enough. Well said Mrs. Reynolds there can be no mistake Wednesday follows Tuesday and Thursday follows Wednesday and so on said Mrs. Reynolds and she said she was still very much occupied with their all having had well completely having had enough, and and said Mrs. Reynolds when Friday follows Thursday and Saturday follows Friday and then they were again at Sunday because Sunday follows Saturday and Monday follows Sunday and there they all were and enough is enough. Mr. Reynolds said it was true, everybody was through, and perhaps Mrs. Reynolds was right and enough was almost more than enough, but

228

said Mr. Reynolds there is nothing to do about it and he said he would have to go and attend to what he had to attend to and Mrs. Reynolds said that she never had said not and no, and Mr. Reynolds said certainly not she never had, and they began another day in their ordinary way and they both knew that although enough was enough they were not through.

Angel Harper was fifty-three and they were not yet through not yet.

Mrs. Reynolds met Annabel Williams who said When the clouds commence to be absorbed instead of drifting it means that the stormy weather is over. Oh yes said Mrs. Reynolds and Mrs. Reynolds said and do you know that the united family of Genevieve's are separating, the four brothers and their sisters have always clung together and now they have quarreled, Andrew has left, Genevieve is leaving and there is nobody left but Fred and Maurice and from having been united and prosperous they are now disunited and unprosperous, it is funny said Mrs. Reynolds that it takes years to build up a business and only a year or two to bring it down. I wish said Mrs. Reynolds that it did not make me too hopeful and she said good-bye and Annabel Williams said good-bye and as she said good-bye she said she had always been hopeful and Mrs. Reynolds said yes it was true that Annabel had always been hopeful and they each of them went away.

Mrs. Reynolds was going home and as she was going home she met her cousin she had a cousin whom she always called cousin, when she met her she said to her and how are you cousin and her cousin said that she was tired, not really tired said Mrs. Reynolds yes really tired said the cousin, you see said the cousin I do not know whether what is happening makes any difference to me or not, and not knowing whether what is happening makes any difference to me or not is very tiring.

Mrs. Reynolds said why not go away and the cousin said there was no use in going away unless she was to stay away and there was no use in staying away because after all she would not know any more wherever she was whether what was happening made any difference to her or whether it did not. Edmund said Mrs. Reynolds oh yes Edmund said the cousin his eyes look angry but he is not angry, he thinks he knows that what is happening makes a difference to him but and the cousin said she felt quite tired nobody does know whether what is happening makes any difference to them or whether it does not. I met somebody to-day said the cousin and when he went away I said I would never see him again, I did not want to see him again because he said things that made me feel quite tired but I do not know very likely I will see him again very likely and Mrs. Reynolds' cousin went home and Mrs. Reynolds went home and it was time to go home even if it was the longest day in the year and it some-times is. It is funny said Mrs. Reynolds there comes a moment Mr. William Williams told me when I am twice as old as my step-daughter, she is sixteen and I am thirty-two, and then every year well she is older and I am not twice as old so do I get younger when she gets older said Mr. William Williams and Mrs. Reyn-olds said anything that happens like that makes my cousin feel as if she were tired because she does not know whether it makes any difference to her, but I know said Mr. William Williams I know that it does make a difference and anything that makes a difference to me makes me feel funny, and Mrs. Reynolds said it was time to go home and if it was time to go home she would go home even if it was the longest day in the year. When she was home Mr. Reynolds came in and she said what is happening and Mr. Reynolds said nothing and then they had dinner and as it was the longest day in the year but nevertheless they did not go to bed until it was dark and then they went to bed and Mrs. Reynolds did not sleep very well and the next day it was morn-ing and she got up late but she did not tell any one.

It was like that said Mrs. Reynolds nothing is going to be hap-pening because nothing is happening and Mrs. Reynolds said it is like that, and she said she was almost going to say it every morning and Mr. Reynolds said yes and it was morning and yesterday was the longest day in the year so today the day was a little shorter, and Mrs. Reynolds said yes.

Mrs. Reynolds met Edmund, she said to him I see why you feel like that suddenly, suddenly you have no hope, I see said Mrs. Reynolds why you feel like that. I have no hope said Mrs. Reynolds suddenly I have no hope, I see said Mrs. Reynolds why you feel like that. I feel like that said Edmund because of what is happening, and I said Mrs. Reynolds feel like that because I feel suddenly that there is no hope. Edmund said that he was irritated, he said that what was happening which was why he had no hope made him feel very irritated. Mrs. Reynolds said and she meant what she said she said she was never irritated, that when suddenly and even if it was suddenly perhaps just as suddenly it would go on she felt that suddenly there was no hope but she was not irritated and anyway she was feeling a little better, she was not feeling that there was any hope but she was feeling a little better and Edmund said he was not feeling any better and even if he would feel better he would be just as irritated as he was and he was irritated by what was happening just as irritated as he was, and so Mrs. Reynolds said she would go home and Edmund went away without saying where he was going and Mrs. Reynolds did not ask him she was so certain that she was feeling just as she had been feeling, she was feeling that there was no hope and that even though she was beginning to feel better she was just feeling that she had suddenly been feeling that there was no hope.

When Angel Harper was fifty-three he did not remember that he had ever been fourteen, did not remember it at all. It did puzzle him that a grandmother a mother and an aunt and their son's grandson and nephew all talked just alike, he knew it was true because it had been true but he did not remember at all that he had been fourteen not now when he was fifty-three. When he was fifty-three he said he forgot Joseph Lane and when he said he forgot Joseph Lane he said that two were more than three and when he said that two were more than three he knew that he could not that is to say that he did not remember having been fourteen, and anything not there made him touch his hair and so he did touch his hair because his having ever been fourteen was not there.

Useless not to be late said Mrs. Reynolds when she met Edmund and Edmund was not really late, he had a great deal to do and he was not really late. If he was late it was because he really had so much to do. Mrs. Reynolds said that she knew that Edmund had a good deal to do but it was useless for him to be late. Anyway said Mrs. Reynolds any date is an anniversary and any anniversary made her sad and glad, and when she was sad and glad she was beginning to have hope and when she came home and Mr. Reynolds was there she said she was beginning not exactly to have hope but she was beginning not to feel as badly about it all not as badly and Mr. Reynolds said he was tired it had been a long day but not Mrs. Reynolds reminded him not the longest day, the longest day was day before yesterday and so Mrs. Reynolds and Mr. Reynolds had dinner and then they listened to the thunder and then they went to bed.

Mrs. Reynolds met Herbert, he was unaccompanied, he said I tender you thirty thanks, he said I wonder and Mrs. Reynolds said and how is the baby Christine, Herbert said she was a wonder well and good-tempered and charming and fearless and generous and tender. Yes said Mrs. Reynolds all the children this year are named Christopher or Christine, Mr. Reynolds says it is natural, 1942 makes anybody think of 1492 and so it is natural, I said it was natural Mr. Reynolds said it was 1942 and you said Mrs. Reynolds how are you. Very well I thank you, said Herbert and how is Sarah said Mrs. Reynolds, suffering a little from eczema said Herbert, that is nerves and nature said Mrs. Reynolds and how are you, I suffer said Herbert I always suffer from insomnia and I have a great many diseases, said Herbert, ah yes said Mrs. Reynolds and your friend Elizabeth Simpson, I have not seen her for a very long time said Herbert but I am seeing her day after tomorrow, of course her occupation as a spy keeps her very busy, oh yes said Mrs. Reynolds and said Herbert she has to give me information, oh yes said Mrs. Reynolds, and how is everything said Mrs. Reynolds, well said Herbert, I do not change my mind, but I feel different, ah yes said Mrs. Reynolds and Herbert said and once more well not once more but yet and again I tender you thirty thanks, and Mrs. Reynolds said and Joseph Lane yes said Herbert, and Angel Harper said Mrs. Reynolds yes, said Herbert, and he said baby Christine was just seven months old today and had just commenced to eat a little juice of calves' liver, yes said Mrs. Reynolds and although there did not seem to be any way of each one of them going their own way, Herbert did go away and Mrs. Reynolds went home, it was not very late and she went out again and as she went out again she met Benjamin Haig, and Benjamin Haig was as always very cheerful and she said to him and how is baby Christopher and he said he was very well a bouncing child and very well. Benjamin had married late in life and immediately had a bouncing baby and he named it Christopher which was natural enough because 1942 would remind any one of 1492 any one at all. Good night said Benjamin to Mrs. Reynolds and Mrs. Reynolds decided she would stay out a little longer and enjoy the fine weather which she did.

She wondered what she would choose, she remembered playing London Bridge is falling down, my fair lady oh, and she remembered that they asked her to choose between a diamond necklace and a wedding dress, and she did not want either one but she had to choose, and now what she should choose, well of course there is and there was Saint Odile and even if she was waiting, that is Mrs. Reynolds was waiting even if she was waiting, she was choosing Saint Odile, she had not weakened, she was still choosing Saint Odile, should there be fighting in the city of cities, and which was it, was said Mrs. Reynolds, was she said Mrs. Reynolds was she still waiting said Mrs. Reynolds and she went home and Mr. Reynolds was there and she said she felt that it might still come true, and Mr. Reynolds said what and Mrs. Reynolds said Saint Odile and Mr. Reynolds said yes very likely and they had dinner shortly after and there was a full moon and they took a long walk and they came home and they went to bed very carefully and Mrs. Reynolds said after all she did not have to decide and they went to sleep carefully and they were quite happy.

Mrs. Reynolds woke up worried, she wondered if she knew what it was that was true. Was it going to be so or was it not, and if it was was it and if it was not was it not, and was she worried because she did not know or because it was not so and she was not certain which day was the day in the month and which week was the week in the month and which month was the month in the year and which year, no said Mrs. Reynolds she could not commence again, not yet nor again, she just could not commence again, so it was best just to be not sure of the day or the week or the month but not the year, the year was here, that was all there was to the year, in fact she began to think that that was all that there was to any year, that it was just here, days and weeks and months were not like that but a year was like that only like that only just like that. She woke up worried and she went to sleep again and when she was asleep again, there was no use worrying, because certainly not necessarily but certainly, certainly, Angel Harper was fifty-three and there was no use being careless about that, Mrs. Reynolds was asleep again, and she was as she was asleep again not only worried but quite certain that it was not what it had been but what it was. When she woke up Mr. Reynolds was awake and Mrs. Reynolds said she was not worried and Mr. Reynolds said that was right and they had better get up and they did get up and that was that.

Mrs. Reynolds met Edmund and she she said to him how are you and he said oh so so and Mrs. Reynolds said it is moonlight at night and when you wake up at night and you see that it is bright, oh dear me said Mrs. Reynolds I know I have nothing to be afraid of but it did give me a fright, what do you think said Mrs. Reynolds is going to happen and Edmund said well it is going to happen but when said Mrs. Reynolds, when said Edmund, yes when said Mrs. Reynolds, Mr. Reynolds says he does not know when, well said Edmund when, and Mrs. Reynolds said well I weakened a little bit that is to say I did not think, I was just annoyed and fussed but now I know Saint Odile is right and it is going to happen soon. Not too soon for me said Edmund turning away, Edmund said he was busy and he was that is to say he was busy. Mrs. Reynolds felt very relieved, she had told somebody and as it was bound to be that way and she told somebody then it was bound to be that way and if she felt in a way perhaps that it was not at all well anyway she had told somebody. In that way she thought Edmund was somebody, yes somebody.

Mrs. Reynolds sometimes to change her mind counted the

234

number of roses she picked, the number of raspberries she bought, the number of violets she had had, violet by violet, that did not change her mind altogether but still just enough and so she thought that what she bought, well said Mrs. Reynolds to Mrs. Green, you like to buy and keep but not to save, yes indeed said Mrs. Green, it is not only the way I feel but it is also the way I do. Yes or no said Mrs. Reynolds and she and Mrs. Green stood there and Mrs. Reynolds did not care and Mrs. Green did care which made them stand there very much longer. Now said Mrs. Green it is very necessary, Yes said Mrs. Reynolds I have commenced all over again to believe in Saint Odile, oh yes said Mrs. Green, and she asked Mrs. Reynolds what day, and Mrs. Reynolds said yesterday and today, and Mrs. Green said oh yes.

It was just like that and neither of them mentioned that Angel Harper was still fifty-three but he was and Mrs. Green if she had thought would have liked to have mentioned Joseph Lane but besides that she did not think of it very much besides that, she did not know his name. Mrs. Reynolds remembered fie fie fie for shame everybody knows his name and they stood there just that much longer and then Mrs. Reynolds went away and Mrs. Green went the other way. How do you do said Mrs. Reynolds and Mrs. Green did not say how do you do not on that day.

Well said Mrs. Reynolds to Mr. Reynolds when she went home well. And Mr. Reynolds looked up and said well. Well said Mrs. Reynolds it is astonishing, I was so astonished that I cannot get over it. What said Mr. Reynolds. Why said Mrs. Reynolds that it is just the same I read a book said Mrs. Reynolds and it is all the same about the same date, well yes the same date and it is the same and now I am only waiting for the fighting in the streets of the city of cities, to believe that Saint Odile is right and of course Saint Odile is right and it is all the same, and said Mrs. Reynolds even if it does not make any difference to me and in a way it does not make any difference to me but I have not a restless feeling but an underground happy feeling that it is all the same, and Angel Harper being fifty-three is all the same, and Joseph Lane not having any age is all the same and you are all the same said Mrs. Reynolds and Mr. Reynolds said well, and Mrs.

Reynolds said yes or no, and Mr. Reynolds said yes yes, and no no, or if you like it better yes no or no yes. Yes said Mrs. Reynolds, yes and nevertheless makes it just the same and Mrs. Reynolds said everybody wished that it was going to rain, and Mrs. Reynolds said it was a shame, that it was not going to rain and Mrs. Reynolds said that dinner was on the table and they ate their dinner and it did not come on to rain, and the longest day in the year was about a month away and anyway Mrs. Reynolds said anyway and Mr. Reynolds said it was time to go to bed even if there was no rain and they went to bed when all was said they went to bed.

PART XII

Angel Harper when he was fifty-three remembered that when he had been fourteen he had been thin and tired, tired and thin and now he was fifty-three and he was not thin and he was fifty-three and he was not tired and everybody else was tired and everybody else was thin and they said that every day they brought a suckling pig for Angel Harper by airplane because it would keep fresher that way and very likely it was not true but they did say that every day he had a suckling pig brought to him in that way.

But why said Mrs. Reynolds and she began to sigh, but why am I disappointed said Mrs. Reynolds. She had just met Edmund and Edmund was very disappointed and Mrs. Reynolds said but why said Mrs. Reynolds why am I disappointed and said Mrs. Reynolds I am disappointed, I thought everything was going to go better but it never does and Mrs. Reynolds said oh my she was disappointed and she was.

There has been said Mrs. Reynolds a turkey stolen, yes said Mr. Reynolds there has been a turkey stolen.

It was a handsome bird but it was not theirs.

Angel Harper when he was fifty-three and he was fifty-three every day morning and late he was fifty-three when he was fifty-three he remembered that when he had been eleven he had felt that he was undersized, he really had not been but he felt he was undersized and he liked to play with water. He was not then when he was eleven he was not interested in thunder and lightning.

237

Now that he was fifty-three then and just then and always then he was fifty-three, now when he was fifty-three he could never remember when it was that he was first interested in thunder and lightning, and it was troubling him, now that he was fifty-three, thunder and lightning was beginning to trouble him, perhaps he had made a mistake to find thunder and lightning interesting, perhaps because after all thunder and lightning was not made to stay it was made to thunder and lighten and then to go away, away away.

Dear me said Mrs. Reynolds did you hear that thunder and did you see that lightning. Yes said Mr. Reynolds but it did not hit anything. No said Mrs. Reynolds but I can smell it and I do not like its smell. Yes said Mr. Reynolds and then it was time for dinner and they ate their dinner and there had not been any rain and there had not been any hail and the ground was not wet and they sat and then they went to bed and slept.

Mrs. Reynolds met Mrs. George, Mrs. George said she would like to do a portrait in crayons of Mrs. Reynolds, she would prefer to do one of her in oil, but she could not paint in oil very well, while she could draw very nicely with crayons, would said Mrs. Reynolds would I have to sit, no said Mrs. George if you prefer if you very much prefer to you can stand. But where said Mrs. Reynolds would I have to stand, well said Mrs. George not in the sun and not in the shade. All right said Mrs. Reynolds and she did. Mrs. George was very well satisfied with the drawing she had done but Mrs. Reynolds did not care for it she said there was no use in showing it to Mr. Reynolds because Mr. Reynolds never looked at it. But said Mrs. George how can you tell until I show it, ah said Mrs. Reynolds, and that was true, Mr. Reynolds never did see it, it was there and he never did see it, he did not refuse to look at it but he did not see it and Mrs. George did not really mind she was used to it and she took it away and she said some day she would come back again and do it again, and sometimes she did come back again and she did do it again and Mrs. Reynolds said thank you and Mrs. George did leave it and Mrs. Reynolds did not want it and Mr. Reynolds did not see it and everybody was satisfied with yesterday when it happened and with tomorrow when it happened and they were just as quiet Mrs. Reynolds was just as quiet and Mr. Reynolds was just as quiet and Mrs. George had never been quiet and she had had four sons and two of them died, one naturally and one naturally enough, and she had two sons left and they had children. Thank you very much said Mrs. George and I am coming again, and sometimes she did and sometimes she did not.

There came they were quite hungry although they had plenty to eat and quite enough money, some friends of William the younger brother of Mr. Reynolds and of his wife Hope. They were thin these two they were husband and wife and important and prosperous although they were small and very thin very very thin.

I wish said Mrs. Reynolds and she did not finish her sentence. It was late that night and Mr. and Mrs. Reynolds were tired and were going to bed and it was late and they were tired and they did go to bed.

Angel Harper was still fifty-three dear me dear me, he better had be fifty-three, and nevertheless he saw it was like a picture book, he saw a door, and in the door, well not in the door, but in the doorway, it was not light and it was not clear but he was there and it was not queer that he was there but was he there well any-way a boy of ten was there and he had a neighbor and he was not born there, he was left there, the wife of the soldier was dead, the soldier was not dead the boy knew how to draw, and he was left, he went to the grave of his mother and he sent a flower that he had plucked on the grave of his mother to his father but his father never answered from anywhere, and the boy was left there, and believe it or not it was true he was there.

Angel Harper closed his eyes and he opened them again and he knew he never had been married and he had never had any children, and, he knew that if he lost a wedding ring and an en-gagement ring in his sleep that is if he dreamed that he had lost them it did not make any difference. Angel Harper sometimes cried when he slept, not always but quite often. He was and is fifty-three.

If I knew about him I would hate him said Mrs. Reynolds and I do know about him and I do hate him said Mrs. Reynolds and if I forgot about him said Mrs. Reynolds and she did not cry in her sleep not Mrs. Reynolds. Angel Harper was fifty-three, and Mrs. Reynolds knew just what to say but she did not cry in her sleep no Mrs. Reynolds did not nor did Mr. Reynolds he did not. They both slept but they did not cry in their sleep.

Angel Harper was fifty-three. The time had come, he did not say that the time had come but he did not say that the time had not come. When he was fifty-three he remembered that when he had been fifteen, he sat at the foot of a telegraph pole, not high up but at the base where he had made himself a seat and there he sat and looked at two very large dolls each one in their doll carriage, and one day as he sat at the bottom of the telegraph pole and looked at the two large dolls in their doll carriages some one, and who was it was it a man or was it a woman who was it said to him, either it is real or it is not real and if it is not real it is not at all real or it is real and it is all real you see it as real and not real but it is not real or not real, it is real, that is to say is it, or it is not real, that is to say is it, but not the two together oh dear no not the two together. Angel Harper when he was fifty-three remembered that when he had been fifteen some one said this to him there where he sat at the foot of the telegraph pole where he had made himself a seat with a curtain and he could look down on two large dolls each one in their doll carriage.

Angel Harper now that he was fifty-three was in opposition, was he in opposition to Joseph Lane, they were not one another, oh dear no although neither of them laughed then, not at all then. Anybody else would say crowd me if you must, but neither of them said crowd me if you must.

Or said Mrs. Reynolds there is no rain.

Mrs. Reynolds was entirely occupied with there being no rain.

What said Mrs. Reynolds will he do, and he do with liquid her hair, he do, and indeed there was no doubt about what will he do.

He do and there was more, of course there was no rain and if there is no rain there is no water and if there is no water there is no green and if there is no green well said Mrs. Reynolds and if there is no green. She knew she did know that this had nothing to do with what he would do, what would he do.

Angel Harper, had no need to wither away.

What said Mrs. Reynolds would he do. And just at that time it was more than a burden to every one it was just as well. Mrs. Reynolds said it was not just as well and if there was no water it was not just as well. There still were some old wells that did have some water. It, said Mrs. Reynolds is just as well.

By that time there was no room. It is said Mrs. Reynolds very strange, and it was true in the last war so many people have been killed and still now there is less room, we might said Mrs. Reynolds easily say that there is no room, there is so little room, that there is no room, it is all full and there is no room. Mrs. Reynolds did say that there was no water and she meant it, there was no rain and so there was no water. Everybody can come to like water sometime. They can even come to give oxen wine, bread and wine, and horses bread and wine, if they need it, and they can even come to glean in the fields because every grain of wheat is precious. They can even. What said Mrs. Reynolds will he do. And she said she meant it and she did mean it.

Something said Mrs. Reynolds is going to happen. A great deal said Mrs. Reynolds has happened but nevertheless said Mrs. Reynolds something is going to happen.

If they gather when they do said Mrs. Reynolds very well said Mrs. Reynolds. It is commencing said Mrs. Reynolds not alone to feel serious but to be serious. Serious what said Emil, serious if it is to be said Mrs. Reynolds and she did not say she felt depressed but she was depressed. There must come a time said Mrs. Reynolds when everybody is depressed and when the time comes when everybody is depressed then it is time to be like that and I said Mrs. Reynolds am like that.

And she was.

She heard some one say that Joseph Lane did say that when it is like that it is bound to change.

But said Mrs. Reynolds is it bound to change, and she decided to go home and Mr. Reynolds was not depressed, he was too gentle to be depressed he was too patient to be depressed he was too ready to go to bed when it was time to go to bed to be depressed and now it was time to go to bed and he went to bed and Mrs. Reynolds went to bed too and she was not quite so depressed, nothing had changed, every night nothing had changed, she said that nothing had changed and Mr. Reynolds and Mrs. Reynolds went to bed and in the morning nothing had changed and they got up and nothing had changed. It was next morning and nothing had changed and Angel Harper was still fifty-three and nothing had changed and Joseph Lane had said that when nothing changed it would not be the same and it was the next morning and nothing had changed.

Mrs. Reynolds said, it was late in the morning and it was still a pleasant day, Mrs. Reynolds said that she would like to see Edmund and Emil and Helen and the little boy whose father had neglected to pay for him but now having been compelled to pay for him was taking him away, Mrs. Reynolds said she would like to see them but today she was going in another direction, she was going where she would be all alone and she said if she were all alone pretty soon that is bye and bye she would begin to be hopeful again, she did have it as a desire as an intention so she said and as a result she would begin to be hopeful and if she were hopeful then why worry. Yes said Mrs. Reynolds and so she went in the other direction and when she went in the other direction she met Andrew Ell. It is a pretty name said Mrs. Reynolds indeed rather a strange name and as she had never met him before she was very much interested and Andrew Ell was unhappy because he was homeless, his mother was homeless but not with him and he had no father and he had no brother and his mother had no woman with her only her brother and her nephew and it was very sad. I never say oh dear said Mrs. Reynolds because there is no use in saying oh dear and said Mrs. Reynolds if there were any use in saying oh dear, oh dear said Mrs. Reynolds and she said how do you do and good-bye to Andrew Ell, and she knew she said she knew and she did know just what it would do. Every month makes it just that much earlier that is makes the night come just

242

that much sooner. Mrs. Reynolds could always believe everything there was to believe.

Mrs. Reynolds went away and then she went home.

She went out again and she saw a man he was a very gentle man and he was a little drunk and he had a dog and he said the dog was only six months old and although he was only six months old he did what he was told, if he told him to come he came and if he told him to go and lie down he went and lay down, and the gentle drunken man said his dog who was only six months did, but did he.

Mrs. Reynolds went home again and she thought about Saint Odile and her prophecy and she felt that it was true that she Mrs. Reynolds had been feeling blue and so she had not said that what Saint Odile had said would come true. But a little well just a little she began to be sure again that it was true it was not too late yet not at all too late yet for the prophecy of Saint Odile to be true.

And Mrs. Reynolds was at home and Mr. Reynolds came home and they had dinner and the stars shone and Mr. Reynolds said and it is true, when the stars are at their brightest they will dim the quickest and they went to bed and the next day it was raining. Enough said.

Dear me yes I do ride a bicycle said Mrs. Reynolds, I have to said Mrs. Reynolds, I want to said Mrs. Reynolds I need to said Mrs. Reynolds and I have to get something to eat for twenty-five men said Mrs. Reynolds. You exaggerate said Miss Winthrop, yes perhaps I do said Mrs. Reynolds but if I do said Mrs. Reynolds then it is true said Mrs. Reynolds.

It was wonderful said neither Mrs. Reynolds nor Miss Winthrop but somebody whose name they did not know, it is wonderful he said that things change. Whether you know it or whether you do not, whether you do not or whether you do well anyway said the man things change so. They look like, and just then they heard singing and they sang, they look like men they look like men they look like men of war.

Oh yes said Miss Winthrop, people have become militarists said Miss Winthrop, and Mrs. Reynolds said they might just as well go home and she meant what she said, they might just as well indeed they might just as well go home. It was not at all singular although nobody was without a home, I have no home said William Ell and he meant what he said.

Mrs. Reynolds went home and when she was at home Mr. Reynolds was there and they had dinner and as there was no more rain, it can happen that there is never again any more rain, when that can happen the moon can shine, and all right, said Mr. Reynolds and as they had had their dinner and they were tired they went to bed.

Mrs. Reynolds said that everything had been changed since yesterday that is if yesterday was two weeks ago which it was. It was.

Mrs. Reynolds said this to every one who passed along. It is most exciting when it begins again. What said some one who was carrying a melon. Everything said Mrs. Reynolds it is not sure yet but, said Mrs. Reynolds and she gave a happy sigh and now I can believe again in Saint Odile, I never stopped believing in Saint Odile but oh dear me and Mrs. Reynolds looked quite excited and asked him if it was a good melon. You can always tell said Mrs. Reynolds and she meant what she said.

Angel Harper remembered that when he had been eleven he had sat in a room with an old woman and a middle-aged woman and a young woman and that he had held his head with his hand and listened to music.

There is said Mrs. Reynolds no accounting for tastes but even if it did not make any difference I would wish that he were dead, and she knew whom she meant, she meant Angel Harper. She was not sure that it would make a difference but she did wish what she said.

She met an elderly gentleman Mr. Eustace and he was interested in water, quite interested in water and he said to Mrs. Reynolds every few years now I began to bother about when it would happen that I would be past driving an automobile anyway in a city and even perhaps in the country and now well now there are no automobiles to drive and I have no bother in deciding when I would be past driving an automobile and now said Mr.

244

Eustace how about water. Well said Mrs. Reynolds and Mr. Eustace said how about water. They decided Mrs. Reynolds and Mr. Eustace that some one should try again and then Mrs. Reynolds went away and she did not leave Mr. Eustace standing because he too had walked away. That said Mrs. Reynolds makes a day and she looked around and indeed it was evening even if it was not raining and she went home to dinner and Mr. Reynolds said he was not tired but he was beginning to wish that he was not used to it, and Mrs. Reynolds knew what he meant and they talked about it but they said and they were right that they had nothing to say about it and they went to bed and tomorrow was the next day and they well they knew whom they meant by they had not gone away. But they might said Mrs. Reynolds and she knew that she was right yes they might.

And now said Mr. Reynolds' younger brother William who was far away let us not forget Joseph Lane even if he is forgotten. Mr. Reynolds' younger brother William felt that way about everything he knew that he would never have worked in a garden to grow vegetables if it had not been for Angel Harper and did he like it. If he did not he did not and if he did he did.

Angel Harper when he was fifty-three and it was a long year a very long a long long year when he was fifty-three remembered that when he was fourteen he gathered together very large fallen leaves and twigs and he remembered that he was very well dressed then when he was gathering fallen leaves and twigs together.

Mrs. Reynolds knew that she was tired of the exercise she was taking in the year that Angel Harper was fifty-three, it was a long year and she was tired of taking all the exercise she was taking all that long year. Mrs. Reynolds said so to some one who stopped and listened to Mrs. Reynolds saying what she had to say about all the exercise that she was taking all this long year and the one listening to Mrs. Reynolds began to laugh and laughed very happily, and Mrs. Reynolds said all the same it was true she was tired of taking all the exercise she was taking all this long year and they both laughed and they both laughed again. Yes they did.

Mrs. Reynolds was tired and she stopped and she and Ephraim Ell stopped together. They even sat down together, Ephraim Ell they called him Eph Ell was a young man tall and sad-looking and a little pale and he felt everything deeply and he taught what he felt and he felt well quite well and he and Mrs. Reynolds met not very often but they did meet. Mrs. Reynolds was just thinking just then of the wife of the captain who had four children. She rode a bicycle and looked unpleasant and just the day before Mrs. Reynolds had seen the colonel, well anyway perhaps they were all back from a vacation, anyway the captain was not stationed here any longer. Anyway Mrs. Reynolds was standing perhaps sitting and talking that is listening to Eph Ell. He did speak slowly carefully and with deliberation but he meant every word he said. The world said Eph Ell is feeling the curse of God upon it and that is because they only thought of their pleasures their material pleasures their material success, they had peace and plenty and liberty and they abused all three and now said Eph Ell now when they have neither peace nor plenty nor liberty, now well do they or do they not realize now when even when they work so hard to give themselves food and the crops are poor because there are either floods or drought do they now begin to doubt if when they once more have peace and plenty and liberty if that time should ever come what said Eph Ell what and he turned and saw his brother Philip and Eph Ell went away. Any day could be a sad day and any day well any day, was the same day or another day and Mrs. Reynolds was thinking about the lack of water and that she wished that the water would run and that when it would run it would be comfortable and when it was comfortable well it was time that she should go home and go home she did it was dinner time and even though it was September it was a very hot evening and Mr. Reynolds was sneezing and Mrs. Reynolds said that she wished that Mr. Reynolds was always well, and Mrs. Reynolds meant what she said and Mrs. Reynolds said it was time to go to bed and Mr. Reynolds said that he did not feel sleepy yet and Mrs. Reynolds said not yet and Mr. Reynolds said no not yet. A little while after they did go to bed and they both did sleep very well.

John Ell was a cousin of Eph and Philip, he liked to conspire. Do you he said to himself do you like to gather a quantity of

246

powder do you like to gather a quantity of arms do you he said like to gather feathers and do you like to gather old hats. Do you he said to himself do you like to gather odds and ends and do you, he suddenly felt that he had done enough. It is not easy he said to himself not easy at all to have quite suddenly done enough. And so he did not rest. He said he had had enough he had done enough nevertheless he did go on conspiring. He did not conspire early and late, he only conspired when he had the time and he did not almost always have the time. He told Mrs. Reynolds all about it. He knew that Mrs. Reynolds always talked but he knew that all the same although she told everybody everything they would never know that he did conspire, she knew he knew, he told she told and he was very bold but all the same and he knew that it was true nobody would know that he had done anything not anybody would know and it was so, nobody did know. Well Mr. Reynolds said John Ell and when he said well Mr. Reynolds he knew it was time for dinner and it was time for dinner and they invited him in and he went in.

When Angel Harper was fifty-four, fifty-four four said Angel Harper what for, and he began to shy away from what there was to say and he said I will take what I give away. And then he remembered that when he had been eleven, he thought very large green leaves did smell of heaven and lemon, they do, too, and so he picked them he was bringing home milk in a pitcher and when he came home to his home, he had a home that is to say he lived alone with his mother his grandmother and his great grandmother or was it an aunt, well anyway whatever there was to say he brought in the leaves and put them the stems of them in the milk pitcher. And when he was fifty-four and he was fifty-four he remembered that when he was eleven some one in passing did not give him either one or two pears, neither one pear nor any pear. When he was fifty-four he did not remember everything but he did remember something. It was all day and he remembered something even if he had to decide about everything which did he do or did he never do. He remembered boohoo meant crying. He did, he did.

Mrs. Reynolds said that thinking about food, what is food

247

where is food and food as food made one nervous. It said Mrs. Reynolds makes me sad that when I am condoling with some one whom I have not seen for such a long time and now she is all alone I think of whether I can buy some food from her. Food said Mrs. Reynolds food makes you think of food and thinking of food makes you ask for food and asking for food makes you nervous and being nervous makes you feel as if you were a beggar and feeling that you are a beggar makes you know what begging is, and begging makes you know you are rich enough to pay, and anyway said Mrs. Reynolds food makes you nervous, yes it does said Mrs. Reynolds and she wished that she was talking to John Ell but actually she was not. He John Ell was far away, he was a deserter, he had deserted, he would desert, and when, when said Mrs. Reynolds and she knew that some were rich and nobody was poor, yes she knew, said Mrs. Reynolds and she knew that she meant what she said. When she was at home she told Mr. Reynolds all about John Ell. Mr. Reynolds said that he had heard it before. I did not tell you said Mrs. Reynolds. No said Mr. Reynolds but said Mr. Reynolds he had heard it before.

All this time well all this time Angel Harper was fifty-four and Joseph Lane was leading a regular life. That is he was very occupied sometimes very much not as well as he had been but ready to meet any one and not at all nervous. He was not changed but nothing was the same. He spoke again but he did not say leave it to me or when this you see you are all to me, no he just said how do you do and very well I thank you and led an ordinary life just like that. This was when Angel Harper was fifty-four and it had so Joseph Lane knew not only not happened before but was not even a bore, it was and this Joseph Lane knew very nearly all the same.

Believe it or not it is true, true, just true.

Mrs. Reynolds dreamed, that a great many came and they were everywhere and they were the right kind and they brought automobiles and essence and things to eat and she was so excited she dropped her glasses and she said in her dream it does not make any difference because now I can buy others. But could she. That is something to know. When she woke up she did not tell Mr. Reynolds and then later she told him and he said that dreams go by contraries but do they. We we we, said Mrs. Reynolds we hope so and she really meant that she did hope so. It took some time to hope so but she did hope so.

Mrs. Reynolds said and they say how can they tell when they will be too old well too old to drive a car in a city if not in the country, and then the war comes and nobody drives that is for pleasure, no nobody drives that is for pleasure and so everything is the same and nobody is to blame and there is no time of day when everybody can say that they will go away. Nobody.

It is extraordinary how many are killed in a war when everybody is dead.

John Ell said this to Mrs. Reynolds and it did not make her sad and it did not make her glad, she said that it was a bother and after all what was the matter and when she said after all what is the matter she meant exactly what she said.

When Mrs. Reynolds woke up the next morning she found herself saying, which when, they rally around, and she wondered if that meant anything, and in a little while she was nervous, if there was no more bad news well then good news would have to come and she found herself saying will have to come and then she woke up and decided not to be nervous again, not yet or again.

Believe it as carefully as you like said Mrs. Reynolds before night, and then she repeated believe it as carefully as you like but there is no necessity not to be alive to that which is certain to be very often not as much repeated. She said she was confused Mrs. Reynolds said she was confused and she meant what she said. Mrs. Reynolds said to Mr. Reynolds John Ell is confusing because I know when he says it is so that it is either so or it is not so, and so when he says anything it is confusing. And Mr. Reynolds said that he was not anxious about anything and Mrs. Reynolds said that that was a comfort and it was cold in the evening and so they went to bed again.

If they do said John Ell. He was not a friend of Mr. Reynolds' younger brother William he just might not have been. Mrs. Reynolds thought at first that he might have been and then she knew that he might not have been.

If they do said John Ell, and not only did he not know all about it but every day he found out something about it that he did not know about it. Mrs. Reynolds did not want to listen and she did want to listen and she did not want to tell Mr. Reynolds in the evening because it might be a worry to him and she did want to tell Mr. Reynolds in the evening because really she knew that it would not be a worry to him and so mostly every evening unless it was the morning and not very often the next evening she told him that John Ell had commenced saying and went on saying If they do.

Could John Ell change If they to when they do, Mrs. Reynolds said this one evening to Mr. Reynolds and Mr. Reynolds did not say anything, they went on eating their dinner and then that evening John Ell came in and Mrs. Reynolds feeling stronger because Mr. Reynolds was with her she said to John Ell will you some time change If they do to when they do and John Ell said it was best to be careful and when he said it was best to be careful he said he meant that it was best to be careful then he said good night and went home and Mr. and Mrs. Reynolds went to bed and they went to sleep early and woke up in the morning.

Nobody knew how not to tell Angel Harper that the mornings were darker. Angel Harper said that no morning was darker and he was not careful to go away as he said that evenings were darker but not mornings.

He was engaged in looking not out of the window but at the ceiling and as he looked at the ceiling he was not anxious because although it was raining the ceiling was not damp. How could it be. Angel Harper was fifty-four and he knew what he said. He was not averse to a downpour but he knew what he said. This is what he said.

It is obvious that if each thing fails everything fails and it is obvious that if everything does not fail then each thing has not failed. Is it obvious he said and he was careful to be in his own hearing when he said obvious. Obvious he said and when he said obvious he said obvious again. He was fifty-four years old and he said it, he said obvious.

When he was fifty-four years old Angel Harper remembered that when he was sixteen he had seen a boy sitting on top of a high wall eating grapes and next to him had been an older one standing on the wall next to him. Then Angel Harper when he had been sixteen had had a bicycle and then he did not remember anything in between.

When Angel Harper was fifty-four he could not shut a door, not because it was raining not because the wind was blowing not because he could not remember anything in between, not because he was not seen but anyway when Angel Harper was fifty-four he could not shut a door. Not shut a door.

Joseph Lane was not there to be in a dream, he liked eggs and animals and he liked what he had not seen, and unexpectedly well not unexpectedly because there is no unexpectedly not for Joseph Lane but anyway all the same there had not been for him the loss of his name not the loss of his name, not all the same.

And so said Mrs. Reynolds and she was pleased to be at home as it was raining Mrs. Reynolds said she had not gone visiting, and if she had had to go visiting she would much rather have stayed at home. Like me she said I would much rather have stayed at home. Mrs. Reynolds knew that she was not nervous because she said she knew that it was true that if Angel Harper should come to be fifty-five, it would be just not more than just just fifty-five and no more not any more. No said Mrs. Reynolds not any more than fifty-four no not any more.

While John Ell was talking she interrupted him. I do said Mrs. Reynolds believe that what Saint Odile said was true, that there would be fighting in the streets of the city of cities, but said John Ell it is not true, not yet anyway. Yes said Mrs. Reynolds, it is true and Mrs. Reynolds was right it is true true for Saint Odile and true for you.

The Jews John Ell said are good prophets. Mrs. Reynolds said that she did not know whether to be fussed or not.

But little by little it did happen. What did happen said Mrs. Reynolds and said Mrs. Reynolds when it happened we began said Mrs. Reynolds little by little to hope a little hope a little hope a little.

Mrs. Reynolds knew that she would rather meet Mr. Vandermeulen, and that said Mrs. Reynolds although upsetting is in the end everything. Mrs. Reynolds sighed a little is in the end everything she said as she sighed a little.

There is no beginning just now said Mrs. Reynolds and that is why said Mrs. Reynolds that we are beginning to hope a little hope a little hope a little.

Angel Harper made a mistake he made a mistake when he went away and he made a mistake when he came and he made a mistake when he went fast and he made a mistake when he slowed down and he made a mistake when he turned around and he made a mistake when he went ahead and he never sat down. So. What is there to say believe it or not what is there to say today. Believe it or not.

PART XIII

Numbers and names nobody blames numbers and names but said Mrs. Reynolds everybody does and they are right. Why not right said Mrs. Reynolds it is the same difference between me and us. And said Mrs. Reynolds and she felt what she said she was talking that way because she was hopeful, and said Mrs. Reynolds and with reason and she meant what she said. She meant what she said when she saw John Ell who was coming that way but she only said how do you do to him because she was very busy just then. She met an important man she did not know she was to meet him and she said to him tell me and he told her. The thing he told her was very important, she had known that Angel Harper would never be fifty-five alive, and she had known why of course why not but now the captain, told her and she told Mr. Reynolds and Mr. Reynolds said it was exciting and it was exciting though it was what they both knew had known and knew and it was true and with a pleasant sigh Mrs. Reynolds said numbers and names nobody blames numbers and names but said Mrs. Reynolds it is true, they do and she was right they do and so naturally that led her to remember Saint Odile and she was sure it was true which it was.

She told John Ell what the captain had told her and John Ell said well and she said but is it not exciting and John Ell said it was exciting enough which it was, it was exciting enough it was exciting stuff and it had all to do with what was past but as Saint Odile knew the past was never past enough.

Angel Harper nearly was not very well very nearly was not very well, nobody said very well because they forgot, they forgot what, they forgot that Angel Harper nearly was not very well.

Now said Mrs. Reynolds we are sure enough and Mr. Reynolds said and he was very careful he said yes I think so.

I heard Mrs. Reynolds said and it was not John Ell but I did hear, that now there was going to be some good news and some bad news but by the end of autumn there was going to be nothing but good news and in six months the news would be so good that there would be no type big enough in any newspaper office to celebrate it, and said Mrs. Reynolds it was not John Ell. Very well said Mr. Reynolds but I am hungry and so said Mrs. Reynolds am I, and said Mrs. Reynolds we will try to eat, and they did try and they succeeded very well and then it was much later almost late enough to make a fire and then they went to bed when everything was said they went to bed and Mrs. Reynolds dreamed about a soldier, a real soldier and that meant that her friends would be helpful and faithful to her and Mr. Reynolds dreamt that he saved some one from drowning and that means that something he was going to undertake would have a great public success and they both were very well satisfied with their dreaming and when they woke up they were beaming. Thank you said a young woman who came in just then and she meant thank you and she said did you sleep well and they said very well I thank you and they were at breakfast then and everybody so Mrs. Reynolds said yes everybody was hoping to be happy.

When Angel Harper was fifty-four he remembered as never before that when he had been thirteen he had dipped water out of a fountain and carried it away to drink it again while the other children around cooked and ate whatever they found. He remembered this very well and then he said oh Hell. As a matter of fact he knew some one whose real name was Victor Hell, he had known him when he had been fourteen and he saw him again and he had never seen him in between. This made him remember now that he was fifty-four made him remember as he had never remembered before the time when he had been thirteen. Nobody knew just what this could mean.

Mrs. Reynolds liked autumn weather, she liked breakfast later she liked warmer clothing she liked high shoes and she liked gloves, but said Mrs. Reynolds and she meant what she said now with all the difficulties and restrictions will I have them. Of course she said I have said but said Mrs. Reynolds and she meant what she said, will I have them.

When Angel Harper was fifty-four he remembered not exactly remembered but he had when he had been thirteen, he had put horse chestnuts with their covers on into water expecting that they would be as large as horse chestnuts and having their horny cover on and they would be he having put them in water they would be would they yes they would he did not say but he acted as he bent over them to pour the water away he acted as if he would say what he could say, and indeed when he was fifty-four he remembered as he never had before but just the same and no one was to blame it was true that he had when he was thirteen and he did not remember although he knew he had a red sweater on and shoes and short pantaloons and all the same and nobody was to blame he did not remember any more when he was fifty-four.

Mrs. Reynolds was tired at night and she wondered she said she did she wondered if a star that was bright turned from red to blue and blue to red and it did and it did every night it did mean that whatever had happened in between, there was going to be war and peace, war again here and peace again here and perhaps peace again everywhere. Why not said Mrs. Reynolds and when she said why not she felt just as tired as not and Mr. Reynolds said better come to bed and Mrs. Reynolds said she was ready for bed and they went to bed.

When he was fifty-four Angel Harper remembered that a very long time before when he was thirteen or more he was going down a hill and in one hand he had a milk can and in the other hand a piece of paper and did they have anything to do with each other of this he could not be certain and besides was there a very little girl. When he was fifty-four he remembered this and he had never remembered it before never before.

Believe it or not said Mrs. Reynolds I have not seen them recently and Mrs. Reynolds explained that by recently she meant yesterday or today not another day. She knew that Mr. Reynolds was disappointed because some one whom he trusted had gone away but nevertheless he would be there every other day. And which he was, and anyway Mr. Reynolds was not disappointed because he did know that it had to happen but all the same although he was not disappointed it was in a kind of a way a disappointment to him. All the same said Mr. Reynolds I have arranged to replace him, but said Mrs. Reynolds, yes said Mr. Reynolds it is not permanent and it is not as satisfactory, but said Mr. Reynolds and Mrs. Reynolds did not want to go away because everybody was not very busy but quite busy that way. If everything was getting more difficult, more difficult said Mrs. Reynolds and she added that she meant more difficult but if it was going to be true that Angel Harper would be fifty-four and no more, would said Mrs. Reynolds would it be thoughtless of them and she pronounced thoughtless with this meaning and she pronounced it she did pronounce it with this meaning. If she said they had the nose-bleed if she said, and if they felt flushed and warm in winter, if she said, and she suddenly remembered that it was weeks since she had seen John Ell and that that was just as well. He was depressing yes he was and she would rather talk to Mary Louise and Charlotte and even Abraham and William. Please do she said when she saw them and they were very pleased. They were making believe that flour was powder, to powder themselves with flour although flour was scarce. Was scarce said Mary Louise and William and Mrs. Reynolds said that the evenings were cold and they were but not very cold.

Mr. Reynolds came home and as soon as she came home they warmed the house had dinner and went to bed nicely.

And now said Mrs. Reynolds I did hear them say that anxiously might be turning into excitedly and if they feel like that then said Mrs. Reynolds I do and she meant what she said.

It is said a very well-known doctor who was kind, how nice

it is. And said Mrs. Reynolds you have relieved their minds and made them happy which he had.

John Ell said A mist in the valley makes a bright night but Mrs. Reynolds was not there to hear him. She was not there but nevertheless it is true a mist in a valley makes a light night.

When Angel Harper was fifty-four and in a little while well not in a little because the time passes slowly but anyway in a little time there is no more. When Angel Harper was fifty-four he remembered that when he was fourteen, his mother came in with a very large package and a smaller one. She was walking and carrying them. He did not go to meet her but he saw her. Later when he was fifty-four he remembered having remembered this thing.

Mrs. Reynolds was not disappointed that when one went another came. She was not at all disappointed and she said she was not at all disappointed. They waited a very long time for one and when he came he did not stay long and before he went away another came, there was always one, and Mrs. Reynolds said that she was not at all disappointed.

Mrs. Reynolds said she was disappointed, she said she had met the brother of Roger, she remembered Roger and although she had not known his brother she was ready to know him now and said Mrs. Reynolds she was disappointed. Mrs. Reynolds said that he had everything to hope for and said Mrs. Reynolds she was disappointed.

Later in the day she came home again and when she went home again she met Mrs. William Ranger and Mrs. William Ranger told her that there were a great many of the women they knew who were going to have children, a great many of them. That said Mrs. Reynolds is necessary to make up for all those who have gone away. Gone away where said Mrs. William Ranger. Just said Mrs. Reynolds gone away.

Mrs. Reynolds was right and she said she would go home again as she had been going and Mr. Reynolds was there and he said it was very satisfactory. And Mrs. Reynolds said dinner was ready and it was ready and it was dark and it was not cold for the season of the year and Mrs. Reynolds said she had not thought once of Angel Harper that day and said Mrs. Reynolds nobody does and she said Mrs. Reynolds said nobody does and it might be time to go to bed, the clocks had stopped and it might be time to go to bed, so they heated the hot water bottles, they liked metal ones and a great many of them in the bed and they went to bed and Mrs. Reynolds had a little trouble in falling asleep but she did fall asleep and she slept well she and Mr. Reynolds did sleep well.

It does said Mrs. Reynolds it does stand still I mean said Mrs. Reynolds time does stand still, she was talking to Octave Mather. He said yes, he had been standing and he sat down, and said Mrs. Reynolds nevertheless I have broken a tooth, really broken it. Mather laughed, yes said Mrs. Reynolds it is not too early in the day to laugh. And then she sighed, she really did sigh, little by little said Mrs. Reynolds we do not, yes said Mather, yes said Mrs. Reynolds yes we have no bananas. No said Mrs. Reynolds we really have no bananas, and that is the way it is with everything and so said Mrs. Reynolds time does stand still. Octave Mather was completely able to agree with her and they both said yes.

When Mrs. Reynolds went home she told Mr. Reynolds that she did like him Mather because when he said yes she felt a little better. Mr. Reynolds said yes and then they went to dinner, this time they went out to dinner, it was better so said Mrs. Reynolds.

A cow did die said Mrs. Reynolds from eating clover, she did swell up and she would have died if they had not killed her. A cow did die said Mrs. Reynolds at the dinner and then they went home and went to bed and Mrs. Reynolds dreamed of a broken tooth and she did not know whether that meant anything.

The next day was as exciting as any day that is what Mrs. Reynolds said the next day.

Monks said Mrs. Reynolds find more mushrooms than most, and said Mrs. Reynolds and she was talking to Octave Mather, did you know John Ell, no said Octave Mather, I said Mrs. Reynolds know him quite well and now he is not here, that is to say said Mrs. Reynolds I do not know where he is. I know you very well she said to Octave Mather and when you are not here you will not be here. No said Octave Mather. You did not said Mrs. Reynolds know John Ell, it was very interesting said Mrs. Reynolds to know John Ell, I did not know said Mrs. Reynolds whether he was conspiring or whether he was not, it is not said Mrs. Reynolds possible just now to know if anybody is conspiring or if they are not and if they are conspiring said Mrs. Reynolds it is not possible to know for what they are conspiring not possible to know said Mrs. Reynolds if they are conspiring or not. No said Octave Mather and then Mrs. Reynolds had other things to say she said she had other things to say but not today and then she asked Octave Mather if he was going away and Octave Mather said he could not say, and Mrs. Reynolds said she had to leave him as she was going to a wedding, and said Mrs. Reynolds at the wedding they say the bridegroom is conspiring and said Mrs. Reynolds he is marrying and everybody knows him but all the same said Mrs. Reynolds everybody says perhaps he is conspiring and said Mrs. Reynolds perhaps he is conspiring and she went away to call for Mr. Reynolds and to go with him to the wedding.

At the wedding some one said, the wife of the captain whose mother is crazy and whose four children are neglected rides a bicycle alone. Yes she does said Mrs. Reynolds.

Little by little said Mrs. Reynolds you expect it and as you expect it said Mrs. Reynolds little by little it is.

It was not said Mrs. Reynolds a very interesting wedding, she said this to Mr. Reynolds at dinner and he was not interested, not said Mrs. Reynolds as interested as that. I hear something said Mrs. Reynolds it was a little later and when they went outside they did hear something and said Mrs. Reynolds it does take some time to know that when I hear something it is something and it is something said Mrs. Reynolds. It made them go to bed a little later than they had the habit of going to bed and they did go to bed a little later.

Mrs. Reynolds said that it was not long to come along and she said she meant by that that any way any day she might wake up and say it is just like that, and not as it is, but as it was. Dear me said Mrs. Reynolds dear me, and then said Mrs. Reynolds dear me we will eat cake, yes said Mrs. Reynolds dear me we will eat cake. And said Mrs. Reynolds we will eat cake together and said Mrs. Reynolds it begins to feel like that it really does and said Mrs. Reynolds I am only waiting for the beginning and said Mrs. Reynolds Saint Odile meant that when she said that. And Mrs. Reynolds remembered it was too early to wake up not that it was very early but as last night was last night she thought she would go to sleep again and sleep tight and she did, all night, which was the morning.

Now that it is coming to an end, said Mrs. Reynolds she was talking to Octave Mather everybody is uncomfortable and everybody is irritated. Whether they have turkeys or not everybody is irritated, those that have turkeys are just as irritated as those who have not said Mrs. Reynolds and Octave Mather said yes. Octave Mather was not talking about turkeys but he intended to talk about turkeys and he said yes. Yes said Mrs. Reynolds and now when everybody has colds everybody is irritated, but really said Mrs. Reynolds everybody is irritated because now it is almost certain to be coming to an end and whether they will be better off or not there it is they are irritated. There was said Mrs. Reynolds Mrs. Christian and she was married to her husband. She had been married to him he was a nice enough man and he was an invalid, and she had married him because every one wanted her to be married to him and she was and she was a devoted wife to him and just at the end well the day before he died she had been so devoted for so long so devoted and had done everything for him and sacrificed everything to him and the day before he died she went out and ordered her mourning and nobody could forgive it and they were right and she was right, it is very hard to wait that last day very hard to wait that last day and now said Mrs. Reynolds everybody is waiting that last day and everybody is irritated. Well said Octave Mather, are you sure it is the last day, well said Mrs. Reynolds nobody is sure it is the last day and if they need it or not everybody is irritated, they can even be poisoned by mushrooms said Mrs. Reynolds they are so irritated and said Mrs. Reynolds and Mrs. Reynolds was not irritated not at all irritated, and said Mrs. Reynolds and she said she liked walnuts and she said she liked quinces only there was no sugar and she said she liked eggs only there were no eggs and she said she was going home to dinner and she went home to dinner and that night they had a very good dinner a very good dinner indeed, yes indeed said Mrs. Reynolds and Mr. Reynolds said yes and then they were very quiet and it began to rain very pleasantly and they were neither too warm nor too cold and then they went to bed.

Angel Harper when he was fifty-four did not remember that he had been born before. He just did not remember at all that he had been born before. It did not make him irritable but it did make him nervous and he said he would not change his mind and he did, he began to remember that he had been born before and that was the day that everything began to get grey, blue and grey and he said he might be white with fright but he had never liked white. When he was fifty-four he did not remember that he had ever had to shut a door, he just did not remember that ever before he had had to shut a door. Nobody said thank you when he went to bed. He was fifty-four, he had been fifty-four before he was just going on being fifty-four. But for how long. Ah that, was where he did not like anybody who felt fat. He did not mind if they were fat, but he did not like anybody who felt fat. Or and he often said so anybody who wore a hat. When Angel Harper was fifty-four he remembered that never before had he felt that it was just as well as not, and so what.

Well said Mrs. Reynolds I like to know that it has not been useless, and just then she sneezed not once or twice but quite often enough. It was neither very late at night or very early in the morning but said Mrs. Reynolds in these days there is nothing and Mrs. Reynolds meant what she said there is nothing to be said about daylight.

Angel Harper when he was fifty-four remembered that a very long time before he was looking tired and he was sitting on a box and he looked as if he was all alone and there were people passing by and a girl was standing by and a woman was behind him and later on it was raining and night was coming and he was sitting on a box and he was looking as if he was tired of standing he was not standing and tired of sitting he was sitting and he was growing he was feeling he was growing and his head was aching and his legs felt too tired for stretching and when Angel Harper was fifty-four he was remembering that this had been happening a very long time before.

A little every day of expecting to go away said Mrs. Reynolds, you can said Mrs. Reynolds change anything for anything, I wonder said Mrs. Reynolds whether it can be done at once because I am very fond of honey and in great quantity said Mrs. Reynolds, she was in quite a crowd there were almost twenty women and one of them had a child, whose tongue was burned because the child had put into its mouth an electric attachment and Mrs. Reynolds was very sorry. By the time they were all gone Mrs. Reynolds was very sorry. Dear me said Mrs. Reynolds if I knew how to be patient and I know how to be impatient I would know that everything is imminent very imminent. She was talking to Octave Mather and he said yes, it is imminent, so imminent that a postman is necessary, just one postman, it is just as imminent as that. Yes said Mrs. Reynolds everything is imminent that is to say that any day Angel Harper will not have a birthday. Not said Octave Mather and he went away and Mrs. Reynolds went home and she had nothing to say but she did say to Mr. Reynolds that it was time that everything was imminent and Mr. Reynolds did say yes it is so.

And then they had dinner this evening they did eat very well, very well and then they felt as much better as they could and although it was late in the autumn the wind was very very warm and they went to bed and slept as heavy as lead and the next morning they were awake very early. But they did not get up, they did not go to sleep again and each one of them read in bed.

Why said Mrs. Reynolds to Andrew Whittier do you look so troubled has anything happened. It is said Andrew Whittier all the fault of my father, mine a little but mostly the fault of my father. He liked to buy drugstores in the country that were not doing very well and then he worked them up to do very well and then he sold them and so he went on until he bought the one here and why I do not know but he stayed on and had a large family and he paid no attention to our education and then he died and I inherited the drugstore and I was always in a drugstore and I made out prescriptions and now all of a sudden they say that I must sell the drugstore right away or be put in prison, because I have been making up prescriptions right along and nobody minded and now, said Andrew Whittier you would suppose in a time like this they would pay less attention rather than more but no not at all I must sell it right away and I do not know what to do or what to say, with a wife and a lot of little children and always having made a living out of a drugstore, and Andrew Whittier said oh dear and Mrs. Reynolds said oh dear it is too bad, and then Mrs. Reynolds said it really was too bad, and it was too bad that Andrew Whittier looked so worn and he said it was too bad and they both said it was too bad and then each one of them went home.

Angel Harper remembered when he was fifty-four that a very very long time before he was thirteen then, it was raining very hard and it was raining he remembered he had then an umbrella when it was raining and he was walking and there were no puddles and he had an umbrella and it was raining very hard. When Angel Harper was fifty-four he remembered that a long time before, before what, before it was raining but when it was raining he had an umbrella and he was walking and there were no troubles.

Mrs. Reynolds when she was going home met Andrew Mather and she said I do remember and she said I do remember that when you see one Andrew you always see two and Andrew Mather said yes and Mrs. Reynolds said yes and then they left one another that is to say Mrs. Reynolds went home and Andrew Mather went another way.

It was unusual was it unusual said Mrs. Reynolds but it does seem as if they were weakening, and Mr. Reynolds said yes, and said Mrs. Reynolds everybody says but said Mrs. Reynolds everybody says it will be worse before it is better and everybody well said Mrs. Reynolds not everybody but said Mrs. Reynolds yes everybody everybody is disappointing, not said Mrs. Reynolds not really disappointing but surprising, and then Mrs. Reynolds decided that it was autumn and autumn was autumn and it was raining, yes said Mr. Reynolds and dinner, dinner is ready said Mrs. Reynolds and we have game not hare but wild rabbit although said Mrs. Reynolds I do not really know that there is a difference even though I know it is and that said Mrs. Reynolds is like everything and they ate their dinner and it was still raining and it was dark and it was still raining and it was bedtime and it was still raining and Mrs. Reynolds said when she liked it she liked to hear it and said Mrs. Reynolds it is disappointing but the change will be a pleasure, what change said Mr. Reynolds, the change said Mrs. Reynolds, going to bed getting up being here not being here, and their weakening really weakening and nobody knowing what is going to happen dear me said Mrs. Reynolds even if it is raining it feels like morning and they did not get up they went to bed because that is what it was it was bedtime.

Mrs. Reynolds said she was excited and she was excited. She saw John Ell and she said to him I am very excited, and said Mrs. Reynolds I know that you know why I am excited and it does excite you too but you do not want it to be true and so it is not exciting to you, and John Ell was as quiet and Mrs. Reynolds said he would be and Mrs. Reynolds said she was excited and she was. She went on and she met Andrew Mather and she said she was excited and he said he knew she was excited and she said to him but you are excited too and he said yes he was but that was nothing new, and she said but you knew that it would be exciting and he said yes he knew, and Mrs. Reynolds said she was going on being excited and she went home and she said to Mr. Reynolds that she was very excited and he said yes but do not be too excited and she said Mrs. Reynolds said yes she would not be too excited and little by little she was less excited and they ate their dinner and she said she was not excited and they went to bed and she said she was not excited she said it was all true and she might would could and was excited but now she was quiet and it was not cold and when all was told, Mrs. Reynolds said she would be excited again and again.

Mrs. Reynolds said they come with a hum they come past and said Mrs. Reynolds there must be so many of them so they do not seem to come fast and they last, and said Mrs. Reynolds and she and Mr. Reynolds woke up at night to hear them in their flight, it is a pleasure said Mrs. Reynolds, oh dear said Mrs. Reynolds it is a pleasure said Mrs. Reynolds and Mr. Reynolds said yes.

Angel Harper when he was fifty-four remembered that his grandmother she might have been his mother but she was not, was not, when he was fourteen she had a bicycle his grandmother who might have been his mother had a bicycle which she rode swiftly. When he was fifty-four and he began to feel funny about not being any more, he remembered that his grandmother who might have been his mother rode a bicycle very swiftly, when he had been fourteen. Angel Harper was fifty-four and so much not any more.

It is finished said Mrs. Reynolds, it is not ended yet but it is finished and said Mrs. Reynolds she was talking and she was glad she was not talking to John Ell she was talking to Andrew Mather, it is finished and the crows are cawing and it is autumn and I am wondering whether and she wondered whether she said she wondered whether whether it would be any different to be able to buy if you have money or not if you have no money. It is said Mrs. Reynolds finished and she went to say it to any one and she did say it to any one and she went home and said it to Mr. Reynolds. Yes said Mr. Reynolds. And now if we have money well not now but later when it is ended as well as finished said Mrs. Reynolds and we can buy and they can want to sell well then said Mrs. Reynolds after the first excitement is over will we like it as well. I suppose so said Mr. Reynolds and it was not cold but it was quite cold enough and there was not much heat and he was beginning to be very sleepy. I suppose so said Mr. Reynolds and then Mrs. Reynolds said she would quiet down and then they would go to bed and so she read a detective story that did not interest her and she did quiet down and then they went to bed.

Yes just as I said said Mrs. Reynolds Angel Harper will not be fifty-five alive. She said it to Oliver Mather and Oliver Mather said yes. Mrs. Reynolds went home to dinner, at dinner she said to Mr. Reynolds, As I said Angel Harper is not fifty-five alive, yes said Mr. Reynolds he is not fifty-five alive. And then they sat until very much later and then they went to bed and Mrs. Reynolds said, Angel Harper is not fifty-five alive, and said Mr. Reynolds Joseph Lane. That said Mrs. Reynolds is another matter and Mrs. Reynolds said and she was very sleepy, Angel Harper is not fifty-five alive and Mr. Reynolds said yes and then they went to sleep very happily together.

Mrs. Reynolds remembered the next morning that she had said that Saint Odile had not been mistaken, and said Mrs. Reynolds she Mrs. Reynolds was not mistaken in believing in Saint Odile because Saint Odile had not been mistaken. Angel Harper was not fifty-five alive.

EPILOGUE

This book is an effort to show the way anybody could feel these years. It is a perfectly ordinary couple living an ordinary life and having ordinary conversations and really not suffering personally from everything that is happening but over them, all over them is the shadow of two men, and then the shadow of one of the two men gets bigger and then blows away and there is no other. There is nothing historical about this book except the state of mind.

BRIM BEAUVAIS (1931)

MOTTO: How could it be a little whatever he liked.

ONCE.

Always excited to say twice.

He came twice and she coughed.

Now I need reason to wonder if she went to say farewell.

It is no pleasure to be angry after in spite of what they like as often better.

She might be once and fanciful but for me she would like a melon better only did she have to not like having to need more of it for her mother.

It is very true that each one of them had a mother and now how about now will he make believe that for and forests are with cold upheld. Some have been irritated to be told about the cold.

It does make a difference if he jiggled.

As soon as to say I like it. That is to say. Finally a word. They will often talk it over. What is the difference between you did and did it. Oh think so kindly.

I like a motto.

Lotto.

Pearls by girls.

Logs by dogs.

Pens by hens.

And suits by fruits.

When should a pencil be a pen and when.

They will marry then.

Coats are principally overcoats. Hasten to overtake them.

It is no ease to have no recollection and why will they come and hasten that is hurry them.

Coats may be then. I know that there are no new ones.

It is very nice to have a lot of money when no one has been heard from.

This is why.

I know what a book is.

Time when I know. What a book is.

Please me. She sees me.

I met many of them and now I have quarrelled with them and those of them all of them of which they will come often with them. So he says.

A great struggle in tenses.

The remarkable attitude.

Boys flourish in religion that is to say if they go to play.

A great many have never heard of it.

The great glory of a simple story is this, if you tell her in a letter tell him that you will sell him. Or may they be critical critical in a crisis or example or perhaps waiting. A true story has no interruption.

So then Beauvais pin them. Oh feel with tears that they are nervous.

Should they think beckoning is welcome if they change beckoning from willing and willing to as welling. Beckoning welling. It wells up in them tearing him in a hurry she would let him. Now think clearly usually ordinarily.

It is wife who is after all very welcome in restating that they will.

But might might be right in laughing. How can Howard often soften in respect to two women.

Beauvais and Howard made it yet in intelligence of not beckoning their account on their account. Our hope is welcome. Show me just why you came.

But of course you will not. Please me.

Beauvais must be appointed. The odds are in his favor. The pleasure is theirs. The most of it is what they like. It will be an annoyance to be introduced.

They no longer need with them. Hatchets can refer to having crossed before which an ocean liner are for them. More nearly.

It does smell of fish but I thought not.

Age why age why did you like.

Beauvais may trust in trusting. They will bedew women with welcome and appointing and it would fain be a circumstance. Which they have. Oh blindness where art thou.

Just be joyful and never nervous. Call a boat a boat. Do be perplexed by uneasiness. She may smile to have it about it.

They have so largely bought all with it. In no complaint. Read happily easily. Ferociously is blemish blame Beauvais. How are ours.

Howard had hold of him. And he stepped on a board. With him. Oh should he be in shadow. It is not necessary to have life ever. In cohesion. How are Howard's words. Be necessary. Be right. Be fairly in shown. No and no they knew all who have him. All who have him.

Chapter I

A boy lit it and it was happily one. Ought she to be delighted to be near him. They must be always better in not to have them seated.

Beauvais should be toward Howard.

Beauvais all very well.

Do they know a swan when she sees one very early in the afternoon lately before one has seen one.

Beauvais should be broken their rule. He was intimidated by an offering. He came to call pearls close. By their wedding. To them.

Beauvais change Beauvais to a deafening wedding from weeding and she knew like that.

Once upon a time a ruffian was married and they thought with them.

It is marvelously adjoining to them. They will be a blemish. More than with feathers they can relish more of them. How are mines made by his liking. He approached she was standing by his liking but what asking of their handling might with withdrawing, it was an incident of not exciting should then.

All this could remind but not now. How about then.

Very prettily incline.

And no moving.

It might be as well before behind with before then.

Them then.

Should accordion is in volumes of very inherent very should be indent so come with intent for velvet invent then.

There is no use in being vacant for wicked without ours.

She very near quiet.

I know I don't know.

Was he as tired as who.

Not the same.

There is no confusion but true.

Get through.

CHAPTER II

Better beeded it comes to be again that they bless them because in them they live with better beeded as she may authorise them.

To establish them they might to endow them with prevalence she may bring that to doubt round and around and about Brim how to fancy Brim. He is eight in anguish. How to fasten burly with for him.

Brim Beauvais has vanish as an addition and they cause. However ours are made. Generous as they color. Off without it. So sew she must be once in a while at a stretch.

Brim Beauvais can be caught. Permanently.

How can you be so pleasant around me.

Was I right to like them young.

Brim Beauvais how do you mention better. Better not. Brim Beauvais how do you mention rather. Rather than with him.

272

Brim Beauvais on account.
Should Brim Beauvais of course.

CHAPTER III

Two two two can you say for two how do you how do you do.
Brim Beauvais makes a curtain be achieve.
It went away this way.
For how many pears.
She prefers him.
Perhaps it is not here any longer.
For in place of it.
As much as when they felt more for me.
She loves me.
Brim Beauvais not having come, we will take it for granted that he is not having that pleasure. Which he could have if he had wanted to be successful as well as hopeful. James always had, said that he would be agreed. Always had said that he would believe not in his name. So sadly treating it as if it was, his hope. I hope that you will be able, to manage it.

BEAUVAIS AND HIS WIFE

A NOVEL

Beauvais is a name to contain happen and a gain in nothing. Beauvais is why.
They will stand. What they wish. Will not. Annoy.
Beauvais and dark the sun-light is dark. They will have had and been naming.
The sun-light is dark. Should many cry. And try. To meet often.
However. If they wish.
Brim Beauvais conscious of which wish to be known where and often.
Brim Beauvais and his wife Florence Brim Beauvais and his wife Florence and bears as well as more they should he would. Many did not come.

273

What has happened. Before. They married.

Brim Beauvais and will. They meet Mathilde and Aesop Amhill. These two were married and jewelry was not the wish they had not the wish they were always. To be known. They were welcome. When they were married they were writing.

Who knows how many were married.

Martha and Bayard Bartlett were married but Martha is not a name Mathilde is a name and Lavinia and even Agnes but not Martha, is not a name. Not Martha.

Frieda and Angelo Knowles were married. Were any of them married and who has known whom.

Brim Beauvais is a friend of aunts and even ready to be grateful. To them. They will exchange partners. He will remain married to Florence.

Partly of necessity it is careless to leave well enough alone.

Just two may marry.

Angelo Knowles and Frieda. He came they came together and afterwards both grew thinner.

Martha and Bayard Bartlett as is the case with many. He came. And was intimate. He knew how many went away in a minute.

William and Genevieve Butler always know any one. They are careless together. Of leaving without them. As they frequently do. For their satisfaction. As we know. It is very likely. That they have to satisfy that and they refresh, by their knowing which way. Any one went. Who might come. With them. How are they. Further.

She might be anxious to try.

It is a time of trial for them. As they are obliging and ready to fashion a home with them. Very much as they were. For them. No one. Is useless. As all of it is in denial. Or courtesy. Or will they.

So much more as politeness.

Chapter II

Who is through. With them.

She makes many a failure and for this they plan to deceive her. He is well-known.

She makes many attempts to deceive her.

By meaning all how strange.

They carried would they.

Arthur Ranger Gurtin and felt fully owned. She knew Agnes Lillian who made many add pleasure to their delight.

It is very easy to change. By labor.

And they nestle fondly for with him. He has gone and it would not matter because they will not inquire.

Brim Beauvais does not ask if it is strange. If it is familiar. To him. Because of which. Their handkerchiefs had meant. That he found them.

In harmony of a situation. If she. Was disappointed in not surprised. In anguish. Over in because for their felt formally.

Should join and shine.

I will go away with her and be a father.

She may be left with me.

Brim Beauvais might be anxious to be a witness. Which is what he is but will he see it without wishing. For them. Forever. Over more very likely.

Do they most and liking merit best.

I do not feel that I know what she thinks.

Yes quietly.

Chapter II

A part of their feeling is in towers having houses. Which they do.

Chapter III

How can it be hoped that will be helped. As it is felt that they will like whatever it is his way. Always.

In the time. In which. There is given very much to do.

Need there be a definition.

I like a mother and a child.

I like a mother and a child said quickly.

All hope of a better yellow is there is hope for practically. For them. In winter.

They return to women and children. And will they be coming. In their way. Advantageously. It is an advantage. Independent. Of extra. Wishes.

Brim Beauvais is married to Florence Anna.

Hours crowd in hours.

All his have heard all from him that he is hers and they are pleased. Occasionally. For them ferocity is soft. Oh so softly will they make it please them too. So made a meadow do. They like to be there at that time. Favorably. In their reaching it favorably. To have lost it whether. They meant it. For them. Too.

Alright they fasten better losses. Brim Beauvais knew that they will remain for them through with it favorably adjusted to them. As well. Brim Beauvais knew it very well.

An incident. Do many please.

On account of in their way joining with and having bay leaves around them with their mine of remind them.

Brim Beauvais came to say that. Think twice. Breathe easily. All of which is. Useless. Brim Beauvais breathe as easy all of which is more useless.

Than ever.

An incident without the perfection of their dependence. They need trials to perfect them. And he breaks down. And he weakens. Because they are more careful.

She met as much yet.

He heard a protection in an analysis of dedication.

Brim Beauvais sign away.

An incident in the life of Frederick. Frederick had been perfectly leave and leaves of a tree. He had been cautiously perfectly for them. They will garnish pleasure by a season and it is as easy. Should it be fired to impatience.

For this an incident.

In the life of Eliza and Johanna or agreed for them to hear.

All four of it showed.

An incident in the life of they met with whom. They he had been pretty well mentioned by three.

I asked are we any different from the rest of them and they meant with them. He answered yes you do. I doubt it.

But what is it that they expect who are angry. Show it allowed and beside. Ours are habits. It is kindly to try to oblige will he deny others with theirs as much as they know for it to have vim. This is what he said. Rightly.

She might do through you. What she did.

How have they. Anybody has had cakes. Should they show.

The strain of that. How outrageous.

Beauvais met a master.

Chapter III

Put and push.

Lightly. They will manage. To push. Which way. They have. As an enterprise.

Beauvais felt that way. Away.

Mean. That thing is mine.

We spoke of Johanna marrying.

Would a couple. Be attracting.

Oh do be careful of souls and pairs of pearls which they know.

She may Florence be plainly. Stated not to. Go away. Oh do thank you. She knows how joining is welcomed.

By them.

Hours of welcome less.

She made a mention. Of this.

Are surprised when surprise hires velvet for flowers. That they may underway as it is for them to like to say. That they do.

Hand in hand is made thoroughly gloved by kindness.

An incident in the life of Eugenia. Eugenia is a girl who has thickened with theirs. As they planned. She bought. What. As alike. It is momentarily all which of what they made Mary Mary do have the absurd allurement of their showing their cake whether with for them. This is a bit of why all of it well welcome as a wish. There would. Be. A girl. And a carpet. He probably sat there. It is not deniable that it is a sign. Of being well.

No one can arrange that Mary should meet Beauvais.

The episode of Robins Porter

They knew they had been not at all agreeable because just as they were to start it was finished. Robins Porter had rendered all this and made it easy at first. He was willing to be able to have them think and waver with and rather just as well that they went. But which. They were at hand. To ask them. To be selfish. About it. The incident which was why Robins Porter thought everything would be to finish was this. He was anxious to please and very wary of the advantage to be taken by their hearing of a mountain. Do be sweet. And hearing of a mountain. Should they plan for their sugar just at first she would like to be angry and have to say blue and green blue two green one and then they had requested white for some and it was after all better. That they had left. The episode of Robins Porter is finished.

Brim Beauvais who wishes will he say that all of it is anxious and every day they will persuade them to have them. Call for them.

Chapter VII

How can it be that they will change two for three. All of which they will judge it is better. To stay. With them.

If you think you do like that. You know that you will have the rest of that. So that they must in all of which it is radically. A rest even. For them. Just as much as when they would like. Which they mean by resting.

And episode in analysis. Will baskets hold everything.

It is at noon that they change. From one side. To the other. After noon they change from one side. To the other.

Brim Beauvais and Agnes Douglas should they think that they have not understood. Or would they rather. Be very happy just as they were.

And would it be all of it very well and alike by means of their. Retaliation. As much so.

It would not be as strange.

And in the meantime.

For them to be sweet.

For them to know.

That they can come.

Home just as well.

As with. For them.

And so they might in the meantime know the differences.

278

Brim Beauvais married Florence Douglas and William Turn-
bul married Mary James. And by and by neither of them were
frightened.

Who can change what they think easily.

But which of it by which of it, is the mention of why. Will they
go. Made necessary. In their instance. They like. What they do.

Please be careful of him.

Remember how many hours each of them spent there.

Chapter Seven

Who holds them from keeping. It away farther away still.

Withholds them.

Beauvais and Richard have not been asked do they love what
they have.

Order and disorder.

Cleanliness.

Reviews.

Better.

Which they will.

They are all very well established. And yet. Might it be an
advantage. To change or should they rest as they are. Would it
matter if it turned out that it was right for them. To succeed in
giving for us with what. They could have. In leaving as well as
remaining all and more for it. It is without doubt not a question. For which they include their satisfaction. Indeed. It is quite
warm.

So that they might find. That we were. Very successful.

Chapter VI

There can be two sounds for them. And she may be very easily
asleep.

Chapter Six

He made it be as prettily as possible their way just as much as to
hide for them that he asks it to be that he wishes to feel it.

But when. Justly. Defied. Lest. They neglect their curtains.
By which in immensely. They can so swiftly read it. For them-

selves. And be very unquiet in which respect they mean in imply as for them. Radiantly more than which they were. Indeed. Very often. It is by this that they put it on high. In pearls. Pearls which do make blue a fish.

But why do you do it.

Chapter Six

Be reclaimed for themselves with their tears as their measure that they will be by themselves as much so as they ever can for them. It is highly obliged. That they do it. For further. That they mean.

Ambrose Winchester made certain that were they waiting they would wait callously with a question. How fortunate.

A chance to have a place that they make theirs with which they cloud their delight.

Brim Beauvais was fortunate. In willing. That they should enjoy. Their closing of their blessing. With this chance. Which may be the equal of it. Or indeed. Be the equal of it. Or perhaps. Be equal to it. Just as much as theirs is. More than they could in a little while ask it very well.

Brim Beauvais was married to Florence Winchester and no one is more willing than they to be virtuous. With which they have in their nervousness. No pleasure. Which. They have. For themselves. Alone. In every way. Very likely. You know they say and they oblige as well as being without any anguish.

Let us think callously of unity.

He is obliged. To banish those. Whom he finds. Disagreeable. Just as well.

As when they feel that it is now and about why they can. Be always very well.

And reasonably. Precious and cautious. Just as much.

Brim Beauvais and his wife Florence. James Sperry and his sister Janet. William Fuller and his sister Dorothy. Jacqueline Richards and her brother Henry. All these are astonishing. More than that in a minute.

280

Chapter VII

Why should he go with him when he stays here for him.

Brim was mentioned without mentioning them. They were usually forgetting that choice is an attention and choosing is frustrating just as others are. Who knows. Just as others are.

Oh can they decide better than beside with their assistance besides more than they tried to have them share as they can with which they are aware of failing. There are three things that make for yes. With them. For which. They may add. And mention. For their kindness. Which is habitual. As they have forgotten. To be certain. In a minute. With their enchaining, forty in their arranging. Which they might. In substance.

For our cloud.

As soon as it has been at once with them. For them. In fortunately.

Partly without it.

It came to happen that on account of distance they looked again. At one. Which is the same as. That they have forgotten some. Of which they had been rather. Careful. Formally.

Rather careful. Continues. And more about it what they consider their fault. No one can join Brim Beauvais again. With them. As he certainly does.

Brim Beauvais was anxiety. For them. In their mistake. Which they manage. To arrange in waiting. They manage to have preferences. Just as he is told. For this and in an appointment it is a declaration that whatever he may be being with them for it which is why they have understood adding as changing. Certainly he meant. All of it a delight. It is just. What they wanted. Because it added. It to that. To oblige them to dictate. Their allowance. And so Brim Beauvais may do this with her.

Chapter Eight

She said a river is near land near water.

Chapter VIII

Put Beauvais where you please and cry will felt. Willed and will felt or Beauvais almost cry.

Just when and why will adding will Beauvais try and will cry.

It is very pleasant in the garden and they look too and see that they are looking too. At him. He is very nearly when they see him. It is only afterwards that they will cry. After him. It is only with him that. They will try. To cry. With them. Nine of them with him. It is only afterwards that they will try. To cry. With them.

Brim Beauvais and a ball where there had been. A pigeon. This is not a fancy this is a fact.

Brim Beauvais could be surprised that the taller and smaller was as active as the taller and smaller was as active. And he went with preparation to cover the situation. Which they added figuratively. And no one asked them anything. Or nearly. Not enough. To oblige them. To have meat. Ready for them. It was after this. All. That is to say. They had already eaten. Every day. Brim Beauvais.

Brim Beauvais makes every one angry.

Just yesterday they were selfish.

Beauvais has made an answer. It is a very good way. This is not an answer. It is a record.

Of what a titled lady does.

Part II

And episode in their agreement.

She said I have known three.

Three when.

That they were better than ever then.

She said it does not matter then.

That they were as much better then then when.

She said with when they resemble or resemble them when.

She said with whether they will or had rather better resemble better resemble them. And so forth. This episode was not so soon finished. As commenced.

The episode continuous and they joke.

Beauvais pleases her and misses being with her.

The episode

Who can be tall. All. Three.

Were they seen near to be. All three. As tall as she. She was careful to be left there where she did more than her share. In devotion. To the cause. Of country. She was never lost and easily filled the post which she needed and it needed. To be filled. At a very great cost. By her. She devoted herself. To the cause. Of her country.

After that what mattered.

Another one who was equally tall. Was not devoted to her country. At all. She was well. Known to be able. To say. It is mine. And it was. And she was dead in bed. Because she loved these. Who were of another country. And so that. Afterwards she was ready to gain. No one could be left to be leaving. That she would have them. If they. Went away. Did they all go away. However and rather he meant. That they were careless. Not in expression.

She was never drowned. Nor indeed in love. In answers. Oh so easily tall. There is no use in wishing that many women were even. Or three.

The episode is finished.

Chapter Eight

Brim Beauvais is not anxious to dance and as it does not happen he will not be famous as successful or thoughtful or in them alone. As they very well know. In place. Of an advantage.

They might be careless of all three. Brim Beauvais, Florence, and Hotchkins and his wife. All three are mercifully spared. So many are anxious and she will very well eat dinner. Here. Not unexpected. And alone. With and which is noticed. And so they like their interruption very nearly all of it was for the best in their liking made easily and gracious. He told them that he liked that they were. Cautious. And that they were. Fairly insistent.

Many many leave with them.

CHAPTER IX

What does he do when he thinks. Of it. With them. Which fortunately makes no difference as they mean to have it lost for them. As much as they do clearly. Which at once. It was more necessary just when they thought about it. For themselves. As they do prudently. It is of no use for them to arouse more than they leave as balance. Just as they do naturally. More than they did. Ultimately. For more than ever. Where they do particularly.

Brim Beauvais surrounded the center with what they could call flowers or only just a flower. For their chance. Made necessary in an ultimate recital of their wanting. It for them. Brim Beauvais felt very well. It is often that a welcome for him and for Florence comes simultaneously just as often. They came at once.

Who does and whom have they heard. Which is it that they add publicly. Nor prudently. In reading with and without resting. With resting. They will leave them for it or as bought. It is very welcome. All of which do. For them to add luckily.

Brim Beauvais was successful in asking it to be a chance. He was successful. In adding. It to be a chance.

He made all of it plainly.

Brim Beauvais left and right for which in there to be a chance. Needed in estimation. Nor for clarion as they look as at a daisy which has on account that she was faintly yes as ever. Do which. Strangely. Leaving fought in pieces. Owned with a joining in their reverence daily.

This is why. They have it as a leaf. As and a leaf. For farther. That she had adjoined their raining in the main where they choose. They choose admirably.

Brim Beauvais and choice.

Brim Beauvais was a man who felt that he knew older than the want of eloquent prestige and caught and further felt in choice gently. Who has heard stern tones. When they like. Florence. Think.

All are changes.

Chapter Nine

An episode introduced for variety.

284

One man is a man. Winning. Two men are two men winning. One man is one man winning. Two men are men winning. Two men who are two men winning are arranging for that creditably. One man one man winning is making winning learning. For their account an episode is made of very pretty laces. Very pretty presents. Very pretty choice. Very pretty choice. Which they have. In discretion. And so they marry. Glass finally is thought. To be welcome. As toast. And for a fugitive they come to go. An episode to tell them so. An episode is kindly. She is not kindly. Nor is their care. Kindly. For them they like. Partly. To have it be. A kindness. Which they do. To them. An obligation. And a relief. Indeed. Not to know. That they very well wish. For everything they have is more than they thought would leave it out. For them. More than they did. An episode is gracious. They had indeed very much rather have been. Cautious. Very much. Rather. Have. Been cautious.

An episode closes. They must have been known to have won. They must. Have been. Anxious. To have some one. Win.

Chapter X

A little yellow flower is fragrant.

Chapter Ten

It was liked that a little yellow flower was fragrant chapter ten.

Chapter X

A remarkable career in which he had been heard. And so. Brim Beauvais was best of all for it for himself. That he would. Leave it. As he had been. Very careful. One at a time. Obliquely. Which made them rise. For them. Fortunately. On their account please measure it once that they may. Share it with them. Just as it was. Remarkably. For which in their allowance. They make spoiling it. A victim. Of their obligation. That they are. Reasonably. Avoiding. To be careful to. Release it from their hold. At once.

Brim Beauvais did the commission.

He asked them to prepare whatever was all of which he would

ask them to compare. Relying. Upon their account. Of the same. That they had undertaken. And so it would be of interest to them.

Brim Beauvais had married Florence. It was not strange to add one. Just by being. In their case. Left to it. In every way a delight. Just in the hope. Of their announcing that. After the violence. Who has. Introduced violence. Into the discussion.

Brim Beauvais made it be perfection. If perfection is good. More perfection is better.

Chapter X

By the time that they are told. That a great many have been held to be very well known as when they have them with them. In the place of their wanting. That they should resign themselves to everything.

Curtains have been left to be only with them. And windows have been. Left. To be without any hindrance to living. And also. They might. Be just as well established with and without their having been very soon only known as hoping to be winning. It might need much encouraging to have them like that a beginning.

Beauvais and trimming. They will be persistent. In the realizing. That they continue. To use men. And women. And who knows who came. Who follows. Who is with them. Who says yes to them. Who after all made them go.

Just then three women saw that they could call and they must not be aware that it could be thought, that they were allowed to have it heard for them. All of this is a necessity. And they wish for everything.

Brim Beauvais had occasion to reach it. Very likely all who had been without their consent left to be reproachful could be thoughtful. It was with their help. That they were able. To have it helped to need more than they could. That was available.

Just when will they come.

Chapter Ten

It was very nearly certain that they had heard of it again.

286

Chapter XI

Just why will he try.

Chapter XI

Brim Beauvais may account for this some day.

Chapter Eleven

Brim Beauvais may appoint them to behave as well as they can under the circumstances. He will realize that it is very well to have them place it there for themselves. They will amuse themselves. And while. They are quiet. They will be openly and with relish leaving it alone. As they might. On account. Of their arrangements.

It will be plainly left to them to try.

Underneath.

It is by them by no means that Brim could never be annoyed. And because. In astonishment. They like. He asked for it. As they lured them. To arrange places. As if it mattered. Very much. Who makes all calls.

It is in union that there is strength. And they divided. And therefor. One of them. Was stronger. Than before. More so. Than before. And which one. Went away. And may they like. To have it intended. That it should be known. Or not.

It is a very long time for which Beauvais asked a minute. He was united and felt himself to be urgent. And he would. Be without doubt. Outwitted.

Or would they narrow it. Would they exchange it. Or only by themselves. For them. And with renown. They knew. That there were clashes. And that no one was to compare what they liked at one time. Or nearly so. For them. Frightened.

Should they mean would they think. Or hope for Susan.

Brim Beauvais married Florence. Florence had a cousin Susan. Susan was only felt to be when he Florence's brother compared one another. Susan is the same as Sarah. And they knew more than ever. That it was very pleasantly rather more than they were alike.

It is by being coveted that she thinks well of them.

An appointment, they are appointed pleasantly. It is more than orderly. Often they think well together of this arrangement. And it is allowed. Without any doubt. Carefully.

Brim Beauvais felt that the occasion warranted his interference. But was it his duty. To be polite. And express his hope. That they would arrange. Never to see them. Which is. What happened. It is ordinarily. Not a question. They will be welcome. They will come. They will be welcome. And as much as ever. Will they have it happen. That they knew. That on this account. They will join. Very fairly. In something. That is undertaken. At once. As a pleasure. And in consequence. Of their having been. A disappointment. Or an opportunity. Of disappointing them immediately. In the meantime. They were as well known. As it is at all necessary to be. Where undoubtedly among themselves. They speak of it. Which is a relish of their advantage. Over others. More than. They enjoyed. In an advantage. Necessarily theirs. This is an autobiography of one of these. And only two. Made it more an occasion. Of interrupting. On their account. Their hope.

Think singly and very often.

Brim Beauvais can easily be lost in counting.

At all events and at this time. All of them whom and because of it they had the occasion to reveal as fairly with themselves safe and safely not more than all of it as they had established. A memory.

She may be reminded instantaneously as an advantage.

Brim Beauvais knew more than as they were. Knew more. Than. As they were.

Brim Beauvais feeling a revelation in instinct. And a pleasure.

Chapter XII

A story can be told if there are conversations. There always is conversation. Whenever they meet. They tell themselves. That they do it. Or they might mutter. But not at all. He waited.

Chapter XII

And then to be then with then not with them. And to be interested and with them. They were perfectly at home with and
without them. Fortunately. It was an undertaking that they had
undertaken with enthusiasm. And they were remarkably adapting the obligation of wondering. Whether they were able. Was
he able. To judge whether he would. Decide. About whether he
was able. To have more of them. None of them. Which were
necessary. As they were. He was often awful. And it is thought
that there were meaning to have them come then with and without him. He was all that they could leave when. They left him.
To themselves. As they were often. Just as sheltered. As on account. Of the sun. Which was why. They had decided. Everything. As very likely. Often. At that time. All who have hold.
Of their exchange in exchanging it for him to beckon them.
Often. To come there. With and without him. Or more con-
stantly than they ever do. In excuse. For which they are without
doubt. Remarkably. At one. With an investigation of a com-
monplace. Revision. Ask them for them. Rather. Which is by the
use. Of elegant. Made natural. And untimely. And then. To have
imagined.

There is no circumstance which necessitates the use of. As
owned in an instance as have been. Recognised. As their permission.

Brim Beauvais can come too. And he will ask too. How do
they manage to feel. That they will. Be very well.

To have renewed seeing him.

Chapter Eleven

It is while they are about it that they feel that they will need it
as a caress. And they might without theirs for them and farther.
As friendship is necessary.

Are you her friend.

Chapter XII

She thinks. That I should. Not mention. What he thinks.

For more than that. They do not care. To amuse themselves.

They give me pencils. At my request.

And at once. They fasten. Upon. My asking. Them. Would they. Be able. To admire without. Finding it out. At once. As they may.

They will illustriously. Suffered themselves. To receive. Them. In charity.

As much as they can.

Which they declare.

They are able to explain.

Whenever. They indicate. That they will not plan. It. For them. Very much more narrowly. As a comfort.

Beauvais. And Brim. And Bliss. And possibly perfection.

Brim Beauvais was married to Florence. He had married. And not at once. As they were very certain. That they would. Bequeath. A wedding.

In them. As they are. In them.

They acknowledge. And they are put. Out of countenance. Just as it is. Advantageously.

No one. Can remind. Theirs. In. Integrity.

Nor should. Nor would. If they mean. That all of it. Is. A recompense. Gratuitously. Just as shun. They shun some of them. But they meet. Some of them. As well. As an invitation. In jeopardy. Which they can. On and allow. In never. Leading. Which is why. Lamentable. Is never a bewildering result.

Brim Beauvais is the result of having nestled in a foreign kingdom.

He has been in intent lent and decorated in allowing variety to think well of when. They meant. To reassure. Him.

Brim Beauvais is always. Profoundly. Influenced by this opinion.

For them fortunately for them they fortunately for them are with them and they are with him. Fortunately. They are. With him.

He fortunately for them is there with them.

They are there with them.

At a distance they are. There. With them.

Brim Beauvais. Made it known. That he had them. As a help.
In their trouble. Which came. Rapidly upon them. In consequence. Of their establishing it. As an obligation. In which.
They questioned something. Individually. And on account. Of
opposition. In the meantime. He went everywhere.

Brim Beauvais married Florence Beauvais. They rested very
happily with the sun shining in the window. As it happened. On
both sides. And they were dreadfully sorry. That it made no
difference. That they were. Very likely. To be able. To have it
happen. That they were. To begin it. As it were. More than they
did. Not in anticipation. Or exactly. So. Shall we mind. What
they do. In this way. More than they had. At once. As in the way.
Of their meaning. All of it. For them. They are often allowed. To
come again. Naturally. As their known. Then. All of it must.
Be. An excuse.

CHAPTER XIII

Watch a watch for them. They will remember to ask ribbon
for ribbon and to resemble them.

They must understand them. They will ask it for them of
him. They will excuse leaving it there for them. They will add
immeasurably to their hope that he will have it left there at that
time for them by him. And so. They must. Make. No mistake.
Because an advantage would be taken. Of any error. That they
committed. In misunderstanding. Exactly. What was meant. By
undertaking. To divide. All of it. Into the parts. Which would
not. Be magnified. By distance. They will call them occasionally
to come here. And see. What they will like. If they have it. Once
in a while. Entirely to themselves.

Brim Beauvais has managed. By a chance. To be perfectly se-
cure. Even doubtfully. In aggression. And they mean. To bother
them. To the degree. Consistent with their announcing. That
they are prized.

Brim Beauvais was married to Florence. Florence is not direct
not directly accustomed. To deduct. From Florence. Which is
in exchange. And adroitly. Who has meant to agree without.
Leaving it with them.

Brim Beauvais is made happy by the dog's dreams. By the dog's dreams. Which makes him. Believe in their startling. As he will be fairly. Thought famous. As the circumstance. Permits.

Brim Beauvais has a chance. To dispose. Of it.

Chapter Fourteen

Who could chew the cud of their thought nervously.

It may be a satisfaction. To disturb. Their relation. To adopted as liberally. As chocolate.

Chickens and cows.

Who allows.

That they will win.

Without doubt.

Weddings.

Brim Beauvais never sings.

Chapter XIV

Brim Beauvais may have a chance to dispose of the rest of their stay. They will go away. Or manage. It industriously. In advance. As they catch it in their flight. It is of no importance that it is better that it is so.

Chapter XV

Brim Beauvais may always go. Away.

Chapter XVI

It is without authority that he has reasoned.

Beauvais is married to Florence.

Chapter Sixteen

Ann and Nell.

Chapter XVII

Brim Beauvais. A lament.

He will be tall. And they. Feel it to make a restitution.

He will fail. If at all.

She must. Be. An addressed. Mention. Of a. Mary. May. A. Mountain.

They will. Grant. For such. And such. Indeed. And. Nervously. It is all. Out. Of a. Mountain.

They must be. Scared. Just now.

In spite. Of their alarm.

Just now.

Very much. Just now.

In spite. Of their alarm. Just now.

Will they mean. Just now.

It is woefully their perfection. With and with. Irreligion. In such. And sections. Of celebrated. Silence. In use. With men and main and when and diminish. All ours are mine.

Brim Beauvais cannot lament.

And they call. Hoping. He will not hear.

As they may. Scare them. In spite of no alarm. They can not be made to harm. Them. Immediately. For they are. Very much. In touch. Of. With them. Without with them. As they scare. Them. In very likely. Ways. It is just. That they will seek. To establish their repose as double. They can. Be known. Without. Any trouble. It is. Effective. To make sounds twice. Should they. Be seen. In reach. And reaching. Come to all. Who have. Gone.

It is a call. To all. Resting. Very well. I thank you.

Chapter Sixteen

Just why. May they cause. Fifteen. To rise. Speedily.

Because they answer. In. As all. It is very well known. Turbot.

Chapter XVI

With wedding Brim. Florence is with him. Brim Beauvais is married to Florence every day. With way and have and stay. Imagine that they. Will. And better. Than. If they had. It. As certain. Brim Beauvais on account of announce.

With a gracious wish they will establish their independence of killing. With a gracious wish. They will establish. Their independence. Of killing.

They may, without anguish, be very often selfish, and they had, established sanction as permission.

And then they were obstinate. And willing. To be selfish. As a wish. Without them. They bought and brought. Only. More than they taught. They were pleasurable. In changing. They were. Embellishing. In persuasion. As ignition. For their quelling. Their. Distribution.

But which. Of excess.

Made it a plea and pleasantly. They mentioned building.

They built themselves. Theirs. Among. Withdrawn. And acting. With a division. For their rarity.

Beauvais and blessed. Because of fright. And should. In course. Of division. As they might.

Chapter XVII

Brim Beauvais could because, and a cause. Of their. And grieving. It is a grief. To be saving. In no obligation. Of their use. With use. Of which. They were. Saying.

Chapter Seventeen

Gone cautiously and question. With what. He said.

They minded. Made by them. To. Belong. In connecting introduced. Connection.

Astonishing can be a covering.

Only do right.

Should they mind.

Chapter XVIII

Leave well enough alone.

Chapter Nineteen

Just cut or put into a cup fifteen made into as many as subdivision. And then they will have as provision. Their immediate welcome in delight. No name made no name made no one. Known no one.

Brim Beauvais should relieve whatever he had begun.

Which made him be better than every one. In their provision. As allowance.

Brim Beauvais should be called shortly Brim Beauvais and not

294

welcome. No one clings to welcome in lions. Or in hearts. Or in welcome. With indifference. Or creditably. Theirs. In producing their joining. This. With them. Immediately. For theirs. Reflexion. That they will. Be welcome. As much as for instance. In redressing. Wrongs.

Have to be careful. To think suddenly. That they will perish. With their attendance. In beguiling. That they shall align. In trusting. In relief. For them. Of their hope. Of lain. Away. By this. That they. Can see. Brim Beauvais. Close. To them.

Better yet. In plenty. Of time. For preparation.

Brim Beauvais meant to keep account. Of whether. It was fragrant. To compare. Older. And younger. In all. The little while. That they were able. To apply for leave. It may be that they. Came in. Noisily.

To often wonder. Whether it would. Be best. To narrow. The research. To their opening. Not too silently. Their bought. Books. Books. Should be given. Not bought. Leave. It as a better felt. Wish. To entertain. Them. As well. As grant. It. To them. In time.

Just why should they ever be anxious.

One of the ways to be taught is this. Brim Beauvais shall miss. Being. With them.

And then. For the time. In which. They prepare. He shall be inclined. To favor it as a reason. In all of it. Incidentally. And bought. Also. No one. Will follow.

So much for that.

Chapter Nineteen

Brim Beauvais married to Florence Anna. Brim Beauvais married to Florence Anna. All made. All. Made. Of all. He thought. Just then. He will. And worship. Walk. Brim Beauvais. Which. Is why. They wish. To once declare. In spite. Of which. They came. To share. It plainly. As they like.

Brim Beauvais shall be welcome well and well. Cordially.
And well.
Cordially.
Brim Beauvais is as knees and need. Well. Well. And cordially.

In conducting Brim Beauvais to this clear and declared reason. For an established. Restfulness. In better. Than before. Left to them. Now. They may. Come to be. All of it. In their despite. To. Say so.

Brim Beauvais may need it. For them.

Chapter XX

Ten may be careful. Of money.

Chapter Twenty-one

Why should mentions be in doubt.

It is a little bit of their defeat that makes them have it come to be a seat. Which they occupy.

With them. Very little. Just as much. As they will have. They will see. To it. For them. Alone. That they have announced. Pride.

They have a great deal of pride in their home.

They have hopes. That at that time. Forty-one and twenty-nine. Make. Thirty-three. In fine. And leap-year. Makes it. Twenty-nine. Who does like. Horses. Who have bits. With which. They ask. Will they have fits. Because they think. That theirs is lost. Which is why. They have asked. The most. Of them.

Which can be purchased. Readily.

Brim Beauvais. Looks like that. To-day.

Left to be told. That an adventure. Is an adventure. To-day.

Forty-nine makes. Sixteen. Excitable. She may. Frequently. Mispronounce. It.

But why will they sing. As they may. With pleasure.

Chapter Twenty-one

With pleasure.

It is a habit to need society.

Chapter XXI

With pleasure.

Nor need they be. Without the token. Of their earnestness.

Fifty-one. With pleasure.

Chapter XXI

They will be met. With pleasure.
And if they accept. The meeting. It will give. Pleasure.

Chapter XXII

They must Brim Beauvais. And Florence. They must. Be perfectly acquired. As an addition. To their. Cultivation. Nor do
they. Need they. Fairly. Furnish. It around. Without their conclusion. And so. They extinguish. Their thought. Their hope.
Their carefulness. Their intrusion. With pleasure.

Should it be mentioned. With pleasure.

In inhabiting. More than they build. Or even in coughing.
More than they like. Nor in withdrawing. Much as they can.
In theirs. In part. In decline. And in flourishing. Theirs. As plants.

It is in decorum that they use their argument.

It is. In decorum. That they use. Their argument. With pleasure.

Should they be idle and antagonistic.

Chapter Twenty-two

It is very. Evident. Made entirely. Carefully. For them. As a
fortune. That they. Conduct it. In a revision. As an instance. Of
their regard. For many. Of their. Fellow-men.

Chapter XXIII

Just as much as a mistake.

Chapter XXIV

It is thus that. They have quarrelled.

Believe me. It is. Indeed it is. Their chance. To reinvite. Their
birthday. Very especially.

Should they decorate a ribbon.

There is a companion.

Brim Beauvais. Has improved.

Chapter Twenty-four

It has become. No disturbance. To accept. Their. Poise.

Nor will they be. Almost welcome. As they shall shame. Those with whom. They have. Been. At an advantage. Made carefully.

Chapter XXV

The history of Brim Beauvais.

He has been very careful. Not to be quarrelled with.

Chapter XXVI

Carry usefulness as an ideal. This is the story.

By accident in returning to their destination they did intend and were a little disappointed in being unable to furnish themselves in the manner they had hope. They had not intended. To return again. As it happened. When they returned. They were told. There had come. As if sent. By them. What they had dimly brought. And this was. An item. It could be a branch of their seeing. That they could. Beggar description.

It was undoubtedly. An error. And it could not be. In the present contentment. Rectified. Although. They could all use. In having to be. Merited. To be thoughtful. Without their permit. In indiscretion. She might amount to that in only briefly calling it to close. Its doors. As they may. Wonder. Should they cover. All who think well of them. With their hope. That they may do. Very well. By those. Who wish. To talk. Is it a wonder. Or might they not all. Have needed. It.

Very slowly.

And not to have. Forgotten.

She may amalgamate change and hate. And he. May amorously. Expect. Their. Representation.

It is undoubtedly unlike a cloud.

Chapter XXVI

Either she may think well of it or he.

Chapter Twenty-seven

Nor hastily. On their account. Will they furnish. Their pleasure. In intermittance. Which they may. Color. As they arise. In their deliberate thought. To be alone.

Chapter XXVIII

Just as many call. As furnish music and water.
Or either. Just as many call. For them. In their delight.
With them. In their delight.
For them. With them. As they. Exchange it. For them. With them. In their exchange. As they. Exchange. It. With them.
They exchange. It. For them.

Chapter XXIX

Did they do it. Without doubt.

Chapter XXIX

Would he be awakened if he were to be alone.
Which they meant.

Chapter Twenty-nine

It is in all a religion. To make them think with things. That they mention. They must. In their habit. Feel very well. As they may. Come. To invent. Their kind. Of arithmetic.
Brim Beauvais. Fortunately. Makes no mistake.
To be as much. As touch.

Chapter XXX

They should indulge. In leaving learning. Their change.
They should indulge. In respecting. Their allowance. Of their hoping. That they will. Underwrite. Their hope. Of their example. Of which. They will allow. In moderation. Their change.
When they are. Thoughtful. They will migrate.
They will ordinarily prepare their method with hope.
Which they will relish.

Chapter Thirty

Brim Beauvais was married. To Florence Anna. She was never appointed and they chose. With reliance. That they had bought. Thoughtfully. In return. Those have. It. Well and pray with their hope of anguish.

They will need silence to employ.

It is after all no useful hope. To have to stand with their wish. No future hope. With which. They will. Stand. With their having. A wish. Of welcome. In hope. And choice.

Chapter Thirty

She might be mentioned as. Much endowed. With pleasure. To be felt. As much allowed.

She would be gathered. As well. As she can. In reasoning. With whatever. They will. And may. That they can. Color it. With joy. In the instance. In which. They felt. Their reunion.

Brim Beauvais is made to be wonderfully. Rested. Any day. With their understanding. Such as they liked.

They may be. More. Naturally. All of it. Which. They allowed. In their reunion. It is. With all. That they. Established. In all. A lesson. To be learned. As teaching. Theirs. On account. For them. In the course. Of their allowance. Which may. Call. Their union. All which is. Made without troubling them. To be adverse. They will follow. Just and by the same. With. And whether. It is beseeching. They may. Follow. With and. Moreover. As they can. In no way blemish. Often. Fortune. Brim Beauvais. Accounts. For this. They. May. Florence and he. They may. Account. For that. In their gayety. In their reasoned plan. Of which. Amiability. And their. Anger. In a way. Never. To be. In an exchange. Of their failing. Made entirely. In such. And because. Of in vain. Brim Beauvais. Is a name. He is made. Of the same. Away. Is a name. He is made. Of that name. All the same. Brim Beauvais. When they came. Rain. Brim Beauvais is a name. They came.

Shall we join them.

FINIS

HOTEL FRANÇOIS Ier (1931)

IT WAS A VERY LITTLE WHILE AND THEY HAD GONE IN
front of it. It was that they had liked it would it bear. It was a
very much adjoined a follower. Flower of an adding where a
follower.

Have I come in. Will in suggestion.

They may like hours in catching.

It is always a pleasure to remember.

Have a habit.

Any name will very well wear better.

All who live round about there.

Have a manner.

The hotel François Ier.

Just winter so.

It is indubitably often that she is as denied to soften help to
when it is in all in midst of which in vehemence to taken given
in a bestowal show than left help in double.

Having noticed often that it is newly noticed which makes older
often.

The world has become smaller and more beautiful.

The world is grown smaller and more beautiful. That is it.

Yes that is it.

If he liked to live elsewhere that was natural.

If he was accompanied.

Place praise places.

But you do.

Partly for you.

Will he he wild in having a room soon. He was not very welcome. Safety in their choice.

Amy whether they thought much of merry. I do marry del Val. I know how many do walk too.

It was a while that they did wait for them to have an apple.

An apple.

She may do this for the Hotel Lion d'Or.

II

Buy me yesterday for they may adhere to coffee.

It is without doubt no pleasure to walk about.

III

The romance of the Hotel François premier is this that it was seen on a Saturday.

IV

In snatches

A little a boy was three, two of them were three others.

She may be right I told her. I thought it well to tell her. They told them. They were avoiding nothing. And so.

Do they and are they will they for them to be remarkable.

Now think.

V

Repose while she does.

VI

An aided advantage in touch with delight.

VII

Just as they will have by nearly whether.

What is the difference between a thing seen and what do you mean.

Regularly in narrative.

Who is interested in Howard's mother or in Kitty's mother or in James as George. Dear James as George.

A target.
Those of course of us who have forgotten war have been mean.
I mean I mean was not spoken of the sun.
Do think of the sun.

VIII

A chance to have no noise in or because.

IX

They change being interested there to being interested there.

Hotel François Ier

To and two to be true.
They will be with me
To have you
To be true to this
And to have them
To be true
They will have them to be true

X

Just as they were ten.

XI

Who made them then.
Which made him.
Do they come then
Welcome
Join and just and join and just join them with and then.
It is very often that they are dissolved in tears.

XII

Should it show where they are mine.
And his care.
It was that they might place them all of them.
Just why they do so.
To call Howard seated.
I never leave Howard.

Hotel White Bird

She may be like that
Do
For me to choose.

II

Our just as assume
Leave riches with her
Are dovetail an origin
With wood.

III

But she
Can go clearly
To pieces
By adding act one
By add may meant scene one.
Left done right and left done.
She will never think in pointing in property inviting.

IV

Just shown as their agent.

V

Just shown.
As their
Agent.

VI

Mutter.

VII

They will read better

VIII

With other

IX

They have known a platter better.
Thank you

My dear

My dear

How are you
This is for you.
Dear
How are you
This is
For you
How are you
My dear
How
My dear
How are you.

II

Love which
Love which
To love which
Which to love which
My dear how are you.

III

Just why they went.
They went
They were to have gone
And they did go
And they went.
What did they do.
How are you
My dear
How do you do
How are you.

IV

Oh choose the better
Oh choose you
Oh choose for you

V

She made it better.

VI

By the choice of more
That is why

My dear
You are
Better
How are you
How do you do
You are better
Two.

VII

She meant well.

VIII

Much better

IX

Very much better
Well.

X

She had eight
As the date
Full date
We date
We have to relate
The cause
Of bringing
It for her
It was light
As weight.
But she enjoyed it.
For it was
Not more than
Not too late

XI

Not at all

XII

She is very well I thank you.

306

For them

Just joined James.

In no way a disappointment.

They must have met with them which was in the capacity to lead and leave.

Our house contains. That is made back with idem. Idem the same just please come and claim our house as a lot which we have in a home. This is what made a pioneer.

Leave a nature to rain.

It makes no difference if they use it.

A narrative oh how often have I thought that a narrative.

How often will a narrative do.

Complain about fifty narratives perfectly.

He is waiting not for his food but for his appointment. Dear dear.

Plenty of bread and butter.

He is waiting not for his food.

Resignation does not mean narrative.

He is to come welcome, as well as having left welcome is not a narrative but foolishly.

I was completely persuaded by Mrs. Tolstoy but she told me.

She was completely persuaded by William but she told me.

How should either have been headed very often.

That is astonishing a narrative and I would so much rather be poetical.

For me.

I love poetical history for me.

I love poetical and still for me.

I love poetical will poetical for me by me.

The best of wishes

He wishes he came away he wishes.

Just why he wishes.

Joined by

He wishes.

A narrative of relieve

He wishes.

307

Think William
Poetical

So few this further.
I will reward
An error
Of regard.

Hotel François Ier

Was there
A surprise
In nearly not to face
Imagine
That the name
Was the same.

I

How far are you not to leave them.

I

With a colored message to know colors were. To know there his coloring there.

I

She made no mistake. To take not only with it. When she came to mend they say.

I

Garments were a separate desire pleasure. She made hours a desired separated measure. With them they actually considered why it is a treasure. Must it become be how even much with pleasure.

I

She used pleasure exactly.

II

They are neither here or there.

II

Or there it mostly widened for in invite there. Them there who how did it. Do this for them.

II

Should it be shown. No how who ever coupled a dog out of a pleasure or round. Around. See me a round. It is polite. Let us congratulate ice rice.

II

They made no mistake to be indifferent. How which come faithfully or. Will it be easy. Not for me.

II

Adjust, add edge to adjoin wine. Wine is a drink. Water. Watered wine. We weigh wine.

III

They must expect one of you.

III

She may expect two of you.

III

What does she expect
You to do.

IV

Come with me and sit with me

V

I am afraid if she waits longer it will do her an injury.

Forests

She liked forests in a pity.

I

With forest too.

II

Will forests do.

III

What is it a pity will forests pretty.

IV

Forests are there

V

Saturday

VI

She must be without it

a

Old when

b

A forest deer

c

Makes it pay me

d

To call her.

With them

When they came in some one was waiting
When they arrived they said something
Some one was waiting when they came in.

Just Church

We stay gathered
With them intentionally
Have they met them
With Church
Just as if in incompetence
It must have leaving weather
As much with confidence
In Church.

Regularity

Be wider with lather
Rather a darkening

Of with gather
That they will
Suffice
Just why
They have this
As mother be occasion
To have rejoiced then ring
A bell soon.
She must be just which they do.
Outright.

Behave

Why cups of butter.
They will
In the morning
Happen
To be fatter.

Articles

Drop him for me.
Does wish.

Tidy

They make her mending large
To have a doll
Do be careless
In hope
Of pointing
Their dispatch
Of hurry
Hurry and come in.
It is of no use.
Hours of trying
That is what breaks
In cups with more rather
Than
They wish.
Do I know whether she has come in or out.

How ours

Very fairly selfish
Some sealed fake ponds
Very much as they hear like
May down in implied
                              Shells
Ears if they accustom to born
With counted help her
I do not think better help is ugly
By which
In win.
Just why a repelled for her
They might in nature
Come for
They caress
A dove tailed
In succeeding.
Nobody knows me.
Our too.

She is my bride

They make safety in seventy plus fourteen. As known as never hearing figures.

What will she see when she hears me.

It is after.
All mine.

Powers in because of up with their resource.

Careful

There is no use in eiderdown
But yes
Leaves which have been that they can win
With yes.

To guess
Would she choose what he would use.
He asked tell her to judge when
And because it is fine.

Allan

Allan Ullman knew me
He was prepared next of kin
To sink and swim
With magnifying carving
Should make
It is well to have held a pillow
Or other corals

At fourteen

It is extraordinary
That she made fourteen
And will make fourteen
And does fourteen sixteen
Gradually
It is extraordinary.

How are they hoping

It is old to think of welcome heavy women
She was fourteen.
They liked to have owls look unlike a pigeon they do look
like. That is a pigeon can be mistaken. For an owl.

How many things happen

A great many things happen

Every time

Every time they mix they make it different women
Who has sung men.
Do be careful of sung.
Checkers among.
Half of them sung.

313

Every time they changed they forgot all they bought.
However they bought.
It is very not useful but exceptional.

A part

Allan Ullman who knew me.
Separately from three his brother mother and father. He knew
me. He said when he knew me he separately regretted one two
three not he.

Our page

How could it be a little whatever he liked.

Morning glories

He made as stable morning glories
For the next to handle
Their regret.
Morning glories were eighteen to the dozen
Forty made fifteen.
Everybody who has been for them.
In add her add coming.
Too many thousands
Have a link with a king.

Francis Rose

Shut up
And stay shut
Where they drink all the better
For families of yet get her
With them in ravishes
Between them with dishes
And they came then with her
In precious labor with love
He may yet get wealth in getting tender
Which they make stronger
With us
Thank you.

How many cakes make jell for jelly
And how many loves make bless
A little flower of rather think better embellishment.
Just why join mass
A mass is a towing to a lock.
At towed they devise
How to a challenge.
Challenge has nothing to do with him.
How are heads held Howard.
She cooked and seized.
Cooked and seized
She cooked and seized.
Forbearance
Cooked and seized.
Bridle is paths.
Just as about a path
Just as a path
Just as a path.
It makes no difference whether four
Ate one.
Sum to sum.
Our adding is more hours.
Ate one
Just as well ate one
Just as well eight one
Just as well eight
One just as well
Eight one.
How much are they like me
Like.
After walked.
Before walked
He made her talk
To have her
Walk
After walked
And leave a walk

Leave walk
Or leave her leave walked.
It is an error
Oh.
Join me
With observation
She may be
Our hour glass
Which we sought
And have not bought
For our hour be
Be an hour for me.
Such is sought
And here bought
For our be
Her be
Err be
Come Francis Rose
Or be
Forty leave fifteen
Thrilled be
Or sought by
It for him
Or for
Her
For him to be
When they may
They may
Shall shelter
They make
Shelter
As they may be
For and to be
Nobody knows how old showers are.
Or how should hours should be.
In inlay should be
That with mean

With be
With held will then
In to be.
What is a square.

She should be

What could it prove
If it made no difference
To them

Dear dog

Dear dog
What do and does it leave
Dear dog.
He likes to see
Dear dog
But did he know it was he.
Leave dear dog where he is
Otherwise it is.
Not satisfied.

With him

Just why they ate
In state
With him.

Why does it come like that

He so happily is present.
When it comes like that.
From him
She so pleasantly is present
When it has come from him.
She so happily is present.
When it comes from him
So happily from him
When it comes so happily out of him.

He says obey

I obey which is to say
They come to-day.
And she closes the door
With delay.
But will
To happen to happen yes.
She sits with him for him
We know the difference

Than

I little thought of how it went
When they were told
It had been better with them
Than
Just yet.

Better heeded

Should rejoice be to arrange
Will they tell they until they are strange
Let them be for me to estrange
That they will until they change
For them will they until they have caught it to arrange
They will estrange
Because they can be blamed for the arrangement of their change
to change and arrange to be strange and well intended to come
to derange them then for them in abundance to them in a vice,
who held them
In a vice
Twice
To them to arrange
For them it is strange
That to them for them
They arrange
In them for a vessel which is meant a book
A book look twice

He held him twice
To make him twice
Shake dice
To be thought tranquil
In their wear
Aware
Come catch with capable
To be to like
A tree
For them capable
Underwent in anger
One
Two
Three
They must be sensibly made with them for them
Three
Ultimately
She might hinder
All of them
Ultimately cornered
All of them as meant
In clouds
Who ate them
Three
Ultimately
Made in generosity
For them to have it
In undertaking
Restively
She might be wonderful
Ultimately
They might in undertaking
Shall he have pleasure
Ultimately
In their recognising
Why they were often
Just as much as three

Which they may would
It may weight wood
For them ultimately
Better than could.
It might be careful
Who has made them
Who might have made them
Ultimately careful
With them.
For them.

BARTHOLEMEW ARNOLD
OR
AFTER THE WAR IS OVER
(1932)

He was named Basket and he could have shaken hands and then what comes after that.

He was called any name that begins differently Abel or Andrew or else by no other name.

Bartholemew was not a name of which they had thought.

A child when they have it will grow fatter very often they worry if it should grow thinner. They had everything to make it thinner and they made it fatter which was a request they made to have it not be thin. A little girl cannot be called Bartholemew altogether.

And then if Bartholemew is not born it does not matter.

This is the life of Bartholemew who was born after.

Bartholemew Arnold had no middle name. His name was Edwin Bartholemew Arnold and he was the younger brother of his sister as a great many are. If they are. They will be restless occasionally. Nor will they be often cooler. They like to like just that.

Bartholemew who have you met or would you come not only if you were better able to be half as selfish. This may be the history of any younger brother who had been held to be one of a large family or only a sister.

May be she will. Be very well. If they like it. It is often as exhausted.

Bartholemew loves life and movement and may be often very often without them. They will call it an indifference in wishes. They will pause or they may cloud it altogether. If they may. They are not anxious.

It is twice that they are perfect.

Bartholemew in order. To be after all. With them. A pleasure.

Who has he met. He has met with whom has he met. Should not be silenced.

It is easy to love better or rather better.

For them or with him.

Should it be a passion.

Bartholemew could love anything which was a different mission. He came again to be often.

This is his history or he likes anything.

Bartholemew will you be young.

The first meeting

It astonished and was one that a shading could be one and no one. Could sent to say it was come. This is the way it came.

Should she be surprised.

If she said yesterday yesterday could he. Always better than vermillion. Or better. They could be carelessness enough now. She was better. A mother was let her. And she would never be now.

Bartholemew strangely.

Did always mother's milk be grey and a milk which held her. She could be better than just guess. It is not dangerous. It is never as dangerous to distress. When they. Could. How. Ever. They will come in interest quickly.

Bartholemew should be in ever as they may not end.

Bartholemew varied.

Should he be received graciously. Or should they complain.

It is not as much. Which indeed they offer as they went.

All who can remember have seen her.

The first meeting

Would she be a little too late. Bartholemew could change to waiting. He had an hour of allowance. He was a little while.

Once unexpectedly.

It is better that is is Bartholemew.

Or may be they like to have been having a little change but no worrying and that is why Bartholemew has not yet been born his sister has and they are all. Very nearly better than as they went. We will wait.

Bartholemew was cautious. He met without any hesitation. And they were engaged.

Finally think that they are beautiful and very little at the first glance.

Bartholemew and his sister. His sister was born first as very often happens very delicately.

She was made to lie beside her mother and they will be indeed in plenty of meaning which need be in looking up where is she. Very beautifully.

She is tall. And very small.

She is very well. Bartholemew may be entertained by being cautious.

He was ruled by their rest.

Or may they say.

A very little one may be tiny Bartholemew may be met as the rest. May be met as the rest. If he is only cautious.

Bartholemew chose what he could do.

They were careful to think well carefully.

Who could and who did have Bartholemew.

One of this was that there were not two.

Bartholemew and never only how do you do because Bartholemew lived to like it and have it to do. He was remained.

A very little chance to have oiled glass or any reason to have it contain. If they help they are not very distressing. Or should she be in a way not spoiled. Or should she. Be. In a way. Not spoiled.

Bartholemew comes to live half way through or just as they knew or they did not know.

Who was alike.

It is often their intelligence which is at fault.

Bartholemew can be called will he or may he they had called

him in and it is not a change to sing signs it is by that that they afterward liked it as new.

Bartholemew can not complain. It is better than never.

But it is always a nuisance.

She liked it bright. And so did he.

But he naturally did not like it so.

Bartholemew was easily not a name.

It is very nearly said. That it is not a name.

Bartholemew can be when they are not lost in which way they go. He is a boy to be a boy clearly. There is a little sister who has appeared first but nobody has questioned. In inviting and they will ask plainly. Have they been thought to make mention of their being needed more than likely. And so Bartholemew is beautifully told.

Who should as they very say better it with their care.

Bartholemew has not, only been met but they will think so. Which they do as their having it could be just once as well.

Now when they will wish it of all things.

May they be thou with how they could often leave it as much. It could be. Or never change. In half. Of the time an allowance.

Bartholemew never would learn latin and greek lately. She could.

He would ask partly.

Or prefer. That they could crowd.

It is often that more than which is all is known.

Bartholemew was born there. Is born there. Lately. As well.

It could be found finally in extra wishes.

Bartholemew oh see.

She was charmed with the dresses of the little baby.

Bartholemew a little. Can be added to her. As she leaves. Allowing for the window. Or with. Cannot be. As extra.

It is quite how or which Bartholemew can be who.

If he had a brother so slowly. A sister. He did not know.

Oh may why. Be returned.

The simple story. Is. That a child who was born was which it came first. And neither how or. Perhaps more.

I would like Bartholemew.

324

The birth of Bartholemew

He is not born. A very pretty charming little girl came to be born in the place of which no one could fancy that it had come. Alright.

Could all be here who heard that he was here not here.

And so Bartholemew cried. Not only. Within itself. Because alternately. He was not coming. Nor had he come. Nearly enough.

Has no one been to see Bartholemew.

Should they be certain to be known to be just as well known. As they will reason. Could it be better just a little baby first. She came. They said they knew her name. But afterward they were not satisfied. Should any one leave guessing a reason to them.

Bartholemew was one of wishes. It is.

Scene one of two

By this which they are rich.

No one or no.

With love for them to have it know.

Oh do you like whatever you say.

Bartholemew is promised.

Be wise for Bartholemew. Ought you to be ought two. It is well named.

Once in a while they like to go and to have it told so. She might be pleased to gain. And so. They lay.

Bartholemew was not religious in no appearance.

Need or knew a church in which not one who went saw which it had been just as well as known Bartholemew.

No one should not remember that the little girl was born first.

Bartholemew can be called one. And they will come to-morrow. Oh how horrid it is to be not allowed to have been both the younger and the elder. Which is it. Do you not like it. Will you not mind it. Will you not get it. Do you not have it. Bartholemew naturally could be in uniform. He was waiting.

All who are prepared like not to say that they will add a wedding to-day. After it a little of it was born. Should they like it. If they are through. Or yes.

Bartholemew should be often quietly. Not by it.

Bartholemew was seen to ask his mother.

She could not say no nor as yet yes. It was too soon.

Bartholemew would prefer yesterday or to-morrow he knows which is better and which is advice. They will be once in a while guilty of no distress. They like to have it done. They lit it one and one. One and one never makes two if there are two. Just now there is one. When will there be another one.

And call it Bartholemew. Or one of not two. They will never know it by name.

Who can be fortunate.

Could it be sweet to congratulate.

She had had her child or two.

She had had one. He was not known.

Sweetly will they be placed.

Do think why they wait. They have not known for which Bartholemew.

She should just smile if she was born already. Or she. Should just smile. If she were born already. Is it not strange that it was St. Bartholemew's day to-day. And he was not born. Oh indeed no he was not born.

Will Bartholemew be three of two.

One two three with she. It is easy to make a mistake. And to be mistaken.

Bartholemew was mistaken. They placed a girl where. If he had been. He would not have been indifferent. Nor would they have been different. But they like a loss.

Bartholemew had not to be had by a mother.

Bartholemew who. Will have no care for you. It is better to have come again. He will come.

Will it will he with they be just with it with him with me as restless.

Why will they shine with all their might.

Could he not having yet been known around like it that at no age could they say have to add it. Can it be likely that they will be older if they see it. See carries across or by having been after made to come as welcome. Change one to one. And they do not know.

Will they be true or through before Bartholemew.

Food for which they had not bought it and this will be Bartholemew's care. Once in a while they come again just as they like. Why is Bartholemew cautious.

But why but why but why will he go.

Or but why did he not come.

Or but why did he come and come.

Bartholemews are often known.

She shall be left to be only here he shall be not only left. This is a question for a guess. Was he or was he a guess. And will he guess. Of course he will. How likely.

Not nearly why they abide by what they like yet.

Or which they mean to pause.

Bartholemew is known as not to minister to their being without them. He may be one although he has not as yet come.

She may well be well be born. And he.

He was very warm when they were very cold.

Should they be thought to be anxious not to be born first.

Which leads not singularly to the ways. I looked and looked and saw. And it was a pleasure if I looked and it was at what I looked and saw.

This may make it soon may be they could be well soon.

It moves as lack of like a moon and they will praise it as as soon. And this was why they changed their hope of making it be ready yet for you.

It was so easy just to like it.

When they exacted little descriptions what did they see.

They saw that nobody said it was ready to be ready to be left.

Now I have this to say yesterday as well as yesterday for yesterday and to-day. I say that they like what I say.

I say that it is true that looking just like you makes it be better and that it is not only true that when they say they may that here and there it is best to be sure that they will be best of

327

any often may they be apprised of how often they can be called. Will you come and be careful.

I think this is why I like to come and look and make it be just as much theirs as most. An easy delay does not make it ask of it to be what they fancy as diminishes.

I could like a simple walk in life and no deceptions. But they will please talk alike. And she may rest when she labors.

It is I hope that I understand and hope to know all of which she says.

I wish to say that the way they tell that they are well is this. Will two think two will.

They could be heard asking why they fastened. In which they play. Oh do be gracious as well as cautious.

I have been thinking of why they know there is a difference between what they like and what they like to hear. Also how often they will say how often they will say they will fasten it as they will like which is more than when they come. There is no sense in asking. Or might she think it was for her.

There is no difference between dim and him. Oh join or join in just as much as may.

They may be content to wonder yet will they not have to have it made to-day as well as yesterday. This can be their belief in no rectification.

I think well of not only telling a thing twice maybe.

It could interest her in them him that it came.

Let us leave ours as best and better. It is not an inconvenience.

I think that I was pleased that I understood what I saw.

This is a case of their leaving.

Now a little time in which to rest.

I have seen that by looking I knew what I knew. That is just yes. They may be their way in their way.

Can happen that she standing there is remaining. Not when they like.

It is all too precautious.

I could I would I should.

Fall means fall or fallen.

And they like out loud with clouds.

328

Which she may very really save for them alone.

How can an hour be their own alone.

And but it is.

I could be always ready.

She will do much alone.

She may be thought to be rich this is how often this is.

Well why do you come in often when they are strong. This makes it less like this.

I have often thought that I have often come to walk.

All should be shared as yellow and blue. They may just as well as wishes. Does it make no difference what they do. All this leads not to fellow but to very well I tell her.

Every year they make more than they made but this not only does make anybody well to wish.

All this makes it very well known.

And now I ask you how many feel well for me.

This makes an add and an embellishment which I like very much. This is why I read first.

I write very well and I tell about how I wish.

This is their increase.

Commence now.

A plan to have a novel follow.

How they asked me what I thought.

What is a romance oh be with me without an adventure. And they will very likely go and see it.

At the entrance of the bay a bay is a body of water not surrounded entirely by land she knew that they were to go straight through.

Oh how often do they wish and wish and wishes.

What do they not tell all they know they do not tell all they know because they know that any others others may or may not go and they may or may not or might not say so.

What is the reason that a commencement is in vain. This is why when I looked at one and one of each one or another I was not only unprepared.

This leads me gradually.

After a while I knew what pauses were.

And so I was perfectly powerless with well well be astonished. She said come quickly. All of which made nobody made a mistake and so it looks like it.

What is it when they say they will rest while they look like it. This is their change.

And so we know that as so many things happened they will not buy more than if it were just that.

This is a full explanation of why they looked together. All of which is in form or a narrative.

This is why they question early if they have come early.

What is the system they say that ought ought to be may they. This is a narrative as an index. It is of no interest to know about it.

Could it be well to be always here to be always here to be always here could it be well to be always here just as they were at that time.

And so it is so when they are behind with their work.

What is what they do not write. They do not write that they knew.

And just so is more than which they had when it is not often.

Could he say every day it looked alike which he was welcome.

It is better to be so tender.

This is why they like hears and made.

It is often thought that love and war may be careful. Just now we have known two doors.

It was a pleasure to think that I did this for her.

What is the best thing they can do the best thing they can do is to buy something.

This makes narrative that is what they are telling not at a stand still.

All which they mean.

Tell any one.

How very soon does one not care that they were there from there or to here or from here to there which perhaps just like it they do or do not change.

This is what I think.

It does not matter who has come when they have only been called first.

330

I am very grateful that they listen not by themselves.

The story which they told they told they do not care who to care.

Let me say just why I come.

I come because she is waiting.

And she comes also.

Leave me to say whatever I like.

I have felt when I have seen them that they were often there.

It is not by the time that there is a cloud of out loud.

I should be very pleased to have them be anxious about me.

It was in this way that it was not now.

Now this is all the difference between what is and what was.

One need not do it but it should be done.

In this way slowly it turns not away and not ever from not being yesterday.

I have been thinking that what makes them this is this.

At one time if they were sitting and not under a leafy tree not at all it was in their costume.

All of which is right.

It is very singular to be often after they went away.

Now think how it came that I was interested.

It is best to know that it is so very often that they will not count. I know how they feel just after every hundred.

It is very likely that love will follow which they call me.

Now listen carefully to how they felt now which they knew.

It makes no difference whether he will order or be loved.

She will be practiced very likely in why they came.

I like a way to cherish.

After waiting and they know will they will they tell it so. To their great astonishment it did. It was told correctly.

I wish to ask is it of any interest now.

A man who can be known often known each as will again I have lost all which they have fastened mildly now why do they add in obstruction it is not which for which they can outlast.

How will they hand or handle what they have not been thought to know.

I wish to leave intelligently for it now.

It is often what they like that makes them leave it alone.

It is when she hears that she knows flattery. I said I liked it.

All who are gained are crossed with their own being a pleasure.

I wish to say that all true stories when they follow an advertisement are exciting. As also when they explain why a woman is named half after a flower in dislike. More also because it is too told that they will heighten by not all alone. She could be early known to cloud.

I wish to say that I understand him.

Well wish it for me wish it for me that I had rather not had hand made.

No one who has been seen has been cautious.

Let me always know that a cow can chew his cud or her cud.

Part II

How they are capable to have it change.

If they that is if I could leave it alone all the time they would be as white while they were there. Let us think how happy we are. Just then they were related.

This makes it do that they will not partly tell differently from which one is who is who.

She could be thought to say it all the same. After I read I was not certain that they lived Easter for me. I wish to say that no one was more anxious.

It is in every way a happiness not to seize it first.

Or which on their account.

All fortunately are told out loud.

Or they may be often occasioned to need no one apiece.

I like everything that happens for them for Monday.

And so they know who they know out loud.

It is very extraordinary that they are not more here than there which they do.

In this to say slowly that she knew where they went.

It is well to be here and not only not here but where. They were painstaking in and on their account.

332

I would like to know just why they were principally there.

Just now I feel that they will not only tell but not be made to be helpful just why they wish.

This was when many thought the same.

This is why everything is changed and they are not to wish again.

What can all who have been Bartholemew do.

The reason that May makes them anxious is that they have been as anxious.

Any other thing which they have been as anxious about is just this.

For or fought. But which they ought.

Or why not be careful.

I have heard it rumored that it was not true.

It could be often said that it is often not there that they are better than even without this. And so they will kiss. All who are often thought of could and cud and better here than there.

It is all mine, coming too fluently.

He has a great hesitation in often too. In very likely. What is the difference between hearing and seeing if both make a claim on Bartholemew.

It is often there that they are very happy.

In which way they changed as much.

I think with Bartholemew that she will regret it all through.

I have often thought that if they think of him as Bartholemew.

It is always less as a use. Or however clouded.

Who will be called better nearer.

Or who may they be outwardly. No wish to wish all of which for Bartholemew.

All dogs are like dogs. Then they do not know when.

Once very often I knew that it was at their place in their place but not noticed as Bartholemew.

Bartholemew is meant.

All which they know as best.

Or which they might as well finish.

Bartholemew may often be just the same.

What has Bartholemew thought.

Bartholemew is not the cause of everything nor will they manage it just now.

One or two of which there is no cause to speak easily.

Bartholemew has not spoken.

It is often not only by their choice but by necessity.

No do not think well of them.

Once upon a time they were not afraid to have it known that it came again.

During which time they may have thought ought of Bartholemew. It was their meaning they withdrew from them in the meantime and very soon across to throw.

How should Bartholemew be framed.

He asked Bartholemew to be mine. Or rather may they happen to order milk for Bartholemew.

If they were ready may she deduce from this preparation. Or rather may they tell it as very likely. It is very robust to be well aware of why they were ready. Just now.

Bartholemew was born but they not only let no one know but they waited.

With which it went it was as well known that they went often.

Bartholemew may not be changed because they come they will not only hope not to differ to expect him but of this it is quite certain. Oh why will they like not only known so much.

Think kindly of use of so much. Or more narrowly in tears. If they will like it again. It is of no importance that they are only not only not selfish. In no man's memory.

Yes who can doubt the truth of their attempt. Or which one fails. They may like it. About when will they come. Often as she intended to like. Better than it. For them it is no fortune. Or on their account.

I think I will sell a wheel a day in this way they who are awkward are not supplied.

Full of why they ask.

Each one is perfect when two are enough.

Now I need not tell you what I am trying to do.

Once when they were willing they were just as comfortable as ever.

No more than Bartholemew.

Bartholemew was anxious to know it.

It is often that they please.

When they may be cautious they may not be anxious.

Once when they were all older Bartholemew was not cared for. It is not known just why he was anxious. It is not only their hope but also their anxiety that filled them they were pleased to be always there and not to be lost just yet. For instance if they were anxious they were equally not wanting to have it be known then. May be all those who were welcome were not only thought of but with it they had not nearly enough or some of it which is what they had as an example. In which case not only was it of no use.

Bartholemew is a place for which they can be no mistake. He is helped with them as the found which it is in their case. They knew that they were to have been here in not their way only but also why they left. It is hopeful to let Bartholemew know.

Should he not be well known not to wait.

It is very soon that they know a noon at noon.

All which he knew when he went away.

Bartholemew was one of the cases which they had in mind. Or not to get away from which they meant.

It is often the father of Bartholemew who is persistent. Or more than how they like. Bartholemew is often that they thought well of it.

Bartholemew they will strangely play as they know it very well. He may be not at all like it.

Bartholemew what of it all is true.

Did you see how I wrote out here Bartholemew was not only known down there. He was not born oh how do you do he was not born.

He owned a Bartholemew by which by this time all for they may not closer it is all bought.

All of which they argue.

They may think that Louis Etienne Marius George will replace

335

Bartholemew but not at all it will not and yet it is very difficult to make a sacrifice.

Bartholemew need not have joined or made it all a pleasure.

Who can be so glad that Bartholemew is not there where Louis is.

It is their own for which they are remarkable.

I would never he would never lose his place.

Flowers make Bartholemew careless he never won to name.

She knew that it was not only here that they were born.

He knew she knew that it was always their plain for them not frugal but an instance. To think two not two Bartholemew.

What would the poor orphans do if there was no military service this has nothing to do with Bartholemew or the disturbance of a rolled ball.

It is very warm if it is not very hot for Bartholemew. Yes dress well.

Nobody needs close doors for him because he will naturally win.

Bartholemew will not say that when it did come to pass they would not only happen to stay which they did he knows how to comfort.

Bartholemew entitled would he or would he not eat pigeon or which he chose when he was deprived. Nobody likes what he likes. Bartholemew may meant to mean him.

From which they thank him from this that indeed better than capability Bartholemew understood too that they should not be patient because of whatever they could or could not do.

No one changes Bartholemew to hope. Or would they do well to relish it.

She sleeps accompanied by the dog Basket while it rains on a Sunday afternoon this makes them neglect Bartholemew for whom a bird sings birds sing or not sing because they like the time Bartholemew has been heard.

Bartholemew may be fought for just why they should wish for this.

Bartholemew do they separate them from not with them or kindly let well enough alone.

336

It is often that they think not why they were known.

If Bartholemew met a woman and she was well to do would she be a woman who had been busy as a woman is busy who is and has done more than that in being there when it is not only best but necessary to do it so as there is nobody else there or not.

Bartholemew is exact. In wishes they may be rich in wishes and riches for them for which they have gone.

Bartholemew may marry a ball.

Bartholemew may not be ferocity as well yesterday.

Or they will as who like Bartholemew will or will or who like Bartholemew they make it please extras better than more of which it is alike because of the Bartholemew they met because she will be well at least for then they can in become not begun nor not one or Bartholemew which may name too play two again they think what it is not only why not they mean fourteen mean.

It is not only known I think I should mention Bartholemew soon may be they do say it is as soon in July too Bartholemew in no case when it is not theirs to try.

Bartholemew not neither or add was he glad.

Why is it all they like in Bartholemew.

Order it for Bartholemew which is not only right but may be not only but at least perhaps will be what they cannot keep from leaving it but which they are at present to do.

Which may Bartholemew do.

Should she be willing to be precious.

Bartholemew could be through not at all not yet.

Just ask them how they have not met Bartholemew.

I never hear Bartholemew say what did he say.

Fortunately Bartholemew is not too anxious to be here.

Why do they mind not having Bartholemew if they do.

She caught or they want Bartholemew as he comes to stay if he might.

But not if as if Bartholemew minded. Bartholemew was wished wish on or of whatever it made it a wish.

Bartholemew may be relieved by a name.

Not only when Bartholemew came did they go.

Bartholemew should not mind currents.

Bartholemew was not restless.

Bartholemew could wait.

No news of Bartholemew who knew that they needed not only their way.

But who acts as if they did if not Bartholemew.

Why should eight be Bartholemew.

Bartholemew could not be stated to have pleased.

If she could add Bartholemew to fairly.

It is not of any use to Bartholemew.

They stretch arrest arrests. No one need know Bartholemew.

Why should Bartholemew be so persistent.

Bartholemew this time did not know what it was like.

Bartholemew to ask what news is there of you.

Or not. Bartholemew.

Kindred Kit to Bartholemew.

It is of not any importance to arrange what they have Bartholemew or higher than if they did know that not only not but a valley could be more than if a wish it were below.

Why did they guess that they would not have Bartholemew.

It is true that Bartholemew never came through.

The End

MARGUERITE
OR
A SIMPLE NOVEL OF HIGH
LIFE
(1932)

IN NORTHERN COUNTRIES A CHILD IS OFTEN ADOPTED.
When it is. There is often something else that happens and either
the child is not well or very well and something else happens. It is
very likely that it is a girl.

Should it be about what they care.

Once once or twice in the northern countries they adopted
a girl. She had a happy childhood and nothing else matters. A
childhood is not happy if nothing else matters. It is just what
they like.

In northern countries if they adopt a child they will be satisfied to be unhappy. If nothing else matters.

In a southern country if a child is well a father is nervous that
is if it is well born as it is well. And they will be seriously well.
Just as it does. It will if it does. It can take any amount of care.

If she could remember that she was adopted would it be more
than any other pleasure or sadness. She was never distressed.

One at a time they being the only one left and so a home is
formally what they do often feel to be very well but not established.

It has often happened that they have been adopted. One may
say it is better to be brought up by one parent than to be adopted.

339

One may say and no one does say or refuses to be thought to be welcomed by any such thing.

In the northern countries they often adopt a child particularly when a couple have been childless.

It was their habit to be childless and so they adopted had adopted one. She was raised as their daughter although in a way it was the one who had adopted her as their legal daughter who was with it as one.

It is her name which is of importance. Sometimes they are legally adopted and in any case they are known by the name. And in this case it was so.

After a little while it ended not disagreeable which made it not a matter of indifference.

She was not appointed nor was she chosen to leave home.

Should she be chosen in adoption not any one is chosen. They adopt one this is often happening in a northern country where it is not very cold and no one is ever frozen. They often adopt a child and they think nothing of having never been accustomed not to have had a child without adoption. And so much for that.

After the adoption the child is with them and there is no difficulty about any one leaving them when either one or the other need not have been left without either one or some other one and without explaining and so they are necessarily bad and they have been very good. It is a satisfaction to come from a small country which is not a big country and which is never really frozen nor is it the country where they will have never been cold in the summer nor hot in the winter the winter is not only cold but the summer which is after the winter is hot and everybody is not certain that it is possible to have a cold winter colder and a warm summer hotter and so they are equal to anything.

It is the custom to adopt a child in a northern country if the couple have not either of them wanted a child and they have not had one earlier and then when it is later they have adopted one. This is not an advantage but it is happy without there being any more than one without any objection and the other not wanting it either.

She was used to callousness, she could be tenderly mused she could accustom and in they are always made comfortable in a different letter.

After adopting they are very kind to the child they have adopted. They do not mean anything or if they are fortunate fortunate and fortunately is a good reason.

From the beginning she and they were likely or just as likely to be adopting.

The way they were happy was this. They were colder and warmer and they were always ready to go in and come out as often and this is altogether. Once in a while they were not more than always careful but this made no difference to Marguerite. No one could adopt oftener. They adopted once. As it happens they adopted she was adopted. This makes her.

It is my might.

One

Marguerite was chosen and once when she was younger she was not so promising.

Now to like her.

She could be happy in not hurrying.

Or could she be happy in not hurrying.

After she left her adopted father and her adopted mother she had not left them. They would never know anything about anything and she would not care nor were they there nor nearly anything. This is natural when it has happened and is happening that she is sad but not worrying. How many can inherit money when some have some and really no one knows anything. And this is not a grievance in believing. She was very happy. Any one is sad. And any one is no one worrying. I like to look at cushions.

See one

It is a sea where they are near a lake and she said they swam there from their nightgown. Or all. They swam there. Not on the sea they were not on the sea. A land that is not on the sea is all that is so nearly that in living she was not threatening but really saying a river to be sad is nearer. And so this was not late in life. But even later.

It is very pretty to have straight hair made curly.

The thing that happened was that she had a habit. Not of being adopted or adopting or adapting but really truly would she like it now was not it dreadful that any one could often only not be sent away. And stay.

The real story of a northern winter is and a northern summer and which they might in vanish. She could always be called for.

In the northern countries adoption is not everything because they are not ever careless. She was adopted when she was quite a little thing. This does not matter. Who always does not matter. Alike does not matter. Who has been never been careless. All about does not matter.

She was adopted and it does not matter. She is now known as never having been careless which they may declare should she be here.

Oh why can they be cared for.

A change of scene and she comes to England.

Why is England not a northern country. It is not a northern country.

She will call either selfish if they come either as selfish.

After or a little other after she is adopted she likes to change about. What does she change about. Nothing at all. She stays as she is.

Once in a while if she likes it not only not better but always as often not better she feels that it is not even a wish. And so she calls money often money. Which made her leave strangeness to be selfish and their on their account their wish. After she had been adopted it might be that she was born always there as not so easily can any one remember anything or not after a while.

It is always their meaning which is a difference between often and open.

In the northern countries they adopt children and children have them to ask everything in the way and at the time and when they have or have been as a morning. And in this way easily of course and in consequence and it was most of the time. She could not remember any trouble.

After she was adopted she lived there. It could not know. They could not change by chance. Any one could get to be twenty-one. Almost more.

After a while any one knew that no one not on account of come again. It is very true that an adopted one is never glad to see her mother because she has not got one. They need never regret everything. She will not be cautious to close.

After she had been adopted they will be thought to swim and sing. They will be light in summer and dark in winter. They will be all alike in respect to everything just as they choose. It is why they had one then. There is plenty of favoritism in singing and swimming but she remembered them both.

Once once or twice the mother.

Or very happy with a girl.

She could in one year every time it would they would be that they had a girl.

Three a girl they adopted a girl. In a northern country.

In a southern country a girl. It made the parents sad. That they had that she had a girl. She was not their parents.

To go back now to the one who was an adopted one going to England. It is very likely that in going to England she went from them. They were not there to be ready. And she left. She did not. Not leave them. They were inquiring. Not if she were leaving. No one could inquire. If she were leaving. Because she had not. Left them. To leave them.

The thing she did was to go to England. And there the struggle for life was not severe.

Just who has been whose.

Marguerite there could expect care. She could be very much better everywhere. Everywhere and there.

After Marguerite had been adopted nobody spoke.

Consider how agreeable adoption is also consider how many hours from England also to please to never to be able to achieve the ambition of really going where they desired it if not any longer they could have been hoped to have her come. After adoption going is going. As much can be said of coming. She was an adopted one. She felt finely.

After every little while she saw why it was not once in a while.

He changed while they changed. She was left alone. England was not as far and she could go. This was after she was left that is to say adopted means having been adopting. There is no reason why they should stop choosing. Who could she called one and one.

It is so easy to feel better.

Marguerite did not feel better. She had been adopted and then later she went to England and there she remained until she left England.

After she returned from England she knew who hesitated.

She was often told that they were wretched. And she made their wishes their wishes. Can any one leave Finland. She did and came to England. After that they will be acquainted.

As I was saying she had been adopted as is the habit in northern countries and after every little while they will beware of their English. They have it very well taught. They will go. They will not decide about everything. It is always thought well that she should go away which she did and stay away which she does. She will be happy if she can say I mean. And they will respect having been in England. And now she is not far away.

She will resume her voyages. She will leave England for France.

And having left England for France she has come to France and having come to France she will long to have been in England as is natural to her station. She will be unique in asking and receiving and not being only but also desired. And so they may go. She has been in England and from England she has come to France and having come to France she will be in a state of enlightenment and no one need because it is prettily desirable and very successful to mention swans and sparrows. Sparrows are not younger than swans.

And so here we are in France and so they say there are more pleasures than rather very often they are separately undertaken to be anxious.

In this way one may unite before and after and because of their betterment.

The melody of which they like they must be always used to

be welcome. And love to rush and pleasantly come back. Or they will. This may be better than their chance of leaving it very well fastened as in a plan.

She may be thought to be thoughtful but she was adopted as is the custom in northern countries.

Be very carefully acquainted with anxiety.

Or do not expose yourself to this as a wish.

Can you see how readily not to agree not to say not to manage to say not to bewilder not to favor or not to gently mind which piously makes theirs be sewn. All of which they will all go to arrange it so.

The three countries in which they have been acquainted but she has not been acquainted with them is or are England Finland and France and Finland comes first.

Every little while they know her better.

It was not only known but it was told. That she knew. That in northern countries they did adopt and were adopted very young or anything. And they plainly made it a difference to have no one like it which is why they were willing to be feeling. It is not strange to be feeling. They will answer and answer anything that is no one who can would ask and answer a question or not at all which is just as returned as vehement they will kindly cry. Or known as announcement. Or complying with custom. The custom. In a northern country is something. Not entirely nothing. Not either just as well. Not with. Or without. Or with them. They will please do.

After she had been adopted she was plainly not wishing but very little in it as it is to do very likely. She could be just as well. And so much a reason for a treasure. They may use treasure and pleasure alike. It is in their way not selfish or grasping.

She may be after a while there.

Remember in Finland Finland is a country. England is a country that is a country which is a comfort and they say they may not only have been but who can say where. England is there. She came to France to stay. And she did.

No one reasons for her reflect what reasons are. Or just did. She makes it be. As well as in they say.

345

And so we begin.

She will change hands because. They will welcome her.

And she will be very capable.

They will make theirs be often. That she is not responsible for being left. And going after all to have them ask what might they do if she had been disappointed. All of which it is in a way inevitable and how dreadful.

Could she be adopted by a country without hope. In a country where they feel that going away is welcome. Does she feel that they will ask. Oh yes and no.

Does all who have been met in vain come with for recuperation.

All made by their meaning. All made without with and also by nor for just as with their meaning. In how to place.

Say why she will welcome surely and be as welcome. A survival of their interesting and after all the north can be called less as very farewell.

She was adopted as if with and by for her father and her mother which she had.

I do borrow and borrows her so and so.

Let us remember that she learned finnish as she was born there of a finnish father and a finnish mother or rather. After the adoption.

Now she went away. Older. After that please mind the cross. And be always with and might have missed her mother. Might not. She had no father. She had no mother.

In England she did not like weddings either. She felt very well.

So may she ask why any one had a blessing all which all of which may be true.

Why will England be happy there. Or might they be there. For in which it is neat or not obliged. It is a cloud that they will exactly furnish meat for butter. And never question why they make messages older. It is not because of their willingness believing rested not as well all of which are allowed. It is by their own way. Own way and is. Being taking. Shall refreshment have with them a time. All this makes adoption forgotten.

Gradually they will lie.

Marguerite prefers to be annoyed to be impatient. She prefers to be disturbed to be here. And here means there. But which she can call. Every little while they are out of it. And she can be remembered and so she is by this never wakened. Any little gift is lighter than at first. And so Marguerite has been in Finland in England and in France. Or be polite.

Can nobody know.

Or why do they. Be always there. For which. They will plan. More of it.

Often not only was she not adopted but not at all. Oh or not at all. They were so indifferent. By that time it was not alone that they were careless. Should he mean to be. It was just that. And just as likely.

She could not betray or doubt. Nor could they betray or doubt. Like that.

It was not often why they went away.

For this for them for which for what they do.

Or just to mention it.

It does not make.

They like it though.

That it could not make not any at all. A difference.

Could having not gone away leave it to them. Or could it. Just as well as they choose. By which I mean. Have I it do at all or very likely. It is by all this that they ought. Which is very well as neglected.

It does not make any difference by what they mean. They like to say hammer.

All of which they could be not out loud. Or very well careful.

Marguerite has no friends. She is not very tall. She will have a sight of there being there. Or not at all.

She is never anxious. To be quite. Persuaded. Or may be. Would they like it if. It was not all of it more than just as much better. It is very quiet when they like.

All this is Marguerite.

And now what does she say.

Marguerite is capable of being born and adopted and leaving just as you like. Or might it be what they will as occasion. Or will they be willing to go. Or might. She be not only without mention. Not of this. Nor only anything. And so they like. What is it that makes everything useful. These are all the day. And this is what she can say. Marguerite can say. That they may. Be alike.

What should Marguerite mean by missing.

All of it by the time they do.

Marguerite was left she does not know by whom. Nor does she know that she was an orphan. She was adopted as is the custom of northern countries very often. She was adopted at once and lived there with and without care. Not that it made any difference. Or was just alike. She had many gifts and was very often. With them. As they like. Neither do they mean that. Which is why they are not careless or very often thinking. That it should be all as well. And so Marguerite was not mistaken nor could be more an object of their seeing. Which could it do. She was not only never married. But they were. Not mistaken. It is not on account. Of this. They can protect and recognise and organise this from that. Which is what is obliging. And so often. Marguerite could often mean known.

Could it be happen to be selfish. And are they comfortable in England. And do they. Ever. Dance after going to their churches where they pray. Or like it. Or how. Do they like it. By which means. They are never after. What I like. Best.

In this way Marguerite has told all she knew. And now she knew that it is in France. Not where they dance. But just as likely.

After a little while she managed to leave a parade. That is they were taught about glasses. And very well if they came last. Could Marguerite be first in her class or lonesome or anxious or pitiful or will not crying or just as much and very nearly eating. Oh thank you.

It is now known that there are hours in Sweden. Also which they like. It is now known that Finland is not a part of Sweden and England is a way. To which they please. Making it do. Like. And alike. By which it is more than forever it is well. To have it known.

348

By the time that they were English and not far away.

By the time that they were not English.

All of which does not recall it more French.

Or every little while.

By or more or who little while.

Marguerite was Finnish she admired everything English she was able not to like the French and in a little while she was here. And had come to stay.

This was not what Marguerite had to say.

Marguerite had been adopted whether she was little or very little and she had been to say so or better. It is not only better not only not to have not to say so. Oh no. She was adopted and was there when she had not been there. There.

In the northern countries and Finland is northern adopting is not often everything. Might they say anything if they might. Please do.

Marguerite was painted pale not while light not white. It is not her wish. She has no wish. She is leaving adopted.

And they like it very well. And they might have it to do. And they will not have it declared. And they will. Once in when there is time. In which. It is so much. As much. Of interest.

When she came.

Marguerite who has or had adopted Marguerite.

Do be or do.

She had an adventure. She came nervously. Or left by that. Where they went in. Or to please.

Every one was patient.

One can.

One cannot lose one's Marguerite.

And she was prayed there. She likes what they can. And do. Go.

Or not.

What can Marguerite do better.

She had done better.

She to find no effort on Saturday to be too much either in England in Finland nor in France. And should be very tired. Not here nor very well there. But mainly with which they will well and never as well though they admire this. She does not know what ten years are.

And so they do not neglect to arrange not a pattern but dishes not a swan but roses not a swan but carrots and nobody laughs.

Or well.

However they will leave it as a finish.

And so how many hours are ours.

Who has been heard to hurry. She will be always not or selfish. They will claim doors.

How can hours or ours be different in Finnish in English and or or in French.

How often do they burst open.

Not white or blue she could be tired on Sunday.

Marguerite was selfish she asked could it be dreadful.

Then they went where they went in.

After all who has not lost one's Marguerite. Or found the time.

Marguerite pleases better than ever. She is more homogeneous.

Could any one guess how many countries are known as present.

Three countries are known as present. In each one I have forgotten but I do not forget.

They will not eliminate industry nor practice. They have manners and places and additions. They will also come as they can.

How are they careful. They are careful not as they are told.

A conversation in English in Finnish and in French can not be held at the same time nor with indifference ever or after a time. They will be proud to be nearly or may they be ever after just like nor either just the same find and finally like it. Might it make no difference to anybody.

Could she sigh by being half of the time just there.

And so may be to doubt it.

She alone knows and there is not that difference. Before they were alike now they are not. May be they are before. Before they are not they are alike. And only often before.

350

She could have a chance by being just and not only there. It made no difference. It was always why. And they could worry. Just by all of it.

Finland is far away. It is easily reached. They will be there. They often cause it to come. England is not far away. Who will not be not only just as they went there. Almost all which. They are alike. It should and did they have it which made it only only is allowed. They will often always which is likely. Once in a while they will not be there. Two are to them.

This way English Finnish and French. Now can all who speak. Speak it.

Marguerite can come every day or else. By the time which they know.

Should have been tries.

That is nice. To not like what she tries.

And so the home of truth is Finland. It is also England. Is it also France.

It is very difficult to remember and forget adoption.

In northern countries who adopted whom. Or would they be refused or would they be worshipped or would they be just as dark as a dog or just as fair as a ribbon and would they like it best if it cost nothing or if it did would they not be better able to be glad if they could not kneel nor either if they did which they could like and alike is fastened. Then they may be fairly said to be often together. Not more than the mother and daughter or is it fair to leave an adopted daughter not home alone only home alone. She could not be called cried. They will be often near to when they cost not in that. No one can lose a daughter not in Finland which is one of those northern countries. Neither one of these is made why they are which is they are happy just which is whether more than they do either not even more only just alike. This is why they pay.

Come in and come to study.

Marguerite a seat.

Is it nicely to be in doubt if it is warmer within and without. Any doubt is dear. She can be hoped.

Finland is a country where purses are given to women or are

given to men or are either given often as enough to children. They will play with purses.

Marguerite was adopted she was often not a mother nor indeed either. She was pure and easily frightened. She had been a little girl. Who were not old were not told nor was she told nor will. They may have been seen to know that a lake in the morning is not near a sea at night. She would so like to cross an ocean and be good humored.

She was a part of readiness. And yet she could not arrange. She was told she was brave and she looks it. For them do they dislike.

How often could no one remember.

She was endowed and not painful she made it prettily and fatigue she was meaning that they would like their taste her taste was shown. It was admired and all who were complimented were pleased.

Marguerite could think well of any noon. She was often called not to come but to stay a while. And like it.

Could they be sure that by adoption any religion changes. Marguerite never asked or asks herself this. This which in a way means that as it is she could never have been to a mountain. Nor will she think that it is that that is lost. Alright who likes tomorrow and with it at night. She has never been painfully timid just timid.

All who can like a house can like a house.

Marguerite will she be sweet in living or failing. Will she be sweet.

Marguerite feels nicely about adopting. She will know better not to adopt often. She will be miserable or just around.

She will be nicely spared. Or well. How is it a cunning to have fine hair. Or be just as well. Or not impatient. Or easily lost. Or with them. It might make time to have them around.

Marguerite was famous. They talked about her. They said will she she has might it mean that and who has been often wanted. Could she be alike. They will not often do more than they do. All who are ours.

Marguerite was made a maid.

352

She changed and came again. She was adopted had been known in the north. They will all like her like that.

No one can ever think any minute.

Marguerite is a life what and then which adopted. A northern country. Is one. In which. They are adopting. They leave it to me.

It is easy to be hours apart. And never move.

She liked it all the time.

When she first began. To smile. It was. Not. All the while. Pretty soon she did not begin. She did not smile oftener.

After every once in a while. They made their happen to make. Have made the any arrangement. It was often just what they had. No one could be more like. It is often very convenient. All who make hour glasses. She might try.

It could not be seen that they were often selfish.

What could she did she having back. Leave all of it at once. We have known that she never left them. They were partly mine. She knew. Which she could.

It is often why they obtain.

Make I make it right with Marguerite.

Marguerite was not stolen. She could come alone.

And so they knew which ever she was having first.

It was always how they liked and often. Knowing as well as she did. Whose could she arrange for. And plead. Might they not just as often try. Just as often as not.

Marguerite was not as often fond of first.

Just why should union try. And may she be called. In union there is strength but more break it. She has passed part of her life here.

Who knows Marguerite. When she comes.

She can forget three countries Finland England and France. Every little while is most.

Can any one forget who has been here. Why certainly in asking them the questions. How many are there who do not come with her. Or will they leave her most. She will apply. And it is their having her here. Which is for them whether. An adoption is clever. It is easy to finish. Without which.

Marguerite was early to bed but she read.

Shall it be why they thought. Does it make any difference when they eat. Will they interfere as they come. Could they come as they would. Who will hope that they do.

Marguerite would never like to mean. She would. She could be seized with displeasure. It is not only but also avoided but not by which they pause. She could. Have heard. Of another country. Which was. Not Finland. Not England. Nor France. Earlier she could. And then she could. And now she could.

All that she could. She either would. And so it pleases and well dreadful. No one should ever quote. Or have it help her.

Marguerite was adopted. So she says. And why should she say she was adopted. People in northern countries can adopt and be adopted.

After that they will leave them. Or if they have. They will leave them. I like that dog. Or they will leave them. But whichever they are. They do not like it. Or going away. Will they be strange. Will they be. Alike.

It is easy to have a difficulty in hearing when they were where. She went to be here. She came to be here. If they came not to be where. They came to be at most where. They were. And so alike.

It is very easy to love wealth and poverty, riches and money, conveniences and plenty, arrangements and anything which they are sure to have there. And they so one like it. Could she be other. Than not happy. In spite of which. She can smile. Wanly. With them. Left at last. Along. Oh why do they like. It.

This is what she had to happen.

Who could remember where she had been could she remember who had been there. Will she remember that she has not been where it is not more than she can have been with known.

Marguerite cannot ask a question.

That is the power of adoption.

So many hours so many houses so many countries so many cities. And with all of them one. Nobody knows London is in England.

She cannot be as fresh as a daisy.

Think wonderfully of there being or so dreadful with wondering of their being which they are wondering or with not only their being. The country that is well-known.

And so. Often.

Every time she says anything she smiles. Nor will she like them. What is there between with them. And we might do. Or say. For them.

And so she came to come. Marguerite is here.

Once there came in these difficult times to sit not at all because she was querulous. Not at all. She was not annoyed or a nuisance. She had a rosy life. She had been adopted and she was not indeed bothered to be devined. They will also call clad. She can be so often particular. Nor will it do that she like dolls. Anybody can hear for her. She was ready to say not younger. It is too often too made too known too well. Anybody can hear needing. Nor can they if they have enough. All these who can hear or need in to meet. Marguerite. It often makes an impression. It should be time to be often. To not to like to that.

Please have Marguerite fancy. More or this which is not only met as known. It is their nicely live.

It is easy to forget a country and countries and to remember for them.

Marguerite has been held mainly for them. She can cook well. So she says. Does. And may be.

It is not nicely to need why they ask.

No one can or does lose their Marguerite. Here she is.

Just why Marguerite was carefully to be known as never seated. And she was not in acres. But she could. Justify please it for them.

No one could think that she would be sure to place a time with that. She was often just as willing as if she were orphan where. There were no orphans. Could she be if she were older. Just as old. She might if she were asked be more than just where. There were but had been one to declare. And now he wants his ball. She would not be interested. She would say. How dreadful. But does this express any emotion. Have adopted children that is a child of adoption have any emotion. Marguerite was never one of three.

She could help this. And like this. With them with for this.

355

Never thank them for this and this. Remember an adoption. And she could not tell when.

She could say she never knew. To whom she could be grateful. And therefor. She was not grateful before. She was able. Not to think more. Than she had. In time. She was very selfish to be welcome.

Once in a while she could remember that her mother and her father had a mother and grandmother. But she never knew. She knew that they were not only more but moreover. She could not feel careless of repair or of despair. Nor could she love those she loved the most. Who can lie. They can easily be cheerful as they say. It is not only that she looks but that she does not look alike. Who can for it say it. Made them not fasten or favorite or aching. She liked why she ate and why she did not eat. She was often fastening and fasting. They may be all be awkward. Or who can be kind. Should it leave it made it that it does not matter or like that.

Once in a while they think well to distinguish. Marguerite can and should be debated. She can be often or for more. And then how is or when it is or when is it or if it is. She can be often with and beside almost met. It is as happy they will find as happy or may be they will accord a crowd. It is not only theirs are silent.

Marguerite was fastened by having been a birthday. She knows the day so in that sense she was not adopted. And by it. They are leaving it in might they can be very should it be mine too. How many years can you be adopted. She never asked that yet although and though all that is well past.

Marguerite was so she said having had given what she said. She was as often a little way in each. A country is a country gone and known. And often. They will celebrate not to like and like that.

Please mind me.

Marguerite is often placed in a seat and by herself if she sits. Gracious and to be kind.

They will abolish a stool.

And she will change a day for a chair. She might be thought for a festival. But no. Northern countries have adoptions. And with a little while. Northern countries do. They may be cold. They may be warm and sunshine. Also which is what she may as like. She can conceal her pause.

Marguerite was wishing. She was not wishing. She was not white and wishing. She was not pale nor brown and wishing. And if it is not night.

Marguerite may be taught right.

She can come away.

It is what happened by a seat. With and will it when she says did. They may do that. The same.

What can conceal a border.

Here we are well.

Anybody having no apprehension and nor intention nor in regard to right or with as by their please. She was always ready to be then to that. I like it. But hours of going aghast. It is very ease to be well with less. Less is it.

No one has the right to whistle in a court.

She could not be wrong. In the wrong.

Oh Marguerite will they be ever told just why they are not bold why they are in the fold. Why they are adopted and who they are like. Marguerite is like Amelia.

Marguerite when she is in pain is plain. When she is heard she is safe when she is blest she is best.

Marguerite is very much indeed why they. Can be best of it as a place wherein they can. It is often they who make the sound that they have not a pleasure in hearing.

Marguerite is very much what they have.

Now all who think about adopting adopt.

She may be very careful that not only all who think about adopting adopt but which they can in all of the way that they disturb.

Why will she be all English all Finnish all French why will she be all Finnish all English all French. Marguerite has the time to hear.

Oh Marguerite will you be planned. Or will you be very much a place. Or will you be a fastening. Or will you be their home.

357

Oh Marguerite who will have been here known for him for them. Or will it be just what they need.

Marguerite for which will they acknowledge.

All who can be just sit still together.

It happened that she had known but was discouraged.

But she was sure and then they came that is she came. To them. Oh will they miss. It.

It is not only that they know but that she knows that she can be a little more than extra.

Marguerite believe me. That you are sweet.

No Marguerite. Believe me that you are there.

Marguerite believe or not as you like.

Marguerite just why should all who are here open the door and declare.

I wonder at it.

Marguerite when can you connect the past with the past. The adopted past with the or a adopted past. And then they will not beside because she moves fairly surely although she may forget.

If caught and coercion are not alike.

Marguerite be careful that you have thought so.

Or Marguerite be careful that you have thought either that they did come or that they have come.

Or could they or could they smile so well.

Marguerite was often right. She said there would be more light.

Indeed she was not often colored to be night. And then she smiled as well as never more. Very often that is. As a place.

Could fifty times they think of Marguerite.

Marguerite was there or she. Was pleasant not as to hair. Not pleasant there. That is delicately fair and yet as dark as when they knew there was a park. Where they were like. A great deal of light is some resemblance.

I like it. Marguerite could be like it.

She could also like it. Although very nearly she at first.

And then arrange. Mountains are a range and also stoves and also will they be so sweet to cattle. Not if they are kept clean.

It is often thought that they will know their merriment.

Marguerite was stationed and was questioned. One thought she could be was frightened. But no. In the morning she was low. But by evening she was really earning morning noon and evening and just alike. She could be frightened of their having meant to dike and not like Finland England and France or so much.

She was often naturally historic.

Or just at a glance.

Now how is there a story without a history. Or a history.

How is there a history without a story.

Her story was that she knew history. She knew when Finland was born not only within but again. She also did know not to know England then not even France.

Afterwards she was in request.

What could more do than south. Not north. Not north or south. Which they may aim. Or commit to claim.

Marguerite never did claim. She asks for a thing in unison. She bestowed pale as their part. And they will. It is either otherwise or they may as well as will. Why they are wholesome. Or just as well apart.

Can she Marguerite be a mean. Between which is that there is a stream. Or with as well.

It is more than kind of her to be here.

Marguerite can almost dream that to be adopted is a dream of not a queen. Or just shortly. She can also prevail upon no one to come when where they will if it is either here or there. Or just alike. Why will they not mean. Come with them quickly. She has been there. Not as it were there.

It is surprising than any one like her could be what is it if they do not ask.

Or just as much a chance.

Can any one think future when they will. She is not to be known as when they come either.

Does she like all who have been here. Marguerite cannot ask questions.

That is not the reason of not adopted or not in the past.

If it could that they were the children she had not almost forgotten.

It is often by that that they will include exclusion. Nor will they call not coming again. Anything is ours like that. So not only with where they and do not it has been often all brought.

Marguerite was a child not younger than most. She will be tall as not tall as less than for most. She will is already shown. That they touch. Or will think it a resolve with fair and very pleased to be a principle. She could not think well of further but further than it went. Should all who come back go. Or stay.

Anyone cannot be adopted and registered. Or not polite in courteousness or just why they will better able to love to have it be. Just what it was not. Like and like for them.

Thank you in kind.

Marguerite no one knows.

It is not often ready to have part three partly. No will she just like having it with not a trouble. It is no trouble.

How do you like what they did.

By why they will be pale.

She is pale. Not as pale. Because it is not known. Why she is not. Oh love to be so.

Marguerite was slowly changing to circumstances. She might be dangerous if she changed. And do they do think so.

It is often called Marguerite to be forgotten.

Why could not Marguerite think that when she came there it would be open. Because she has had experience that when she came there it would be open. Just as get yes.

It is not why she was as she was but only longer.

Marguerite in fruition. And all of it not a distress to a pleasure.

She could be called not nor neither careful nor caution. In syllables no one renounces.

Marguerite all filled with then. She has been dangerous not to danger nor to weather.

All who have been told nothing are not knowing. All of it doubtless.

Marguerite will she mean that nobody knows she has no adventures but experience. Nobody knows. She knows. She knows all made of knows or knowledge all will be known as knows. It is of no importance.

All white is not alike or paleness increasing.

Should it have shown or shone with accents brighten, she could be happy if she was not better known. How is she better known. By having been in many places without their cost.

And now act as if Marguerite could converse and have things happen.

She was adopted and not starved.

She was born before she was adopted and not starved.

She was born and not starved.

She was left more than adopted and not starved and not here known.

All apples all dogs all suns and all places and all oranges and all dinners and all deers are not starved and all not adopted and all not known and all not clouded and all not taken and all not a trouble and all not liked and all not beside and all not kind. And all.

She was born and not starved adopted and not starved here and not starved there and not starved known and not starved again and not starved and only. She was not starved and so a heroine.

This is a story of Marguerite.

From head to feet.

And a love of what she asked. Was why they came.

But she might be just as well be happy.

Marguerite was mentioned as sweet.

But not as sweet Marguerite because just for this. Or with just for this.

All out to be inclined to be praised for. What she does. Or not.

Marguerite then had this happen.

Just why they like what they say.

Marguerite was always there in not a disappointment. If they went away to stay or to go. Could she go. When they went away to stay. This would happen not to go. It would happen that she was not only not to go but not to stay. This is how Marguerite could find out.

How could she like what she did.

Marguerite when she was sure could learn Finnish that is to

say she was Finnish and could learn English if she did learn English she could learn french. And as much.

All who are around are reasonable.

And this is what all who like like it.

How many things happen. Not any of a great many things do as well as more do not by that or which happen. It is just alike not that. Is it why they like what they wish. It is not often that they allow for or with wishes. All of which is made to stay. Not to increase or to inquire which for and then needed yesterday.

How can they be called English french or Finnish. By that.

Marguerite was awakened to yesterday and not yet.

Marguerite she could say that dogs dribble as they lay. Or on account of it.

What could her feelings be. If this is all of three or more often.

She may be used to recklessness but not at all not at all used or to be used to it or not at all to be used to recklessness or not at all to be used to it.

What is the name the character the surname and the occupation of Marguerite. Does it make any difference. Will she be known. Can she come again. Is it useful as well as necessary. Do they do not do as they like it. Or may she not be always there. What is her name. Marguerite is her name. What is her surname. What is her surname what difference is it what is her surname what difference does it make.

How could she be not frightened or not frightening or not well.

Marguerite made carefully apart. Her name of Marguerite is a rare name.

It can be repeated it does will and can say that the name a name if a name to be that name is a rare name and so she is so kind and the best of which nearly which and only which it is.

Marguerite is her name was it given to her does she remember her mother her grandmother her uncle or what. Anyway it is her name. And she knows well which she knows that rarely which she knows.

Marguerite may feel afresh that it is twice as a life.

And they think thanks.

Was Marguerite known as not or was she in a care or was she be which and ever which makes it be all.

She could recover. And recover.

So that Marguerite is not toothless and fevered she is just pale and fair. And so it has been not only mine but mine. And Marguerite will not feel that there is any or an in occasionally. Not that she has pain. There is no pain in complain or in fair or in there. No explain in not here nor in not here nor in not here which is not there. It is better to be fearful than to be tremulous. Oh yes.

Marguerite found many hours. Or easily plain or easily past or easily why or easily gain. They hope not for better times often.

Marguerite was not born for ages. It is a common name. One has known a Marguerite just yes.

Marguerite which they are willing but then they could not always know one that has was adopted. But then northern northern people often adopt children. Children are not motherless. They are fatherless. They are not fatherless. Nor uncleless nor indeed a date in which they do not meet. They are always without change. Who can be in search of a father without a mother. Even if the grandmother had known that no one was dead. And so they were accounted for. It should be rarely that they do engage.

Marguerite was known to be often. That they were with their and on their account. Oh nicely now.

She was adopted and they dropped the name not she. It was rare. She was to be no dupe to fancy. She was to be known older she was to be which they can have if they fancy it. No one taught to be alike. It was just as plainly taught as when they mentioned. Marguerite can be so sweetly in a swoon.

All taught not only not but left to how so naturally to fill a swan with butter. Oh swan.

This makes Marguerite complete but not how she was born.

She was born the children of more than one. And so more likely. It was more likely that she would like not it what is it that it made not be this as born.

She was born and so she away. Let alone. It is nice what they like with remain. She was adopted by them as could be not children. Children are known as such. She was not happy but very pleased. Very pleased and very well seen and played. And they could judge.

Will she be known. Not unless it may they it we they they we say. She is not here. So she came to be. Known to have the place and the pay oh yes to say. How kindly. They should frighten.

It is once in a while an occasion. More she can do.

Marguerite was adopted very nearly and she could leave very nearly and go very nearly when she did not come. There could be nothing. Done. By her known with her as her resolution.

She sneezed but not from pleasure but in spite of their refusal but this has nothing whatever to do with Marguerite.

Or like it quite as well.

She may be exercised by their thinking just as well of it.

And now Marguerite who will think well of wealth and a wreath.

Marguerite has been warned to be close not to be with them with these not to wonder when they will and when they were near nor which by which they mean leave it or leave it here.

Marguerite may be an instance of why they liked the name or which they had or why they smile or when they will or be or is it not or just the same. Marguerite is always made. Leave it to her to end the same as when she will and when she will and will and can.

She thinks very well of why she is selfish. Who has hopes of in the end of the spring. She has not because she knows if she has known they will leave him and it will be most nefarious. Or will she just yet. Suit it. She may be thought to be obliged and in their way. They may not be alike. All of which she knows now.

Marguerite has almost forgotten adoption but not yet. She has almost forgotten that they might. But not yet. She has almost forgotten all one day. She has almost forgotten all one day but not yet. She has almost but not yet forgotten that it is not whichever they are for. And so the hours crowd.

She would be so sweet soon if she were known at noon.

Is it not best for Marguerite to say. She has been well reconciled to be abruptly at noon. Seen. They may care not to scare but she has forgotten that is not forgotten in between. And this leads to so much.

Marguerite was born a Finn that is to say on the border which is near the Russian border and they thought or ordered that she was not there when she was adopted because she was adopted as is common in northern countries but she might have known.

On account of which they may be often more than all alike on account of which they are not.

If she went away if she came to stay she was Finnish.

After a while it is an example that she looked like this. It is easy to understand. They may account for more than in and noon.

Should they challenge Finland to be England.

Marguerite was born in Finland not in England. She was in England not in Finland. She was in France.

Just when she was to be sure that she would do if they understood that she was not to be thought hurried as she was not through just then she was by no means not alone.

Why is why yes.

She has not been adopted by distress. She had not been adopted not again not when. Oh yes she knew who were how many how many who were through.

She knew they were fresh in pleasure but not in there. She knew that they could leave and learn and pay and fasten but not in there. She knew that they were kind and careful and all and she but not in there. All the rest of it she knew. How did she know. She knew. She had left home adopted when she was young and now there was some time since then. All this she knew. They were there to arrange. May be not. May be they do. May be they call. May be they have printed what was not known. May be not.

She may be said to be thoroughly content to see more which is why it is nobody's fault that she does not love what they do not say for them presently.

Think of how Marguerite was not willing to be famous, it was why she went that she knew that she came and she would not ease or release what is not that no one is which it is that they remember in which they do not manage to blame.

Why this when that is perfect.

365

Marguerite was born in Finland near the border of Russia and she was well when she had but she not only knew but could not remember. After she was as is frequent in northern countries adopted by a married couple she was adopted for the sake of the mother who did not care for her. This can happen when in Finland which is a northern country they adopt some one which again is not only not often but quite often done in such a northern country. Finland is a northern country just as often.

After the death of the mother which was sure to happen later she left the father which was what will be nearly earlier. After which just alike.

This is England. Who told any one that England was across the water. Who told any one that any England was anywhere across wherever there was water. She likes England better than France and why. Because she knows why.

Marguerite could be born it is not a cup which is forlorn nor a cup measured it is not a cup measured nor may she make a mistake since which it is all read. She knows that if it is said so she finds it not only there but there.

Marguerite what will become of any one adopted. Marguerite what will become of any one adopted.

Marguerite has not this to answer oh no she has not this to answer.

Marguerite what will become of any one who has been adopted and is now not one who has been adopted. Marguerite has not this to answer either.

Marguerite will not settle anything because there is no waiting in adopting. If one is adopted one is not waiting and so they realise that ice which is cold is welcome to believe that she makes it be good with them alone that they like what they admire. Often one says does she know. Can no one who is told be waiting with which they come to wish which for a dish. It is easy to say no I do not like it if it is so. Nor indeed do they collect publicly more than once for once. She may be often with and without a wish. All of which they could reconcile more abundantly. Just why they are. All is my best.

It is often that they end before.

366

She might be why with all of which.

Are and are not is not are they otherwise like it in possession. After which I like it green. This is not only because of whys but because of yes. And she was nearly in no case. It is often that nobody knows how.

All which she likes because all which she may they think he said it like that.

Marguerite was afraid of a rose.

Or was she why she came.

Oh dear Marguerite was afraid she could be taught with which she came.

May be she be lawful.

It was well to adopt. Could it.

It was well that they knew did not know that she could not be seen waiting. Nobody can be seen waiting sometime. For this they like it for that.

Marguerite was born in Finland.

Why are they there when they are born. Or may be they will feel well and be well until which they may not at all very careful. All should be thought.

Will she feel well if she agrees with them or is with them or is agrees with them.

Marguerite was not strong she preferred kneeling to standing or not sitting or standing or not kneeling or kneeling and not waiting. This might be because she was made to be believe it of her that she will not be.

May they account that for her.

Marguerite was never married. She could keep it as if she were not so or not in any sense likely at all likely. Could those who have been adopted marry.

Once when her hair was fine she was one at a time and always.

Oh think so well of it and wishes.

Marguerite had not fair hair it was fair but she was dark in Finland not dark in England not dark in France.

North east south west home is best that is what she hears them say.

Marguerite shall be not known not to be placed where they

367

do whatever they do like. She is not anxious not to hear something that is not only all not to her credit but very likely more often than not at all doubly likely.

She was never disagreeable in thought.

How can they reasonably feel better without it ever not only not having been bought.

Will they remember that yesterday it could if she did say that not any one properly could be necessary to go not only not away but not their way.

If she was adopted which does not differ from if she were adopted she would not then be after more often more than any other after all.

It is often not so and not so often and not only not so but not so soon and not sewn nor as soothing to be adopted and which is a difference between next to and next to this. She is adopted and she is not interested in any one. And so they make her be careful to be fatigued that is she reminds herself.

To be so sorry not to have after all been there which is the same as remarkable.

How can there be an exercise of adoption with and without question which she may if she does like.

In northern countries they do adopt. Children.

Marguerite could cry and not to love to die. Marguerite could cry and often enough to pull through not likely to not need it to not to be without it as she had not been through without it not it without for you. She having been adopted and not leaving for not left could be all so nicely faded to not a ground. A ground is plainly what they like often while they think what they do like. She is not known instantly that they make it do sooner.

It is very well to be an advantage or just as likely.

What could Marguerite do if everybody was anxious.

They should be thought to be always well when they came after as they might cause it.

Marguerite was born in Finland and admired Sweden. She was born nearly where they had been but she was not only not used to it.

All of which they feel like it.

368

She was adopted by a husband and wife but they did not remember alike. It was of no use not to be well and selfish and she never minded it. She could hear it at all. And they were liked. After she left before that they were not there not only not as needing but in which case. She left Finland for England where she learned English. She learned English and left England and she came to France but although she tried she did not learn french.

She said to say it to have it to be she said she had none and she had some.

It was not by asking after anxious wishes that she was obliged to be back.

She could be nearer to it or not.

She would be better to be or not.

This is how they could wait.

Every day Marguerite waited she waited to see if she were not going and so they could not abandon waiting.

Because by the time that she cherished all or more readily what she not only knew she was made often not that she did not know that is allow that she had sent it away. By this. Could they in some country ask them this.

Marguerite earned money in Finland in England and in France. She liked England she sent money to Finland and she stayed in France.

Always when I am through she is not only through but not commenced.

Marguerite says that in Finland she floated upon ice.

All which is made to pull a praise for progress.

Let me hear you say that Marguerite is usual every day.

This is a history of her day.

She wakes up in the morning and nearly. Always ought to.

After she accepts not only not a wedding but effectively to repeat all which is bought. For this they do not call her early nor does she come with not forever running. It is quite quietly that she said yes.

Marguerite has been a privilege and a pleasure in the beginning and often that sameness has become inconstant. Does she love. She says but that may be because by that she passes France and

369

England because by that she repasses Finland. Because by that no hope of pleasure makes any thing this there this delight. It is awfully often all. She can be caught with dated pleasure. Every little once in a while a pause. She recounts. How many hours before to-day may make two an afternoon. Her life is reasonable without economy. By which means she remains fortunately there or theirs alone.

A very likely home is Finland. Marguerite was born in Finland near the borders of Russia and there she came to France but neither directly or even not more placed as a departure carefully. She came again. It is often as exciting not to pray as to stay.

She might be thought to be cross because she opened the name not on the same day.

Or with it inclined.

It is past that they understood.

This is a history of her life she could be even ever if she cried.

The fortunes and misfortunes of Marguerite. Marguerite had no misfortunes. The misfortunes and fortunes of Marguerite. Marguerite had no fortunes. And why had she no fortunes. Why had she not any misfortunes.

Marguerite was born in Finland and she was not often mistaken by that. She had been engaged to England and there she was praiseworthy. She had been recalled to France that is just as well she had never been there before. After that any one could not be very fortunate for their belief. She believed she would as she was not known once. It is very easy not to be deceitful.

There is not any home for Marguerite a home town means something but not something else.

It is by which by me that Marguerite can see that she can say that when she looks and it is a pleasure that she can say not only not yesterday.

Marguerite was employed to be all of which they knew she was employed scarcely as to blame.

This was her unhappy experience.

Now let us think woefully of nationality. A nationality is this she does not know how not to receive more knowledge that not as bliss that not not only not and not to miss which she knew she knew that she could be blamed and paid for as if in defence not only of herself but many and more kind. Who could know that she would not say so say that she knew that they could come never to come. She refused to see them.

Was she known to have a dream without danger. Or was she not known.

Marguerite she suggests not Marguerite because marguerites although not attractive not only attractive are smaller as well as faithful they are not because there has been some mistake only in names.

Now this is telling it truly. She was born in Finland and not as many might think not truly of her mother which is her father because she does not care to know. She always thinks of it of which it is so.

She might keep it not only from not being so. Every time it is said it is always the same even when it is added. She was born in Finland and this is near the Russian border which she thinks is exactly her name. Her name is now not any different at any one time. She was born and the name is the name of her grandmother but this she knows but is not certain which.

Marguerite has not come back again when she has been or not.

Marguerite could be in imagination not born in Finland nor either or not. It is not.

She has been born in Finland which she admires she admires the country by way of which she made England for a change. Nobody sought for her.

She was born in Finland when she was old enough after having lived in Finland she went to England. In Finland she had been old enough so that after England she came to France. This is where she is now. All sorts of differences do not matter nor can they make it which it is not known for which it is not known or really better it does not matter.

She left Finland for England and she left England for France not to be in England not to be in France not yet or rather not to have not been in Finland not in England not in France.

She could be meant to be born in Finland when she says goodbye to France. In saying all this she does not miss one country.

This is what they like to do.

Marguerite was adopted as is the custom in a northern country. She was not less than all of which. She may be fortunate or fought more but not as likely as that they were never more around than when she was alone which after all was not right there not only with it. It was why she was born not for it really she could know but she had not wanted not only not to know but without doubt. How very much and also how very often.

She was born in Finland. She left Finland and went to England. She was often in England after she had been in Finland and not back again. It is not very likely that they were often there.

She was waiting for no dog. She had been left not by them but by leaving. She would be often found in tears not without reason.

Marguerite was often happily better.

What is it. She was born in Finland and in Finland they do not thank that is in England they thank and also not only in France.

She had been born with care. She had come away from there and had been adopted by a man and woman that she called mother and father naturally and not unfortunately. She was not unfortunate either. By which she meant nothing.

Do do be sure that she is here.

Many things that have happened in her life are these. She would not say. What is it when you ask. She was not born in vain in Finland nor did she in vain go to England nor in a way in vain did she come to France. All these succeeded one another. And oftentimes she would not be conscious that this was past. Because quite naturally these countries were there in a way to her they might since without calculation there is no prostration they might not only follow it alone. She who was not blind because she had that beauty thoughtfully could be not known. I have often said I will not mention her.

In every likelihood nobody can do harm. She was born in the country where she had not visited nor had she failed very likely.

I will now tell why she came. She could not do otherwise nor could she leave it as a reason moreover formerly there is no such pleasure as a touch.

372

It is very often true that no one in Finland was born in England. This may not be carried away. And now I ask. Will she furnish us.

And so no one is silent in her presence not even as much so.

She was not only in England and in France. Very likely they are thoroughly better than any commencement immediately.

The great question is can any one very immediately stay away.

At least no one is blamed.

She is often always there. On no account. But which will gradually know its worth.

It is not often that not as well she spoke she called it the dog she called him the man she called her the woman and they were each and all not averse not to be welcome which she is if wishes. Are derived.

And so they may. She was born in Finland near Russia and England and France and she may without that difference. Having blamed others or not now. And so they need never please her either. But she need not leave it for this nevertheless.

I can no longer remember how she says what she says.

Finis

Or who will be called better nearer.

Finis

WHAT DOES SHE SEE
WHEN SHE SHUTS HER
EYES

A NOVEL [1936]

IT IS VERY MERITORIOUS TO WORK VERY HARD IN A GARDEN equally so when there is good weather and something grows or when there is very bad weather and nothing grows.

When she shuts her eyes she sees the green things among which she has been working and then as she falls asleep she sees them a little different. The green things then have black roots and the black roots have red stems and then she is exhausted.

Naturally as she works in the garden she grows strawberries and raspberries and she eats them and sometimes the dog eats them and for days after he is not well and finally he is so weak he cannot stand but in a little while he is ready to eat again.

And so a day is not really a day because each day is like another day and they begin to have nothing. She herself was in mourning because her mother had died, her grandmother was dead before her mother died and her father had curly hair and took off his hat so that his eyes could see that somebody had stopped to talk with him.

It is a pleasure to be afraid of nothing. If they have no children they are not afraid of anything.

A good many of them only have one child and that is not the same as not having any children. If they are married and have no children then they are afraid. But if they are not married and have no child then they are not afraid.

Never having seen him before he becomes your servant and lives in the house and just as intimate as if he had been a father or children. It is funny that, there seems to be so much need of having always known anybody and he comes to answer an advertisement and you never saw him before and there you live in the house with him.

After all nothing changes but the weather and when she shuts her eyes she does not see clouds or sky but she sees woods and green things growing.

So the characters in this novel are the ones who walk in the fields and lose their dog and the ones who do not walk in the fields because they have no cows.

But everybody likes to know their name. Their name is Gabrielle and Therese and Bertha and Henry Maximilian Arthur and Genevieve and at any time they have happened to be happy.

Chapter I

How often could they be afraid.

Gabrielle said to any one, I like to say sleep well to each one, and he does like to say it.

He likes to do one thing at a time a long time.

More sky in why why do they not like to have clouds be that color.

Remember anything being atrocious.

And then once in a while it rains. If it rains at the wrong time there is no fruit if it rains at the right time there are no roses. But if it rains at the wrong time then the wild roses last a long time and are dark in color darker than white.

And this makes Henry Maximilian Arthur smile. It is just like the weather to be agreeable because it can be hot enough and so it might just as well not be hot yet. Which it is not.

And therefore Henry Maximilian Arthur is not restless nor is he turned around.

376

Chapter II

She grew sweet peas and carrots and beets. She grew tomatoes and roses and pinks and she grew pumpkins and corn and beans. She did not grow salad or turnips nor camelias nor nasturtiums but nasturtiums do grow and so do hortensias and heliotrope and fuchsias and peonies. After she was very careful she refused to pay more than they were worth and this brings Henry Maximilian Arthur to the contemplation of money. He might even not then throw it away. He might. After all he clings very tightly to what he has. But not to money because about there is no need. Money is needful those who can move about. And as yet Henry Maximilian Arthur does not do so.

No matter who has left him where he is no matter no matter who has left him where he is no matter. There he is.

No matter. It does not matter that no one has left any one where he is. It does not matter.

All birds look as if they enjoyed themselves and all birds look as if they looked as if they enjoyed themselves.

Better is not different than does it matter. It is better even if it does not matter.

Once in a while Henry Maximilian Arthur was caressed by Theresa. When Theresa caressed Henry Maximilian Arthur Henry Maximilian Arthur liked it as well as he liked it better. That is what is the way in which it was that it did as well as it did not matter.

Grasses grow and they make a shadow so just as grasses grow.

Henry Maximilian Arthur could be tickled by grasses as they grow and he could not caress but he could be caressed by Theresa as well as be tickled by grasses as they grow, when grass is cut it is called hay.

A year of grass is a year of alas. When grass grows that is all that grows but grass is grass and alas is alas.

One evening morning Henry Maximilian Arthur was awake. Once every morning he was awake and Theresa was not there and when Theresa came Henry Maximilian Arthur was there just the same.

377

That is what adding means and a cow. Henry Maximilian Arthur had no need of a cow. Theresa did Theresa had need of a cow, but a cow died and that was a loss a loss of a cow and the loss of the value of the cow and to replace the cow there had to be a medium-sized cow and a very small cow. But Henry Maximilian Arthur did not share the anxiety.

S